"THE KLINGONS," INSISTED DR. McCOY, "ARE CHILDREN COMPARED TO THESE ASSASSINS. . . ."

"The Ssani won't negotiate. Not with the government, not with us, not with anybody."

Commodore Montoya leaned back in her chair. "Dr. McCoy is right, gentlemen. It would be a mistake to underestimate the difficulty of what the Federation is asking of you."

"However?" suggested Kirk.

"However," said Montoya, "we are still asking."

Look for STAR TREK Fiction from Pocket Books

Star Trek: The Original Series

Star Trek: The Next Generation

Star Trek: Deep Space Nine

STAR TREK®

SHADOWS ON THE SUN

MICHAEL JAN FRIEDMAN

POCKET BOOKS

New York   London   Toronto   Sydney   Tokyo   Singapore

This book is a work of fiction. Names, characters, places and incidents are products of the author's imagination or are used fictitiously. Any resemblance to actual events or locales or persons, living or dead, is entirely coincidental.

POCKET BOOKS, a division of Simon & Schuster Inc. 1230 Avenue of the Americas, New York, NY 10020

STAR TREK is a Registered Trademark of Paramount Pictures.

This book is published by Pocket Books, a division of Simon & Schuster Inc., under exclusive license from Paramount Pictures.

Library of Congress Catalog Card Number: 93-84538

ISBN: 0-671-86910-8

First Pocket Books paperback printing July 1994

10 9 8 7 6 5 4 3 2 1

POCKET and colophon are registered trademarks of Simon & Schuster Inc.

Printed in the U.S.A.

For my father-in-law, Marvin Laxer,
who never took no for an answer

ACKNOWLEDGMENTS

☆

When I was young, I really detested the idea of becoming a doctor. My mom and dad would of course suggest it from time to time, as was their sworn duty as Jewish parents. But the medical profession never appealed to me, never beckoned, never caught my eye. Looking back, my parents say it was probably because they wanted me to become a doctor that made me so dead set against it.

In any case, as an eleven-year-old sitting cross-legged in front of the television set, I always felt a lot closer to the character of Captain Kirk than to that of Leonard McCoy. After all, McCoy was just a physician. Nothing much heroic about that. He didn't get into fistfights very often, he almost never got the girl, and—well, he just didn't seem very happy, did he?

Spock was kind of cool and aloof. Scotty got to tinker with things. Sulu was an expert swordsman. But McCoy?

All he got to do was practice medicine. And medicine was the stuff I hated.

It wasn't until I got older that I realized the mark DeForest Kelley and his character had left on my psyche. Not because McCoy was a doctor necessarily, but because he was a human being in the finest sense of the word. Fallible, ill-tempered on occasion, contrary, and far too vulnerable, but also devoted, tenacious, and courageous in a way that means more to me now than any Kirk-style derring-do.

I see these qualities in the best people I know—people who stubbornly hold on to their ideals, people who remain true to a higher principle when they could get away with a lot less. Funny enough, some of them are doctors.

For instance, Dr. Keith Ditkowsky of New York's Long Island Jewish Medical Center and Dr. Seth Asser of the University of California at San Diego, who have long been my sources of information regarding things medical. Also Dr. Michael Ziegelbaum of Greak Neck, who officially joined the brain trust when he helped me develop the concept of bloodfire.

As always, I owe thanks to a lot of other people as well. Dave Stern, for caring enough about this manuscript to put me through the ringer. Kevin Ryan, for his patience when I called to gripe about how depressed I was getting while writing the darn thing. Bob Greenberger, for giving me so many good excuses to goof off when the task seemed intolerable. And Paula Block, for her trust and cooperation.

To my son, Brett, who just the other day told me he wanted to be a *writer,* of all things, making my fatherly heart swell with pride. (Of course, I think he should be a first baseman, but that's another story entirely.)

Acknowledgments

To my mom and dad, of course. To Lorraine, Carol and What's-his-name, Lois and Cliff, Lori and Lee, Patti and Marc, and all the little ones: Fara, Eric, Amy, Craig, Matthew, and Jared.

To the Guys, for giving me a chance to let off steam without inhibition. To my Friday night card game, for being good enough to relieve me of my royalties about as quickly as I receive them. And to Roseann Caputo, for giving me the opportunity to contribute to as worthy a cause as Make-A-Wish.

Finally (I've saved the best for last, of course), I want to thank my wife, Joan, for her understanding and forbearance during that month and a half of husbandless late nights and weekends. If you don't know how I feel about Joan now, I trust you will by the time you've finished this book. She and Jocelyn have a lot in common, you see, and in many cases the feelings I ascribe to McCoy are my own. So in many more ways than one, this book couldn't have been written without her.

Michael Jan Friedman
Port Washington, New York
April 1993

HISTORIAN'S NOTE

This story begins shortly after the events that took place in *Star Trek VI: The Undiscovered Country.*

Book One

— ☆ —

McCOY

ONE

☆

On the Federation member-planet Ssan, there is a drop of blood.

It quivers for a moment in the breeze from an open window and then falls into the large, white, quarry-tile basin below it. Disturbing the blood and water that have already mingled there, the drop creates a series of concentric circles that radiate to the limits of the basin's walls and then shiver into nothingness.

A meter or so above the basin, there is a man-sized bench seat, also made of white quarry tiles. Laid on its back across the length of the bench seat, there is a male corpse in a bathrobe of the palest blue, illuminated by the morning light from the open window. The robe is made of soft, Ssani silk, woven by worms in the mountains of the southernmost continent. The corpse's skin, all that is visible of it, is almost as pale as the robe; its tiny, indigo eyes have rolled

3

up beneath the bony brows of its hairless head, which is tilted back over the edge of the platform.

A slender thread of blood, as red as a perfect ruby, runs from the corner of the corpse's open mouth. It traces a languorous, loving trail across a clean-shaven cheek to the bottom of a long, bulbous earlobe—a physical characteristic typical of the Ssana. There, the trickle of blood collects and forms yet another drop.

Before it became an empty vessel, this body housed the spirit of Thur Cambralos, master governor of Pitur, Ssan's largest city-state. Until a very short time ago, he was the single most powerful political figure on the planet. He will continue to be thought of that way for another few minutes, until his lifeless flesh is discovered by a servant.

Except for the thin trickle of blood, there is no mark of violence on the corpse, no outward sign of the death that overtook it. But then, one would not expect there to be.

On the Federation member-planet Ssan, assassination is an art unto itself.

Retirement.

Leonard McCoy, chief medical officer of the *Enterprise,* mulled the word over as he stared at the featureless ceiling of his bedroom. It was so heavy, so final. Like the clash of a wooden gavel in some old-fashioned courtroom.

Boom.

I hereby sentence you to the rest of your life. And may God have mercy on your soul.

Frowning, he pulled away his bedcovers, then sat up and swung his feet around in a single movement. Across the floor, standing against the far wall, was his nemesis: a metallic gray storage container, identical to the one every officer on the ship had been given for his or her personal effects.

He'd put off dealing with the container for days now. Once, not so long ago, he had been looking forward to retirement. But that was before his dealings with the Klingon called Chang. In opposing the traitor and his plot, the doctor had been forcibly reminded of how exciting and satisfying life on a starship could be.

On the other hand, it also left one open to experiences like the one he'd had on Rura Penthe, the Klingon asteroid archipelago. McCoy shivered just thinking about the place, with its murderous cold and its flesh-carving winds.

But that wasn't the reason he'd decided to go ahead with his retirement after all. He just couldn't picture himself serving on another vessel or taking orders from some whippersnapper of a captain. He just couldn't contemplate starting all over again.

If he'd had some better options, he certainly would have considered them—but he didn't. So, getting to his feet, he padded across the floor and faced the storage container like a man.

The thing was empty—painfully empty, he might have said, except it would be more painful to him when it was full. Looking around, he found a shelf full of medical monograph tapes that he'd accumulated over the years.

Most of the tapes were written by people he'd never met. Maybe now that he'd have nothing else to do, he could visit with some of them—talk some shop, get to see how planetbound physicians spend their time.

He shook his head. Who was he kidding? At this point in his life, he had about as much in common with a planetbound doctor as a Romulan had in common with an inchworm. Come to think of it, maybe less. Not that he wasn't interested in the science behind the monographs —on the contrary. But when the scientific talk was over, he'd be longing for a view of the stars streaming by at warp three, not a tour of some old geezer's research lab.

McCoy sighed. Come on, he told himself. A journey of a thousand miles begins with a single step.

Slowly, deliberately, he went over to the shelf and picked up a few tapes in either hand. Then he returned to the storage container and placed the tapes inside.

There, he thought. It's a beginning. Hell, maybe someday I'll look back and wonder why I didn't retire earlier.

Yeah, he thought. Maybe someday. About the same time pigs learn to fly.

At the house of Kimm Dathrabin, master governor of the Ssani city-state Tanul, there is a knock at the door.

"Yes?" a servant says, opening the door and peering at the visitor, whom he does not know.

"My name is Harn Baraffin," the visitor tells him. "I come with news from Pel Sarennos, second governor of Pitur. Is Master Governor Dathrabin at home?"

"He is," says the servant, "but he is occupied."

"This is urgent," Baraffin interjects. "It concerns Master Governor Cambralos." Then, glancing about and speaking in a quieter, more confidential tone: "The master governor has been assassinated."

The servant considers this information. The very reason his master decided not to see visitors was to protect himself from assassination. But if Cambralos has been killed, he would surely wish to hear the details of it.

"Very well," the servant says, motioning the emissary inside. "Come with me."

Careful to lock the door behind him, he guides the visitor through the large foyer, past the pair of armed bodyguards, and up the broad, winding stairs to the house's second floor. Making his way past a set of celebrated tapestries depicting the development of the rule of law in Tanul, the servant shows his charge to the very door of the master governor's suite, where two more armed guards stand.

"It is all right," the servant tells the guards. "He is an emissary from Pitur, with news."

The guards eye the visitor suspiciously. One of them produces a flat, plastic stick with what looks like a square piece of sponge at the end. The sponge has been treated to react to the presence of certain chemicals.

"Spit," says the guard.

The emissary works up a drop of spittle and allows it to fall on the piece of sponge. The guard holds the stick up to the light. There is no change in the color of the sponge.

He nods to the servant. "You may go in," he says.

Without further discussion, the servant opens the door and escorts the visitor inside. The walls of the suite are adorned with a different kind of tapestry, the subject matter more entertaining than edifying. A thousand years earlier, they were the property of a slavemaster who specialized in imaginative young concubines.

Even under the present circumstances, the emissary cannot help but gaze at the tapestries. Grunting softly but derisively, the servant advances to the other side of the room, where he knocks softly on an arched door.

"Yes?" comes the master governor's reply.

"There is someone to see you," the servant says. "From Pitur—with news of Master Governor Cambralos."

Seconds later, the door opens and the master governor's bulk fills the space. He looks past the servant and finds the emissary at the other end of the room. Then he glances back at his servant. "He has been screened?"

The servant nods. "He has."

Looking more confident, the master governor crosses the room. "You have news for me?" he asks.

"*Master Governor Cambralos has been assassinated in his bathing room,*" the emissary replies.

Dathrabin curses beneath his breath. "*When?*" he asks.

"*Last night. Shortly after dark, it is believed.*"

"*Then Sarennos is in charge?*"

"*That is correct. He hired me to bring the news to you.*"

"*I see. We will have to meet soon, then, Sarennos and I. There were a number of . . . understandings between Cambralos and myself. Trivial things, mostly, but . . .*" He clears his throat, remembering the company in which he is thinking out loud. "*In any case, you must tell him to get in touch with me.*"

"*I will tell him, Master Governor,*" the emissary replies. "*Will that be all?*"

"*Yes—unless you can suggest a way to rid us of Shil Andrachis and his ruffians.*"

The servant takes that as his cue. Indicating the door, he ushers the visitor in the proper direction. But just as they reach it, the Pitura stops and looks back.

"*Master Governor?*" the emissary says. "*There was one more thing.*"

"*And that is?*" Dathrabin asks.

"*This,*" the visitor tells him. And before the servant can draw another breath, much less intervene, the Pitura moves across the room, faster than the servant would have believed possible, and leaps, driving his heel into the center of the master governor's forehead.

For a moment, Dathrabin staggers. Then he falls backward, like a great tree cut at its base. There is no doubt that the blow was fatal; assassins do not make mistakes.

The servant is stunned. He finds that he is frozen in place, unable to move.

"*I will not kill you,*" the assassin whispers. "*Unless you make it necessary.*"

The servant agrees. Remaining still, he watches the

assassin step over his victim to avoid Holarnis's shadow. Then, bending down, the Ssana uses his knuckles to rap the master governor in four places—the forehead, the center of his chest and the heel of either foot.

As the servant knows, they are the residence-places of the soul. The assassin is driving off the remnants of Holarnis's earthly spirit.

Then, apparently satisfied, the Ssana rises and advances to the window, shrugging off his robes as he goes. Underneath, he is wearing a less ornate set of clothes—more appropriate for slipping down the side of the building and through the streets without drawing attention.

The servant knows that there are two guards out there, but they will be no match for the assassin, particularly since they do not expect an attack from above. He could scream and improve their chances, but he is not a courageous man.

The assassin turns back and glances at him. "Don't you want to know?" he asks.

The servant shakes his head. "Know?" he croaks.

"Why the guard's test did not expose me," the assassin says. Taking the servant's silence for an affirmative response, he removes a tiny bladder from his mouth and squeezes the contents out. He watches the servant's reaction as it drips slowly to the floor.

"Cambralos's own saliva. It was the High Assassin's idea. Rather appropriate, don't you think?"

He chuckles and then, without hesitation, turns and leaps through the open window.

Captain James T. Kirk stared at the rather austere, dark-haired image on the forward viewscreen and leaned forward in his command chair. His mouth had gone inexplicably dry.

"Would you repeat that, Commodore?" he asked.

On the viewscreen, Commodore Montoya, a petite woman with strong cheekbones and braided raven-black hair, nodded. "You're to meet me here at Starbase Twelve, Captain. Upon your arrival, I'll brief you on the details of your mission."

Kirk grunted. "That's what I thought you said."

At the navigation console, Pavel Chekov turned away from his controls and shot the captain a querulous look. At the helm, Ensign Joe Christiano darted a glance at Kirk as well. The captain didn't have to see Uhura to know she was just as surprised as the rest of them.

Montoya must have noticed the reaction on the bridge. "I can understand your confusion," she told Kirk. "Your last orders were to report to Earth, to be decommissioned as scheduled. Basically, that hasn't changed. But since neither you nor any of your officers are scheduled to retire for another couple of weeks, Starfleet wants you to make a little detour along the way."

The captain nodded. "Acknowledged, Commodore." He felt the roil of conflicting emotions as he turned to Chekov. "Set a course for Starbase Twelve, Commander."

"Aye-aye, sair," said the Russian, putting aside the curiosity that must have been consuming him as he swiveled around again to perform his task.

Kirk fixed his gaze on Montoya again. "Is it permitted to ask where you'll be sending us?" he queried.

"You'll be serving as a diplomatic envoy to Alpha Gederix Four, a planet the natives call Ssan," she said.

The captain shrugged. He'd never heard of the place, though the computer could certainly give him its location and some historical background.

"In any case," said the woman on the screen, "I'll see you shortly. Montoya out."

No sooner had the commodore's image faded than a

buzz permeated the atmosphere of the bridge. Kirk looked around at his officers, who discontinued their muttered conversations.

"I don't *know* why we've suddenly been taken out of mothballs," he told them, answering the question in all their minds. "But for those of you who were disappointed at our decommissioning, I wouldn't get my hopes up. As the commodore said, this is only a short detour."

The captain felt a pang as he said that—the same kind of pang he'd experienced three months ago, when Uhura had notified them of the decision to scrap the *Enterprise* in the first place. Since that time, he'd come to accept their fate. He'd even come to look forward to his well-earned retirement—an endless series of long, lazy days with his once and present lover, Carol Marcus.

But the thought of another mission, another chance to see places and people he'd never seen before . . . coming so unexpectedly, at the eleventh hour . . . it had a kind of poetic justice to it. As if fate were rewarding an old warhorse for services faithfully rendered.

Even if it *was* only as a diplomatic envoy.

Suddenly, Kirk felt compelled to share the news. "Mr. Chekov," he announced, "you have the conn."

And before Chekov could even begin to signal his assent, the captain was heading for the turbolift.

"So it has come to this," Zar Holarnis says, his voice strangely flat. "Merciful deity. How could we let another High Assassin come to power?"

Holarnis, the blade-thin master governor of the city-state Larol, is in his Hall of Governance, surrounded by his second and third governors, his advisers, and his security officer. All know his question is largely rhetorical, and so they do not answer.

"Four master governors in the space of one day," Holarnis continues. *"Cambralos, Dathrabin, Lefarnus . . . and now Kinshaian."*

"They will strike here next," says his security officer.

"Merciful deity," Holarnis repeats.

Again, no one speaks—not even his second governor, who is normally full of ideas. The great hall whispers something, but it is unintelligible.

"We must strengthen our defenses," the security officer begins hesitantly. *"More men—and not just in the building but in the surrounding streets."*

Holarnis snorts and looks up at him. *"Do you think Cambralos didn't have guards? Or Lafarnus?"* He shakes his head. *"No amount of security will keep Andrachis's murderers out."*

The security officer frowns. *"Then what do you propose? Surrender?"*

The master governor glares at him. *"Of course not,"* says Holarnis. *"But sitting around here would be worse than surrender. I have to go somewhere else—somewhere they will not find me."*

The security officer grunts. *"Now? When they will be watching the Hall of Governance?"*

"Tithranus is right," an adviser says of the security officer. *"If they see you leaving, they will follow. And then you will have no chance at all."*

"Perhaps," responds the master governor, *"if I leave alone. But what if I send out six or seven hovercars—all well guarded, all with polarized windows? How will Andrachis know which one is mine?"*

They look from one to the other, all around the table. The third governor nods. Before long they are all nodding, all except the security chief. But even he seems satisfied with the strategy up to a point.

"A good plan," confirms the second governor.

"I will make the arrangements," pledges the security chief.

"But do you have a destination?" asks an adviser.

"I do, of course," replies Holarnis. *"But I will share that only with Tithranus."*

There is some squirming around the table. Suspicions flicker in the eyes of those assembled.

"But, Master Governor," says the third governor. *"Surely we can all be trusted with such information. If we should need you . . ."*

"Then you may inform me, and I will apprise the master," responds the security chief.

"That is correct," agrees Holarnis. *"If you need me, Tithranus will know where to find me."* He sighs. *"Mind you, it is not that I lack trust in any of you. But I must leave as few chinks in my armor as possible."*

"Do not be concerned about us," the second governor assures him. *"Our egos will heal. The only matter of any importance is your survival, Master Governor."*

For the first time since the beginning of this meeting, Holarnis allows himself a shadow of a smile. *"Thank you, Penarthil. With any luck, I will not need to take such precautions for long."*

The second governor respectfully inclines his head. *"With any luck,"* he echoes, but, at least to the master governor's ears, he does not sound altogether optimistic.

McCoy sat down on his anteroom couch and contemplated the matched set of *phornicia* shells that he had removed from their place on the wall.

The shells, pink, intricate and undeniably beautiful, symbolized the healing arts on Magistor Seven as the caduceus did on Earth. The Magistori said that if you put a *phornicia* shell to your ear, you could hear the voices of all those whose lives had been saved by their physicians.

Abruptly, his thoughts were interrupted by the sound of chimes. "Come on in," he said.

As the doors shooshed open, they revealed the familiar figure of Jim Kirk. Smiling congenially, the captain stepped inside.

The doctor smiled too, but only halfheartedly. As his friend crossed the room, he held up the shells.

"Nice, aren't they?" he remarked.

Kirk considered them and nodded. "As nice as the ones you lost on the *first Enterprise.*"

McCoy sighed and looked down—past the shells this time. On the floor near his feet lay the ominous gray storage container. The thing already contained a few monograph tapes, not to mention a prized bottle of Saurian brandy. He placed the *phornicia* shells in the container, then shook his head. "Always did hate to pack," he muttered.

"Bones?" said Kirk.

The doctor looked up. There was unmistakable excitement evident in the captain's expression—puzzling, given the fact that they'd soon be saying good-bye not only to the ship but to each other.

"What is it?" he asked.

"Listen to this," said Kirk. He licked his lips. "We've got ourselves a mission."

As far as McCoy was concerned, his friend might as well have just spoken perfect Klingon. "What . . . ?"

Kirk smiled again. "A mission, Bones. We're not through yet. They want us to help out one last time."

"Who does?" asked McCoy, getting to his feet.

"Commodore Montoya at Starbase Twelve."

14

The doctor absorbed the information—or tried to. Somehow it just didn't want to sink in.

"But . . . why in blazes *us,* Jim? Not that I'm looking a gift horse in the mouth, mind you. I mean, I could stand one last hurrah—provided it doesn't lead to Rura Penthe the way the last one did."

"But Starfleet has any number of ships in this sector," agreed the captain. "So why pick on a ship that's already been put out to pasture?"

McCoy grunted. "They didn't tell you anything *about* this mission? Anything that might have given you a clue?"

Kirk shook his head. "Not yet. Only that we're to serve as a diplomatic envoy to a place called Alpha Gederix Four. Of course, its inhabitants call it . . . Bones, is something wrong?"

McCoy could feel the color drain from his face. He could feel his Adam's apple crawl the length of his throat and then come down again like the hammer of doom.

"Ssan," he said, in a voice suddenly full of bitterness. "They call it Ssan."

Kirk's brow creased. "You've been there before."

"I certainly have," the doctor replied. He suddenly saw how all the pieces fit together, and he was less than pleased with the picture they made.

"I think I know now why they picked us for this mission, Jim. Because they wanted someone who'd had some extended experience with the Ssana . . . and was still wearing a Starfleet uniform. And I'm one of the few officers in the Federation who fits that description."

"I see," responded the captain. "So, we owe this mission to you," he concluded, obviously trying to inject a little levity into what was gradually turning into an unexpectedly grim situation.

"Seems that way," the doctor agreed.

He took a breath, then let it out, as images he'd done his best to forget came flitting back to him. He swallowed a second time as the memories began to come back to him.

"But before it's over," McCoy said, "you might not be so all-fired grateful about it."

In the capital of the city-state Larol, the Ssana called Shil Andrachis stands in an open-air market, pretending to study a water-filled tray of sprouts. But he is really considering the building across the street.

The building is the Hall of Governance, the residence of Master Governor Holarnis. By now, Holarnis will have heard of the assassination of his fellow master governors in other city-states. He will have begun to make plans that will enable him to survive as his peers did not.

It is Andrachis's job to make sure that Holarnis's plans come to nothing. He vows that he will not fail in this task.

After all, Holarnis is just a master governor. And Andrachis is the High Assassin.

TWO

☆

"Poor bastard," rasped McCoy.

He grimaced at the charred and twisted wreckage of Master Governor Holarnis's hovercar, as depicted on the undersized monitor in the center of the briefing room table. Leaning closer, he saw a splash of red blood on the jagged shards of a shattered window but no other sign that anything alive had ever been inside the mass of blackened metal.

"He never had a chance," McCoy added.

"As you know, Doctor," said Commodore Montoya, "that was the whole point. These assassins are quite thorough."

Montoya sat on the far side of the table, behind the single-screen monitor. There was no need for her to see these pictures anymore; no doubt she'd already had a bellyful of them.

On McCoy's immediate right, Jim Kirk grunted in assent. "Thorough, all right. And you say all seven of the hovercars that went out that day suffered the same fate?"

Montoya nodded. "All seven, Captain. Holarnis thought he was confusing them, since they usually work alone. He didn't anticipate the assassins' ability to adjust to the situation."

Her gaze moved from Kirk's face to Spock's, who—from McCoy's perspective—sat beyond the captain along the curve of the table. Like his longtime companions, the Vulcan was intent on the image of death and destruction but, unlike them, he displayed no outward sign of sympathy for the hovercars' occupants.

"At the time of his death," the commodore continued, "Holarnis was the highest-ranking government official on Ssan. That honor has now fallen to Meladion, the master governor of Orthun. Of course, subspace communications aren't as quick as we'd like them to be. By now Meladion may have been assassinated as well."

On McCoy's left, Scotty shook his head and swore softly. "Nice bunch o' folks," he said, his voice dripping with irony.

Spock, however, took in the information with perfect equanimity, the same equanimity he'd shown years ago when he realized that an entire shipload of his people on the U.S.S. *Intrepid* had perished all at once.

"Unfortunate," was all the response the Vulcan could muster.

"Unfortunate?" the doctor echoed. He shook his head in mock amazement. "Don't get all teary-eyed on us, Spock. I mean, we're talking about people *dying,* for god's sake—not the cake at my granddaughter's birthday party."

"I beg your pardon, Doctor?" said Montoya. She

probably didn't know what else to say. After all, she hadn't served with Spock for the last twenty years. She didn't know how he'd react to the verbal jab.

"It's all right," McCoy assured her, settling back into his seat. "It's an old story, and one that'll probably never have a satisfactory ending."

"In other words," Kirk told her, placing a hand on the doctor's arm, "you may proceed with the briefing—with my apologies for the interruption."

"Actually," said the commodore, "it's I who should apologize, Captain, for forcing you to postpone your retirements for this mission. But considering Dr. McCoy's measure of experience with the Ssana, and your own record of success in resolving violent conflicts . . ."

"No problem at all," replied Kirk. "I don't think any of us has quite come to accept the decision to decommission the *Enterprise*, so taking her out one last time won't be too great a hardship."

Montoya smiled thinly. "Good." She tapped a panel in a small control console built into the table, and the image on the screen shifted.

"Alpha Gederix Four," said the commodore, pointing to the fertile, cloud-swathed world on the monitor. "Known to its inhabitants as Ssan. A planet with a long and time-honored tradition of legal assassination."

Spock frowned. "Institutionalized murder. A means of political control, I assume?"

McCoy shook his head and opened his mouth to answer. But Montoya beat him to it.

"The assassins wouldn't call it murder, Mr. Spock. To their way of thinking, when they kill, they're performing a religious act."

Spock raised an eyebrow.

"A religious act?" Kirk asked.

"Think of them as a cult, Jim," McCoy said. "They have a specific function to fulfill in society, with ceremonies to observe, even initiation rites to undergo."

Montoya nodded. "Becoming an assassin involves subjecting oneself to physical, biochemical changes. When those changes are finished, the person isn't Ssani anymore but . . . something else."

McCoy shuddered, remembering. Montoya was right. Assassins weren't like other Ssani. They weren't like any other race he'd ever met.

"It makes no sense to me," Scotty interrupted. "How something like that develops—"

"The institution's been around forever," McCoy answered. "It evolved out of the Ssani tendency toward multiple births—twins is the norm there, and triplets aren't uncommon at all—and as a way of combating wild population growth."

"Survival of the fittest," Kirk said.

Montoya nodded. "Assassins have always been held in the highest regard on Ssan. Up until about forty years ago, when a wave of new-age thinkers started convincing the people to break with tradition. Not only would they begin to practice birth control, a heretofore unheard of idea— though the technology had long been available—but they would begin to phase out the institution of assassination." A pause. "The institution fought back."

Again, Montoya tapped at her controls. And again, the image changed.

Now they were looking at a picture of a Ssana. Like all his planet's people, he had long, bulbous earlobes and tiny, indigo eyes set deep beneath bony brows—eyes that stared in that glassy way McCoy had come to associate with the dead.

But then, even without that clue, the doctor would have

known the Ssana was deceased. After all, he recognized the individual and knew that no one had ever taken a picture of him while he lived.

"This," said Montoya, "is—or rather was—Li Moboron. As Ssan's High Assassin, he took exception to the new, progressive government, which was considering, among other things, an invitation to join the United Federation of Planets."

"Exception?" McCoy chuckled bitterly. "It was a blasted holy war."

"As the doctor says," Montoya amended without blinking, "it was a holy war—a wave of wholesale assassinations. To combat it, the government hired a small army of counterassassins. After a long and bloody conflict, in which the Federation sometimes helped out with disaster control, the government emerged victorious and instituted its reforms. Birth control became widespread. And assassination was outlawed."

"Outlawed?" echoed Kirk. "How did the government break that news to its hired guns?"

"Not very well," said McCoy.

Montoya shot him a glance this time, like a warning volley across his bow. A reminder that she was the one providing the briefing and that unless he had any relevant questions, he'd best keep his mouth shut.

Normally the doctor would have taken that as a challenge. But he had to concede that the woman had a point. The situation on Ssan was no laughing matter; best to be as businesslike as possible.

Montoya cleared her throat. "At first, there were surprisingly few repercussions. But as time went by, the surviving assassins—on both sides—formed a series of secret cults, and it was these cults that preserved the concept of the assassin in Ssani society. Of course, they had their differences. Without government sanction, each group had to create its own definition of what an assassin should be. Some were naturally more militant than others."

"They lacked a leader," observed Spock, "someone who could unite the cults."

"Exactly," said the commodore.

Once more she hit her control panel. This time the sight that greeted them was that of a flat metal disk with a symbol rendered on its face in red.

"That cross you see is a stylized dagger," explained Montoya. "The circle represents Alpha Gederix, the sun. It's the emblem of the High Assassin. We found this at the wreck that contained the master governor's body."

McCoy straightened and cursed beneath his breath. He hadn't grasped the magnitude of this. He hadn't grasped it at all.

When Montoya had shown them Holarnis's hovercar, he'd thought it was the work of an individual cult—and Lord knew, that would have been bad enough. But if someone had gotten himself named High Assassin . . .

"That suggests two things," said the commodore. "First, that the assassins had somehow determined which of the cars Holarnis was in and destroyed the others simply as a warning against those who'd try to protect assassin targets."

"And second," McCoy snarled, "that there's a new Li Moboron around."

Montoya turned her attention to the doctor again, but if she harbored any resentment, it evaporated quickly before the horror that must have been etched into his face.

"He calls himself Shil Andrachis," she told them. "A protégé of the last High Assassin, if his propaganda can be believed. His goal? To roll back the reforms—all of them—and to restore the assassins' tradition to Ssan."

"And that's why Holarnis—and the others—were murdered?" asked Kirk. "Because they wouldn't do as he asked?"

The commodore nodded. "Today's master governors were probably teenagers when Moboron and his movement were demolished. After four decades, the Ssana may have forgotten how ruthless these people could be. In any case, they don't have the option of fighting fire with fire this time—or more accurately, assassin with assassin. All the assassins are working for Andrachis."

"Which is where we come in," Scotty noted. "And this time, to supply more than just disaster control."

"True," said Montoya. "You're to find the assassin leadership and negotiate a peaceful settlement with Andrachis—before these isolated assassinations evolve into mass slaughters, as they did forty years ago."

McCoy shook his head. "Forget it."

The others looked at him as if he'd committed a murder himself. Spock cocked an eyebrow. Kirk just frowned.

"Bones," said the captain, "a year ago, I wouldn't have bet a plugged nickel that we'd see a détente between the Federation and the godforsaken Klingons in our lifetime. But we *did,* didn't we?"

Jim didn't get it. But then, he had never been on Ssan. He hadn't seen the things McCoy had.

"The Klingons," insisted the doctor, "are *children* compared to these assassins. Li Moboron would sooner have fallen on his blade than negotiated. And if this Andrachis character is his protégé, he won't negotiate either. Not with the government, not with us, not with *anybody.*"

The commodore leaned back in her chair and fixed the chief medical officer with her gaze. "Doctor McCoy is right, gentlemen. It would be a mistake to underestimate the difficulty of what the Federation is asking of you."

"However?" suggested Kirk.

"However," said Montoya, "we are still asking. I will apprise Admiral Jovanovich of the doctor's concerns, but the mission goes on. Any other questions?"

Before McCoy could answer, Kirk said, "None, Commodore. I think we've heard all we need to hear."

By the time they returned to the starbase's transporter room, McCoy's scowl had deepened considerably—though even a half hour ago, Kirk wouldn't have believed that possible. Hell, the doctor wasn't even complaining about having to let someone "shoot his atoms halfway across the galaxy."

"Good luck," said the commodore, who'd graciously volunteered to see them off.

"Men make their own luck," commented the captain, eliciting a crinkling at the corners of Montoya's mouth that he took for a smile.

Brave words, he told himself. But it was difficult feeling brave while his chief medical officer was in such a funk.

But hell . . . they'd faced tough situations before, hadn't they? And McCoy had never been as gloomy as he was now, not by half. Was it just that Bones was feeling older and less prepared for something like this? Had their close brush on that Klingon penal asteroid taken more out of him than he'd admitted?

Or was there something else? Something about Ssan that he still hadn't let out of the bag? As Montoya's transporter chief whisked them to their ship, Kirk wondered about that.

Strange that in twenty-seven years of serving shoulder to shoulder, McCoy hadn't described Ssan to the captain in any detail before. Especially since his stay there was his first real mission in space.

After all they'd been through together on the *Enterprise*—both the original and now *Enterprise*-A—Kirk would have thought he knew everything there was to know about his friend Bones. It seemed there were still some stories left untold between them . . . some secrets left unspoken.

Perhaps it was time to dredge up some of those secrets, for the doctor's sake. As a friend, it was the captain's duty. to help him get them off his chest. Of course, McCoy might tell him it was none of his business. But that wasn't going to stop him from giving it a try.

A moment later, the transport was complete. The captain's companions began to step down from the *Enterprise*'s transporter platform.

"Uh . . . Spock?"

The Vulcan turned to him. "Yes, Captain?"

"I'd like you to take the conn," Kirk told him. "I'm going to"—he glanced in McCoy's direction—"relax for a while."

The first officer inclined his head. "As you wish, sir."

Having made that arrangement, the captain caught up with McCoy, who was already halfway out of the room. "Bones," he said, "wait up."

The doctor glanced over his shoulder. "What now?" he asked.

"How about a drink?" Kirk suggested.

McCoy looked at him, emotions flitting behind his pale blue eyes like some kind of exotic, alien insects. "A drink?" He shook his head. "Sorry, Jim. Not right now. I don't feel much like being bartender-slash-psychiatrist."

The captain smiled. "You misunderstand. I'm volunteering to be the bartender this time." A pause. "You look like you could use one."

The doctor considered the offer for a moment. "Sure," he said at last. "Why the blazes not?"

As they emerged into the corridor together, Kirk planted a hand on McCoy's shoulder. "As I recall," he said, "you like your brandy at room temperature, right?"

"Two degrees above," the doctor reminded him dourly.

"Two degrees above. That's what I *meant* to say," the captain assured him.

McCoy swallowed, felt the fire of the brandy warm his insides, and looked over the rim of his glass at Kirk. His friend was watching to see if the liquor had taken the edge off his frustration. And maybe it had at that.

"Well?" asked the captain, breaking a long silence.

Bones shrugged, feeling too ornery to be diplomatic. "It's not Saurian."

Kirk's gaze darkened. "How chivalrous of you to say so, Doctor. And just when I was starting to feel like a good host."

Stung by the remark, McCoy snorted. "I guess it's not that bad. Aw, hell . . . it's not bad at all." He swirled the remnants of the liquid around in his glass. "The mood I'm in, even the Saurian chancellor's private stock wouldn't impress me."

"You're in a mood?" The captain shrugged. "I guess I hadn't noticed."

The doctor glared at him. "You know what?" he said. "You're a lousy bartender *and* a lousy psychiatrist. You don't bait your patients, for god's sake. You bring them out slowly. *Gently.*"

The captain held a hand up. "You're absolutely right, Bones. I stand corrected." He leaned forward, meeting his companion's gaze. "Now why don't you tell me, slowly, and gently, what the blazes is on your mind."

McCoy sighed and looked away. He really didn't want to talk about this now. Or ever, for that matter.

"It's about Ssan," the captain prompted.

"I already told you about Ssan," said the doctor, putting on an air of annoyance, though he knew it would do him no good. Kirk wasn't about to give up.

"You didn't tell me everything," the captain pressed. "Not by a long shot. I want to hear the rest of it."

McCoy thought a moment. "All right," he said finally. "It's true, I suppose. I didn't tell you everything about that place." He found a spot on the wall behind Kirk to stare at. "Hell, there isn't that much more to tell. Just that it was a bad time for me. And I made a lot of bad choices I've had to live with the rest of my life."

"What kind of choices?" asked Kirk.

McCoy glared at him. "You're relentless, aren't you?"

"It's in my job description," the captain advised him.

The doctor harrumphed. "How about some more of that mediocre brandy you were serving?"

Kirk reached for the carafe on the table at his side and leaned forward. Bones held out his glass and watched the captain refill it.

"What kind of choices . . ." McCoy echoed reflectively. What kind indeed.

He tossed back the brandy, letting it sink into all his crevices. Then he looked at his friend again, no longer feeling quite so cornered.

"The kind that get people killed," he said evenly.

Kirk shook his head, still not understanding. "You mean you made a mistake?"

The doctor ran the fingers of one hand through his thick gray hair. "Good question," he said. "I wish I had a good answer." He thought for a moment, allowing the memories, good and bad, to well up inside him. "I guess," he went on, "some people might say it was a mistake. Me?" He thought some more. "I'm *still* not sure."

The captain sat back in his chair. "It's a little difficult to discuss something without knowing what it is you're discussing. Some details might help."

McCoy nodded. "You want details? Okay. Picture yourself at the tender age of twenty-six. Fresh out of medical school, a trainee on his first mission. And one of your best—"

The intercom buzzer went off before the doctor could finish his sentence. The captain walked over to the intercom panel.

"Kirk here," he replied. "Is that you, Spock?"

There was a pause on the other end. "It is indeed, Captain."

Kirk smiled faintly in appreciation of his own sixth sense. "What can I do for you?"

"We have just communicated with Commodore Montoya . . ." the Vulcan began.

The captain exchanged looks with his chief medical officer. "But we only left the starbase a few minutes ago," he said.

"Quite true," Spock agreed. "However, she had enough time to reflect on Dr. McCoy's remarks to decide that we needed help in our efforts at diplomacy. As luck would have it—her words, not mine—one of the preeminent diplomatic teams in the Federation happens to be in this sector, awaiting a new assignment. The commodore took it upon herself to engage their services on our behalf."

"Diplomatic team . . ." muttered the doctor. As far as he was concerned, diplomats were somewhere on the evolutionary scale between a slug . . . and another slug.

And here it had been his own comments that had prompted Montoya to provide them with diplomatic assistance. Talk about your bitter ironies, he mused.

"Did the commodore say which team it would be?" asked the captain. There were several, after all, and some were better than others.

"She did," confirmed Spock. "The name she gave was Treadway. Clay and Jocelyn Treadway."

Treadway, McCoy repeated inwardly. Suddenly he found himself smiling.

But it wasn't out of happiness. It was the kind of smile that comes when a person can't quite take it anymore, when he finds it somehow easier to laugh than to cry.

Kirk looked at him, no doubt wondering what had prompted his friend's sudden change in demeanor. "What's so funny?" he asked.

"I beg your pardon?" said Spock.

"We'll go over this later," Kirk told his first officer. Applying pressure to the panel a second time, he broke the connection.

McCoy felt his stomach muscles contract painfully, as if something had grabbed him from inside and wouldn't let go. Treadway, he repeated inwardly. *Treadway.*

Still grinning like a crazy person, the doctor set down his glass and lowered his face into his hands. "Of all the blasted diplomats in the galaxy, why did it have to be *them?*"

Kirk's eyes narrowed. "You know them, Bones?"

Raising his head, the doctor leveled a blistering glare at him. "You're damned right I know them." He could feel his mouth twist with undiluted hatred. "Jocelyn Treadway is my ex-wife, Jim. And Clay Treadway is the man who married her."

The captain swallowed involuntarily. "Jocelyn," he

muttered. "Of course. But it's been so long since . . ." He paused awkwardly.

"My godforsaken ex-wife," McCoy repeated. He was overcome with genuine misery—the kind he'd experienced in their worst moments on Rura Penthe. "Damn it, Jim, if this isn't the mission from *hell,* I don't know what is."

THREE

☆

"I knew this was going to happen someday," said McCoy.
"I just knew it." He looked up at Kirk. "If I stayed in
Starfleet long enough, if they kept on mediating from
planet to planet, the chances of our running into one
another would get greater and greater and . . ."

"You knew?" asked the captain. "You knew Jocelyn
had remarried, that she was in the diplomatic corps?"

"Damned right I knew," he said softly. "Joanna told
me. Not on purpose, mind you. She wouldn't have done
that to me." He picked up his glass again and took
another sip of brandy. It wasn't Saurian, that was for sure.
But right now, he didn't mind the feel of the liquor
burning in his throat. He wiped his lips and set the glass
down.

"One shore leave, it just leaked out. We were all sitting
around carving up the turkey and Joanna was talking to
Conner, my grandson—"

31

"I know who Conner is," Kirk reminded him gently.

The doctor harrumphed. "Yes. Of course you do. Anyway, he couldn't have been more than two at the time. He asked where his grandmother was, and Joanna told him she was off on Chadric Seven, helping the Chadricans see eye-to-eye." He half-smiled. "Eye-to-eye—get it?"

The captain nodded. "I get it, Bones."

The Chadricans were cyclopean, like a half-dozen other sentient species in the known galaxy. It was the kind of joke only someone like Joanna, who'd been out in space, could have made.

"I guess," Bones went on, "she must have forgotten for a moment that I was sitting there. When she realized what she'd said, she turned three shades of purple. But it was too late. The cat was out of the bag. That's when I asked her what in heaven's name had possessed her mother to join the diplomatic corps."

"And she told you about Clay Treadway?"

McCoy shook his head. "No. She refused. She knew what a wreck it would have made me." He paused. "But Conner wasn't so merciful, bless his pointy little head. He came right out and told me that Grandma had married Mr. Treadway, and they'd gone off into space together."

The captain frowned. "Lord, Bones. Conner's twelve now. That means you've known about this for a decade."

"And I didn't tell you. I know." He grew angry suddenly. "Well, I don't have to tell you *everything*," he snapped.

But as soon as he'd let the words escape, he was sorry for them. He winced at his own volatility.

"It's okay," Kirk told him. "You're right. You *don't* have to tell me everything."

McCoy sighed. "I couldn't, Jim. It hurt even to think about Jocelyn remarrying. But to say it out loud . . . even to you . . ." He sighed again, a little louder. "I just wasn't strong enough for that."

Kirk leaned forward and clapped his longtime comrade on the shoulder. "No apologies necessary, Bones. We've all got a few skeletons in the closet."

"Thanks," he said sheepishly. And then: "Jim? Would it . . . I mean . . . ?"

Kirk appeared to know what his chief medical officer was trying to say. "Would it be all right," he finished, "if you didn't have to be there to greet the Treadways when they beam on board?"

Scowling, McCoy nodded. "Yes," he said. "That."

Kirk smiled.

"Spock and I can lay out the welcome mat by ourselves," he assured the doctor. "In fact, we'll deal with the Treadways every step of the way. You don't have to get involved with them at all, if that's the way you prefer it."

McCoy sighed and averted his eyes. "I'd appreciate that," he mumbled. Then he remembered: "Wait a minute. I'm supposed to be the expert on Ssan around here. How can I—?"

"Don't give it a second thought," Kirk interrupted. "If the Treadways are as good as Montoya says, we may not need you at all. And if I have a question, I can always ask. Anyway, I've survived without you on several occasions. I think I can pull it off just one more time."

The captain smiled. McCoy supposed he should smile back. But he couldn't. His senses were gradually drifting to another place and time. To a town in Georgia and a certain hot summer afternoon.

Suddenly the doctor felt the need to stand up, to shrug off the past. Kirk looked at him with a measure of concern.

McCoy said, "I think I'd better be going. You're going to want to make arrangements for our guests and all."

Truth to tell, there wasn't very much to do. They both knew that. But he wanted to be alone right now—and Jim knew him well enough not to stand in his way.

Hell, Jim had had more than his share of loss over the years, what with the deaths of his son and his brother . . . and Miramanee . . . and so many others he probably couldn't count them all. He knew what it was like to need some solitude, some time to put things in perspective.

Putting down his brandy, McCoy managed a bit of a smile. "I'll see you later," he told Kirk.

"Ya know where to find me," the captain said.

And, feeling more than a little out of kilter, McCoy beat a hasty retreat from his friend's quarters.

Jocelyn Treadway bit her lip nervously. When Commodore Montoya had asked her and her husband to undertake this mission, she'd thought about declining. After all, it was more than a little awkward.

However, Clay had insisted that they go. He'd reminded her that they'd joined the diplomatic service to do a job, and that the situation on Ssan fairly cried out for someone with their talents at mediation.

It had struck her as strange that her husband would be so adamant about it. But then, Clay had developed a very strong sense of duty over the years; it wouldn't have been the first time he'd put an assignment before his own welfare.

So in the end, she'd gone along with it. But now, as she waited alongside her husband on the transporter pad of the *Potemkin,* she began to wonder if she'd made the right decision.

"You'll like working with Jim Kirk," said Captain Gladstone, as her bearded transporter operator exchanged coordinates with his counterpart on the *Enterprise.* Gladstone was a tall, well-built blonde, whose good humor seemed as irrepressible as the ample curves beneath the surface of her uniform.

"So I've heard," replied Clay, gracing the captain with a flash of his perfect teeth. "Best in the business and all that—present company excepted, of course." His mustache, reddish gold and neatly trimmed, widened to accentuate his smile. Unconsciously, he ran his fingers through his thick, dark hair.

Her husband didn't mean to flirt, Jocelyn knew. It was a reflex, something he'd been doing practically since birth. Nor did it make her the least bit hot under the collar. Jealousy was for fillies.

Not that she had much reason to be jealous, Jocelyn remarked inwardly. True, her hair had gone mostly gray and she'd acquired a few wrinkles here and there, but her dark blue eyes still turned men's heads. Some men's, anyway.

Abruptly, the transporter operator looked up. "Looks like we're all ready," he told Gladstone.

The captain nodded. "Thanks, Jonesy." Turning back to the Treadways—but mostly to Clay, Jocelyn thought—Gladstone inclined her head in a sort of salute. "Good hunting," she wished them.

It's not a hunt, Jocelyn mused. It's a mediation. The two activities couldn't possibly be farther apart.

But then she caught herself. Be fair, she thought. The woman didn't mean anything by the remark. Gladstone's no more trigger-happy than any other commanding officer in Starfleet. You're just on edge.

Because of where you're going. And who you're going to see there.

And maybe, she conceded, despite her protestations to the contrary, just a mite jealous as well.

As if he'd read her thought, Clay turned his smile on her. And if it had been flirtatious before, it was full of something a whole lot more intimate now, more devoted.

Jocelyn sighed. Her husband's little flirtations never went anywhere. He was as faithful as the planets in their orbits—that, at least, had never been a problem.

She looked around. Where in *hell* was that transporter effect already?

She'd barely finished asking her silent question when she realized she was no longer in the transporter room of the *Potemkin*. Her surroundings were virtually identical, but Gladstone and the man she called Jonesy had disappeared and been replaced by a new set of faces. Fortunately, none of them were *his*.

Not that she wouldn't have to see him eventually, Jocelyn knew. But if she had her druthers, she preferred that it be later rather than sooner.

She and her husband descended from the platform together. Funny, she mused. No matter how many times she transported, it always made her feel a little uncomfortable. Of course, she wouldn't tell anyone that.

Jim Kirk stepped forward and held out his hand to Clay, who was closer to him. "Ambassador Treadway," he said. "Welcome aboard."

"Captain Kirk. The pleasure's all mine." Clay turned to indicate Jocelyn. "And you know my wife, I take it."

The captain nodded, greeting Jocelyn in turn. "Nice to see you again."

Kirk was no longer the bright-eyed, bushy-tailed youngster Jocelyn remembered. If the years hadn't exactly been unkind to him, they'd still left some subtle signs of their passing: a few lines in his face, a few streaks of gray in his hair.

But he hadn't become a very good liar. He wasn't glad to see her at all, she knew—no gladder than he'd been thirty years ago. Jim Kirk had seen the pain she'd inflicted on his friend: he couldn't remember that and be genuinely pleased at her presence on the ship.

Not that she'd gotten any enjoyment out of seeing her ex-husband beaten down that way. Lord knew, the last thing she wanted in the world was to hurt someone she'd loved the way she'd loved him.

"Nice to see you again, too," she told the captain. Unfortunately, she found, she didn't mean it any more than he did.

Kirk gestured to introduce them to another uniformed figure, who'd been standing in the shadows near the transporter console up until then. "This is Mr. Spock," he said. "My first officer."

A Vulcan, Jocelyn noted. Good. It always made their job a good deal easier when there was a Vulcan aboard. That way, they wouldn't have to be the voice of reason all by themselves.

She didn't expect Spock to shake hands with them, the way the captain had. He didn't. "I trust your efforts on Risa were successful?" he asked, taking in both Jocelyn and her husband at a single glance.

"Very successful," Clay assured him. "Fifty years from now, no one'll ever know there was a war there."

"In fact," said Jocelyn, "there's talk of making it a vacation planet. Might not be a bad idea either, now that the natives have quit killing each other for a while."

The Vulcan turned to Kirk. "The Risans were involved in a nearly continuous round of armed conflicts for the last decade. Twice before, the Federation had failed to bring the two sides to the bargaining table."

The captain nodded, doing his best to look impressed, but Jocelyn could tell that he had other things on his mind—like the mess on Ssan, for instance.

"I'd like to hear more," he told Spock, "but I'll bet our guests would like to freshen up before immersing themselves in work again." Turning to the negotiators, he said: "We've set aside a class-one suite for you, if that's all right."

Clay cleared his throat. Jocelyn could feel the blood rushing to her face.

"Actually," she told the captain, "we would prefer two suites."

That plainly took Kirk by surprise. "Two?" he repeated.

"Yes," said Jocelyn. "My husband and I . . . require separate quarters, Captain. The quartermaster on the *Potemkin* was to have apprised you of that."

Now it was Kirk's turn to redden. "I apologize for the oversight," he replied. "I'll see to it that you're assigned individual suites immediately."

"Adjoining suites will be fine," said Clay, trying his best to cover his embarrassment. He glanced at Jocelyn to make sure she had no objection.

Not that she *could* object, without making a bigger scene than was necessary. Nodding, she gave the idea her blessing—though truth to tell, it would have been kinder for her to take something on the other end of the ship.

Kindness and cruelty, she thought. Why had she always been so much better at the latter than the former?

"Adjoining suites it is," the captain confirmed. Without looking at the Vulcan, he asked, "Would you see to it, Mr. Spock?"

The first officer nodded. Returning his attention to the Treadways, he said, "Would you come with me, please?"

"Absolutely," responded Clay, rapidly rebuilding his facade of confidence and casual authority. "We're with you, Mr. Spock."

Studiously avoiding Kirk's eyes, lest she find something she didn't want to see there, Jocelyn fell into step beside her husband and followed the Vulcan out of the transporter room.

Uhura was having lunch with Pavel Chekov in one of the *Enterprise's* rec lounges. As he got up to get them some coffee, she couldn't help but overhear the banter at the next table.

"Attractive?" echoed Joe Christiano, the ensign who had only recently been assigned to the bridge. "You bet. I mean, for an older woman, of course."

"She's attractive for a woman of any age," argued Dennehy, one of Scotty's fledgling engineers.

Wouldn't it be nice, thought Uhura, if they were talking about me? I don't even think I'd mind the "older woman" disclaimer.

"And those eyes," commented Christiano. "What color is that?"

"Sort of a . . . blue-gray," decided Dennehy. "A really *nice* blue-gray."

Oh well, Uhura mused, I guess they're talking about someone else.

"You know what I heard?" said the ensign.

"No," replied Dennehy. "What?"

Chekov chose that moment to arrive with their coffees. As he set them down on the table, he shook his head from side to side.

"You know," he sighed, "I never thought I vould miss this tasteless sludge the food units spit out. But when I thought ve had all served on our last mission together, even this coffee suddenly seemed—"

"Ssh," hissed Uhura. She tilted her head meaningfully toward the side of the room where Christiano and Dennehy were sitting.

Chekov just looked at her, obviously puzzled. "Vhat's the matter?" he asked.

"Nothing," she told him. "Just sit down and be quiet." And again, she tilted her head to indicate the two young men.

The security chief followed her gesture but couldn't quite see what she was up to. Nonetheless, he did as he was told. He'd known Uhura too long to question her reasons for doing things.

"The doctor's *wife?*" exclaimed Dennehy, barely suppressing his surprise.

"Ex-wife," corrected Christiano. "Apparently, they were divorced a long time ago. A very long time, in fact—maybe forty years."

"You're kidding me," accused the engineer.

"No, I'm not," said Christiano. "The captain and Mr. Spock were talking about it on the bridge. You know, when they didn't think anyone was listening."

Dennehy shook his head. "Dr. McCoy and Jocelyn Treadway. Hard to believe the old coot could ever have interested her, you know? Or that . . ."

Uhura never heard the rest of the engineer's comment, because Chekov didn't let her. Pushing his chair out from under the table, he got up and walked across the room to where Dennehy and Christiano were seated.

It took a moment for the objects of his attention to

realize that the security chief was headed their way. But as soon as they did, they clammed up.

Planting the heels of his palms on the table between the ensign and the engineer, Chekov leaned forward and fixed them with his gaze. Even from her vantage point on the other side of the lounge, Uhura could see how the two had paled.

"Let's get a few thinks straight," said Pavel, his voice a harsh rasp. His head swiveled toward the ensign. "First of all, Mr. Christiano, what is discussed on the bridge stays on the bridge—whether it's clessified information or the time of day. Is thet understood?"

The ensign's head bobbed up and down. "Yes, sir."

Chekov then turned to Dennehy. "And as for your description of Dr. McCoy as an 'old coot,' I do not care for it. I do not care for it at all."

The engineer nodded earnestly. "Acknowledged, sir."

"Doctor McCoy was saving lives even before your parents vere born," Chekov reminded them. "He is the most decorated medical officer in the fleet. If I vere you, I vould remember that next time I vas tempted to refer to him in less than flettering terms."

Dennehy nodded even faster. "Absolutely, sir."

The security chief looked from one to the other of them. "If I ever hear such an outrageous, debasing conversation between the two of you again, I vill see to it thet your next assignment is the supply run to Goliardh Seven. Am I making myself clear?"

Christiano's Adam's apple traveled up and down his throat. "Very clear, sir."

Apparently satisfied, Chekov straightened, tugged down dramatically on his tunic, and returned to Uhura's table. She felt an impulse to applaud his performance but restrained herself.

"There," he said, as he sat down. "Thet should put a lid on any embarrassing gossip about Dr. McCoy and his ex-vife." Chekov glanced at the two young men appraisingly. "At least, I hope it vill."

Uhura smiled. "You know something, Pavel? You're the best friend a ship's doctor—or for that matter, a ship's communications officer—could have."

Chekov smiled back and lifted his coffee mug in salute. "As usual, Uhura, you are absolutely right."

For what had to have been the fiftieth time, McCoy removed a shiny, new medical tricorder from one of sickbay's specially built supply drawers. Mechanically, he put the device through a rigorous self-diagnostic process and, like each and every one of its shiny, new predecessors, the unit checked out just fine.

The chief medical officer knew full well how unnecessary this all was. After all, he'd had his staff check all the equipment from tricorders to bio-beds just a couple of weeks ago, strictly to satisfy Starfleet regulations. And it was so rare for even the most hellish contraption to go on the blink these days, even that had seemed a bit frivolous to him.

Yet the alternative, going out into the ship's corridors and turbolifts, its bridge and its rec lounges and its botanical gardens—in short, taking part in the public life of the *Enterprise*—had been so terrifying, he'd preferred to sequester himself in sickbay every waking hour of the last two days.

Because somewhere on this vessel was Jocelyn. Not a memory but the real thing. The thought unnerved him as no Klingon disruptor ever could. Damn, all a disruptor could do was kill him; Jocelyn could do far worse, as McCoy could testify at length.

Wasn't that why he'd gone out into space in the first place? To get away from her? To escape the very notion of her? And here she'd followed him to what he'd thought was his ultimate refuge, invading his privacy, shattering the fragile cocoon of calm and certainty he'd spent years constructing so carefully about himself.

Anger flashed through the doctor like a bolt of electricity. What right did she have? Hadn't she done enough to him?

Without meaning to, he slammed his fist down on the unyielding metal surface of the supply cabinet. It was the sharp report of colliding surfaces more than the impact itself that reminded him of the tricorder still in his hand.

Cursing aloud, he checked the thing's readout and saw nothing but digital gibberish. Obviously he'd damaged its delicate internals.

"Great," he muttered. "Keep it up and you won't have to check the equipment. You'll *know* it's broken."

It was time to get out of here, he told himself. This was no way for a man to live. He had to find himself some sentient company or go berserk. Tossing the broken tricorder into one of the repair bins, he stripped off his lab coat, hung it on an empty hook, and headed purposefully for the exit doors.

He was already well out into the corridor before he even thought about where he was going. Certainly not in the direction of the library; it was the first place one would look for a diplomat, given their love of information on comparative civilizations. And not toward any of the conference rooms, either; the only thing those people liked better than reading about alien cultures was talking about them.

He snapped his fingers as inspiration gripped him. I know, he thought. The engine room. There's always someone down there, and it's almost always Scotty. Here on the *Enterprise*-A, he's got a lot less to worry about than he used to. I can probably shoot the bull with him for as long as I want.

And it would take his mind off Jocelyn, as his tricorder diagnostics had failed to do. Yup, that's what he'd do all right. He'd visit Scotty.

As luck would have it, the first turbolift he encountered was ready and waiting for him. His approach triggered the sensor built into the bulkhead and the lift doors slid aside for him.

"Engineering," he commanded.

The doors slid closed again. Massaging a crick at the base of his neck—one he'd no doubt developed scrutinizing all those blasted tricorders—McCoy tried to imagine his journey down through the bowels of the ship. And across as well, he reminded himself. Sickbay was quite a way forward of engineering, after all.

Moments later, he reached his destination: the corridor right outside Mr. Scott's domain. Stepping out of the lift compartment, he focused on the doors that led into that arcane and wondrous place.

At long last, the doctor felt safe. Nothing down here except the engines and an extra gymnasium with which some bright young ship designer had no doubt filled an otherwise useless space. No chance that he'd run into—

"Leonard?"

McCoy froze at the sound. A trickle of ice water made its horribly cold and deliberate journey down the middle of his back. And even before he turned to look over his shoulder and identify the source, he knew who it was.

"Jocelyn," he said, his voice surprisingly clear and steady.

Giving in to an undeniable curiosity, he saw that she

was just as he remembered her. Well, maybe not quite. Her hair, once a dark, unadulterated brown that had reminded him of fine, ground coffee, was shot through with waves of silver-gray. And there were wrinkles at the corners of her mouth, at the bridge of her finely sculpted nose and around her eyes.

But it was still Jocelyn, the slim, compact girl he'd once seen across a high school dance floor and marveled at. The same girl he'd fallen head over hard-rubber heels in love with.

It wasn't until the first moment of shock and wonderment passed that he realized she was wearing a form-fitting scarlet exercise outfit. Or that there was a fine sheen of perspiration on her face, accumulating in beads at her hairline.

"Been to the gym, I see," he told her. As before, his voice was strong and even, strangely not even hinting at the trembling in his soul.

Returning the scrutiny, she nodded. "That's right," she said absently. "And you?"

The doctor swallowed. This was absurd. They were exchanging banalities as if they hardly knew each other . . . as if they hadn't shared a marriage bed or given birth to a child once upon a time. As if she hadn't ripped his heart out one fateful day and changed both their lives forever.

Nonetheless, he couldn't get himself off the established course. "Engineering," he replied. "To see Mr. Scott."

To try to take my mind off you, he remarked. But only silently, only to himself.

Her forehead puckered ever so slightly. "How . . . how are you?" she asked, her voice faltering a bit—though that could certainly have been the result of her exertions in the gym.

McCoy shrugged. How was he? "Not bad," he said, "for a man significantly past his prime. For someone who obviously hasn't taken care of himself the way you have."

Jocelyn seemed taken aback by the comment. "You seem to have taken care of yourself just fine," she observed. And she wasn't just being polite, he realized with a start. She really meant it.

"Thanks," he told her, meaning it just as much.

"Don't mention it." A pause, as her expression changed to one of concern. "Leonard, you haven't been . . . hiding from me, have you?"

"Hiding?" he echoed, as if it were the most ridiculous thing he'd ever heard.

"Because I don't want that," she went on, not falling for his act in the least. "This is your ship, your home. I'm an invader here. I know that."

"You're nothing of the sort," he assured her, lying through his teeth. "You're here because you've got a job to do. And this place is no more mine than it is the Klingon emperor's. It belongs to Starfleet."

"No," she insisted, the ripple in her brow becoming more pronounced. "I mean it. I didn't come here to make you uncomfortable. I don't want you to think you have to avoid me." Her lips went taut. "I wish there were some way I could—"

"Could what?" asked a deep, masculine voice.

Both of them turned, to see Clay Treadway standing a little way down the corridor. He was smiling generously, making light of the situation, but his stance was unmistakable, at least to McCoy.

It said: This is my woman, stay away from her or face the consequences. Anyone who thought mankind had evolved much in the last several million years might have changed their mind if they could have seen the look in the man's eye.

The doctor didn't budge, though. The blood rushed to his face, but he stayed right where he was. Maybe with someone else, it would have been out of sheer orneriness. But with Clay Treadway, it was something that ran much deeper. Something like out-and-out, blind, rampaging hatred—and for a damned good reason.

"Clay," declared Jocelyn, as if to break the tension. But if that was her intent, it didn't work. Had the two men been elk, they would have locked antlers and gone at it right there in the corridor.

As it was, the newcomer didn't give even a hint of lowering his head and charging. He merely inclined his head in a friendly sort of way and uttered a single word: "Leonard."

Of course, the way he said it, it came out more like a dismissal, the way one would address an inferior. But then, that was nothing new. Clay had been talking to him that way since they were boys back in Georgia.

McCoy's teeth ground together. They hadn't seen each other in more than forty years, but they were picking up right where they left off. Except for the irreducible fact that Clay had already won the contest—won it hands down, in fact—and that no matter what the doctor did now, he couldn't alter that fact.

"You haven't changed a bit," McCoy noted. It wasn't a compliment.

But the other man seemed not to know that. Or if he did, he chose to ignore the information, because his smile only broadened.

"Why, thanks," he told the doctor. "Kind of you to say so, Leonard." Then, turning to Jocelyn, he said, "I was waiting for you up in the library. I thought we'd made plans to go over those Ssani protocols."

Jocelyn made a small, strangled sound of frustration. "You're absolutely right. I'm sorry, Clay. I just lost track of the time."

"It's my fault," offered McCoy, addressing his ex-wife. The last blasted thing he'd *ever* do was apologize to Clay. "I'm afraid I've held you up."

"That's okay," said the other man, as if the apology had been directed at him after all. "No harm done." He looked at Jocelyn again. "I just asked around until I found someone who'd seen you headed this way in your gym togs. Now shall we go?"

There was something strange in Clay's voice—strange and unfamiliar. After a moment, the doctor thought he knew what it was.

His suggestion that they go wasn't a suggestion at all, was it? It was a plea for cooperation. Maybe it didn't show in the man's face or his demeanor, but he wasn't entirely certain that his wife would come along.

No. That's ridiculous, McCoy mused. Clay's had Jocelyn wrapped around his finger for years. Then again, wasn't it possible that things had changed? That the shoe was on the other foot now?

The very idea made the doctor want to laugh out loud. But of course, he was probably misreading the situation. He wasn't a very good judge of these things and never had been.

More than likely, he'd just heard that tone in Clay's voice because he wanted to hear it. Because, more than anything, he wanted the bastard to suffer the way he had suffered.

Frowning slightly, Jocelyn nodded in response to her husband's invitation. "I suppose," she said.

But not enthusiastically, McCoy noticed. She was going, but she didn't really want to go. What she really wanted was to stay and talk. To him. Not to Clay. To *him*.

Abruptly, something stiffened in the vicinity of the doctor's backbone. What am I doing? he asked himself. What am I thinking? That after all these years, I'm going to win Jocelyn back?

It was preposterous. Worse, it was dangerous. It had taken him nearly half a century to get over her. There was nothing in the galaxy that could make him risk opening those old wounds again.

And yet, he thought, gazing at her still-lovely face and form. And yet . . .

Jocelyn smiled a small, tight smile. "Nice seeing you, Leonard. Perhaps we'll run into each other again sometime."

There—in her eyes. A flicker of emotion. A hint of what he used to see there in the old days, in the golden afternoons and the velvet nights.

Clay must have noticed it too, because he took Jocelyn by the arm and gently but firmly aimed her toward the turbolift. And with a last, brief look of apology—or was it regret?—she let her husband guide her into the compartment.

As the doors hissed closed behind them, McCoy could feel his heart start to hammer against his ribs harder and harder, until he got so lightheaded he thought he might faint. Reaching out to the nearest bulkhead for support, the doctor waited for the sensation to pass.

But it didn't, not entirely. Even though the hammering stopped, there was still an ache there. And he knew that there was only one thing in the universe that could cure it.

The question was, did he really want this? Even if he hadn't imagined the look in her eyes, even if he could have her back as he imagined, did he want to leave himself open to the pain of losing her again? Hell, it hadn't worked for them the first time. What made him think it would work any better now?

McCoy stood there for a long time, seeking answers. But by the time he stirred himself and went up to his cabin, he still didn't have any good ones.

FOUR

☆

Kirk had hardly taken a single step into McCoy's quarters before he had a pretty good idea of why the doctor had called him here. After all, he'd seen his friend in good times and bad, but he'd never seen him quite like this.

McCoy was standing at his bar, drinking from the same bottle of brandy that he'd packed away before the news came of their mission to Ssan. From the look of his complexion, he'd started on the bottle some time ago.

The captain allowed the doors to close behind him before he offered his sage bit of advice. "Getting drunk's not going to solve anything, Bones."

The doctor turned to him and quirked an unexpected smile. "No," he agreed, slurring his words just a bit, "it's not. But hell, it sure makes it a lot easier to forget the problem."

Kirk frowned. "You're the psychiatrist. What would you tell me if our positions were reversed?"

McCoy grunted. "That she's just a woman. That you'll get over it."

"And you'd be right," the captain asserted.

The doctor shook his head. "Nope. I'd be lying like a rug. But don't let that stop you from saying it, if it makes you feel better."

Moving to McCoy's side, Kirk reached for his friend's glass and wrested it from his grip. "The idea," he said, "is to make you feel better."

The doctor hadn't offered any resistance, but he glared at the captain now with bloodshot eyes. "Where are you going with that blasted brandy?"

Spilling the contents into the sink, Kirk set the glass down on the counter. "Me, Bones? I'm not going anywhere. At least until you tell me what set you off this way."

McCoy ran his fingers through his hair and stared into space. For a moment, he said nothing, and then: "I saw her, Jim. I saw her in the corridor outside engineering."

The captain sat down next to his chief medical officer. "Go on."

McCoy chuckled. "Funny. I went there because it was the last place I thought I'd run into her, and there she was." His forehead ridged over with the memory. "Looking as beautiful as the day I married her—sap that I am."

Kirk sighed. He could only imagine what the other man was going through. "Did you talk?"

The doctor nodded. "For the first time in thirty years. Not that we said a whole lot." A pause. "She asked if I was avoiding her."

The captain winced. "Pretty blunt, huh?"

"Yup. She told me I shouldn't be hiding from her. That she was the invader here and she knew it. And then . . ."

"And then what?"

"Then Clay showed up, and a strange thing happened." McCoy licked his lips. "I got the distinct feeling that she was more eager for my company than his." He turned to Kirk. "That is pretty strange, isn't it?"

The captain knew better than to answer a rhetorical question, but he had to agree. It *was* pretty strange. That is, if the doctor was reporting a fact and not just some wishful thinking.

Then he remembered that the Treadways had asked for separate quarters. Kirk swallowed. What if McCoy's perceptions were on the money? What if Jocelyn really had desired the doctor's company more than her husband's?

If that were the case, Bones deserved to know about the rift between Jocelyn and her husband. And the captain wasn't prohibited from sharing the information, since it hadn't been told to him in confidence. Hell, all McCoy or anyone else would have to do is check with the computer and they could find out for themselves.

That wasn't what made him hesitate. It was the certain knowledge that he'd be spurring his friend on to pursue his ex-wife's affections. And he wasn't sure he wanted to do that, given the way things had turned out last time.

In the end, however, he decided he couldn't keep the information to himself. Bones was a big boy. All Kirk could do was give him all the tools he needed to make his decision and then hope he'd make the right one.

"Bones, there's something you should know," he said at last.

"Oh yeah?" replied the doctor. "What's that? The assassins have blown up Ssan and we're supposed to go home after all?"

The captain shook his head. "No, nothing like that. The other day, when the Treadways arrived in the transporter room, they asked for separate accommodations. Separate quarters."

As the import of the statement sunk in, McCoy's eyes slowly widened. He sank into his chair. "You're not joshing me, are you, Jim?"

"Not when it comes to something like this," Kirk assured him.

The doctor's brow furrowed and he raised a knuckle to his lips. "Separate quarters," he muttered pensively, as if the phrase held all the secrets of the universe. But then, for him, maybe it did. "Separate damned quarters," he muttered again.

"But not divorced," the captain added. "She's still his wife, Bones." He went on—because he had to, because he couldn't let his friend go into this with blinders on. "This may be a glitch in their relationship, nothing more. A brief moment of dissatisfaction in an otherwise enduring marriage."

"And when the moment's over," McCoy continued, "I'll be the odd man out. Again. That's what you're saying, right?"

"It's a possibility," Kirk maintained.

The doctor took a breath, let it out. "In other words," he said, "if you were me, you'd run for the hills."

The captain shrugged. "I can't say. I'm not Leonard McCoy. And as much as I'd like to help, I can't make this choice for him."

His friend harrumphed. "I'm a grandfather, for god's sake. At my age, I should be playing it safe, not putting my soul on the line like this. I should be sipping iced tea on a damned veranda, enjoying my retirement." His eyes narrowed suddenly. "The problem is, I can't help but feel that Jocelyn should be sitting beside me, sipping an iced tea of her own."

Kirk let some time pass before he asked, "What are you going to do, Bones?"

McCoy thought for a moment, choices flickering before his eyes like stars shooting by at warp speed. Finally, he said, "I don't know, Jim. I just don't know."

"Mr. Scott?"

The sound of his name, spoken by the captain's familiar voice, cut through the noise of the warp engines. Taking just a moment to finish the task at hand, Scotty replaced the panel over the naked transfer electronics in the bulkhead.

Then he turned and saw that Kirk had brought a couple of visitors down to engineering with him. Scott didn't know their faces, but he was able to guess their identities.

Getting up off his knees, he wiped his hands on the front of his Starfleet-issue coveralls—not that one could get all that dirty repairing an optical data conduit, but old habits die hard—and held one out to the aristocratic-looking man with the dark hair and reddish mustache.

"Montgomery Scott, at yer service."

The man gripped the engineer's hand warmly. "Clay Treadway, at yours." He gestured to the woman standing beside him. "And this is my wife—"

"Jocelyn Treadway," the woman interjected, holding out a hand of her own. Scotty grasped it, smiling ever so slightly at her spunk.

So this was McCoy's one-time spouse. He didn't have to look far to know what the doctor had seen in her.

"Good to meet you," she said. "As you're no doubt aware, Mr. Scott, we've been assigned to handle the situation on Ssan. And to that end, we have a request to make of you."

"Request away, lass. Whatever it is, I'm sure I've done

it before—or something like it. Ye dinnae spend yer entire life on a starship without learnin' a few tricks, now do ye?"

Kirk chuckled. "No, Mr. Scott, you don't. However, what we're asking for is a good deal more straightforward than some of the requests made of you in the past. In fact, it's the kind of thing Spock would normally have taken care of if he wasn't already beaming down with me."

"I see," said the engineer. His eyes narrowed; he still had three more data conduits to go over, and he wasn't getting any younger. "And what exactly is it ye'd have me do, sir?"

"Well," said Kirk, "you know from our briefing that we're supposed to negotiate a peaceful settlement with the assassins. But before we can even attempt it, we have to find them. And given their talents at concealment, that's easier said than done."

"Fortunately," Treadway offered, "there is a way to pick them out from the general population. These assassins are different from other Ssani. They carry something in their blood that allows them to make more efficient use of their physical resources—and therefore makes them better at their chosen profession. The colloquial name for it is 'bloodfire.'"

Scotty was beginning to see where this was going. "I dinnae suppose this bloodfire can be picked up by, oh . . . say, a sensor scan? Especially when it's concentrated over a relatively small area, as would be the case at the assassins' stronghold?"

"You're catching on," Treadway remarked approvingly.

There was something about his manner that Scotty didn't like. Something oily, he thought. Or was it just the fact that he was married to a friend's ex-wife?

"Providing, of course," the engineer amended, "that ye

can find some loyal soul willing to sit by a console and look for it."

"In fact," replied Jocelyn, "ship's computer can do most of the work analyzing the sensor results, which would leave our hypothetical loyal soul free to tackle anything else that required his attention. All he'd have to do is check the data every now and then."

Scott grunted good-naturedly. "I see why ye're in the diplomatic corps, lass." Then, turning to the captain, he said, "I'd be glad to help out, sir. Just show me what to look for before we make orbit."

Kirk nodded. "Much obliged, Scotty."

"Yes, Scotty," echoed the diplomat. "Much obliged."

The engineer cast Treadway a withering look. He didn't let just anyone call him Scotty. That was a privilege one had to earn.

"Aye," was all the response he cared to make. And without another word, he went back to his work. Out of the corner of his eye, he could see the captain ushering the diplomats out of engineering.

It was only after they were out of earshot that Scotty snorted indignantly. "Much obliged *indeed,*" he muttered.

Captain's Personal Log, Stardate 9587.2:
    We're not more than half an hour away from Alpha Gederix Four. In a little while, I'll meet Spock, Uhura, and the Treadways in the transporter room, where we'll beam down to meet with the Ssani heads of state.
    As for my friend Dr. McCoy, he hasn't been seen outside of sickbay for the last couple of days. If anything, he's avoiding his ex-wife even more studiously than before.
    Though he hasn't actually come out and told

me so, nor have I asked, it's fairly obvious that he's decided to avoid temptation — and to let any possibility of a rapprochement with Jocelyn fall by the wayside.

Perhaps it's better this way. After all, it took McCoy several long, painful years to get over his breakup with her the first time. In some ways, I'd say, he still hasn't gotten over it.

At any rate, I'm going to do everything I can to respect his solitude. As I know only too well, there are times when a man needs his friends around him — but in the case of Leonard McCoy, I don't think this is one of those times.

Nem Antronic, master governor of Tanul for seven whole days now in the wake of Kimm Dathrabin's demise, looked up at his Federation visitors and wondered if any of them really appreciated the difficulty of what he and his fellow master governors were asking of them.

"We've helped handle crises as difficult as this one before, I assure you," said the human called Clay Treadway.

"You have," Antronic echoed, somewhat less than enthusiastically.

"We have," the human repeated. "And we haven't lost a patient yet. So let's just get down to business, shall we?"

The one called James Kirk frowned. Did that mean he was evincing disapproval of Clay Treadway's promises?

Antronic hoped so. All this inordinate confidence was unsettling. It made him feel as if they were talking about some other situation on some other world entirely.

"You've told the Federation that the assassins want

only one thing," ventured the other Treadway—the female, Jocelyn. "And that's the restoration of assassination as a viable institution on Ssan."

Pel Sarennos, who had replaced Thur Cambralos as master governor of Pitur, nodded vigorously. "That is their goal. And they will stop at nothing to achieve it," he added.

"Are you sure?" asked Jocelyn Treadway.

Antronic and Sarennos looked at one another, then at their colleague Dur Manarba of Orthun. "We are as sure as we can be," Sarennos answered. "Do you have information to the contrary?"

"No," said Clay Treadway. "But terrorists like Shil Andrachis usually have some sort of fallback position. A compromise, in other words, which they'll consider if push comes to shove."

Antronic sighed—quietly, so that none of their visitors would notice his mounting despair. But the Vulcan, the one called Spock, noticed anyway.

"That may be true of other situations," he interjected, glancing pointedly at Clay Treadway. "However, I wonder if that is true of the situation at hand."

"It is *not,*" Sarennos stated emphatically. "There is no fallback position. There is only the return of the assassin to our society."

The male Treadway stroked the peculiarly human growth of hair beneath his nose. "Very well then. Let's talk about their tactics. As I understand it, twelve master governors have been killed since this reign of terror began. Now—"

"Thirteen," corrected Antronic. "The master governor of Festur was killed less than an hour ago."

"Thirteen," the human conceded. "The point is, this

Shil Andrachis has so far restricted his actions to individual murders, the kind of activity assassins used to engage in before those activities were outlawed."

"That is correct," Manarba told him, perhaps a bit impatiently. "What is your point, Mr. Treadway?"

The human continued to stroke his growth of hair. "Didn't Li Moboron, who is said to be Andrachis's mentor, begin his assassin war in a similar way?"

Antronic winced. It was extremely impolite to answer a question with a question. Apparently Clay Treadway did not know this. Or was he, for some reason, trying to insult Master Governor Manarba?

To Manarba's credit, he did not return the affront in kind. "Li Moboron did exactly the same thing—at first. Then, when his demands were still not met, he turned to mass executions."

"He bombed public buildings," expanded Jocelyn Treadway, "in the hope that Ssani society would grind to a halt."

Antronic agreed that this was so. "But I still do not see the point of your argument," he admitted.

Clay Treadway leaned forward across the table around which they were seated. "What I'm saying is that, so far, Andrachis's tactics are identical to Moboron's. But does that mean that they necessarily have to remain identical?"

The master governors exchanged glances. The answer was obviously a negative one. But so what?

Without waiting for an actual reply, the human forged on. "What if Shil Andrachis has no intention of waging his war the way his predecessor did? Remember, Ssan is a different world today—a world that has learned to live without the concept of assassination. Will the population come to fear Shil Andrachis so much that they'll embrace a patently outmoded institution?"

"Or," said Jocelyn Treadway, picking up where her mate left off, "will they reject the institution all the more? And knowing this—because if we can figure this out, surely he can too—why would Andrachis pick the general population as a target for his violence?"

"Perhaps he will not," Manarba conceded.

Clay Treadway smiled. "Exactly. My guess is that he'll never escalate this conflict to the point where there's wholesale slaughter, as in the old days. Rather, he'll continue to target government figures. His motive? To force you to change the laws and legally condone assassination again."

Sarennos grunted. "That is all very well reasoned," he judged. "All very logical. Nonetheless, you are quite wrong."

The human looked at him as if he'd just turned into a ripe piece of exotic fruit. "Wrong?" he repeated. "In what way?"

"How many ways are there?" asked Sarennos. "You have made the mistake of imputing to the assassins an expectation that is altogether inappropriate."

Manarba nodded. "They do not kill our colleagues— and perhaps us as well, in time—because they hope to be accepted in any real sense. Mind you, they would not balk if Ssan were to renew its approval of assassination as a viable institution. But they do not seriously anticipate it."

James Kirk, who had only been listening for the last several minutes, chose that moment to pose a question. "Yet you said they wish to see the role of assassin restored to Ssani society. That they would stop at nothing to achieve that."

"That is true," agreed Manarba. "But not through anyone's acceptance. Shil Andrachis and his people seek to reinstitute the killing art by performing it. In their minds, the act itself is a worthwhile goal."

The woman called Uhura grunted. "Then they kill simply to assert their right to do so. And even if it doesn't force you to change any laws, they'll have accomplished their purpose. They'll have defied the reforms the master governors put in place forty years ago."

Her Vulcan companion nodded. "And there is no way to predict what course of action Shil Andrachis will follow. If he considers change unlikely, he need not worry about public opinion—so incidents of mass murder may take place after all. Or he may recognize the killing of government figures as a more pure form of assassination and simply continue to kill them until he is stopped."

"The most dangerous sort of enemy," James Kirk observed. "One who doesn't mind losing as long as he takes his adversary down with him."

Antronic breathed a sigh of relief. At least a couple of these offworlders understood their problem. Now maybe they could do something about it.

But Clay Treadway was shaking his head from side to side. "No," he insisted. "With all due respect, Master Governors, I believe you're mistaken."

Sarennos shot Antronic a look of indignation. It was clear he did not take kindly to the human's display of arrogance.

However, the diplomat seemed not to notice. "You may believe that the assassins have no real goals—that they are simply making a political statement of some kind. But all such statements have at their root a desire for change. What we must discover is an alternate path to the change

Andrachis desires." Treadway attempted a small smile. "I assure you, this situation is not as black and white as it may seem to you."

"You are certain of this," said Sarennos, who was starting to lose his temper. His voice trembled slightly as he spoke. "Even though you are from another world, another civilization. You understand our assassins better than we do."

This time, Clay Treadway appeared to comprehend the extent to which he was insulting the master governors. Inclining his head to demonstrate the appropriate degree of humility, he seemed ready to apologize.

But what he said was: "It appears that we are again at an impasse. Under the circumstances, I think we should simply move on to another topic—one on which we're less likely to be at odds."

In other words, Antronic mused, the human was not admitting that he had been wrong about anything or that the master governors had been right. He was merely proceeding as if their conversation had not taken place.

"For instance," Clay Treadway asked them, "how much solidarity are we likely to find among the assassins? Are they all unshakably loyal to Andrachis? Or are there some schisms we can take advantage of?"

It was a better question than the first two, Antronic had to admit. But by now the human had lost the confidence of the master governors. Nor was he likely to regain it without a full and elaborate apology.

Stifling his feelings as best he could, Antronic prepared to give the human diplomat an answer. However, he was interrupted by Manarba.

"We were told that there would be someone named McCoy among you—one who had had experience with

Ssan in the past." The master governor of Orthun looked from one of their visitors to another. "Where is this McCoy?"

While Antronic could not be sure, having never seen a human before today, it seemed to him that Clay Treadwell's face turned a different color.

"The one called McCoy," replied the diplomat, "is otherwise engaged. In any case, his experience would not help us here in our discussions. He has no formal training in interaction with alien cultures."

Rejecting Clay Treadwell's answer, Manarba turned to James Kirk. "Sometimes formal training is not as good as experience," he pointed out.

"Sometimes," the human echoed—apparently in agreement. "However," he added, "as Mr. Treadway indicated, Leonard McCoy's presence is neither necessary nor obtainable. I'm sorry."

Manarba frowned, expressing the reaction of his colleagues as well. "So am I, James Kirk. So am I."

FIVE

☆

As the captain found himself in the familiar surroundings of the *Enterprise*'s transporter room, alongside Spock, Uhura, and the diplomatic team, he nodded to Scotty, who'd executed the transport himself. Knowing the chief engineer had some advantages, Kirk remarked inwardly.

"Welcome back," said the Scot. "How did it go?"

Before Kirk could tell him, Clay Treadway supplied the answer. "Not too badly, Mr. Scott. Things were a little shaky at the beginning there, but the meeting eventually became a productive one."

As the man descended from the transporter platform, his wife lagged behind him by a step. Judging from the expression the captain glimpsed on her face, he gathered that she didn't entirely agree with Treadway's assessment of the situation but was too professional to mention it in public.

On the other hand, Kirk mused, he had no doubt she'd

discuss it with him in private. Jocelyn had never seemed to him to be the type to keep her frustrations bottled up inside her.

"If you have no objection, sir," said Spock, "I would like to spend some time in the ship's library. It appears that I did not understand the Ssana's problem as well as I thought."

The captain nodded. "Whatever you deem necessary," he told his first officer. "We're all going to have to understand the Ssana a little better from here on in, I'm afraid."

"Amen to that," remarked Uhura, frowning as she watched the Treadways depart through the exit doors. "In fact, I'd like to accompany you, Mr. Spock, assuming that's all right."

The Vulcan cocked an eyebrow. "I cannot see any reason why it would *not* be all right," he assured her.

It was the closest Spock had ever come to chivalry, in Kirk's memory. He and Uhura smiled at the same time. Was it possible that his pointed-eared friend was starting to mellow after all these years?

A moment later the doors swooshed open and then closed again behind Spock and Uhura. That left the captain all alone with his chief engineer.

Crossing the floor to where Scotty stood, dutifully maintaining his post, Kirk asked the question that was in the back of all returning captains' minds: "And how are things going up here?"

"A lot better, I think, then they went down there," replied the engineer. He screwed up his face in an expression of disgust. "Mr. Treadway's comments notwithstanding."

"Better?" the captain echoed.

"That's right, sir." Scott's expression changed. "I think

we may've located the assassins' lair," he announced with some pride. "Of course, I'll want to check and recheck the results, but our initial scan looks promising."

Kirk clapped him on the shoulder. "Excellent, Scotty. I'm glad *something* went right today. If you need me, I'll be in my quarters, taking a nice, hot shower."

"Er, actually, sir . . ." the engineer began.

The captain paused. "Yes, Scotty?"

The man frowned. "Dr. McCoy asked me to tell ye he'd like to see ye when ye got back. It sounded like it was pretty important—at least to him, sir."

Kirk smiled and nodded. "Thanks, Mr. Scott. I suppose my shower can wait."

And wondering what McCoy might have on his mind, the captain exited the transporter room to find out.

Jocelyn waited until she and her husband were both safely inside the turbolift compartment to shoot him an angry glance. As the doors closed behind them, he looked back with the innocence of a newborn colt.

It was a look she'd seen before, a look that had worked its magic and disarmed her in the past. But it wasn't going to do that now.

"What the hell did you think you were doing down there?" she demanded.

Clay shrugged. "My job, of course. What do you think I was doing?"

She shook her head. "Damned if I know. Those Ssana were ready to get up and walk out on you. You couldn't have alienated them any more if you'd spit on their ancestral burial grounds."

Her husband looked at her askance. "You don't think you might be exaggerating a bit, Joc? The only things I said were those that needed saying. What's worse—to be polite and mess up the mediation effort because we don't know who we're dealing with? Or to be a little brusque and accomplish something for these people?"

Clay had always had a way of making stinkweed sound like sugarcane. That was part of what made him so good at mediation. Once he had both parties in the same room together, he could generally sweet-talk them into seeing eye-to-eye.

But Jocelyn could usually see through him when he was applying his powers of persuasion. And as far as she could tell, he was being sincere about this. On the other hand, sincere didn't necessarily mean right.

"You didn't listen to them," she insisted. "You didn't even give the appearance of listening to them."

"You're right," he told her. "If you disagree with someone, it's better to let them know it right off the bat. That's what I did—I let them know it." He paused to brush a strand of hair off her forehead. "Come to think of it, you let them know it pretty good yourself."

She pulled her head back, allowing the strand to fall loose again. Frowning, she tucked it behind her ear. "The only reason I said what I did is to back you up—to maintain a united front. I didn't want to risk losing their confidence altogether."

"Was that the reason?" Clay asked her, his eyes searching hers. "The only reason?"

Jocelyn could feel her eyes narrowing. "What do you mean?"

Her husband shrugged. "I don't know. For a little while there, I got the feeling you were simply standing by your man."

A strange thing happened then. Even though she knew Clay was referring to himself, Jocelyn saw someone else flash before her mind's eye. And the someone she saw was Leonard McCoy.

She recalled their meeting in the corridor the other day. She recalled the way he looked—all brave and awkward at once—when she told him not to play the hermit on her account.

At the time, that look had brought back the memory of a sweet summer night and a shy young man with big blue eyes. And as she recalled her meeting with Leonard outside engineering, memory redoubled on itself, and she saw and smelled and felt that summer evening all over again.

She would have liked to stay and talk, but Clay had interrupted. And then Leonard had done exactly what she'd asked him not to—he'd gone and hidden himself away again. And seeing that, she had taken the hint. She had—

". . . old Leonard, eh?"

Startled out of her reverie, Jocelyn blurted, "What?"

Clay looked at her wonderingly. "I said it was funny to hear the Ssana ask for old Leonard—as if he were going to be of any real use to them." His look intensified. "Or weren't you listening?"

Feeling her cheeks grow hot with embarrassment, Jocelyn took the offensive. "Don't try to change the subject," she told her husband. "Next time we meet with the Ssana, I want you to be more deferential. More respectful."

That was all they needed, she assured herself. They were basically on the right path when it came to the Ssana; a little mutual trust was all that was lacking.

He thought about it. "Fine," he replied at last. "For you. After all," he reminded her, "we are a team, aren't we?"

Turning away from him, she let the question go unanswered. Fortunately, the lift doors opened a second later, letting them out into the corridor just outside their accommodations.

Wishing to avoid any further conversation, Jocelyn headed straight for her quarters. But she didn't get halfway before she heard Clay call out her name.

Still flushed, she turned to face him again. "Yes?"

He gazed at her as if he knew she'd donned a veil and he was trying his best to pierce it. But after a while, he seemed to give up.

"Nothing," he said at last.

Tapping the security plate outside her door, she let herself into her suite. At last her thoughts were her own. And she could remember whatever she wished to remember.

As Kirk entered sickbay, he couldn't help but remark to himself on the place's air of organization and efficiency. If McCoy's mind was in a state of turmoil and disarray, one certainly couldn't tell by the surroundings in which he worked.

The first person the captain encountered there, however, wasn't McCoy. It was a pretty, redheaded nurse, the kind that, at one time in Kirk's life, would certainly have given rise to the idea of a cozy, candlelight dinner. As it was, however, he was quite happy with the thought of Carol Marcus's company at the end of this final mission, and he forcibly submerged his natural inclinations.

"Is the doctor in?" he asked.

The nurse turned and smiled at him. "Yes, sir." She tilted her head to indicate the laboratory portion of the facility. "He's in there, with Dr. DeLeon. They're probably discussing some monograph or something."

As Kirk made his way to the lab area he heard voices all right, and one of them was definitely McCoy's. As was often the case when it came to medical conversations, he had little or no idea what the devil they were talking about.

"It didn't look like a virus," Bones was saying. "But Lord knows, it sure spread like a virus. So I had to assume it *was* a virus."

"Then what?" asked the younger doctor, a slender, fine-boned man with jet black hair and a thick mustache.

"I went through every damned record in the place," McCoy explained. "Actually, we *all* went through them, trying to learn as much as we could about the thing. Not that that was easy, mind you, what with those kids running around and the blotches on my face getting bigger by the minute."

Abruptly, Kirk realized which malady Bones was referring to. The years seemed to fall away like so much dust and he saw himself on Miri's world again, watching helplessly as Bones searched for a cure to whatever hideous malady Miri's forebears had invented in their search for immortality.

"Finally," said McCoy, "I isolated the bug. Mean-looking son of a gun, too. Unfortunately, there was no time to—"

Suddenly he noticed the captain standing there in the entrance to the lab alcove. Smiling self-consciously, he turned back to DeLeon and jerked a thumb over his shoulder.

"Maybe I ought to let *him* tell it," he jibed.

Kirk shook his head. "Not me, Doctor. I was in a haze from the time you started talking about antidotes until someone pressed a hypospray against my arm."

Bones chuckled dryly. "Sure you were. As I recall, we

never would have had the chance to use any hyposprays if you hadn't won those kids over."

"With Miri's help," Kirk amended.

McCoy shrugged. "Whatever." Then he leaned closer to DeLeon. "The truth is," he remarked in a stage whisper, "I would've perished a hundred times over if not for that elderly gentleman in the captain's uniform. But I don't let him know that. I'm afraid it'll give him a swelled head."

The younger doctor turned to Kirk and chuckled. He'd better, thought the captain. Elderly gentleman indeed.

Turning to Bones, he said: "You called?"

His eyes losing a little of their mischievous glitter, McCoy nodded. Placing an avuncular hand on DeLeon's shoulder, he promised: "We'll continue this some other time. Ship's business, you understand."

DeLeon nodded. "Of course. I'll see you later, Doctor."

Both Kirk and Bones watched him go. Then the captain confronted his friend. "Ship's business?" he echoed.

McCoy shrugged. "Not exactly, though I've been on this ship so long, it feels like my business and her business are inextricably intertwined."

Kirk smiled good-naturedly. "Poetry, Doctor? From *you?*"

Bones frowned. "Cut it out, Jim. I didn't ask you here to have you make fun of me. Lord knows, I've been on enough of an emotional roller coaster these days without my best friend taking shots at me, too."

The captain held his hands up, as if to show McCoy that they were empty of weapons. "Sorry," he said. "I come in peace. What can I do for you, Bones?"

His chief medical officer looked away and cleared his throat. "So how did you folks do? Down on Ssan, I mean?"

Kirk couldn't quite suppress a sigh. "It could have gone worse," he reported. "And then again, it could've gone better."

McCoy's eyes sought his. "In other words, our friends the Treadways didn't understand the Ssana as well as you'd hoped."

The captain nodded judiciously. "I'd say that about sums it up. Clay, in particular, seemed to have his own ideas. And when the Ssana disagreed with them, he chalked it up to their limited perspective."

The doctor cursed beneath his breath. "Isn't that just like him, too? Always thinking he knows more than anyone else, even when we were in high school." He paused. "Did I tell you I knew him back that far?"

Kirk shook his head. "Not in so many words, no. But I gathered that you'd known him for some time before he married Jocelyn."

McCoy's bright blue eyes glazed over for a moment. Then he nodded. "For some time, all right. For a long some time."

"Anyway," the captain resumed, "we seemed to iron things out before we left. I think it'll go pretty well from here on in."

The doctor looked at him. "There's something you're not telling me," he decided. "What is it? Come on now, Jim, I want to know."

Kirk grunted. "Well, at one point, after Treadway had thoroughly insulted their intelligence, one of the master governors asked for you. He seemed to think you might have a better handle on the situation—particularly in regard to the assassins' motivations."

McCoy's frown deepened. "You know," he said, "this may surprise you, but I was thinking the very same thing. I was thinking about how foreign the Ssani sensibility can be to anyone who hasn't experienced it before. And I was feeling guilty for not putting my personal hangups aside and doing what Starfleet meant me to do when they gave me this uniform."

The captain didn't respond at first. He didn't want to push his friend in either direction—toward Ssan and Jocelyn or away from them. Then, finally, he found the right words.

"The choice is yours, Bones. It's been yours all along."

McCoy harrumphed. "Just this once," he balked, "couldn't you make the damned decision for me? You are the captain, you know."

"I'm aware of that," Kirk replied.

"You could order me to go."

"I'm aware of that, too." But he wouldn't give that order, and Bones knew it.

Suddenly they were interrupted by a piping from the intercom unit on the nearest bulkhead. Getting up to answer it, the doctor placed his hand over the touch-sensitive plate and said, "McCoy here."

"Actually, I vas looking for the captain, sir." It was Chekov's voice, of course. Kirk would have recognized it even in a sandstorm on Rigel XII. "It seems Mr. Treadvay has called a meeting exectly one hour from now to discuss Commander Scott's findings."

"Findings?" repeated the doctor.

The captain nodded. "Scotty thinks he's located the assassins' lair—though he wanted some time to be sure. Apparently, our friend the diplomat has decided not to wait until then to plan our next move." Crossing to the intercom, he said, "Acknowledged, Commander. You can tell Mr. Treadway that all appropriate personnel will be present."

"Aye, sair. Thank you, sair. Chekov out."

Turning away from the intercom mechanism, Kirk smiled apologetically at McCoy. "Looks like I've got a meeting to convene," he remarked. "I guess I'd better go round up the troops."

But there was a question left unanswered. It hung in the air between them, allowing neither of them to ignore it.

Was McCoy going to be one of those troops? Or was Kirk going to have to plod on without him?

In the flickering light of a cooking fire, amid the crackle of sizzling uterra fat and the sharp smell of leathery flesh and the occasional pop of bursting bones, High Assassin Shil Andrachis inspects the faces of his followers.

He has to comb them carefully to find an assassin who fought in the wars—either with Li Moboron or against him. Those who follow Andrachis in his holy effort are mostly children, the youngest of them barely eighteen summers old. But then, he reminds himself, he was a child himself when he answered Li Moboron's call all those long, empty years ago.

Unlike him, however, these eager young Ssana will never have to hide their art—will never have to repress it in the face of a society that has discarded its most ancient traditions. The way of the assassin is emerging from the filth that has been heaped on it, thanks to Andrachis and others like him, who would not or could not give up the glory of their fathers. And like it or not, society will be forced to remember them.

As he watches, a blade glows a feverish red in the tumultuous firelight. But the reflection is too strong, the surface too polished. Andrachis frowns at the indiscretion.

"Cor," he says simply.

The youth's eyes rise to meet his leader's. "Yes, tir-Andrachis?" It is plain he has no idea what he has done.

The older Ssana casts his gaze in the direction of the knife. "Your weapon, Assassin. In days past, your ancestors used it to kill the most powerful men of their time. Is it to be used now to skin the gristle off uterra bones?"

Lakandir's mouth hangs open. A curt, barking laugh comes from one of the few veterans within earshot and echoes under the cavern's low roof. But the rest of them, like the one who had committed the impropriety, look puzzled.

"How is it," asks the young man with what appears to be genuine ignorance, "that our knives may cut uterra flesh when the beasts are on the wing, emblazoned against the sky—and not resting in our cooking fire?"

Again, the veteran laughs, though this time, not at Lakandir. This time he is amused by the sharply honed common sense behind the question.

But of course, there can be only one answer. And common sense has nothing to do with it.

"Because," Andrachis says, "that is the way it has always been done. An assassin's blade is for killing, and killing only. Its sole duty is to dispatch its victims' souls."

The young man takes the admonition in stride, showing not the least bit of embarrassment. His small, dark eyes remain steady, unperturbed. But then, Cor Lakandir is cut from a different cloth than that of his comrades.

He joined them less than a year ago. Not like all the other young firebrands, who were drawn to the den in small packs, complete with their own, self-chosen leaders, until Andrachis found it necessary to teach them that a den could have only one master.

No, Lakandir came by himself, the way the old-timers

arrived—sniffing out the scent of rebellion and adventure and honor, searching for a completeness they could barely remember.

In Andrachis's eyes, that in itself marked Lakandir as someone to watch. That and the fact that the youth reminded him of someone. It was only after he had gotten to know Lakandir better that he realized the someone was himself.

More than once, Andrachis has thought about the future of his movement, where it might go if it went anywhere at all. And he has recognized the need for a successor, someone who can take over when he is killed or has simply grown too old to lead.

He has come to believe that Cor Lakandir is as good a choice as any. Not now, of course, not before he has learned more of people and how to gain their loyalty—but someday. That is why it bothers him so much that the youth should be so ignorant of tradition. And even worse, that he should question it even after being apprised of it.

Andrachis tells himself he has not dragged the assassins' art out of obscurity into light to see it survive only in a corrupted form. That would dishonor the memory of Li Moboron and all the other master assassins this world has known down through the ages. Before he will see their heritage become something mundane and unrecognizable, he will destroy it himself.

"Are you sure you want to be part of this?" asked Kirk.

McCoy nodded, matching his captain's gait step for step as they negotiated the long, straight corridor between the turbolift and the main conference room. Their footfalls echoed from bulkhead to bulkhead.

"I'm positive, Jim. In fact, I've never been more

positive of anything in my life. It's time for me to stop acting like a whipped puppy and start pulling my weight again."

He frowned, steeling himself for what was ahead. It wouldn't be easy, but then, who'd ever told him it was supposed to be?

"After all," the doctor went on, "I *am* the expert on Ssan around here. That's why they gave us this godforsaken mission in the first place, isn't it?"

Kirk smiled an encouraging smile. "I believe so, yes." A pause. "Good to have you aboard again, Bones."

McCoy harrumphed, doing his best to act like the professional he was cracked up to be. "Don't make a big deal of it," he instructed. "I'm just getting involved in something I should've been involved in all along. It's not like I've come up with a cure for Russhton syndrome or anything like that."

Suddenly the conference room doors were directly in front of them. The captain stopped short, giving his friend one last chance to back out of the deal.

But McCoy wasn't going to take any more charity. Taking a deep breath, he forged ahead, through the instantly parting doors and into the room.

For a moment he took in the glances and expressions that met his appearance. Looks of happiness from Scotty, Chekov, and Uhura and one of seeming indifference from Spock, though the doctor knew better. Clay was good at concealing things, but not so good that he didn't give away a touch of annoyance and maybe of jealousy as well.

As for Jocelyn, it was hard to tell what was in her mind. Surprise? Probably. Admiration? Less probably. Passion? He wouldn't even venture a guess.

"Well then," said Kirk. "If we're all here, let's get

started." As he took his place at the head of the table, he turned to his chief engineer. "Scotty, why don't you tell us what you've found."

"Aye, sir," replied the Scot. He addressed the group as a whole. "Apparently, the data's sound; our little vigil's paid off. It turns out there's a concentration of biochemically altered Ssana in a mountainous area in the northernmost reaches of the largest continent—a good two hundred kilometers from the nearest major population center."

Activating the hologram projector in the center of the table, he brought up a miniature of Ssan. There was a red dot in the northern hemisphere to indicate the site where the assassins were holed up.

"Two hundred kilometers," Spock repeated thoughtfully. "Close enough to inject themselves into the mainstream of Ssani civilization when necessary. But far enough away so that no one is likely to stumble onto their whereabouts." He nodded. "Admirable."

"Be that as it may," Scotty continued, "now that we know where they are, we can direct a message to them and begin the mediation process."

The captain turned to Uhura. "Any problems with sending a narrowcast comm beam to the location Mr. Scott has described?"

The communications officer shook her head. "It's a rocky place," she said, "and the Ssana are reporting some storms in the vicinity. But I've gotten around worse."

Kirk nodded. "Excellent, Lieutenant." He focused on the Treadways next. "We'll need to formulate a message, something the assassin leadership will respond to. And let's make it short, in case Lieutenant Uhura has more trouble getting through than she anticipates."

Clay Treadway gazed appraisingly at the holographic representation of Ssan and shook his head. "I don't think so," he said.

The captain looked at him. "I beg your pardon?"

The diplomat took in the room with one sweeping glance—a practiced gesture that included not only the captain but all his officers as well. He seemed as sure of himself as a man could be.

"It won't work," Clay elaborated.

Chekov leaned forward. "And vhy not, if I may ask?"

The diplomat was completely unflustered. "Because," he said, "Ssani assassins respect two things: courage and cleverness. That's pretty obvious in the literature we studied en route. And the approach Captain Kirk is espousing doesn't particularly smack of either quality."

McCoy could see the muscles working in Kirk's jaw. But as always, he kept his emotions in check.

"You'd like to propose an alternative?" the captain suggested.

"Indeed I would," said Clay. "It seems to me that the only way to begin any kind of meaningful peace negotiations with these people is in *person.*"

The doctor was shaking his head before he knew it. "That's insane," he muttered.

Clay didn't even do him the courtesy of acknowledging him. But McCoy's wasn't the only opposition to his comment.

"In other vords," Chekov paraphrased, "beam down and meet vith them face to face?" He sent a sour look in Kirk's direction. "Is that vise, sir? These people have more than adequately demonstrated their affinity for cold-blooded murder. Vhy vould they not carve *us* up the vay they carved up their own governors?"

"There's always that chance," Jocelyn interjected. "But

then, we in the diplomatic corps often have to accept an element of risk in our work. Sometimes it's the difference between success and failure."

Bones couldn't believe she was siding with Clay on this. Was her devotion to duty clouding her judgment? Or was it some renewed devotion to her husband that was responsible for it?

"There is no question," said Spock, who'd remained silent up to that point, "that risk is a valuable tool in theory. The question is whether it will gain us any advantage in the instance at hand."

"I believe it will," Clay maintained. "However, I will not ask anyone to join us if they believe otherwise."

"Us?" asked McCoy.

The diplomat finally turned to him. "Yes," he answered. "My wife and myself." When Jocelyn made no move to disagree, Clay directed his attention to Kirk again. "You and Captain Spock are welcome to come along if you wish—with or without security personnel. However, there's no amount of security that will be sufficient to protect us, I assure you."

"You've got *that* right," the doctor barked. Suddenly he was on his feet, leaning over the table until he was less than a meter away from Clay Treadway's face. "What you're talking about is suicide, damn it!"

"Bones!" The captain's admonishment cut through the tension-filled air like a phaser beam through butter. "That's enough!"

But McCoy wasn't going to be shut up so easily. "It's not *nearly* enough," he insisted, still glaring at his rival. "You can't just beam down into a blasted assassins' den. You'll be cold meat before you even get a chance to tell them why you're there."

"Perhaps," said the diplomat, unflinchingly stubborn.

"Or could it be you're selling us short, Doctor? You know, this isn't the first time my wife and I have ventured into a dangerous situation and defused it."

My wife. Not yours—mine. McCoy wanted to take the man's too handsome face and tear it apart.

"You just don't get it," he snarled. "You've never been on Ssan. You don't know what these assassins are like." He jabbed at his own chest. "But I do. I've seen their handiwork up close and personal. And believe me, you don't want to get within fifty feet of them."

"Bones . . ."

This time Kirk's tone was a little softer, a little more understanding. And the doctor responded to it, though his gaze remained riveted to Clay's. Unclenching his teeth, he took a deep breath.

"Sorry, Jim. But I'd be derelict in my duty if I didn't speak up." He turned to Jocelyn, hoping that she, at least, would see the sense in what he was saying. "Anyone who thinks he's going to visit a bunch of assassins in their lair and come out alive is the worst kind of fool."

His ex-wife didn't say a thing. Apparently she was every bit as bent on getting herself killed as her damned husband was.

"You've made your case, Bones," the captain stated flatly. "Now take your seat or so help me, I'll have you escorted out of here."

McCoy glanced in Kirk's direction and saw that he meant it. Scowling, he did as he was told. With decorum restored, the captain cleared his throat and announced his decision.

"I have no choice," he said, "but to give considerable weight to Dr. McCoy's input. After all, as he so aptly points out, he's the only one of us who's ever been to Ssan; he knows Shil Andrachis's people better than anyone else on this ship, and if he says it's too dangerous, it no doubt is." A beat. "But even without Dr. McCoy, I would recognize the problems involved in beaming down to the assassins' stronghold. And in my opinion, the risks outweigh the potential for successful mediation."

The diplomat took a sudden interest in his fingernails. "I see," he responded. "And that's your final word on the subject?"

"It is," Kirk told him.

Clay looked up. "In that case, I'm forced to take command of this mission by virtue of Starfleet Order Nine-five-seven. I assume you're familiar with it, Captain?"

Kirk frowned. "Naturally," he said softly. "But it's not a wise course, Mr. Treadway. If you've been reading your monographs, you know that diplomatic envoys who do what you're doing usually end up regretting it."

"Usually," Clay agreed. "In fact, you were involved in many of those case histories yourself, as I recall. However, my wife and I are not the usual breed of diplomats. I'm betting we'll have less occasion for regret than you think."

The captain looked as if he'd liked to have argued the point further, but he knew it wouldn't get him anywhere. McCoy knew it too. This wasn't the first time he'd dealt with Clay Treadway. The man was as stubborn as they came and always had been.

Kirk turned to Scotty. "Arrange an early morning beam-down," he said reluctantly. "For the Treadways, myself, Captain Spock, and a couple of security officers whom Mr. Chekov will select."

Just as reluctantly, Scotty nodded. "Aye, sir. Whatever ye say."

"This is the craziest thing I've ever heard," McCoy blurted.

"I doubt it," the diplomat returned. "Even I've heard crazier, and you've been in space a lot longer than I have."

The doctor absorbed the humiliation with which Clay had loaded the remark. He had to keep his head, he told himself. For Jocelyn's sake.

"All right," he said. "Then at least let me come along. I've had experience with the Ssana. Maybe I can help." He licked his lips. "Starfleet thought so."

Clay regarded him for a moment, as if he was considering it. But when he was done, he shook his head.

"I don't think so," he told McCoy. "I know what Starfleet thought, but I disagree. This is no mission for a doctor."

Bones shot a glance at the captain, an appeal for help. But Kirk's expression said that he had no help to give.

The doctor turned to Clay again. "Damn it," he snapped, "it's not just your life, Treadway. It's your wife's life too, and those of four other good people."

"I'm well aware of that," the diplomat replied, getting to his feet.

McCoy felt his anger surging again. He stood too, his hands balling into fists. "You can't *do* this!" he growled.

Clay's smile seemed to come easily to him. It was undeniably polite, with just the tiniest hint of triumphant spite in it. "I believe I just have," he said reasonably.

And left.

Jocelyn hesitated for a moment, her eyes locked on McCoy—but only for a moment. Then she followed her husband out of the conference room.

By degrees the doctor's anger cooled, became something manageable. Gradually he regained his equilibrium and remembered that he wasn't alone. Looking around, he saw his friends gazing up at him from around the table with varying degrees of sympathy.

McCoy tried to smile, but it didn't work out very well. "I . . ." He shook his head. What was the point of trying to explain? These people knew him better than he knew himself. If they didn't already understand what had just happened here, they never would.

"Bones—" began the captain.

The doctor held up a hand. "Don't," he said peremptorily. And pulling together what shreds of dignity he had left, he made his somber exit.

SIX

☆

Shil Andrachis is peering into the long, dancing flames of the assassins' still burning fire. It warms his face, his knees, his hands.

As is their custom, he and his followers have remained in a circle about the fire for some time after the completion of their meal, to talk, to share ambitions, to give honor to their predecessors in the form of stories.

He has just begun telling one such story, about an assassin who was given the order to kill his own aged parents. The assassin's name was Hordin Mandris, or so Andrachis heard long ago in the camp of Li Moboron.

"The one who gave the order," the High Assassin relates, "was a master governor of Orthun and the worst type of administrator. He had sold out his city-state's prosperity in order to increase his personal wealth. When Hordin Mandris's parents took him to task for it, calling for his

overthrow, he knew he had to act quickly. And Mandris himself was the best assassin in the district.

"As one loyal to his calling, the assassin had no choice but to carry out the task for which he had been retained. Even though his mother and father cried out for mercy— even though his heart felt as if it would break in two—he rewarded those who had given him life with a bloody death.

"Of course, to an assassin's way of thinking, Mandris had done his parents a favor. He had removed them from the lands of the living. He had cleansed their souls in the waters of honor. Still, he could not help but see the greed that had motivated the master governor and continued to motivate him. Nor could he ignore the fact that he had paved the way for further crimes against the city-state of Orthun.

"So, after he had dispatched his mother and father, Mandris went straightaway to the house of the master governor. And with the same blood-slick knife he had used to bring honor to his parents, he brought honor to the administrator as well."

There are smiles around the fire. The story, Andrachis notes with some satisfaction, has been well received.

Afterward, there is silence for a time, as the assassins consider the story from the various ethical angles it presents. This gives Andrachis a certain degree of satisfaction as well.

"Tir-Andrachis?" says a voice.

The High Assassin shrugs off the fetters of thought and eyes the one who spoke. It is Ars Rondorrin, the oldest Ssana here—a man who claims to have served Li Moboron's predecessor, the legendary Dal Biminoth.

It was Rondorrin who killed Thur Cambralos, master governor of Pitur. Given a most difficult assignment, he accomplished it with great skill and efficiency. Biminoth would have approved.

"Yes, Ars? Speak, old dagger."

The assassin casts a gnawed wingbone into the fire. A small cloud of sparks rises in angry reply and scatters into oblivion.

"By now," *observes Rondorrin,* "the master governors must have called their precious Federation. And it will not be long before the offworlders answer their call." *A pause, during which Andrachis imagines he can hear the flapping of uterra wings outside their den.* "We should have a plan to deal with them, should we not?"

The High Assassin nods. "You speak sensibly, brother. Last time the offworlders came, during the wars, they were restricted to providing medical assistance. This time, Ssan is a member of their Federation; there is no such restriction."

"I have heard that they have weapons of their own," *notes Lakandir. He looks around at the other young Ssana.* "Powerful weapons, which can destroy a man in the blink of an eye."

Andrachis shrugs, making a face to show that he is less than impressed. It is important that he keep up his followers' confidence. Early in his training, his father told him that no one could beat an assassin except himself. And like all his father's bits of wisdom, he has taken it to heart.

"A weapon is only as dangerous as the one who wields it," *he comments.* "And the Federation offworlders are not a dangerous people."

"Not dangerous?" *echoes one of the younger Ssana.*

Andrachis shakes his head slowly from side to side, so that his earlobes barely brush the sides of his neck. It was precisely the way Li Moboron had done it—the result of long practice before a thousand mirrors.

"In fact," he goes on, "I can say from firsthand experience that they are weaklings, hardly fit to bathe an assassin's feet." He pauses, remembering. "With one or two exceptions. But they are just that—exceptions. The majority of these people are no more of a threat to us than the master governors' security forces."

"And we know how ineffectual they are!" one of the veterans chimes in. It is a Ssana who fought on the other side in the wars.

For all Andrachis knew, it was he who gave the man the scar that runs from above one eyebrow to his chin. But they are all on the same side now.

Making eye contact with the veteran, Andrachis acknowledges the support. The assassin smiles in reply.

Then Cor Lakandir speaks up. It was inevitable, the High Assassin told himself. The youth never shies away from a topic of importance.

"I understand they have more than just weapons," he notes, addressing the group as a whole. "They have advanced detection technologies. Ways of finding people who don't want to be found." A beat, for effect. "Like us, for instance."

There is murmuring and an exchange of glances among the young ones. Andrachis knows it is his obligation to quell the storm before it gets out of control. Certainly that is what Li Moboron would have done.

But not with words, the High Assassin muses, recalling something he saw only a few moments earlier. His predecessor always achieved more with a gesture. And so will he.

Spotting a thick shankbone that has not yet completely charred over, he reaches into the flames with his bare hand and takes hold of it. The scorching heat sears his skin. The pain makes his eyes sting and his gorge rise. But

*he maintains control of himself and, with the utmost
dignity, removes the bone from the fire.*

*Even rescued from the blaze, the thing burns like an
instrument of torture, such as those feudal lords used on
their enemies in ancient times. But Andrachis holds on to
it, making a point not to look at it—or he might lose heart
at the sight of his singed flesh.*

*"The offworlders may find us," he says to all assembled
there, to all the indigo eyes that glint in the firelight. "They
may track us to our lair. But when they get here . . ."*

*Grasping the uterra bone in both hands, he breaks it in
half with a sharp, resounding crack. It echoes throughout
the cavern as he hoped it would. Then he casts the pieces
back into the flames, sending up a mighty swarm of orange
sparks that writhe for a moment and are gone.*

*"We will break them like the slenderest uterra bone and
send them back to the star-shot nothingness that spawned
them."*

Captain Kirk was staring at the forward viewscreen,
with its dramatic sweep of brown-and-white Ssani real
estate. But his mind was on the advisement he'd just
received from his chief engineer.

"A problem, Scotty? What kind of problem?"

"Well, sir, I've run a profile of the terrain in the vicinity
of the assassins' hideaway, and it's chock-full of
maldinium."

Kirk thought for a moment. "Maldinium? The stuff
that caused all those transport glitches back on Gamma
Caius Seven?"

"The very same," Scotty confirmed. "And it looks
like we're going to have the very same kinds of glitches
if we try to beam a landing party directly into the
caverns."

"Actually," said the captain, "that's not a problem at all, Mr. Scott. The last thing I want to do is make a sudden appearance in the assassins' midst. It's not wise to surprise someone who prides himself on his prowess with several varieties of deadly weapons."

Then again, it wasn't wise to visit the assassins at all. But he'd been around that block already, and it was clear that the Treadways weren't about to give an inch.

"What I can do," Scotty offered, "is beam ye down to a point just outside the hideaway—perhaps a thousand meters from what appears to be the main entrance. Then ye can make as gradual an approach as ye like."

Kirk nodded, even though Mr. Scott couldn't see it. "Perfect," he replied. "That way we won't be encouraging anyone to mistake our intentions."

"And if our diplomatic colleagues complain that our approach is nae as courageous as they'd like?" asked the engineer.

The captain smiled. "You'll advise them about the maldinium," he answered. "Just as you advised me."

"Aye, sir," Scotty agreed. Kirk imagined that he was smiling too. "Have a pleasant evening, sir. And a good night's sleep."

"You too, Mr. Scott. Kirk out."

McCoy couldn't sleep. For the last few hours he'd been tossing in his bed like a catfish that someone had caught and decided to keep for dinner.

But it wasn't he who'd swallowed the damned hook. It was Jim. And Spock.

And Jocelyn.

In a fit of frustration, he tore away his covers and swung his legs out of bed. It was no use, he thought, as his bare feet touched down on the carpeted floor. As long as he knew that his friends were beaming down into what could be terrible danger, he wasn't going to get any rest.

If only he'd been able to convince that blasted Clay Treadway to let him tag along. If only he hadn't made such a scene in the conference room—the kind that made him look like more of a liability than a help.

If only this, if only that. His life was full of such stuff. If his marriage hadn't failed as it had, if the cure for his father's pyrrhoneuritis hadn't come a heartbreaking few months too late, if there had been a way to save Edith Keeler's life without throwing history into a bloody turmoil . . .

And so on and so forth. But there was no sense crying over spilt lives. Things were what they were, you couldn't go back and make them any different. You might as well—

Suddenly he heard chimes ringing. For a moment he wondered if he was imagining it. Then he realized that there was someone outside his door, setting off the built-in sensor beam.

"Of all the crazy . . ."

Why would someone be standing out there at this hour? If there was a medical emergency, why hadn't they just called him on ship's intercom?

Crossing to his closet, he pulled out his robe, wrapped it around himself, and went out into the anteroom. The chimes were still ringing, undaunted.

"All right, all right," he rasped. "Come in, damn it."

The doors opened. And what the doctor saw took his breath away.

"I hope I'm not interrupting anything," said his visitor. "It's just that I couldn't sleep. And I had a feeling you couldn't either."

It took him a second or two to find his voice. "You were

right," he confirmed. "I couldn't." Feeling awkward, he indicated his quarters with a sweep of his arm. "Won't you, er, come in?"

"Thanks," she told him. And with a strange expression on her face, Jocelyn entered, the folds of her low-cut, powder blue shift whispering around her. The doors closed behind her with a soft shoosh.

"It's not much—" the doctor began.

"Don't," she said, cutting him off, no doubt more abruptly than she'd meant to. She smiled at him politely. "Sorry. All I meant was, it's a lot more than not much. It's you. It's everything you've become since—"

She stopped herself. But he finished the thought for her. Hell, someone had to.

"Since you drove me out into space."

Jocelyn nodded. "Yes. Since I did that." She frowned, obviously feeling guilty about that. And why not? She damned well deserved to feel guilty, thought McCoy.

But what he said was, "Can I get you anything? A drink, maybe?"

She looked grateful. "Sure. I don't suppose you've got any wine?"

McCoy shook his head. "Brandy?" he offered.

"Brandy would be fine," she assured him.

As the doctor moved to the bar to secure a bottle— something a little less fierce than the Saurian variety— Jocelyn sat down on one of his stools and resumed her exploration of the place. She had pulled her hair back on one side, he noticed, just the way she wore it the first time he met her.

He tried not to stare at her, tried not to examine her the way she was examining her surroundings. But it wasn't easy. First off, there was the dress. And second, there was Jocelyn herself.

What was she doing here, at this hour, dressed like that? Didn't she know what would be going through his mind? Or hadn't she thought about that in her craving for late-night company?

Whoa, he thought. Get a grip, McCoy. The woman's got a tough mission ahead of her. And barring her husband, with whom she's no longer sharing quarters, she doesn't really know anybody here.

Sure, he told himself. That's it. She just wants to talk. This is the twenty-third century, for god's sake. The fact that a woman's come to visit a man late at night doesn't mean it's time for a hormone upheaval. Particularly when the man and the woman have shared the kind of history we've shared.

Suddenly Jocelyn turned to him, surprising him. He almost dropped the bottle of brandy.

"Leonard?"

Her eyes were aglimmer with light from somewhere in the room, but her tone was matter-of-fact, almost businesslike.

"Mm?" he replied, gratefully turning his attention to finding a couple of glasses. He expected her to ask about the *phornicia* shells or some other such memento of his travels.

She didn't.

"Would you hold me?" she asked, in that same casual voice.

McCoy looked up from behind the bar. He could feel his pulse starting to pound the way it had the other day in the corridor outside engineering.

"Please?" she added, smiling a needful smile.

In the deep and overwhelming silence that followed, the doctor heard a dull thud, followed by a gurgling sound.

Numbly looking down, he saw—as if from a great height —that he'd dropped the brandy bottle after all, and its contents were forming an ever-expanding pool on the tightly woven carpet.

"Oh God," exclaimed Jocelyn.

In a blur of motion, she circumnavigated the bar, bent down, and snatched the bottle off the floor. A moment later, McCoy found himself kneeling as well, reaching inside the bar to grab a sponge.

His hand found the sponge about the same time Jocelyn's fingertips found his chin. Slowly but firmly, she turned his face toward hers. And kissed him, warmly and deeply, as if none of the bad things that had happened to them had ever come to pass.

But they *had*, he reminded himself forcibly. They *had*. He would always feel the sharp, cutting edge of that pain, that resentment. He would always ache with the memory of that fateful day.

Yes, countered part of him—and so what? Was that a reason to prolong the agony? To nurture it like an ugly, hateful pet? Was that a reason to deny himself a second chance, to deny *her* one?

Jocelyn's hair smelled like the jonquils in her father's backyard, sugar-sweet and lazy. Her hands felt like the season's first cotton on his shoulders, on his face. And they were stronger arguments than any of the ones inside his head.

Returning her kiss, McCoy found himself being swept out on a raging current, the point of no return looming up ahead. A moment later, he was even with it.

And then, suddenly, he pulled away from her.

"What's wrong?" asked Jocelyn, her disappointment showing in her eyes.

"I can't do this," he said. More than anything else in the galaxy, more than life itself, he wanted her back. But not this way.

Her brow creased. "Why not?"

He looked at her. "Because it's wrong," he told her. "You're not my wife." And then, though it cut him to the bone to say it: "You're *his.*"

Jocelyn shook her head. "No, Leonard. Not anymore. Not in any real sense of the word."

"I can't," he insisted, caught up in the throes of an almost physical suffering, nightmare images assaulting him one after the other until his eyes started burning in their sockets. "It would be too much like . . . like . . ."

Before he knew it, there was a cool forefinger against his lips. It was hers.

"Don't say it," she begged him. "There's no need." A long sigh. "You're right. We can't do this. Not now, not this way."

He wanted her as he'd never wanted anyone. He wanted to fall with her to the floor, spilling over like the brandy. But it couldn't happen. It just couldn't.

Kissing him on the cheek, Jocelyn laid her forehead against it. Then she got to her feet, replaced the bottle on the bar, and—with one last look of regret—left his quarters.

McCoy cursed. His face fell into his hands.

He should have known better than to let it go so far, he told himself. He should have *known.*

Clay Treadway couldn't understand it. He'd been standing in front of Jocelyn's door for what had to be five or six minutes now, waiting for her to at least acknowledge his presence out here.

There were a few things he wanted to go over with her

before their transport the next morning. A few details he wanted to nail down before they undertook to confront the assassins on their home ground.

He waited a little longer, but there was no answer from within. And Jocelyn *had* to be inside. At this hour, there was nowhere else she could have been.

Clay grunted. Obviously he wasn't getting anywhere by being patient. He had to figure out what was wrong and set it straight. Frowning, he took stock of the situation.

Was it possible that the sensor in the bulkhead hadn't detected his presence? Or that, having detected it, the mechanism that made the chiming sound had failed to announce him?

Certainly it was possible. But he had never, in all the ten years or so he'd been traveling on starships, experienced a malfunction of this sort. So what did that leave him with? Had Jocelyn simply fallen into a sleep too deep for the chimes to wake her from?

Or maybe something had happened to her. Maybe she'd had a medical problem overnight and was lying there in her bed, hanging onto life by a thread . . .

No. He got a firm hold on his runaway imagination. Jocelyn was in perfect health. There was nothing wrong with her on that count.

And as far as this problem they were having with their marriage . . . that would pass. Eventually, in the fullness of time, she would come to her senses and wonder what in the world could have made her want her freedom after all they'd had together.

That was one of the reasons he'd wanted to get her aboard the *Enterprise.* To remind Jocelyn of what she used to have and show her how much better she'd done since then. To put things into perspective for her.

But that brought him back to square one. If she wasn't

in trouble, if the sensor wasn't on the blink, then where was she? Feeling stupid and hoping no one was watching, Clay rapped on the door's duranium hide with his knuckles.

He wasn't sure it would even be audible inside Jocelyn's quarters, but he had to do something, didn't he? He couldn't just wait out here forever.

Abruptly, out of the corner of his eye, he caught sight of someone coming this way from one end of the corridor—a woman, he thought. He was too embarrassed to turn and see who it was, so he just rubbed his hands together and waited for the person to go away.

The newcomer was less than five meters away before Clay sensed something familiar about her. It was only then that he ventured a glance—

And saw that it was Jocelyn.

She looked at him with something strange in her eyes, something he had never seen there before. It was a mixture of carelessness and guilt, happiness and sorrow, hope and regret. And it jarred Clay like a physical blow.

"Where've you been?" he asked her in a hollow voice. But he suspected he already knew the answer. Somehow, he feared, he'd miscalculated—and badly.

"If you're here to talk about our mission," she said, sidestepping the question entirely, "I'm all ears. Otherwise, we should both get some sleep."

Clay bit his lip. It took him a moment or two to regain his composure.

"There are a few details . . ." he replied woodenly.

Jocelyn nodded. "Good. Come on in."

And without any further discussion of where she'd been, or with whom, she entered her quarters; the security mechanism, preset to recognize her, opened the doors a fraction of a second before she would have walked into them.

Still numb with hurt and anger, Clay followed her inside.

Kirk muttered a rather elaborate curse that he'd picked up as a young officer on Tierenios Four. It described the fate of certain farm produce during the worst part of the rainy season.

Spock, who was standing beside him in full cold-weather gear on the transporter platform, cocked an eyebrow, as if he'd observed a phenomenon of true cultural interest. It was a distinctly Vulcan form of sarcasm.

On the other side of the room, Scotty frowned at the chronometer on his console. As his eyes rose, they met the captain's.

"I know," Kirk commented. He was starting to feel uncomfortably warm in his thermal jacket. "They're late."

"They are human," his first officer reminded him.

"I'm human, too," Kirk pointed out. He indicated the two security officers behind them with a tilt of his head. "So are Peterson and Diaz. Are *we* late? No." He sighed. "It's nice to be in the diplomatic corps. Remind me to consider it in my next incarnation."

As deadpan as ever, Spock said, "I will."

Still not as well versed on the nuances of Vulcan mysticism as he would have liked, the captain was about to ask his friend what he meant by that remark. But he was interrupted by the sound of the transporter room doors sliding aside.

A moment later, Clay and Jocelyn Treadway entered

from the corridor and strode across the breadth of the facility as one. Without a word of apology or even a recognition of their tardiness, they took the two empty places on the platform and assumed postures of readiness.

Kirk glanced at Spock. Ever so slightly, Spock shrugged. He sensed the air of tension between the diplomats as well, but he had no more explanation for it than the captain did.

Something must have happened the night before, Kirk mused, or perhaps even that morning. But he had no idea what it was, nor for that matter was it any of his affair.

After all, what took place between the Treadways was the Treadways' business—until it began to compromise their effectiveness in carrying out this mission.

So far they'd just been late for beam-down. He would let it pass, but he would also be damned sure to keep an eye on them.

"Energize," he told Scotty.

"Aye, sir," replied the engineer.

Working his controls with inspired ease, he activated the transporter mechanism. The unit hummed almost imperceptibly as energy accumulated in all the right places.

Then, before Kirk knew it, they were standing on a rocky shelf overlooking a long, snaking valley choked with snow. His breath froze and hung for a while on the windless air in front of him. The sky was a flawless blue thinning to mint green at the horizon.

I guess we're not in Kansas anymore, he mused.

"Which way is the assassins' hideout?" asked Treadway, probably remembering that he'd taken charge of this effort the day before.

Peterson, a slim, clean-shaven man who had reportedly impressed Chekov with his easygoing attitude, shaded his eyes and pointed to a spot directly below the bright orange disc of Alpha Gederix.

"That way," he replied. "If we stay on this shelf, it'll be about—"

"A thousand meters," Treadway interjected. "Thank you, crewman."

Peterson's jaw muscles rippled, but he took the snub in stride. "No problem, sir."

Diaz, stockier and darker than his fellow security officer, was consulting his tricorder in the meantime. He looked up at the captain.

"Mr. Scott was right," he reported. "There's a lot of maldinium around. That means they can sneak up on us and we'd never know it."

Kirk smiled. "That's why you're here, Mr. Diaz. To make sure our friends the assassins don't get the drop on us."

The security man frowned ever so slightly. "Right," he answered.

Right, the captain echoed inwardly. But just to make sure, he patted the phaser in his lower-right-side jacket pocket, before setting off in the direction of the assassins' lair.

Spock fell into step right beside him as he made his way along the shelf. Peterson and Diaz fanned out on either side of them. The Treadways, who had apparently fallen silent again, brought up the rear.

As Kirk walked, he took in the craggy grandeur of the scenery. Plenty of good rock climbing around here, he noted. Maybe someday, after the assassin problem had been cleared up, he would come back and put his old bones to the test.

"This is not El Capitan," observed Spock. He looked around. "It is much colder here." A sideways glance at the captain. "And there would be no one around to rescue you when you fell."

Kirk chuckled; it sounded louder than he'd expected in the taut, chilly air. His first officer was making a reference to a time some years back, just before their run-in with Spock's brother Sybok. The captain had been free-climbing a sheer mountain face in the old Yosemite National Park when he'd lost his footing and plunged to his death.

Or certainly *would* have, had it not been for his Vulcan companion, who'd had the foresight to literally hang around in a pair of levitation boots. Spock had caught his friend and commanding officer by the ankle mere inches from the ground.

"You know me too well, Spock," remarked Kirk.

"Perhaps you are right," the Vulcan agreed amiably. "And vice versa. However, it is too late to alter that situation now."

"I suppose you're right," said the captain. "Short of—"

Suddenly he heard the sound of someone gagging. Grabbing Spock's arm with one hand, he pulled his phaser out with the other. He didn't think about it, he just moved instinctively.

In the next second, however, he traced the gagging sound to its source. Off on their left flank, Diaz was staggering in the snow, his hands clutching his neck as if he were trying to strangle himself.

"What in the name of sanity is going on here?" cried Treadway.

Kirk already had an inkling. Whirling, he started to close the dozen or so paces between him and the bewildered diplomats, but Spock beat him to the punch. Taking advantage of his superior reflexes, the Vulcan launched himself through the air and took both Treadways down at once.

By then Diaz had sunk to his knees, and the snow in front of him was flecked with bright, hot drops of blood. As his hands lost their strength, they fell to his sides, revealing the hilt of the knife that had lodged in the vicinity of his Adam's apple. Then he fell forward and was still.

Swearing sharply, the captain drew his phaser and hunkered down. In less time than it took to blink, he had scanned the rocky shelf and the snow-covered slope just above it. Diaz had been nearest to the slope; the knife had to have been thrown from there.

Sure enough, there were several footprints in the snow to show the approach of the security officer's killer— but not a sign of the killer himself. Obviously, Kirk told himself, they weren't dealing with any amateurs here.

In his younger days the captain might have tried to make it over to the security man's body, just to make sure there was no hope for him. But he was older and wiser now; he knew a corpse when he saw one.

Instead he turned to look back over his shoulder at Spock and the Treadways. Like Kirk, the Vulcan had armed himself and was doing his best to shield the diplomats from their unseen antagonists. What's more, they were all too willing to be shielded.

"Spock," rasped the captain. He asked a silent question with his eyes: *Where?*

The Vulcan shook his head. He didn't have the answer either.

Nor did Peterson, Kirk learned with a glance. Crouched below them on the valley side, he gripped his phaser tightly, his mouth a thin, hard line. When his darting eyes met the captain's, there was an understandable amount of fear in them.

No reason to wait another second, Kirk decided. Removing his communicator from his jacket, he flipped it open with a practiced snap of his wrist.

"Kirk to transporter room," he whispered, his mouth touching the device's hard, synthetic mouthpiece. Still no sign of the enemy, he noted. But then, there had been no warning before they cut down Diaz, either.

"Scott here, sir," came the reply. "Is everything all right?"

Unfortunately, there was no time to give the engineer all the details. "Beam us back up," hissed the captain. *"Now."*

But he never heard Scotty's reply. It was drowned out by a deep-throated cry from Peterson, who had suddenly sprouted a short, gray metal bolt between his spine and his shoulder blade.

A moment later, their stony ledge was rife with white-garbed figures, all moving with incredible speed and precision. Kirk whirled just in the nick of time to see an assassin coming at the back of his neck with a sickle-type weapon.

He didn't have a chance to really take aim. He just raised his phaser in the Ssana's general direction and fired. Luckily, the captain hit his mark, sending the assassin flying backward in a burst of red light.

Kirk turned to Spock again just as the Vulcan pressed the trigger on his own weapon. The phased-light beam blazed a lurid trail through the frigid air; a pair of Ssana grunted, twisted in midair, and fell face first on the coarse surface of the ledge.

Another ghostly white form came at Spock from behind, but he was already aiming his phaser elsewhere and wouldn't see the assassin before it was too late. A second time the captain fired, and the Vulcan's would-be killer fell victim to the beam's stunning force.

Still, there was no way they could cut them all down. There were far too many of them and they were moving much too quickly, weaving an invisible web that would ultimately catch the offworlders in its strands.

Trying to track a couple of the Ssana as they slithered and spun, Kirk released his weapon's stored energy a third time and a fourth, but missed with both shots. And before he could get off a fifth, he felt something hit him with bone-crushing force in the side of the head.

The whole world lurched sickeningly. As blood filled his mouth, the captain felt something cold against his cheek and realized it was the ledge. He attempted to raise his head but it was shoved back down against the rock again.

Steeling himself against the pain, Kirk lashed out with one booted foot and hit something solid. He turned and peered through a thick, red haze, saw a hooded figure roll away from him—and past the figure, on the far side of the shelf, Spock was spinning like a dervish, still bravely defending the diplomats.

Good for you, he thought, cheering the Vulcan as he pulled the threads of consciousness back together. Good for you, Spock.

Then, before the captain's horrified eyes, something big and white came hurtling toward his first officer and hit him square in the center of his back, catapulting him forward, almost making him drop his phaser. Before the Vulcan could recover, another assassin snapped his head back with a high, whirling kick. And a third toppled him with a sweep at his ankle.

That left the unarmed Treadways unprotected. As one assassin grabbed Jocelyn by her arm and pulled her away, her husband tried to intervene. But a moment later, another Ssana slammed into Clay from the side, sending him sprawling toward Spock.

Abruptly, Kirk realized why they were being toyed with this way. The assassins meant to take some prisoners, though he couldn't think quite clearly enough to figure out why. Planting the heels of his gloved hands against the rock, he tried to get up to give Jocelyn some help if no one else could.

To his surprise, no one stopped him. Staggering to his feet, he sighted on the captive woman and lurched across the shelf, weaponless and weak-kneed, not certain what in blazes he would do when he got to her.

Probably get yourself hammered into the ground, he mused. Probably get them so angry at you that they decide to take one less hostage.

That's when he saw something in the corner of his eye—a radiance, a shimmer that he recognized all too slowly but recognized nonetheless. Following the effect to its source, he saw a cylinder of corruscating, electric blue energy build around his first officer and Clay Treadway.

Before the assassins could reach out for them, before they even knew what was happening, Spock and his companion and the energy cylinder all were gone. Scotty had finally pulled them out of this bloody mess.

The captain smiled with relief, knowing his own escape couldn't be far behind. He waited for the wintry shelf and its squad of assassins to vanish, to yield to the warm, familiar surroundings of the *Enterprise*'s transporter room. But a second went by, and another, and still it hadn't happened.

He turned around, trying to determine what had gone wrong. Through a network of snow white antagonists, Kirk saw only one familiar face, Jocelyn's, reflecting his confusion. Her eyes were wide with horror.

They'd been left behind.

Book Two

SSAN

ONE

☆

"Sorry," said McCoy, his insistent, twenty-six-year-old voice echoing in the near-empty rec room of the U.S.S. *Republic.* "I don't buy it. Not for a minute."

He gazed across the dusky red tabletop at Merlin Carver, the brown-skinned man who'd become the closest friend he had in space, and shook his head.

"Murder is murder is murder, Merlin. End of story."

Carver waved away the suggestion. "Not on Ssan. Assassination is a cultural imperative. And Moboron sees himself as an agent of that imperative."

McCoy snorted. "And that makes it all right? As long as he raises the flag of cultural imperative, he can do anything he wants?"

Carver leaned forward in his chair. "Listen, I'm every bit as repulsed by his reign of terror as you are. I'd have to be made of stone not to be. But I'm not Ssani, I'm human. And as such, I'm in no position to judge him."

McCoy swore beneath his breath. "Merlin, that's the biggest load of hooey I ever heard. I don't have to be a brick to know a nice old building when I see one. And I don't have to be a Ssana to know that what Moboron's doing is a crime against nature."

"Against whose nature?"

"Against anyone's nature."

Carver grunted scornfully, his nostrils flaring. "Come on, Leonard, you can't expect other races to behave the way we do. They don't eat what we eat. They don't wear what we wear. Some of them don't even procreate the way we procreate. So why should they be obliged to fit into our parochial notions of morality?"

"Parochial?" McCoy rasped, leaning forward as well. "What's parochial about defending a person's right to exist?"

As he posed the question, he saw the doors to the rec room slide open and admit the other three members of their deepspace training unit—Warren Huang, Paco Jiminez, and Janice Taylor. Noticing McCoy and Carver, they headed for their table.

"Nothing," responded Carver, his voice rising in volume—as yet unaware that they were expecting company. "As long as he or she cares to exercise that right. But people have been known to waive it for what they perceive as the greater good. I'm sure you can find examples of that in any civilization you care to take a look at, Earth's being no exception. In fact—"

"Arguing philosophy again?" asked Taylor, stopping Carver in midstream and causing his head to snap around. "It seems that's all you boys do lately."

Jiminez smiled, showing off his perfect teeth. "Yeah. What are we, the five most promising young doctors in Starfleet or a debating society?"

"What's the flap about this time?" pursued Taylor. "How many angels can dance on the edge of a dilithium crystal?"

"No," said McCoy. "It's about Ssan."

Huang nodded, looking cherubic despite himself. "Oh. That."

McCoy harrumphed. "Merlin here thinks that their little assassination games are perfectly all right."

"By *their* standards," Carver added. "And Leonard is telling me that they shouldn't be able to do whatever they want to do, even if it is their planet."

"That's right," McCoy confirmed, feeling his cheeks start to heat up. "They shouldn't be able to kill one another. Life is sacred, on Ssan or anywhere else."

"Why?" asked Carver. "Because we say it is? Don't the Ssana get a vote? Or maybe their opinions don't count?"

"Right and wrong isn't a matter of opinion," McCoy told him, starting to get exasperated. "It's an absolute. And killing people is wrong."

"But isn't that philosophy at odds with the Prime Directive?" asked Huang. "According to that, we're supposed to resist the temptation to impose our ideas of morality on anyone outside the Federation even if they're committing what we think are the worst atrocities imaginable."

McCoy scowled at the Asian, who, to his credit, barely flinched. When they'd begun their deepspace training together, Huang had often seemed to wither under the intensity of McCoy's stare.

"You're confusing morality with law, Warren. The *law* says we can't interfere with another culture. But that doesn't mean we have to condone everything that happens in that culture. Or say that it's right."

"McCoy's got a point," decided Jiminez, pulling out a

chair and straddling it. "Take the postatomic era on Earth. Remember what the courts were like back then? The kind of justice they doled out?"

"Those courts were an aberration," commented Taylor, her green eyes narrowing. "You can't use that as an example."

"Why not?" pressed McCoy. He could feel his anger increasing by the second. "Who are we to say what's an aberration and what's not? According to Merlin, we're not even qualified to hold up a yardstick."

"That's not what I meant," responded Carver.

"That's what you said," Jiminez reminded him. "Either our opinions about morality count for something or they don't. You can't have it both ways."

"Damned right," McCoy chimed in.

Huang turned to Carver. "I think he's got you there, Merlin."

Carver shot a glance at Huang, his eyes blazing. "Stuff it, Warren."

The Asian smiled. "I reserve my right to reject that advice," he quipped. "Regardless of whether it is based on an absolute standard or not."

That broke the tension. It got a chuckle out of Carver, not to mention McCoy himself, pretty much defusing the whole situation.

"Good point, Warren," said Carver, pushing a chair in Huang's direction. "But I still think you should stuff it." He turned to McCoy. "And you too, Leonard. Just on general principles."

McCoy put on his best mad-scientist look. "You know, Merlin, I don't normally do lobotomies. But in your case, I might make an exception."

"Charming," observed Taylor, pulling out her own chair. "Just charming."

For a moment or two there was silence. An easy and companionable silence, in which McCoy remembered how much he liked all of them, especially Carver. When they weren't arguing philosophy, that is.

"So," said Jiminez evenly. "Is anyone else as scared out of his wits as I am?"

Carver's mouth curled into an ironic grin. "You mean about beaming down into that bloodbath in Pitur?"

Jiminez looked at him as if in disbelief. "Forget the bloodbath, my friend. That's just part of the job. I mean about serving under Vinnie Bando."

McCoy held out his hands. "What about him?"

His fellow trainees turned to him as one. McCoy felt himself shifting uncomfortably under the scrutiny.

"You haven't heard?" said Taylor. "Vincent Bando's the toughest chief medical officer this side of Alpha Centauri. He'd just as soon eat your liver as look at you."

"All in all, an interesting dietary practice," noted Huang.

"Come on," said McCoy. "How bad could he really be?"

No one answered. But Taylor patted his hand as if he was her patient and she was about to tell him he only had a few days left.

McCoy sighed. "That bad, huh?"

"Worse," commented Jiminez. "A friend of my brother's served under Bando on the *Constellation.* Said it was the sorriest year of his life—and he was only there for a couple of months."

"Bando's mean enough under normal circumstances," added Huang. "But saddled with a massive disaster-control effort like the one in Pitur . . ." He winced dramatically. "And to think I could have been an engineer."

McCoy realized that his mouth was hanging open and closed it. A Southern gentleman did not gape; his father had taught him that, though the lesson had obviously not taken as well as it should have.

"Well," he said finally, "I came out here to take my mind off my sack of troubles. It looks like this Doctor Bando will provide all the distractions a man could ask for."

There were a couple of murmured responses, but no one in the room really knew what to say to that. They never did, not even Merlin, who knew a bit more than any of the others about McCoy's reasons for fleeing Earth.

On one hand, McCoy regretted throwing a wet blanket on the conversation. But he also couldn't help taking a perverse pleasure in their discomfort.

Hell, why deny it? He *liked* playing martyr. It made him feel as if he'd achieved a higher rung on the ladder of experience, as if the scars he carried from his failed marriage had graced him with some sort of moral superiority.

Not that he wouldn't have gladly traded his martyrdom for the way things used to be . . . for the kind of life that once stretched out before him like a well-paved street lined with big, white houses and fragrant, old peach trees. But unfortunately, that wasn't an option anymore.

Jocelyn had seen to that.

Usually it was Carver who broke the ice after one of McCoy's little "bon mots." This time, he didn't get the chance. The ship's intercom beat him to it.

"This is Captain Hillios," said the commanding officer of the *Republic* in a voice somehow both melodic and authoritative. "Medical trainees McCoy, Carver, Taylor, Huang, and Jiminez are to report to Transporter Room

One in thirty minutes. Repeat: thirty minutes. We're in shouting distance of Ssan."

McCoy watched Carver's Adam's apple climb the inside of his throat. Then he looked around at the others, confirming the bond that had developed among them—a bond that seemed a great deal more important now that Ssan was no longer just an abstract concept.

"Thirty minutes," echoed Huang. "Barely enough time to put on some clean underwear."

But the man's voice came out flat and listless, McCoy thought. Like a mint julep left sitting too long in the sun.

By the time they reached the transporter room, Jiminez had come up with a name for their group.

"The Ssanitation Detail," he said, smirking. "What do you think?"

McCoy nodded. "I like it."

"Me too," agreed Huang. "It's got just the right mixture of bravado and morbid fascination."

Taylor glanced at him. "You sound like a theater critic," she observed.

Huang shrugged. "I told you I missed my calling."

As they approached the transporter platform, McCoy stole a glance at the transporter operator on duty. To his dismay, he saw that it was Sorenson, a junior officer who'd joined the *Republic* about the same time as the medical trainees.

"What's the matter?" asked Carver.

"Nothing's the matter," McCoy assured him.

"Come on," said his friend. "This is Merlin you're talking to. You look like you just lost two pints of blood."

McCoy frowned. "I don't like transporters," he mumbled, so the others wouldn't overhear.

"Excuse me?" replied Carver, leaning closer.

"I said I don't like *transporters*," McCoy repeated.

The other man looked at him, a smile playing at the corners of his mouth. "Don't tell me you're afraid you'll get your atoms scrambled."

McCoy's frown deepened. "That's exactly what I'm—"

The doors to the transporter room opened abruptly, and Captain Hillios walked in, surveying the medical trainees from beneath her sweep of copper-colored hair. Instinctively, McCoy stood up a little straighter on the platform.

The captain's gaze fell on each of them in turn. "Well," she said, "at least you all showed up. In my last batch of medical trainees, I had someone who couldn't stand the thought of beaming off the ship—if you can imagine such a thing in this day and age."

McCoy felt Carver's elbow poking him in the ribs. Fortunately, they were in the second row and not immediately visible to Hillios. With his own elbow, he moved Carver's aside.

"In any case," said the captain, "I wish you all luck. From the reports I've seen, it's no picnic down there." Turning to the transporter operator, she nodded. "Prepare to transport, Mr. Sorenson."

"Aye-aye, Captain," said Sorenson.

As he fiddled with his control board, McCoy could feel his muscles tighten painfully. It wasn't just that he hated transporters. He hated *all* machines on which men's lives depended. The transporter just happened to fit into that category.

"Energize," Hillios commanded.

McCoy shut his eyes tight. The hum of the transporter mechanism rose in pitch, though after a while he could barely hear it over the grinding of his teeth.

A moment later, he imagined he could feel the indescribable cold of space thrilling through his bones, sinking a thousand tiny claws into his flesh. No, not cold, he realized. Heat. *Terrible* heat.

"My God," said Carver, standing beside him.

McCoy opened his eyes and saw a spectacle of devastation the likes of which he'd never seen before and hoped never to see again.

"My God," someone else said, echoing Carver's words. It took a moment before McCoy realized that someone was he.

From the looks of the beam-down site, it had once been the city-state Pitur's council chamber, made of rich, marbled stones selected for their pink and pale blue hues, draped with deep purple tapestries and carpeted in thick, white Ssani cloud moss. It had once been a stage for Ssani lawmakers as they paced back and forth, reshaping their society with new, progressive laws.

Once . . .

Now it was a bloody, flaming shambles. A charnel house filled to the rafters with the dead and the dying. A bedlam of sorrow and pain and surrender.

Whatever had happened here had torn up the slabs that comprised the walls, leaving them scarred and even crumbled in some places. The windows had shattered into a thousand tiny shards, the tapestries hung in fiery tatters, and the mossy carpet underfoot had turned crimson with the blood of its masters.

Up until now, "disaster control" had merely been a phrase, a concept. Now its meaning came home with mind-numbing force.

There were medical personnel, but not enough. Not nearly enough. This chamber must have been crowded wall-to-wall when disaster struck.

McCoy just stared. It didn't seem possible that there could be so much suffering in one place. So many people crying out for help . . .

"Watch out!"

McCoy whirled reflexively at the sound, just in time to see someone dressed in the blue and black of a CMO come crashing into him, knocking him backward. For a moment, he tried to stop himself from falling, but it was no use. The weight of the other man was just too much for him to bear.

As the trainee fell, smashing the back of his head against a marble fragment, he caught a glimpse of something bright and terrible. It was a flag—a heavy, blazing flag—and it landed on the floor in exactly the spot where he'd been standing.

Before McCoy could comprehend the full import of what had happened, he felt fingers digging into the fabric of his medical tunic. Taking hold, they lifted him to his feet.

And he found himself locked eye-to-eye with the man who had knocked him down. He got a vague impression of blunt, squared-off features, a close-cropped brush of iron gray hair and a hard, thin-lipped mouth.

Then the man thrust him away. "You've got to keep your eyes *open,* Doctor. I'm a little too busy these days to be your nursemaid."

Bando, a voice whispered in McCoy's brain. Vincent Bando. It had to be. He was the only CMO assigned to Ssan, wasn't he?

"Yessir," muttered McCoy, still stunned from the blow to the back of his head.

Scowling, the stocky CMO pointed to a clot of wounded Ssana clustered around a cascade of fallen stones. "Over there," he growled. The expression on his face said that he was used to being obeyed.

McCoy followed the gesture, swallowed. But somehow he couldn't get his feet to move. He couldn't get his body to accept where it was or what it had to do there.

"Yessir," he said again, even more lamely than before, wide-eyed, blinking at the smoke that stung his eyes.

Bando's scowl deepened as he leaned in close. "What's the matter, Doctor? Haven't you ever been in Hell before?" His mouth twisted into something like a savage grin. "Now get a move on!"

The last few words, shouted in McCoy's face, did the trick. They were like a physical blow. Clenching his teeth against the acrid smell of charred skin, the trainee made his way through the wreckage of the council chamber.

Behind him, the CMO was rousting the others as he'd rousted McCoy. But that was just background noise. As McCoy approached the group of victims to which Bando had gestured, he could feel his training coming to the fore. He could feel himself starting to think like a doctor.

There were five of the Ssana. Two were obviously dead and a third was well on his way. But the other two looked as if there was a chance they might be saved.

As McCoy knelt beside the nearest Ssana, he swallowed. Up close, the stench of the man's ruined flesh was almost overpowering. Gagging, fighting down his lunch, he opened his shoulder bag and took out his tricorder.

It confirmed his initial assessment: burns over thirty percent of the Ssana's body, broken bones, shallow shrapnel wounds. But vital signs were good. And the patient was young, even younger than McCoy himself. With some help, he'd pull through.

As the doctor put his tricorder down and reached for

his hypospray, the Ssana's tiny eyes opened and fixed on him. They were a dark shade of indigo, almost black, beneath a thick brow that was creased and furrowed with pain.

Noting the hypospray, the Ssana shook his head as much as he could, which wasn't much at all. "No," he breathed. "No . . ."

"It's all right," said McCoy. "I'm here to help you."

The Ssana shook his head again. "Leave me," he rasped, his voice cutting through the noise all around them. It had taken a great and agonizing effort for him to speak with such authority.

But why? Why didn't he want to be helped? Was he just dazed, not thinking straight? Or was it something else?

"Leave me," he repeated in a pleading tone, his over-size earlobes shuddering with the intensity of his helplessness.

McCoy swallowed. "I can't," he insisted. "I'm a doctor."

The Ssana raised his hand toward McCoy's face, but the appendage never made it all the way. And when it fell, it came to rest on the body beside him.

It was that of the other survivor, a woman who was hurt nearly as badly as he was. McCoy wondered if the woman meant something to him or if he was simply being chivalrous, even under such horrific circumstances.

From a medical standpoint, it really didn't matter which patient he started out with. They were in roughly the same sort of shape. And there was time enough to save both of them, barring any unforeseen complications.

So, despite the Ssana's harsh and tortured protests, he set his hypo for colerium, the anesthesia that worked best on these people, and injected it into the man's arm. As he realized what McCoy was doing, the Ssana grabbed his wrist, but it was too late. The effects of the drug were nearly instantaneous.

Even so, his grip on McCoy didn't relax one bit. Marveling at his patient's force of will, the doctor broke the Ssana's grip and turned his attention to the female. As it turned out, her injuries weren't quite as bad as he'd thought at first glance. Allowing for her lesser body weight, he administered a slightly smaller dose of colerium.

Then he set to work placing dermaplast patches over the worst of their wounds. In a matter of minutes, he'd stopped the bleeding, such as it was. Now it was just a matter of getting them to a medical facility.

Leaning back, McCoy found that his eyes were full of soot. He used his sleeve to try to wipe some of it away, but it made the situation even worse; a moment later, his eyes were stinging with acid tears.

So when he heard the sound of a distant rumble, he had only his ears to tell him where it was coming from at first. Blinking desperately, he cleared his vision enough to see the direction in which everyone's head had turned.

Through one of the ruined window openings in the chamber walls, McCoy could see a distant tower half in flames. And he was certain that it hadn't been in flames a few minutes ago.

That was the moment, he'd recall later, when he got his first real taste of what it was like to serve on the planet Ssan in the time of the Assassin Wars. It was one thing to work under adverse conditions, even to risk one's life in the process. But it was quite another to see another beacon of death being lit before you'd put out the flames in the last one.

Bando rounded on them. "All right," he said, his eyes a startling red, his voice hoarse from breathing in smoke for who knew how long. "Let's stop gawking and finish up here. Looks like Moboron's making sure we don't get bored today."

McCoy didn't have to be told twice. Removing his communicator from his belt, he flipped it open. "McCoy to Federation Medical Facility One. Two to beam over."

He got a response a couple of seconds later. "Acknowledged, McCoy. Bet you're thrilled you got this assignment."

The trainee frowned at the black humor. He had a feeling he'd be hearing plenty of it before he left this world.

As he waited for the transport to take place, he heard one of his patients murmur something. Looking down, he saw that the woman was still asleep. But the man had somehow managed to open his eyes again.

The hatred in them was as big a shock to McCoy as anything he'd seen so far. The Ssana looked as if he'd have liked to rip the human's throat out with his bare teeth.

He must be delirious, the trainee told himself. Why else would he be looking that way at someone who'd just saved his life?

And more importantly, how could he still be conscious? *Did I somehow screw up the colerium dosage?*

Fortunately, he didn't have to wonder for very long. A moment later, the transporter effect created an aura around both survivors, and in the space of another heartbeat, they were gone.

TWO

☆

McCoy sat on his haunches, his back resting against a stone wall in Pitur's benighted government square, and peered through the confluence of gray smoke that had collected overhead. The complex's four abandoned towers were barely visible against the darkened sky, except where they were outlined by dying, orange embers.

There were no longer any living Ssana in the area. Those who had escaped injury had been evacuated; the wounded had been beamed away by Federation transporters. Most of the dead had been carried down as well, although it wouldn't be until morning, which was still an hour or so away, that the authorities would send teams to search through the rubble for the rest of the bodies.

At this point, the blue-and-black-suited figures that milled around in the square were all offworlders, Starfleet doctors and medical trainees in various stages of physical and mental fatigue. To McCoy's smoke-stung eyes, they looked like ghouls lingering at the scene of mortal disaster long after the last drop of blood had dried up.

"What do you think?" asked Carver.

McCoy turned at the sound of his name, wincing at the crick he'd developed in his neck, and scanned the face of his friend, who was squatting beside him. Merlin looked like he'd pulled a week's worth of all-nighters.

"About what?" asked McCoy. His voice was flat, passionless. It sounded to him as if someone else were speaking.

"About how long the man's going to keep us here," said Carver, a little impatiently, as if it should have been obvious what he was talking about.

McCoy shrugged. "I don't know." He thought for a moment. "Bando said he wanted us ready just in case Moboron wasn't quite finished. But it's been a while since we beamed over the last of the casualties."

His friend nodded. "That's what I'm saying. I mean, we've been going for—what? Seventeen hours now? Pretty soon we'll be no good to anybody." He sighed. "We've got to get some sleep. We can't wait forever for Moboron to make his move."

McCoy grunted. "Funny," he said. "Seems like years since we had that discussion about assassin philosophy."

Carver squinted at him, perhaps waiting for the other man to begin the discussion anew, now that they'd had a chance to see the fruits of that philosophy firsthand. But McCoy refrained. He was just too damned tired.

They heard the clatter of footfalls on the paving stones nearby and turned their heads at the same time. It was Taylor, Huang, and Jiminez, who'd been pumping some of the veteran doctors for an idea of how long they'd have to remain here.

"Well?" asked Carver, as his fellow trainees hunkered down in front of them.

Jiminez shook his head. "No way to tell, they say. It seems it's not just a matter of saving lives. Bando takes this business personally."

"That's right," said Taylor. "It's like it's him versus Li Moboron. A game of one-on-one. And from what his doctors say, he hates like hell to lose."

Huang smiled tautly. "Lovely fellow, that Bando. Everything we'd heard and more." He raised his bloodshot eyes to the smoke-clotted heavens. "I wonder what the sunrises are like around here. I have a feeling we'll be seeing a lot of them."

Carver chuckled humorlessly. "What do you know? Even Warren Huang has a dark side."

"Wait a minute," said McCoy. He blinked, not exactly sure of what he'd seen. Then he saw it again and pointed to the center of the square. "They're beaming out."

The others followed his gesture. "You're right," said Taylor. "Well, at least some of us are leaving."

"But where are they going?" asked Carver. "To the dormitories? Or another disaster site?"

"Beats the hell out of me," said Jiminez. "Maybe we ought to—"

He stopped in mid-sentence, and McCoy saw why. Suddenly they weren't in the square anymore. They were in a huge, sterile-looking, softly lit ward full of biobeds. The biobeds were occupied by the Ssana whose lives they'd been saving since mid-afternoon.

"Oh Lord," said Carver. "What now?"

One of Bando's veterans approached them. The woman looked as tired as they felt, but somehow she seemed to be bearing up under it better than they were.

"I know," she said. "You've had it. You want to take a hot shower and go to bed. So do I, but this is Ssan. You've got to help check the survivors first. Bando's orders."

"Bando's orders," Jiminez repeated numbly.

"That's right," the woman assured him. She indicated the far lefthand corner of the hall. "You've all got assignments down there. You'll find your names logged in beside the vital signs. From now on those patients are your responsibility and no one else's."

"No one else's," muttered Jiminez.

The woman sized the trainee up. "We're understaffed here, Mister. We make do." She smiled wanly. "But don't worry. Once you get started, it'll go quicker than you think."

As she turned on her heel and left them standing there, Carver scanned the hall and swallowed. "I haven't got the strength for this now," he told the others.

"Maybe next time, we shouldn't save quite so many," quipped Jiminez.

"Maybe we shouldn't save any at all," Taylor grumbled softly, obviously not appreciating her colleague's remark. "Then we can keep more regular hours."

Jiminez frowned, turning to face her. "It's a joke, Janice. You remember what a joke is, don't you?"

Taylor flushed at the remark. She was about to answer when Huang stepped between them.

"Easy, Doctor," he told Taylor. "Haven't we had enough casualties for one night?"

McCoy put a hand on Jiminez's shoulder. "Warren's right," he said, "as much as I hate to admit it. We're all bushed. We can barely think straight. And Jiminez couldn't think straight even before this."

Jiminez leveled a narrow-eyed look at his fellow

trainee. "I'd take offense at that," he rumbled in mock anger, "if I could remember what it was you just said."

"We'd better get started," Carver reminded them, far from eagerly. But it did the trick. Taking the lead, he guided them through the army of biobeds to the area the woman had pointed out to them.

As they made their way through the ranks of the wounded, who were cocooned like dormant insects in their metallic-fiber blankets, McCoy found himself feeling more at home. After all, his father was a doctor back in Georgia. He'd been trekking up and down hospital corridors before he was old enough to talk, helping to cheer the patients with his devilish smile and confound the nurses with his antics.

Tired as he was, he told himself, he could handle this. It was the kind of doctoring he was used to, the kind he'd seen his father practice for as long as he could remember: one-on-one, physician and patient, in a setting conducive to compassion and contemplation.

Not the insanity of exploding towers and the screams of the dying. Not the horror of splintered bones and blood spattered on smooth, cold stones.

This was healing. This was medicine. This he could do, he knew, even with his eyes closed . . . although it wouldn't hurt to keep them open.

Approaching the first of the beds that had his name included in its biosigns display, he forgot about his friends for the moment and leaned in to get a better look at his first patient. It was a woman, the very first one he'd treated on his arrival here.

The Ssana was still unconscious. No surprise there; colerium was famous for the long-lasting nature of its effects, and he'd given her a healthy dose. But her color was good, the shards of debris in her wounds had been removed, the new dermaplast patches were holding nicely, and the readout above showed that all her vital signs were stable.

Not a bad job, he told himself, if I do say so myself. Brushing a loose lock of hair off her forehead, he smiled and programmed the biobed to take a blood sample, just to make certain there were no complications. Then he went on down the line.

His next patient was the one he'd found lying next to the woman. He too was well on the road to recovery, his biosigns steady, his color restored, his patches showing not the slightest sign of rejection.

And unlike the last time McCoy had seen him, he was blissfully unconscious. Apparently the colerium he'd administered had taken effect after all, if a little more slowly than he'd expected. Maybe the hypohead was faulty, he mused. Arranging for a blood sample, he started to move to the next bed.

"Doctor?"

It took McCoy a moment to realize that he was the physician being addressed. He turned and saw a thin male nurse with hair the color of straw approaching.

"Yes?" said the trainee.

The nurse indicated the Ssana with a jerk of his head. "It's him, sir. He's been . . . well, he's been growling."

McCoy looked at the man askance. "I beg your pardon?" he replied.

The nurse frowned. "Growling, sir. Not constantly, of course, but from time to time—enough to get me worried. And once, I think his eyes opened." He peered at McCoy. "I have to admit, I haven't been here very long. But this is the first time I've ever seen anybody take a shot of colerium and show signs of coming out of it."

The trainee cast a glance at the Ssana and bit his lip. First the man takes too long to succumb. Then he resists the drug enough to make guttural noises. Could it be that it wasn't the fault of the hypohead after all? Or for that matter the size of the dose?

"Thanks for letting me know," he told the nurse. "You did the right thing."

The burly man nodded. "So what do you think it could be?" he asked. "I mean, what's different about him?"

McCoy snorted. "I don't know the answer," he told the nurse. "Maybe something will turn up in his blood-chemistry results." He clapped the man on the shoulder. "Right now, however, we're both needed elsewhere."

The nurse grunted and went about his business, though he was still plainly curious. And for his part, McCoy proceeded to the next biobed assigned to him. But for the next half hour or so, which is how long it took him to make his rounds, he was still plagued by the question of how his patient had defied the effects of a drug as powerful as colerium.

Standing in the Federation-outfitted lab just down the hall from the convalescent ward, McCoy peered at the screen of his bioscanner, checked his blood-chemistry results for the third time, and sighed. He'd hoped to come out of this endeavor with some answers. But all he'd succeeded in doing was generating more questions.

None of this was making sense, he told himself. Maybe there was something wrong with the bioscanner itself. After all, the device wasn't exactly state of the art.

Initiating a diagnostic cycle, he waited for a few seconds. Then the results materialized on the monitor, where bright green graphics overlaid a blackness as impenetrable as space itself.

No detectable malfunctions. Everything was in working order. So there really was an anomaly in the patient's blood sample that he'd never seen before. And somehow it was linked to the Ssana's ability to fight the effects of the colerium.

For a moment McCoy caught a glimpse of himself on the screen. The expression reflected there was one of discomfort—the kind one might see on a boy sweating in his stiff-collared Sunday best when he'd rather be splashing in a cool, granite swimmin' hole.

I do hate it when things don't go according to plan, he mused. Always have, always will. That's one of the things that make me so hard to live with.

Or so Jocelyn had told him. But that was long ago and far away.

Looking back over his shoulder, he scanned the lab. Together with the ward itself and the medical team's dormitories, it took up an entire floor of what was still one of Pitur's most prominent hospitals.

At first the Ssani doctors in the facility had balked at making room for the offworlders. But then they'd seen the Federation's level of technology and its ability to save lives, and the complaints had abruptly stopped.

Unfortunately, even Federation technology couldn't tell McCoy what he wanted to know right now. No—what he *needed* to know.

Carver and Huang, his partners on this late-afternoon shift, were just across the way, intent on their own bioscanners. There were other doctors present as well, but none quite so close to him.

McCoy grunted. Asking for help was another thing he hated. But in the present case, he didn't seem to have much of a choice.

"Merlin? Warren?"

His fellow trainees turned away from their respective scanners. They looked surprised and maybe a little pleased at the interruption. After all, blood analysis was normally pretty boring work.

Leave it to me to find some excitement in it, McCoy mused.

"What's up?" asked Carver.

"C'mere for a minute," said McCoy, "and I'll show you."

As they approached, he stepped away from his monitor and gestured for them to take a look. They complied—first Carver, then Huang. Each of them came away with a puzzled expression.

Merlin stroked his chin. "It doesn't make sense. With a virus that widespread in his system, there should be some kind of response—some white blood cell movement, something." He stroked his chin some more. "It's as if the virus has found a way to become accepted."

"A symbiote?" suggested Huang. "There's some precedent for that, on Delanath Four, though that was in an invertebrate. Still . . ."

"To complicate the matter even more," said McCoy, "the patient seems to have a resistance to colerium. In fact, that was my main agenda in looking at his blood results—to try to explain that resistance." He paused. "Interesting, huh?"

"Very interesting," agreed Huang. "You've put the machine through a diagnostic mode?"

McCoy scowled at him. No other answer was needed.

"Of course you did," said Huang. "I feel worthless for even asking."

"So what've we got here?" asked Carver. "A Ssana with

a marked resistance to colerium and a virus that his body doesn't seem to recognize. On the face of it, I'd say the virus is counteracting the drug, absorbing or attacking it."

"That's the simplest explanation," noted Huang. "But to these humble ears, it sounds *too* simple. More likely, the virus is—"

"What's going on here?"

Their heads all snapped around at the same time. In the short time they'd been here, they'd all come to react instinctively to the voice of their commanding officer.

McCoy saw the way Bando was looking at them and swallowed, though not as loudly as Huang. Carver was the first to recover.

"We seem to have isolated an anomaly," said the trainee. "A virus . . ."

Bando's brow creased and he stepped forward to scan McCoy's monitor. Carver and Huang got out of his way with admirable quickness.

"Damn," said the CMO. He straightened and looked at them. "You know what you've got here?"

McCoy shook his head, wondering if even that was too much of a response to what was obviously a rhetorical question. But Carver actually went so far as to say something.

"What, sir?"

The muscles in Bando's face went taut. "A blasted *assassin,* that's what. A coldblooded, murdering assassin."

McCoy didn't understand. His expression must have communicated that fact eloquently, because the CMO provided an explanation.

"The natives call it bloodfire—not as an indication of the host's discomfort but as a description of the way one reacts under its influence. In instances of physical stress, it stimulates the adrenal medulla, or what passes for an adrenal medulla in a Ssana. The result?" Bando looked like he'd just eaten something that had gone bad a couple of days ago. "Supernormal increases in the speed and force of the heartbeat; dilation of the airways to facilitate an incredible rate of breathing and oxygenation; a widening of the vessels supplying blood to the skeletal muscles. In short, the individual becomes a superman."

McCoy saw where the CMO was going with this. So did Huang, apparently.

"The assassins take it to enhance their physical powers," said the Asian. "To become—"

"Killing machines," Bando finished for him. "For the last twelve hundred years, they've celebrated their first kill by exposing themselves to the virus. And if there are any long-term ill effects, they usually don't live long enough to experience them."

For a moment, the muscles in the CMO's jaw worked. Then he slowly turned to face McCoy, fixing him with a stare that could have cracked a dilithium crystal.

"Congratulations," he told the trainee. "You saved the life of the Ssana who destroyed that council chamber— and most of the people in it."

Outside, it was dark. McCoy could see that through the occasional rectangular windows. But inside, overhead lights defied the star-shrouded gloom, giving each doctor all the illumination he needed to make his rounds of the patients assigned to him.

The first time he had done this, at the end of that seemingly interminable night, McCoy had treated each Ssana with sympathy, with compassion. And why not? None of them had deserved their injuries. They were victims.

Or so he thought. But now, when it came to at least one of his patients, he knew better. And in case he was tempted to forget, all he had to do was take a look at the Ssani guard who stood in the corridor just outside the ward, visible through the transparent plastic of the north-facing door.

Bando had actually requested two guards, and that they be assassins themselves. However, the authorities had pointed to their need to deploy their resources—and especially their assassins—in the ongoing struggle with Li Moboron. In the end, they had sent over only one guard, and a normal one at that. Bando hadn't liked it, but he had called it "better than nothing."

McCoy felt a stiffening of his spine as he approached the Ssana with the virus known as bloodfire in his veins. It took an effort of will for him to mask his disgust . . . his outright revulsion . . . at this being who could contemplate murder as easily as someone else might admire a sunset.

As if he knew he was being watched, the assassin's eyelids fluttered open. At first the indigo orbs were glassy, out of focus. But with startling alacrity, they found McCoy and fastened on the sight of him.

The human peered into the unfathomable depths of the Ssana's personal darkness. He couldn't help but feel that if he stared hard enough, long enough, he'd find an explanation there, an understanding of what could compel one sentient being to destroy another sentient being.

Despite the colerium, the assassin's lips moved. He seemed to be trying to say something, to communicate. Out of curiosity as much as duty, McCoy bent closer to hear.

But it wasn't a word the Ssana had been attempting to get out. Suddenly the writhing lips puckered and, with unexpected force, blew warm spittle into the human's face.

Anger exploded in McCoy's brain. For a moment he didn't see a patient, someone who needed his help. All he could make out through a haze of throbbing, white-hot fury was an antagonist—an enemy—whose windpipe he would have liked to crush with his bare hands.

There was no fear in the Ssana's eyes. In fact, there was something like humor, like pleasure. And maybe even a hint of relief.

In the end, that's what tamed the raging, twisting thing in McCoy's gut: the recognition that he was playing right into the bastard's hands.

Not the oath he'd taken to heal the sick and preserve life wherever possible. Not the precept of do unto others taught to him by his mother and father back on Earth, though later he would tell himself that those things would have curbed him as well.

Perhaps the details didn't matter. The fact was, he stopped short of doing violence to the Ssana. Trembling, cursing, he wiped the spittle off his face with his sleeve and did his best to take charge of himself.

It wasn't easy. What's more, the Ssana knew it. And to let McCoy know he knew, he grinned at him.

But the human wasn't about to be tempted a second time. Glancing at the biobed's life-sign monitor to make sure nothing was amiss, he turned his back on his patient. But he could feel the wounded man's eyes boring into the back of his neck as he retreated.

McCoy took a deep breath, let it out. Damn, he thought, still shuddering with spent emotion. For a moment he'd been reduced to the predator that still lurked in his civilized psyche. He'd been lowered to the level of a killer.

How could one sentient being destroy another sentient being? Perhaps his patient was intent on teaching him the answer.

In any case, if he'd had any doubts that Bando had been right about the Ssana's identity, he had none now. The assassin had dispelled them with remarkable efficiency.

THREE

☆

"A counterstrike?" echoed McCoy, trying to rub the sleep out of his eyes. His bare feet were cold on the bare metal of the floor.

Bud Glavin, a narrow, sharp-edged doctor with sad brown eyes and thinning red hair, nodded to confirm that the trainee had heard correctly. "That's the way this war goes, my friend. Moboron hits the government, the government hits Moboron. And we get the privilege of cleaning up the mess."

His voice echoed in the dormitory room. Crammed as it was with metal beds for all the male doctors under Bando's command, it still somehow managed to sound like a big, empty shuttle hangar.

"Where did they find them?" asked Jiminez, from his perch atop a second-level bunk. His long, dark hair was in almost comical disarray.

"In an abandoned farm building out in the country," said Glavin. "It was a relic—barely able to stand on its own—but that didn't keep Moboron's people from using it as an explosives warehouse. When the government's assassins surprised them, they were getting ready for their next round of attacks."

"Casualties?" asked Carver, sitting cross-legged on his bed.

Glavin shook his head. "None that we have to worry about this time. Apparently the government's bunch came out without a scratch. And there weren't any survivors among the enemy." He scowled, deepening the lines in the skin around his mouth. "I guess that's why they call them assassins."

McCoy cursed beneath his breath. The others just frowned.

"Anyway," Glavin told them, "the reason I woke you is to put you on alert. According to Bando, our friend Moboron isn't going to take this lying down. He'll retaliate sometime in the next twelve hours or so."

"That's Bando's estimate?" asked Carver.

"And my own," replied Glavin. "I've been here as long as anyone. And I can tell you, Li Moboron doesn't waste any time when it comes to killing people."

Huang was standing at the foot of his bunk, his arms wrapped around himself against the chill. He looked sleepier than any of them. "Thanks for the good tidings," he muttered.

The older man looked at him and cracked a lopsided smile. "Don't mention it, rookie." And, having discharged his responsibility, he made for the exit.

The trainees looked at one another. "In other words," said Jiminez, "get ready for another damned bloodbath."

"I think that was the gist of it all right," agreed Carver.

"Wait a minute," said Huang, scanning the other trainees' faces with a disturbed expression on his own. He looked wide awake suddenly, as if he'd just remembered something important. "I thought the assassins were the *bad* guys."

McCoy leaned back into his pillows, shook his head, and sighed. "Didn't you read the historical data file, Warren?"

Huang's cheeks turned ruddy. "I must have overlooked it in my concentration on Ssani biology. A grievous error, I see, which I can only hope you will feel inclined to correct."

McCoy grunted. "In a nutshell, Li Moboron's assassins are the bad guys. The government's assassins are the good guys." He paused, darting a glance at his friend Merlin. "Of course, you could argue that an assassin is a bad guy no matter *which* side he's on . . ."

"But that's another discussion entirely," said Carver. "As we know from sad experience. Right?"

McCoy bit the inside of his lip. His ego still stung from the humiliation he'd suffered at the hands of his "favorite" patient. If he wasn't inclined to detest assassins before, he certainly had reason enough now.

But he refrained from venting his anger. Merlin was right. They weren't going to solve anything by reviving their conversation. And besides, they were talking about politics now, not philosophy.

"You see," explained Jiminez, dropping his chin over the edge of his top-bunk mattress, "assassins haven't historically acted as a revolutionary army. They were individuals available for hire to the highest bidder—freelance contractors, really. And since there were no laws against assassination, they were usually successful contractors."

"That's right," said Carver. "Then the current government came in and threatened to change the laws, and all hell broke loose. A bunch of the more traditional assassins banded together to create havoc in an effort to convince the government that what it was doing was wrong."

"And that," Jiminez added, "is when the government decided to fight fire with fire."

Huang thought for a moment. "That doesn't make sense," he decided. "If the government wins, doesn't that put all assassins out of business, including the ones now fighting on the government's side?"

"It certainly does," McCoy responded. "But since the institution of legalized murder started on Ssan, no assassin has ever been forced to think about the implications of his mission. In fact, they're not *allowed* to think about them. Their only responsibility is to do the job assigned to them. And that's what the assassins fighting on the government's behalf are doing now—the best job they can. No more, no less."

"Exactly," remarked Jiminez. "And if it's their fellow assassins they're supposed to kill, that's all right as far as they're concerned. Assassins have been hired to kill each other before."

"But they're thwarting their own best interests," Huang insisted.

"Maybe," Carver told him. "But they've got no choice. Assassins aren't permitted to turn down an assignment, no matter who it is they're supposed to kill. Even if it means they may never kill again."

"An honest day's work for an honest day's pay," said Jiminez, giving the phrase an ironic twist. "At least from their point of view."

Huang's forehead wrinkled. "I will never neglect to

read a historical data file again. Not when there is so much one can miss."

Jiminez stretched out his arms. "Well," he said, half-yawning, "I don't think we can stay in bed any longer, much as I'd like to." He swung his legs over the side of his bunk with an air of resignation. "Okay now. Sick people, here I come."

Not a very appealing prospect, McCoy thought. And even less so when one of those sick people happened to be scum.

As Jiminez dropped to the floor, McCoy cast a glance at Carver. His friend noticed the look and shrugged.

"Hey, now," he said straight-faced, "don't look at me, Leonard old buddy. It wasn't Merlin Carver who told you to pick an assassin for a patient."

McCoy snorted. "True," he said, tucking his head under the top bunk as he got to his feet. "But you didn't tell me not to, either."

All told, McCoy had nine patients to look after. Six of them had suffered wounds less severe than those of the nameless assassin. Four of the six would be discharged in the next couple of days. Two of the four were probably well enough to go home immediately and no doubt would have if their beds were needed by worse cases.

Yet McCoy looked after all the rest of his charges before he got around to the assassin. He couldn't help it; the idea of treating the man just made his skin crawl. And even when he finally got around to it, he found he couldn't look the Ssana in the face without anger bubbling up inside him again.

So he concentrated on the biosigns monitor above the bed and wordlessly, as objectively as possible, did his job.

"You hate me," said the assassin.

It took the trainee by surprise. Not just the words themselves but the clarity and strength of the man's voice—no doubt a result of the parasitical bloodfire that flowed through his veins.

Nonetheless, McCoy managed to keep his eyes off the assassin's face. Saying nothing, he went about his business, fastidiously checking each biolevel and logging it in for future reference.

The Ssana grunted, apparently seeing through the human's indifference. "You are right to hate me," he said. "I am your enemy. And not just because we are on different sides of a political conflict."

McCoy frowned, trying to focus on his patient's heart rate and remember what the norms were for this race. Hell, he'd known them last night, hadn't he? How could he have forgotten?

This would be a lot easier, he thought, if the bastard hadn't suddenly developed an appetite for conversation. But no matter. He'd grit his teeth and get through it—as if he had a choice.

"We are enemies," the Ssana went on, his tone as reasonable as all get-out, "the way certain species in nature are enemies, the survival of one inimical to the survival of the other. Enemies by virtue of instinct. Enemies in the blood."

McCoy pressed his lips together. He wouldn't get suckered into a discussion of divergent philosophies. He *wouldn't*.

This wasn't Merl Carver lying beside him. This was an inhuman killer, a madman, a fanatic. By answering the Ssana, he knew, he would be reducing a heinous crime to a matter of personal preference.

"You would like to see me dead," the Ssana told him, in

an unexpectedly inviting way. "In fact, there is nothing you would like better."

It was a strange thing to say, and an even stranger way to say it. But McCoy still resisted the idea of conversation with this slime devil.

"So . . . why not do it, human? Why not kill me?" The Ssana whispered in words so precise they seemed to insinuate themselves directly into the trainee's brain.

That's when McCoy looked away from the monitor and peered into the assassin's face. The expression he saw there was very different from what the Ssana's tone had suggested.

It was like looking into the eyes of some jungle predator as it closed in on its kill. Except the kill was . . . itself?

"What?" was all he could say.

"Kill me," the assassin snarled. "End my worthless life."

Strangely numb, McCoy shook his head. "No," he replied.

The man's mouth twisted cruelly. "But why not? Do I not deserve to die? Have I failed to kill enough Ssana for your taste? Or do you wish to see me whole again, so I may strive to kill some more?"

The human found himself smiling, of all things. "Are you out of your mind? Why do you want me to kill you?"

Suddenly he felt the Ssana's fingers close around his wrist, just as they had back in the council chamber. But this time the assassin's grip was even tighter, even more painful.

It made McCoy glance at the sedative readout, expecting to find that the Ssana hadn't been getting his prescribed dosage. But the readout showed that everything was in order. And then, cursing himself for a fool, McCoy remembered: the bloodfire.

Checking the other readouts, he confirmed it. The Ssana's heart and respiratory levels were up, considerably higher than they should have been, given the presence of the colerium.

Looking back at his patient, McCoy tore his wrist free. The Ssana's expression didn't change. It was still a mask of cruelty, as if cold fires raged just underneath the veneer of his burned and lacerated flesh.

"Why do I want you to kill me?" the assassin repeated. "Because you have wronged me. You have shamed me by preserving my life. And the only way you can make amends—to me, to yourself, to the ruling principle of nature—is to destroy the life you saved."

For all its intensity, the Ssana's appeal was almost hypnotic. McCoy found himself being lulled by it, trapped in it . . .

He shook himself free. "No," he insisted. He could feel beads of cold sweat standing out on his forehead. He wiped them away with the back of his hand. "I won't kill you. I won't even consider it."

"You lie," said the Ssana. "You are considering it right now."

"That's absurd," McCoy told him. The sweat was building up on his forehead again. "I'm a doctor. I don't kill people. I help them."

"Even if they don't want to be helped? Even if it makes them want to rend their flesh from their bones to know that an offworlder had a hand in their salvation?"

Ah. So *that* was it. It wasn't just the idea of being saved that the Ssana found so onerous. It was the idea of an offworlder being responsible for it.

Somehow that bias made the human mad. It gave him strength. Steeling himself, he met the assassin's gaze and returned it measure for measure.

"Look here," McCoy said, surprising himself with the ring of authority in his voice. "I understand your shame. I understand what drives you to convince me to kill you. But to be honest with you, I don't give a damn."

The Ssana's indigo eyes narrowed. Apparently he hadn't expected that.

"You see," the human went on, "as a physician, I've got my own kind of shame to worry about. And I'd be shamed from top to bottom if I let somebody die just because he wanted to."

The assassin didn't answer. He just stared at him.

McCoy straightened up. "Now, after you walk out of here, I wash my hands of you. What you do at that point is your own business—or rather, yours and the government's. But until then, I'm going to do everything in my power to see to it that you survive. Got it?"

For a moment the assassin seemed to be weighing the resolve behind the human's words. Then he simply turned away, as if further conversation was beneath him, though he couldn't disguise the volcanic flame that burned in the depths of his Ssani soul.

Something in McCoy derived satisfaction from that small, subtle victory. And not just because he was standing up for what he believed in but because, ultimately, the Ssana had been right.

Deep down, McCoy *did* hate him—for the lives he'd taken as well as the callousness with which he'd done it. And if it made the assassin's blood boil to see his life saved by an offworlder . . . well, that was just a little bonus they hadn't mentioned in medical school.

Noting the last of his patient's biodata, McCoy got up and turned his back on the assassin. After all, he had reports to file. And from what he understood, Bando was pretty strict about such things getting in on time.

Not that that was any surprise. The chief medical officer was pretty strict about almost every—

"McCoy!" came a guttural cry, slicing through the carefully controlled atmosphere of the ward. The trainee traced it to its source and saw Bando himself standing at the entranceway, staring at him. The man's expression was unreadable, but that didn't give McCoy any solace.

Had Bando been watching him? For how long? Had he seen McCoy avoid the assassin? Had he seen him almost fall prey to the Ssana's hypnotic snare?

McCoy had a fleeting vision from his boyhood back in Georgia: one of the wildly colored butterflies in the collection of his friend Skippy Manwaring, pinned to a piece of smooth, white cardboard. He'd been fascinated by the thing, by the idea of something being skewered by a huge pin, with no hope of redemption, not ever.

But try as he might, he couldn't ever quite imagine himself as that butterfly. At least, not until now.

As he cleared his throat, McCoy was preternaturally aware that everyone in the place was looking at him. Not only the doctors, but most of the patients as well. But the pair of eyes that bothered him the most were the CMO's.

"Yes, sir?" he replied at last. His voice sounded meek compared to his commanding officer's.

With a single finger, Bando beckoned to him. Impaled on the man's gaze, McCoy crossed the ward and followed Bando into the corridor beyond.

Bando wasn't one to mince words. But then, McCoy thought, maybe that was good. He wouldn't have to wonder for long what he'd done wrong.

"You know," said the gray-haired man, "I didn't like you from the first time I laid eyes on you. And the fact that you pulled an assassin out of that tower didn't make me like you any better."

McCoy swallowed. This sounded worse than he'd imagined, and his career rested squarely in the CMO's hands. One word from Bando and he'd be plying his trade on a Mars-orbit tug.

And Mars was too close to Earth for McCoy's tastes. A good many light-years too close.

"Of course," Bando continued, "first impressions can be deceiving. Sometimes the biggest wimp turns out to be the best doctor in the long run." His eyes narrowed. "So I give everybody a chance. And I mean *everybody.*"

There was a long pause. McCoy writhed inwardly under the man's scrutiny, but he kept his mouth shut. Trying to fashion an answer, any answer, seemed like the wrong move right now.

"Even so," said Bando, "you didn't do anything to change my mind about you. And if I were a betting man, I'd have bet heavily that you weren't going to."

Suddenly, Bando's face seemed to lose its tension . . . to crease in unexpected places. My God, thought McCoy. I think the old buzzard's *smiling* at me.

"Until today," Bando told him. "I saw you with that murdering bastard of an assassin, McCoy. I saw him try to bait you, try to draw you in so he could sell you on his damned philosophy. Am I right?"

Numbly, the trainee nodded. "You're right," he confirmed.

"But you stood your ground. And better than that, you told him off. I saw the look in his face, McCoy. You don't see that look on an assassin very often. It means"—he savored the thought—"that they've lost. And they detest the thought of losing anything."

The trainee shook his head. "You mean you . . . like what happened?"

Bando nodded slowly, the muscles in his temples working. "I like it a lot, McCoy. And you know why? Because it takes more than compassion to make a good doctor. It takes anger too, and plenty of it. Anger at the circumstances that create the misery you've got to deal with. Anger at the people who create those circumstances. Anger at the whole damned cosmos, for giving birth to the kind of beings who could be so miserable in the first place. They don't tell you that in med school, I know, but, hell in a handbasket, they should."

The older man's eyes glinted in the overhead lighting. If McCoy didn't know better, he would have sworn that the glints were sparks.

"I'm happy to say I was wrong about you," said Bando. "You're going to make it here on Ssan, Doctor. You're going to make it, period."

Well, how about that, McCoy thought. I'm not going to be serving on that Mars-orbit tug after all.

"Thank you, sir," he told Bando. "It's good to hear that."

"It's good to be able to say it," the CMO insisted. "Carry on, Dr. McCoy." Clapping the trainee on the shoulder, he continued on down the corridor, his footfalls resounding from wall to wall.

McCoy grinned like a kid. Merlin wouldn't believe this in a million years.

"Bando said *what?*"

Merl's face was a mirror of his disbelief. Nor did the other trainees in the lab look any more credulous than their colleague.

"What he said," McCoy told them all, "was that he

liked the way I stood up to that assassin. He said he liked it a lot. And that it wasn't only natural to get angry, it was good. In fact, it made me a better doctor."

Taylor shook her head. "Son of a gun. There's a human side to Bando after all."

"And he smiled?" asked Huang. "He really smiled?"

McCoy shrugged. "I'm no expert, mind you, but it looked like a smile to me."

"Hey," said Jiminez, "maybe we could ask him to do it again. You know, so we can decide for ourselves."

"Yeah," said Taylor. "Right."

"So you're the CMO's fair-haired boy now," observed Huang with mock craftiness. "Does that mean you get two desserts?"

McCoy frowned, but without rancor. "At least. You don't expect me to get angry at my patients on an empty stomach, do you?"

"Nah," said Jiminez. "That would be inhumane, wouldn't it?"

"Inhumane all right," echoed Carver. But he wasn't laughing with the rest of them.

McCoy looked at him. "What's eating you?"

Merl hesitated a moment before answering. "I don't get it is all," he said finally.

"Get what?" prodded McCoy.

"How you could be so proud of yourself. I mean, being angry makes you a better doctor? Give me a break."

"Uh-oh," said Jiminez. "I smell another philosophy seminar."

"Me too," said Huang, "and speaking of breaks, I think I'm due for one." He glanced meaningfully at Taylor and Jiminez. "Anybody care to join me?"

Taylor cleared her throat. "Sure, why not? You've seen one microbe, you've seen them all."

And as McCoy withstood his friend Carver's scrutiny, their fellow trainees filed out of the lab. "See what you've done?" he jibed. "And just when I was starting to feel popular."

Merlin muttered a curse. "You know," he said, "I never would have thought a little praise could turn your head so far around."

McCoy bristled. "And what's that supposed to mean? That I should have given in to that assassin and killed him?"

"Of course not," Carver retorted, his voice rising a notch in volume. "But the fact that you didn't isn't exactly justification for a medal. I mean, what's the big deal? You stood up to someone who wasn't even standing up *with* you."

"An assassin," McCoy reminded him.

"But a helpless one," Merlin added. "And a patient, for god's sake. Someone you're supposed to be healing, not locking antlers with."

"Locking . . .?" McCoy couldn't believe he was hearing this, even from Carver. And then he realized why his friend was acting this way. "You're jealous, aren't you?"

"Of what?" asked Merl, his voice going up another notch. "Congratulations from a man who's lost sight of what he's doing here? You've heard what they say about him, Leonard. Bando thinks he's one of the principals in this war. He thinks Li Moboron's on one side and he's on the other. The healing part, the compassion part, that's all become incidental to him."

"He's up to his elbows in blood," McCoy countered, his voice getting louder along with his friend's. "What do you expect?"

Carver's eyes widened. "You're defending him now?"

"No," McCoy insisted—though he was defending him, wasn't he? "I'm just setting the record straight is all."

"How about setting the record straight on your patient . . . Doctor?"

That stung. "In what way?" McCoy asked.

"You think it's some kind of laughing matter when your patient asks you to kill him?" Merlin took a step toward him. "You think that's something to snicker about with your friends?"

McCoy could feel the blood rushing to his face. Enough was enough.

"I wasn't snickering at anybody," he snarled. "I was just—"

"Just what? Just ridiculing some local customs?"

Suddenly McCoy saw what was happening, and he said so. "That's what this is all about, isn't it? We're back to the same old argument."

Carver pounded his fist on the metal lab table beside him. "No. This isn't just about philosophy anymore, Leonard. This is about you—and what kind of doctor you want to be. My kind, or his kind. Because if it's his kind, I don't want any part of it."

McCoy swallowed. "Is this some kind of ultimatum, Merl?"

"It's what I said it is," Carver insisted. "A choice. *Your* choice."

That's when McCoy's anger got the better of him. After all, who was Merlin Carver to preach to him? What had he been through to earn that right?

A wrecked marriage? No way. A daughter who'd probably never know him? Not even close.

"Go to hell," he told his friend.

For a moment Merlin's mouth went taut. Then, with

agonizing slowness, he shook his head. "No," he told McCoy. *"You* go to hell."

And as if he didn't trust himself to stick around, the man turned and stalked out of the laboratory, leaving McCoy with the taste of ashes in his mouth.

"Well," he said to no one in particular, his voice swallowed up in the sudden emptiness of the lab, "I guess I told him off, didn't I?"

FOUR

☆

Bud Glavin had been right about Li Moboron's counterstrike. Less than eleven hours after his assassins' nest was destroyed, the rebel leader returned the favor. With a vengeance.

This time his target was the sprawling, single-story barracks of the city police force. The government-aligned assassins, who knew the tactics and abilities of their adversaries better than anyone, had declined to congregate in a public place. But the police, in their pride and naïveté about how far the dissidents would go, had opted to sleep where they always slept.

It proved their undoing.

As soon as McCoy beamed down, his senses were assaulted—by the din of Ssani voices raised in a tremulous wail of pain, by the garish sight of blood spattered liberally on a broad sea of broken rafters. But he didn't

155

freeze. He'd already had his fiery baptism in the realities of this war.

"All right!" Bando shouted over the din, as a second wave transported down, including the rest of the trainees. "Spread out, and use your tricorders! We may have to do some digging this time!"

Even before the CMO had finished, McCoy was wading through the debris, shading his eyes from the sunlight that came through the ruined roof in slanting, golden shafts. Inside of five steps, he found a man who was still alive and knelt beside him.

"Bastards," the Ssana hissed, clenching his teeth against the pain of a shattered leg. "Never even saw them coming."

"Quiet," barked McCoy. "Save your strength." He scowled at the level of cell damage registered on the tiny tricorder readout. "Looks like you're going to need it."

"Bastards," the man muttered again—and then screamed as the trainee applied a hypo to his injured leg. Pounding his fist against a chunk of seared wood, he screwed up his indigo eyes and squeezed tears from them.

It took only a moment for the colerium to take hold. Satisfied that his patient was in no immediate danger, McCoy stood up again and looked around.

He didn't like what he saw. Of the twenty doctors that had beamed down, only two-thirds of them were hard at work on newly acquired patients. The others were standing around, looking disgustedly at their tricorders or at piles of dead Ssana, crushed beneath fallen beams and masonry.

If the job Moboron did on the government buildings had been horrible, his work on these barracks was positively staggering. Back at the government plaza, Moboron had permitted a fair number of survivors; here, he'd made no such concession.

"Damn it," spat Taylor, not more than a few meters from McCoy. She was standing astride a Ssana who was well past her help. "Damn it to hell."

It was terrible to have to transport into something like this. But it was worse when there was hardly anything here for one to do.

And no one was taking it harder than Vinnie Bando. He was shoving aside splintered pieces of wood, kicking at rubble, and cursing volubly, looking for all the world like a lion who'd come home to find his den destroyed and his family hacked to pieces.

He's lost this one, McCoy told himself. Moboron had been too thorough; he'd carried the battle before Bando could even take the field.

"This stinks," the CMO roared. "You hear me?" He took in the whole place with one sweeping glare. "This stinks! Next time we get here faster, understand? Next time we *beat* those murdering bastards!"

It wasn't the anguished cry of a healer, McCoy knew. It was the bellicose cry of a warrior, a man whose pride had been stung and who would tolerate no more of it. Removing his communicator from his belt, the trainee prepared to use it.

Then he realized he wasn't the only one watching the CMO's tirade. On the far side of Bando, almost hidden by his bulk, Merlin Carver was staring at him too.

No—not staring *at* him, McCoy realized. Staring *past* him. At his fellow medical trainee, Leonard McCoy. And the look on his face wasn't one of horror. It was one of accusation.

Merlin had told him that Vinnie Bando was a lost soul,

someone who had forgotten why he was here. And the CMO was doing his best, it seemed, to prove Merlin right.

Forcing himself to avert his eyes, McCoy flipped open his communicator. "McCoy to Fed Med One." He'd lapsed into the abbreviated language used around the facility without even thinking about it. "Just one this time," he added.

"Acknowledged," came the reply. "And locked on. Better luck next time, trainee."

As McCoy watched the transporter effect claim his patient, he scowled. He hadn't been here long, but he had a feeling next time wasn't going to be any better than this time.

Halfway from the medical facility's transporter room to the patient ward, McCoy bumped into another of the nurses, a big, muscular specimen with arms as thick as the trainee's waist. He'd run into the man once or twice before.

What was his name again? Cauley? No, Curley. Burly Curley, McCoy mused. He smiled at his little private joke. It felt good, too, after the horror of what he'd just been trudging through.

The nurse smiled back. "Headed for the ward?" he asked.

"Yup," said McCoy. "You?"

Curley shrugged. "Where else?" His smile faded. "Bando let you off early?"

"Mm," McCoy replied. Their footfalls echoed in the austerity of the corridor. "That is, if you call six hours early."

"Six hours is nothing," said the nurse. His pale blue eyes asked a silent question, which he soon after translated into something audible. "What's the matter? Did you get sick?"

The trainee shook his head. "Nope. There just wasn't any point in hanging around any longer. Everybody's coming back."

Curley's brow creased over. "Everybody? After only six hours?"

"Uh-huh," McCoy confirmed. "I'm just the first, because I dug out the first survivor, I guess."

As they came out onto the ward, he found himself feeling a little incomplete. He was supposed to have brought more of the living home with him. Unfortunately, it hadn't worked out that way.

"Our assassin friends were more meticulous than usual," McCoy went on. "There just weren't many live bodies to go around."

The nurse swallowed. "You mean the patients we've gotten so far—that's it? That's all of them?"

McCoy frowned. "That's it, all right."

"Damn," said Curley, taking the lead as they made their way among the biobeds. And then: "Must have been a slaughterhouse."

"It was," the trainee agreed. Not that one could describe it in a single word, but *slaughterhouse* probably came as close as any.

"Your patients are over here," said the nurse, "right?"

"Right," responded McCoy.

He let Curley continue to lead the way. It meant one less thing he had to think about. Funny. He felt as emotionally drained now as he had his first time on the ward, even though he'd been out at the disaster site more than twice as long the last time. Frustration took a lot out of a person, he decided.

"By the way," asked McCoy, "the patient I sent in before . . . ?"

The nurse tilted his head to one side. "Over here," he said, making a turn at the next intersection. "With all your others."

A moment later, the trainee found himself confronted by the sight of his newest charge. The colerium-sedated Ssana was tucked away beneath his metallic blanket, neat as you please, insulated from the pain within as much as from airborne germs without. The only way his wounded leg could become infected was if something attacked his whole body, and the biosigns display would warn them of that well before it became serious.

"Thanks," McCoy told Burly Curley.

The man waved back at the trainee without looking at him and homed in on a patient who had kicked loose her covers. With one expert motion, Curley tucked them back into place and went on.

Turning back to his own patient, McCoy looked up at the Ssana's vital signs readout. Everything was where it should be, he noted. Respiration, pulse, neural activity, all at optimum levels.

Of course, with all that damage to the Ssana's leg, the trainee would have to watch him carefully. Bone cells were a little more ornery than soft-tissue cells; they didn't always regenerate in the proper formation. But for now, the situation was as good as McCoy could hope for.

Glancing over his shoulder to get his bearings, his eyes met those of the wounded man's immediate neighbor, and he felt a sudden surge of anger. It figures, McCoy remarked inwardly. The nurses had deposited the newcomer in the nearest empty bed—right next to the bloody assassin.

But if that came as a surprise to McCoy, the look on the killer's face was an even bigger surprise. Far from the haughty sneer he'd come to associate with the man, what McCoy saw now was an expression of concern. Of sympathy, he might have said, if he didn't know better.

Frowning, he turned his back on the assassin again. Even though he'd won their last little sortie, he didn't care to look at the man any more than he absolutely had to.

"Doctor?"

McCoy clenched his teeth. Unfortunately, he couldn't just ignore the Ssana. As Merlin had pointed out, he was still a patient.

Turning slowly, he met the assassin's gaze. "Yes?"

The Ssana tilted his head to indicate his new neighbor. "He is a police officer, is he not?"

"I don't see what business that is of yours," said the human.

The assassin looked at him for a moment, then nodded. "I thought so. Moboron must have destroyed the city barracks." A pause. "My grandfather was a police officer. Poorly paid, ill-respected by his wealthy employers in the government. Yet he did his job; he was as dedicated to it as I am to mine." Another pause. "He would not have been glad to see his fellow officers and their sleeping places destroyed."

McCoy saw his patient wince a little. At the image of destruction? He didn't think so, given what the assassin had done. Then at what? Memories of his police officer grandfather? At how he'd been looked down on by his superiors?

The doctor could identify with that. His own grandfather had been a low-level technician at a medical technology company. Never very good at what he did, he was always on the verge of getting fired and therefore always kowtowing to his superiors in the hope that they'd keep him on.

That's why he'd wanted his sons, McCoy's father and uncle, to be medical men, the kind of people who used the instruments his company manufactured. It was a way of finally getting some respect.

But even if he and his patient had something in common in their backgrounds, it didn't make McCoy feel any more sympathy for him. The Ssana was still a killer, still a monster as far as the human was concerned.

"The city barracks," mused the assassin. "That was one of the targets Moboron preferred to leave for last." He pondered the implications of his deduction. "Then he must have been retaliating for something. Perhaps the discovery of one of our strongholds? And its subsequent devastation?"

McCoy's ears perked up as he listened. A couple of the nurses could have discussed all that within earshot of the Ssana. But if he'd really figured it out from nothing more than the sight of the injured police officer . . .

Then he knew his organization pretty well. Knew Moboron pretty well, too.

If that was so, it might not be a bad idea to get better acquainted with him, despite McCoy's revulsion for the man. After all, what were his personal feelings compared with an opportunity to dig up strategic information that might end up saving some Ssani lives?

Turning to his neighbor again, the assassin's brow puckered. "We do not like doing this," he said. "We do not like it at all." An angry sigh. "Explosive devices are for the weak, the untutored. Their use brings dishonor to the user."

"Then why do it?" asked McCoy.

The Ssana fixed him with his tiny indigo eyes. "Because we have no other choice," he replied evenly. "The government wishes to make us extinct." He gazed at the human appraisingly. "Tell me, Doctor, what would you do if someone tried to make you extinct? What lengths might you go to in order to ensure the survival of your kind?"

McCoy shook his head. "That's different," he pointed out. "Your assassins aren't an entire race. They're a cult, a tiny fraction of the population."

The Ssana smiled thinly. "I see. Then it is the size of the group that determines its right to survive."

The trainee could feel his temples working. This assassin really knew how to push his buttons, didn't he? But if McCoy were to have any chance of extracting anything important from the man, he'd have to keep his emotions in check.

"Numbers aren't the issue here," he insisted—but calmly. "I don't think anyone would bother to outlaw your practices, to deprive you of what you see as your rights, if they didn't abrogate the rights of others."

"Of others?" echoed the Ssana.

McCoy nodded. "Your people want to live free of the fear that they'll be assassinated. Is that so difficult to understand?"

The Ssana shook his head. "No, it is not difficult at all. The question is whether or not that condition should be granted to them."

"It seems pretty straightforward to me," said the human.

"But you are not a Ssana," his patient pointed out. "Perhaps in your Federation, our insitution of assassination is frowned on."

"It is," McCoy assured him.

"I gathered as much. But in the context of Ssani

civilization, Ssani history, assassination is not a thing that deprives one of his or her rights. It *is* a right, perhaps the most essential and valuable and sacred of all rights."

The trainee shook his head. "The right to die?"

The Ssana shrugged. "In a very specific sense, yes. The right to die according to tradition. With honor. With the sort of dignity that can only accrue to the victim of a ritual assassination."

McCoy grunted derisively—though not too derisively, he hoped. He didn't want to put the assassin off completely. But he also didn't want to appear too nice all of a sudden, or the Ssana would suspect he was up to something.

Just keep the conversation going, he told himself. And hope that the bastard slips up somewhere along the line.

"Let me get this straight," he said. "You're telling me that it's a privilege to be the victim of an assassination?"

"That is correct," agreed his patient.

"And what if the victims don't see it that way?" McCoy argued. "What if that's a privilege they can do without?"

The Ssana smiled that thin-lipped smile again. "No one on Ssan asked that question until your Federation meddled in our affairs. You have infected us with your presence, with your ideas."

"Not true," the human told him. "The Federation doesn't meddle. It offers."

"Different words, but they describe the same thing." His patient's eyes took on a harder cast. "Nonetheless, assassination is a right. A victim may not look forward to it. A victim may even try to avoid it. But it is the right of the victim to be a victim."

McCoy looked at him askance. "That's absurd."

"By your standards," amended the assassin. "Not by ours."

He sounded like Merlin, thought the trainee. As if right and wrong were a local phenomenon, something that changed with the temperature or the altitude or the color of the sky.

"You have heard this before?" asked the Ssana, a little surprised. Damn, thought McCoy. He's not *too* perceptive, is he?

"Look," said the human, ignoring his patient's observation, "I just don't buy it. How could something be a natural right if it's rejected by the individual it's supposed to benefit?"

The assassin thought for a moment. "Knowing so little of your society, it is difficult for me to answer that question." Then his eyes widened noticeably. "Wait. What does your homeworld government think of suicide?"

"It frowns on it," McCoy replied.

"Merely frowns?" prodded the Ssana.

The trainee scowled. "All right. Not just frowns. Prohibits. So what?"

"Does a person not have a right to die by their own hand?"

McCoy swallowed. He thought he saw now where his patient was going with this. "No," he conceded. "Not according to the law he doesn't."

"So the government is enforcing his right to live," the assassin concluded. "Even if it is contrary to his wishes. Even if it is a right he does not choose to exercise."

The human had to admit that that was the case. And also that his patient was one hell of a lawyer. He'd have made old Judge Bernhard back in Georgia sit up and take notice.

"I believe," said the Ssana, "that I have opened your eyes—at least a bit." He glanced uneasily at the wounded man on the next biobed. "Not that it will make any difference, in the long run. But at least one of you will know what it is you are helping to destroy."

McCoy tried to think of a response and couldn't. He just stood there, albeit reluctantly, sharing some of his patient's frustration. He knew he wasn't wrong about this. It *couldn't* be right to kill people, especially when they didn't want to be killed. And yet . . .

Unexpectedly, the Ssana looked up at him. "Will you speak with me again?" he asked. "Later, perhaps? Or tomorrow?"

McCoy had intended to speak with him again. But he hadn't anticipated such willingness on the part of the assassin. He nodded.

"Yes," he assured the Ssana. "We'll speak again." And with a last glance at the newcomer's biodata—just to be sure—he made his weary way to the dormitory.

FIVE

☆

Vincent Bando didn't spend much time in his office. It was obvious not only from the very thin layer of dust that covered the furniture here, but from the way he sat in his chair. He didn't look comfortable, McCoy observed. He didn't look right.

"As you know, I get right to the point," said the CMO, cracking his knuckles purposefully as he gazed at the trainee across his old, metal desk, a relic left over from the previous generation of Ssani administrators. "I saw you talking with that assassin again. At length. I want to know why."

There was no rancor in Bando's voice, no suspicion. Apparently McCoy had earned the benefit of the doubt with his earlier stunt. On the other hand, the trainee knew, the man across the desk was the what-have-you-done-for-me-lately type. The trainee wasn't going to get by for long on the basis of one good performance.

Clearing his throat, he replied, "The right to live. The right to die."

The CMO's brow furrowed. "What?"

"It doesn't matter," McCoy assured him. "Not really. The only reason I was talking to him at all was to see if I could get any information out of him." He leaned forward, meeting Bando's rapier scrutiny undaunted. "You see, he knows Li Moboron—how he thinks, what he's liable to do next. And our man is bored lying in that bed all day. He's starved for conversation."

"For something to get his blood pumping a little," Bando remarked.

"Exactly. If I can satisfy that need in him—"

"He may inadvertently tell you something that'll help in the fight against Moboron," the older man finished.

"That's right," said McCoy. "I mean, there's no guarantee, but I thought it was worth a shot. And anyway, what have I got to lose?"

Bando took a breath and let it out as he pondered the question. For a second or two, his eyes looked strangely vacant. Then they hardened again. "Nothing," he decided. "Nothing at all."

That night at dinner, McCoy ate with Jiminez. Carver, Huang, and Taylor sat on the other side of the room.

"This is ridiculous," said McCoy. "No, scratch ridiculous. It's plain stupid."

Jiminez shrugged. "What can I say? Merlin's not exactly your biggest fan right now."

"But just because he and I have a problem doesn't mean the rest of you have to suffer for it."

Jiminez shook his head as he took in a mouthful of Ssani legumes. "I'm not suffering," he mumbled around his food. "Do I look like I'm suffering?"

"You know what I mean," McCoy told him. "We all went to school together. We all shipped out together. We should all be eating together."

"Try telling that to Carver," said Jiminez. He kept his eyes on his plate. "And . . . well, Taylor too."

McCoy looked at him. "Taylor too?" He gazed across the room at her. "What in blazes does she have against me?"

His fellow trainee sighed. "Seems she's decided ol' Merlin's got a point about your bedside manner. If you ask me, she's just upset about the scarcity of survivors the last time out and the prospect that we'll see more of that in the near future, and she's taking out her frustrations on the most convenient target. But the upshot is that you're a barbarian in her book as well."

"Great," said McCoy. "Just great. As if I was responsible for what happened in those blasted barracks."

"Maybe not," responded Jiminez. "But the old supply and demand principle is at work here."

"Supply and demand?" echoed McCoy.

Jiminez nodded. "An economic theory that was popular about three hundred years ago. The idea was that, everything else being equal, rareties were more valuable than things in plentiful supply. That's how it is with the patients around this ward, I think. If we had a lot more of them, your treatment of the assassin wouldn't stand out like such a sore thumb. But because survivors may be few and far between from now on, every patient seems that much more precious. And it becomes that much more important that we deal with them according to the book, even if one of them is a murdering assassin."

Still watching Taylor, McCoy considered the theory. "Interesting," he replied. "But I still wish Taylor had told me about her feelings to my face."

"I recommended that," said Jiminez. "But as I said, she was a little upset. Maybe in a day or two she'll feel otherwise." He smiled, with a bit of an effort. "Now can we eat in some semblance of peace? You haven't touched your greens, you know. And hell, they're almost edible."

But McCoy wasn't thinking about greens. "I suppose Huang doesn't approve of me anymore either," he remarked, ignoring the other man's attempt to distract him.

Jiminez frowned at McCoy's stubbornness. "Actually, Warren hasn't said anything one way or the other. But when I told him I was going to join you for dinner, he just sort of looked away." A pause. "I guess you can draw your own conclusions."

McCoy's eyes narrowed. "Then why is it you're not shunning me the way they are?"

The other trainee grunted. "Let's just say my standards aren't very high and leave it at that, shall we? Now, as I recall, we were eating dinner. That's a custom that usually involves looking at one another while we talk."

. McCoy tore his eyes away from Carver's table. "Sorry," he said. "So how are things going on your end of the ward?"

Jiminez poked his fork into a mound of flaked meat. "About as well as can be expected. I'll be discharging two patients tomorrow, right on schedule. I was hoping for three, but the woman with the broken wrist seems to have suffered some nerve damage the biobed didn't pick up. I'm going to have to do some microsurgery before she leaves." He raised the meat to his mouth, trying to work up some enthusiasm for it. "And on your end?"

"Just ducky," McCoy replied. He was still stinging a little from his rejection at the hands of Taylor and Huang. "Like you, I've got a couple of patients ready to go home.

And the others aren't throwing me any curves I can't handle."

Jiminez chewed away for a little while. Then he asked, "How's your assassin? Last time I looked, he'd mellowed out a bit. He was, you know, less feisty than before."

"I suppose," said McCoy. He considered the other man for a moment. "Can you keep a secret?" he asked.

Jiminez tilted his head to one side. "That depends," he said honestly, "on what it is. I mean, if you're going to join the assassin brotherhood or something, then you should probably keep it under your hat."

McCoy smiled cynically. "Don't worry, it's nothing like that, though it is about assassins." He lowered his voice to a conspiratorial murmur. "But more than that, it's about saving lives."

"I'm always interested in doing that," Jiminez told him, lowering his voice as well.

"Of course, this isn't the kind of life-saving they taught us about back in school. This is the kind where you use information instead of a tricorder and a hypospray."

The other man's brows knit. "Information," he repeated.

"Damned right."

"And where do you get this information?"

"Where else? From my friend the assassin. He seems to be pretty well tuned in to Li Moboron's strategy, Paco. I've already begun to lay some groundwork to get him to trust me. If I can keep it up, who knows? Maybe he'll tell me something that'll end this assassins' war a little sooner."

Jiminez regarded him. "So this assassin is a tool. A means to an end."

McCoy didn't like the sound of that and said so.

"Nonetheless," said Jiminez, "that's what he is, at least, from your point of view. A tool, like a neuroscalpel. Except he's also your patient."

McCoy felt the blood rushing to his face. "Now just a minute here, Paco—"

The other man's eyes flashed dark fire. "No," he interrupted, his voice unexpectedly sharp and biting. *"You* wait a minute, Leonard. Don't you see what you're doing? You're betraying the oath you took when you graduated from med school. Your first duty is to the patient—not some abstract idea of the societal good."

"Abstract?" McCoy felt himself choking on his own anger. "My God, Paco, you've seen those people. Those bodies. If we can keep any more of them from getting hurt, from getting killed, isn't that worth a little subterfuge?"

Jiminez shook his head. "You just don't get it, do you? You're not a politician, Leonard. You're not a general. You're a doctor. And doctors are supposed to worry about healing—period. When we start worrying about something else, we stop being healers."

"Semantics," McCoy hissed.

"Maybe I'm not as good as Carver at arguing philosophy," Jiminez conceded. "But I can tell you this: there are reasons that doctors aren't supposed to meddle in the kinds of things you're meddling in." He stood up and looked down sadly at his fellow trainee. "If that's your secret, maybe you'd better keep it to yourself, all right?"

As McCoy watched open-mouthed, Jiminez picked up his tray and took it to the other side of the room. At first, it seemed he was going to sit down with Carver and the others, but he didn't. He walked right past them and dumped the remainder of his meal in the disposal unit. Then he exited through the sliding doors of the cafeteria.

Despite the lack of commotion, however, Jiminez's gesture was noticed. By Carver. By Taylor and Huang. And by some of the veteran doctors. One by one, they all turned to glance at McCoy.

Cursing beneath his breath, the trainee shut them out. He didn't need or want their approval. The chief medical officer had told him he was doing the right thing. What other endorsement did he need?

Grimacing at the slightly acrid smell of the Ssani greens he'd been avoiding up until now, he lifted a forkful to his mouth. And with forced composure, he ate them. They tasted the way he felt: bitter.

At least I don't do anything halfway, McCoy mused. Now I've managed to alienate everybody.

Sometime during the night, McCoy woke in a cold sweat. His breathing was loud in his ears, so loud it should have woken everyone in the dormitory.

But no one else seemed to be awake. As he looked around, he confirmed it: everyone was sleeping the sleep of the just.

Everyone except him. He shrugged off the implications of that observation and tried to remember what his dream had been about. After all, there had to have been a dream, right? You didn't bolt out of a dead sleep unless you'd been dreaming something pretty bad.

But for the life of him, he couldn't remember it. He closed his eyes and tried to conjure an image out of the enforced darkness. Nothing happened.

Sighing, he lowered himself back into bed. Go to sleep, he insisted silently. You've got another long day ahead of you. And if there's another attack, you might not get any rest for a long time. So go to sleep, damn it.

Unfortunately, whatever had woken him was still flitting around in his system, turning on all the lights and inviting the neighbors over. And McCoy knew from long experience that when he felt this way, there was no strategy that would do him any good.

He was up for the night. Mumbling a curse, he swung his legs out of bed and massaged his bloodshot eyes. Then, reaching for his uniform on the clothes tree beside him, he stood up and slipped it on. His boots came last, the sturdy, leatherlike material lending him a sense of stability.

Finally, he stood and made his way out of the dorm. Down the corridor, past Bando's unlit office and the cafeteria, toward the dimly lit egress at the end of it, and finally into the ward full of wounded Ssana.

As always, there was a Ssani guard just inside the entrance, but not the one McCoy was used to seeing during the day. The guard's eyes were the only thing that moved as the trainee walked in. Satisfied that he wasn't an assassin, the Ssana resumed his silent vigil.

On the other side of the ward, one of the veteran physicians scanned a readout above one of the newer patients. Noticing McCoy out of the corner of his eye, the man turned to look at him. His eyebrows shot up in a silent question: What are you doing here at this hour?

The trainee didn't have a good answer. All he could do was hold his hands up in a gesture of helplessness and mouth the words: Can't sleep.

The veteran smiled benignly and went back to what he was doing. No doubt he'd seen this kind of thing before. McCoy couldn't have been the first young doctor who'd walked the night after a few days of this place.

Then he thought he felt a third set of eyes on him—not the guard's, not the doctor's, but those of someone else.

The trainee looked around, but he had a hard time locating them. In fact, he was ready to chalk it up to his imagination.

That's when he happened to glance down the aisle where the assassin's bed was located and saw a glint of light reflecting from two small, indigo orbs. Of course, McCoy told himself. Who else?

Negotiating a path among the rows of sleeping Ssana, he finally reached the assassin's side. The man was wide awake.

"What's the matter?" asked the human. "Trouble sleeping?"

"No more than you," said his patient. "But then, assassins need less sleep than other Ssana to begin with. I hope the same is true of physicians."

McCoy snorted softly. "No such luck," he said.

The assassin nodded. His eyes seemed to look right into him.

"You know, Doctor, I have been thinking about the things we said. About how I could best explain our position to you."

"Is that what's been keeping you up?" asked McCoy.

The Ssana smiled thinly. "Perhaps." A pause. "Tell me, what do you know of Li Moboron?"

McCoy took the time to choose his words carefully. "That he's the leader of your group. That he hates the idea of assassination being outlawed, as you do. And that, judging from the bloody results I've seen, he's pretty damned good at what he does."

"All true, of course," his patient replied. "But did you also know that Li Moboron is a poet? A man of remarkable sensitivity and bountiful expression?"

The human looked at him. "I find that hard to believe,"

175

he admitted with all honesty. "Murderous intent and heartfelt compassion don't seem to fit into the same package."

"Even on Ssan," said the assassin. "Nonetheless, Li Moboron is one package into which both qualities do fit. Perhaps that is why he is our leader—because he has managed to combine and reconcile those two disparate traits into a single, superior intellect."

McCoy frowned, seeing that the Ssana needed a little prodding. "Your point?"

"That to comprehend things Ssani, you must listen with the heart as well as the mind. That you must know the assassin in all his aspects before you can presume to pass judgment on him."

The trainee's heart leapt a little. Now they were getting somewhere. "All right," he responded. "I'm listening."

His patient closed his indigo eyes and recited a verse from memory: "We are all shadows on the sun, obscuring its holy light, its perfection. To take a life is to allow the heavenly glory to shine that much brighter."

A pretty ghastly thought, McCoy remarked inwardly. And he didn't care much for the level of artistry either, although to a Ssana's ear, it might have sounded a lot better.

The assassin opened his eyes. "Do you understand?"

The human sighed. "Not as well as you'd like me to, I'll bet. I mean, I can grasp the image and everything. It's just that in my experience, it doesn't have much validity."

Now it was the Ssana's turn to frown. "You cannot conceive of the sun as a symbol of a higher spiritual reality? At least on a figurative basis?"

"It's not that," McCoy told him. "It's the idea of life marring that reality in some way. It seems to me that without people to believe in it, to lend it significance, there is no spiritual plane. So every person deleted from the equation would, to use your imagery, make the sun shine *less* brightly."

The assassin pondered that for a moment. "It seems our cultures are further apart than I thought."

"Seems like it," McCoy agreed, as disappointed as his patient. So far, he'd come away with nothing even vaguely useful in the war against Moboron. "So is that why you became an assassin in the first place? Because this philosophy appealed to you?"

His patient shrugged. "My father was an assassin. I saw what he did and I respected it, perhaps because I respected him. It was only later, after I had made my first kill and experienced my bloodfire dream, that I realized the beauty and complexity of the doctrines I had embraced."

"Bloodfire . . . dream?" the trainee repeated.

"Yes. After one is infected with the holy virus, there is a period of fever, of brief but powerful visions. Occasionally one does not survive this time. But those who do carry with them the vitality of their visions for the rest of their lives."

"Interesting," said the human. "And what kind of things did you see?"

The Ssana's eyes lost their focus and his mouth pulled up a bit at the corners. "I was on a plateau in the northern mountains, spread-eagled on my back, my wrists and ankles tied with leather thongs to stakes driven into cracks in the stone. A uterra—one of the predatory flyers that infest the mountains—swooped down at me with hunger in his eyes, intending to eat my insides. But at the last moment, he stopped.

"Then, far from rending my flesh from my bones, he gnawed his own leg off. And taking it up in his beak, he fed it to me as if I were one of his young. He was making a sacrifice of himself, you see. He had recognized that, of the two of us, I was the better killer. And he gave of his flesh to make sure I survived my ordeal."

The corners of his mouth pulled up a little more. "It was a strong vision—perhaps the strongest my father had ever heard of. The uterra is an excellent hunter, Doctor. When one visits an assassin in his dream, it is an omen of great things to come. And when a uterra sacrifices himself that an assassin may live, it is a sign of . . ."

His voice trailed off and the almost-smile faded. Suddenly, his eyes fixed on the human with renewed intensity. "Why are you here, Doctor?"

That caught McCoy a little off-guard. "You mean in a spiritual sense?"

The assassin shook his head. "I mean on Ssan. In your Starfleet. In space. Why did you leave your world in the first place?"

The trainee cleared his throat self-consciously. He really didn't want to get into all that. But on the other hand, he didn't want to lose his peephole into the mind of Li Moboron.

"That's a personal question," he said at last.

"So it is," the Ssana confirmed. "But I have discussed my bloodfire dream with you. Nothing is more personal than that."

"What happened to our discussion of your leader's poetry?"

"I no longer think that is a road worth traveling. I wish to know about *you.*"

McCoy swallowed. "There's not much to tell. I wanted to be a physician, so here I am."

"But could you not have practiced your medicine on

your homeworld? What I am asking is, why did you come out here to do it?"

Why indeed. That was something the trainee hadn't discussed in detail with anyone—not even Carver, when they'd still been on speaking terms.

Oh, he'd mentioned that his marriage had broken up, of course. But he hadn't told anybody why. Nor had he planned to—until now.

McCoy looked around to see who else might be listening. There weren't any other doctors around, trainee level or otherwise. No one to eavesdrop on a private conversation.

Certainly, he could have fabricated a lie. But he was afraid that the assassin would see through it and stop trusting him. And besides, he realized he wanted to tell someone what had happened. He'd wanted to for some time now.

Here was a chance to tell someone who'd be leaving in a couple of days, someone he'd never have to face again. McCoy licked his lips.

"I left Earth," he said very slowly, "because I had to. Because I had no other choice in the matter."

His patient's brow creased. "You had to? Were you fleeing the law?"

McCoy shook his head. "No. Not the law. Something far worse, where I come from."

And in the next few minutes, he described what had happened. It was difficult to say the words that brought the memory back to mind but not as difficult as he'd thought it would be. And in the end, it actually felt good.

Throughout, the Ssana had only listened. He hadn't commented. He hadn't judged. He had only absorbed McCoy's tale with a look of compassion, the same kind of look he'd bestowed on his neighbor from the police barracks.

"So there you have it," said the human. "Not a pretty picture."

"No," the assassin agreed. "And that is what propelled you into space? The desire to forget what you saw that day?"

"That was it," McCoy confirmed.

His patient's nostrils flared wide. "Had it been me," he said, "I do not think I would have taken it half as well as you did."

"What would you have done differently?" the human asked.

The Ssana thought for a long moment, blinking as the scene unfolded before his mind's eye. Then he focused on McCoy again.

"Nothing you would approve of," he answered at last.

SIX

☆

The next morning, McCoy was bleary-eyed and a little lightheaded from his late-night foray, but he still had patients to see. As before, he saved his examination of the assassin for last.

But this time it was for an entirely different reason. This time he was actually looking forward to their conversation.

It surprised McCoy that this should be so. The Ssana was still a killer, still someone who stood in opposition to everything the trainee believed in. And it was true that he had only begun talking to the assassin in the first place in order to gain information about Li Moboron.

Yet somewhere along the line, without meaning to, he had developed a rapport with the Ssana, maybe even a rudimentary respect. The two of them had bridged a chasm McCoy would have once called too wide and deep. And even if their perspectives could never be reconciled, there was something undeniably satisfying about the opportunity to air them.

"You look tired," observed the assassin, as the trainee approached.

"I am," McCoy conceded. "Very."

"But you do not shirk your duties as a result. That is good."

The human shrugged. "Would you?"

His patient shook his head. "Most assuredly, I would not."

This seemed like as good a time as any to try to pump the Ssana for some information. Trying not to show his eagerness, McCoy scanned the biosign readout for a moment or two. Then he said: "What would you be doing now if you weren't lying there in that bed? I mean, what does an assassin do when he's not plying his trade?"

The Ssana smiled his customary, thin-lipped smile. "An assassin is always plying his trade," he replied. "That is, if he hopes to be a good assassin. But as for your question . . ." He grunted. "If I were with Li Moboron, I would probably be mapping out the site of our next strike. Or perhaps the strike after that."

"He plans that far ahead?" asked McCoy, pulling aside the metallic blanket to check again on how his patient's wounds were healing.

The burns were coming along quite well, though the shrapnel wounds were a bit behind the pace he had expected. But only a bit, nothing to be concerned about.

"He is Li Moboron," the Ssana replied simply. "As the chief assassin of all Ssan, he—more than anyone—would know that assassination is all in the planning. Anyone can kill, but to do so quickly and efficiently, and with a minimum of danger, one must be an expert planner."

"Do tell," said the trainee, pretending to listen with

only one ear as he put the blanket back where he found it. "Then Moboron knew in advance that he was going to destroy the police barracks?"

"It was one of his options," the assassin amended. "Which option he elects to exercise depends on the situation. If the government's people had not found and wiped out ours, Li Moboron would more than likely have moved in another, less devastating direction. But you left him no choice."

"Uh-huh," McCoy responded. He was making progress, he supposed, but it was awfully slow. Did he dare make his inquiries more pointed, at the risk of unveiling his purpose and maybe blowing the whole game?

He pondered the question for several long, tense moments. And in the meantime, his patient asked a question of his own.

"Tell me, Doctor, do you remember my request early on . . . that you kill me?"

He referred to it so matter-of-factly, he might have been talking about whether or not it was likely to rain that evening. Or what some old codger had gotten his wife for their golden wedding anniversary.

"Yes," said McCoy. "I do."

"Yet you have not heard me repeat it. And you have not asked me why."

"All right," the human remarked. "I'll bite. Why haven't you asked me to kill you since then?"

"Because it would not change the loathsome fact that you preserved my life. Whatever dishonor I have suffered is irrevocable; my death would not mitigate it. Given that set of circumstances, it is preferable for me to survive and, even in my shame, to continue to further the assassins' cause."

McCoy looked at him askance. "Further the assassins'

183

cause?" he repeated. "Does that mean you plan to escape?"

The Ssana nodded. "Of course. If not from here, then from whatever facility they bring me to. It is only a matter of time."

The trainee swallowed as he heard the certainty in his patient's voice. The assassin believed every word of it. And McCoy wasn't entirely sure he didn't believe it as well.

"Really," he said, for lack of a better response.

"Really," the Ssana assured him.

"Really," said Bando.

McCoy nodded. "That's what he said. Sooner or later, he'd escape from whatever facility the government placed him in." He paused. "Of course, you'd expect him to say something like that. He's an assassin."

The CMO frowned, emphasizing the deep, carved lines around his mouth. "What about the information you were going to dig up on Li Moboron? Any progress there?"

There was a note of surliness in Bando's tone that caught the trainee a little off-guard. After all, the man had been so encouraging in their previous conversations.

But then, Bando's attitude probably had nothing to do with McCoy. Maybe the man was just starting to show some cracks. After all, with a job like his—constantly waiting for some bloody massacre, never knowing when it would come—it was a wonder he wasn't howling at the Ssani moon on a regular basis.

"None to speak of," the trainee replied. "He did tell me that Moboron plans his strikes well in advance and then decides which place to hit depending on the circumstances. But I haven't been able to get an inkling yet of which places those might be."

Bando grunted. "And when do you think you might be able to do that?"

McCoy felt his face grow hot. "I . . . I don't know. I mean, I could try to be more direct with him, but I don't want to—"

"Then *be* more direct," said the CMO. He squirmed in his chair. "The government just found another of Moboron's hiding places. It was a clean sweep, not a single rebel left standing." A beat. "I guess you've been here long enough to know what comes next."

The trainee recalled Taylor's face back at the police barracks, as she took in the slaughter and cursed her helplessness. He remembered the splashes of blood on the splintered beams. He nodded.

"Unfortunately," said McCoy, "I just saw all my patients. And he—the assassin, I mean—knows I'm not due for another visit until this evening."

Bando leaned forward over his old, metal desk. "If we're going to get anything from that patient of yours, we've got to get it while it still does us some good. This evening might be too late. You understand?"

"I understand," said McCoy.

He waited a little more than an hour so his visit wouldn't seem too suspicious. Then, tricorder in hand, McCoy entered the critical care ward and started going through the pantomime he'd devised in Bando's office.

To avoid diverging from established practice, he went to the assassin's bed only after he'd checked all the others. Playing his tricorder over the Ssana, he glanced at the biosigns displayed on the screen above the patient.

"Something wrong?" asked the assassin.

McCoy turned his gaze on his tiny tricorder readout and then looked to the bed's display again. He shook his head appraisingly from side to side.

"Doesn't appear to be," he remarked. Then, putting the tricorder away, he smiled in a perfunctory sort of way. "Just a routine check is all. These biobeds don't always hold up as well as we'd like."

"And this one?" prodded the Ssana. He didn't seem particularly concerned, just curious.

"Still humming along just fine," McCoy told him. "I get the exact same readings on my tricorder. The bad news is you're no better off than I thought you were. The good news is you're no worse, either."

His patient looked around the ward at the other doctors. To give McCoy's ploy some additional credibility, Bando had recruited Carver and Huang to go through the same motions as their fellow trainee. They'd started a little bit later, so they still had a couple of beds to go.

Noticing McCoy's scrutiny, Carver shot him a deadpan look. There was no way the assassin could glean its meaning, but McCoy understood perfectly. Merlin had made it clear he didn't approve of doctors' deceiving patients. And to be part of that deception was anathema to him.

On the other hand, he wasn't going to disobey Bando's orders and foul up McCoy's little subterfuge. Carver had too much respect for the chain of command to do anything like that—too much respect for the laws of Starfleet, regardless of who had been empowered to carry them out.

"Incidentally," McCoy interjected, taking on a more sober demeanor, "I've heard a rumor. Some bad news for your side, if it's true."

"And what is this rumor?" the Ssana inquired, his voice slow and even.

"That assassins attacked a government armory on the other side of the capitol and were stopped before they could do any damage. Apparently none of your people escaped."

McCoy's patient shook his head. "Do not place any faith in the verity of this story. Li Moboron has not included any armories among his targets. Nor would he."

"How can you be so sure?" asked the human. "You haven't been with him for several days now. He could have changed his mind."

"No," the Ssana insisted. "Li Moboron would know that there is no point in attacking an armory. It is a place of things; for a price, things can be replaced. Flesh and blood cannot. It is only with flesh and blood that one may fashion a convincing argument."

"I see," said McCoy. He had the feeling he was finally getting somewhere. "Then maybe I'm wrong. Maybe it was some other place."

"The air-shuttle terminal?" suggested the assassin.

McCoy felt his heart leap. He was definitely getting somewhere.

"Maybe that was it," he agreed.

"Or the history museum? There is an exhibit there on stone-age cultures. It will be crowded—dense with targets for our assassins."

The human was starting to feel giddy. It was as if he'd hit the mother lode.

"Or perhaps the library? Thousands of Ssana use it each day, do they not? Li Moboron could not help but consider it."

Suddenly McCoy got a bad feeling. A feeling that he was being played for a fool.

"You're mocking me," he told his patient.

The Ssana shook his head. *"Mocking* is too harsh a word, Doctor. I am merely telling you that I see through your tactic. And that it will not work." He smiled grimly. "You must remember, I am an assassin. Trickery is second nature to me. And there is nothing more difficult than tricking a trickster."

McCoy could feel himself betrayed by the blood that suffused his cheeks. He searched for words and couldn't find any. But it didn't really matter anymore, did it? The jig was up.

Finally finding his voice, he said, "You're right. I was trying to deceive you. But only to save lives—Ssani lives." He indicated the patient in the next biobed. "When he came in, you seemed concerned. You seemed sorry for him." He licked his lips. "There are going to be a lot more like him soon."

The assassin's eyes narrowed. "You are telling me that another of our dens was discovered?"

The human nodded. "And wiped out. My superior expects your superior to follow up with a massacre to end all massacres. That is, unless you help me out."

"Help you out," the Ssana echoed. "You mean tell you where Li Moboron will strike. Betray my comrades. My cause."

McCoy could feel the anger come rushing up into his throat, threatening to choke him. "Damn it," he snarled, "we're talking about lives here! We're talking about people like you and me who can be saved if we act now!"

The assassin looked at him. His expression was one of empathy, as if he could feel the human's pain. And seeing that, McCoy thought for a moment that his patient would answer his heartfelt plea.

But he had spent a fair amount of time with this Ssana. He should have known better.

"I believe," said the assassin, "we have had this conversation before." He shook his head, obviously unhappy at his inability to give McCoy the answer he wanted. "I cannot help you, Doctor."

"Can't?" McCoy spat. "Or just won't?"

His patient met his angry gaze. "Cannot," he insisted. "Or have you failed to hear what I have been telling you these last few days? About my beliefs? About my people's beliefs?"

The human could feel his teeth grinding together. His temper was a molten flood, a river of lava that obliterated any outcropping of rational thought in its path.

"I've been listening, all right," he growled. "I've been listening to claptrap and double-talk, in the hope that I could learn something useful, some small bit of information that would help put an end to this senseless, stupid bloodshed. But I can see now that I was wasting my time."

The assassin's brows knit over his tiny indigo orbs. "In other words," he concluded, "our conversations were merely ploys? Not genuine discussions of right and wrong but attempts to maneuver me into a betrayal of all I hold sacred?"

The way he said it made McCoy feel ashamed of himself. As if he was the one at fault here. As if he was the murderer and not the other way around.

Obviously his eyes said as much, because his patient's expression changed. The sympathy, the compassion were gone. They had been replaced with a hard mask of resentment.

"How enlightening," the Ssana commented, in carefully measured tones. "Here I thought I could not easily be tricked. And yet, you tricked me after all." He glared at the physician. "You have earned my respect, offworlder, though not, I think, with regard to the qualities you would be respected for."

As McCoy began to frame an answer, he suddenly remembered that he and the assassin weren't alone. Looking up, he realized that some of his other patients were looking at him.

And not only his patients. Across the ward, Carver was staring at him too. And Huang as well, though he tried not to show it.

"I burn with humiliation for you, Doctor," said the assassin. "I believed I had found someone like me—someone who believed in a principle so strongly he was willing to die for it. But I see that you are someone else—someone willing to bend his oath to fit the circumstances." His temples worked. "You brought dishonor to me when you would not let me die. But it is nothing compared to the dishonor you have brought down on yourself."

McCoy wanted to lash out at the Ssana. He wanted to call him a bloody-handed murderer who had no business judging others. And he might have—except for the fact that the bastard was right.

Merlin had been right also. And so had Taylor and Jiminez and Huang. He had forgotten that he was a doctor and tried to be something else, and now all he had to show for it was a raw, red conscience that felt like it had been dipped in saltwater.

And if it had worked? If he had gotten the information he'd wanted and saved some Ssani lives in the process? Would he be feeling better now or worse? Would the gain have made it all right or, in some way he couldn't quite fit words to, would it have made it even more wrong?

He didn't know. He didn't care. All he could see right now were the accusing eyes of his colleagues. And, of course, those of the assassin. More than anything, he wanted to be free of them.

With that one thought firmly in mind, McCoy turned and walked toward the exit, and he didn't slow down until he was well past it and into the corridor beyond, leaving the Ssani guard staring after him.

He couldn't face Bando right away. He couldn't. Not with his thoughts all confused and jumbled like this. He had to get control of himself. He had to remember who he was and why he was here.

Picking his head up from the sink, where he'd been running it under a torrent of cold water, McCoy brushed away a lock of wet hair and looked at himself in the mirror. He didn't like what he saw.

A man for whom the end justified the means. A man who'd traded ethics for unforgiving logic and honor for expediency, to whom the individual had become merely a number in an equation, and a very small number at that.

It had taken a murdering marauder to set him straight, but he saw it now. Saw how little he belonged out here in space, far from the peaceful valleys of his Georgian home, where someone weak of character could be tempted to forget all he'd learned and become a piece on the chessboard of war.

Bando had encouraged him, certainly. But the choice had been his. And despite the advice of his friends, he'd made the wrong one.

But it wasn't too late, was it? He could still redeem himself, set the record straight. He could still embrace the oath that he'd once taken so much to heart, in the evergreen days before . . .

His eyes narrowed. Never mind all that. Never mind *her*.

He had a report to make to the CMO, and there was no time like the present. Wiping the water from his face, McCoy stalked out of the lavatory and into the corridor beyond. The stretch ahead of him, usually busy, was empty right now. His footfalls echoed sharply, like tiny cracks of thunder, until he pulled up in front of Bando's office.

The door was open. The CMO looked up from his computer monitor and met the trainee's gaze squarely. "Have you got something?" he asked.

"He saw right through me," McCoy said flatly.

The older man cursed. "How?"

"I pushed too hard," the trainee explained. "He saw what I was doing and refused to reveal anything useful. And when I tried to appeal to his nobler instincts, he told me I should be ashamed of myself, that I had violated my trust as a doctor by trying to deceive him."

Bando grunted derisively. "That's rich. He goes around killing innocent people and then lectures *you* about morality."

McCoy looked at his superior. "And you know what?" he said. "He was right."

The CMO's brow creased down the middle. He leaned forward, as if uncertain that he'd heard correctly.

"What?" he got out at last.

"I said he was right. I *was* violating my trust. But I'm not going to do it anymore. Not even if the assassins burn all of Ssan down around us. I'm a doctor, not a spy, sir. And from now on, a doctor is all I want to be."

Bando glared at him. "You know," he rumbled, "I didn't ask you to do this, McCoy. It wasn't my initiative. Sure, when you came to me with it, I thought you were on to something. But it was *your* idea." He paused, his jaw muscles working frantically. "Now you mope in here and tell me your damned plan didn't work. And because you're not man enough to take the blame yourself, you're trying to pin it on me."

The trainee shook his head. That wasn't at all what he'd intended. "No," he insisted. "This isn't about blame. It's about—"

He never finished his sentence. It was drowned out by the roar of a huge explosion, felt in his bones as much as heard. And then another.

"My God." Bando looked up at the ceiling, his eyes fairly popping out of his head. "They're *here.*"

Stunned as he was, it took McCoy a moment or two to realize what the CMO was talking about. Then it hit him.

This building was the target of the assassins' next attack. And the next attack was *now*.

SEVEN

At first McCoy thought the disaster survivors' ward—*his*
ward—was the one under attack. Then, just before he and
his colleagues were beamed to the attack point, he learned
the location of the assassins' true target.

The knowledge made his blood freeze. No being, no
matter how cruel, could do what Moboron's assassins
were said to be doing. It just wasn't possible.

Then McCoy beamed down to the attack point alongside Bando and a couple of his veterans, and he saw how
naive he had been. It didn't matter how much horror one
had witnessed, he realized. There was always a worse
horror beyond that.

What met his eyes had until minutes ago been a
children's ward. A place for society's innocents to heal
from injuries, from illness, from surgical procedures. But
Li Moboron had performed his own brand of surgery on

the place, and now the immature throats of the dying filled the debris-clotted air with thin, high-pitched wails.

Kneeling, the trainee placed his fingertips against the neck of a girl no older than his own daughter, half-buried in the rubble of a collapsed wall. She was beautiful in a fragile sort of way, more slender than she should have been. Perhaps it was an illness that had made her so thin; perhaps that was what had brought her here.

She would no longer have to worry about any illnesses, he told himself. She would no longer have to worry about anything. Closing her eyes, he got up and made his way farther into the heart of the disaster.

The cries grew louder, but all McCoy could see before him were corpses. A boy here, a girl there. Just beyond them, an infant. He could feel a pounding in his temples that seemed to grow fiercer with every step he took. But there were no living Ssana, no one he could help.

Then, suddenly, something came flying at him out of the flames and the billowing smoke. Unprepared for it, he fell over backward trying to absorb its momentum, tumbled while clutching the projectile to him.

It sobbed with its whole body. As McCoy righted himself, he looked down into its Ssani face and saw that it was a boy. The youngster was bleeding from a deep cut in his ridged brow, his indigo eyes wide with fear and shock, his breathing labored and ragged. Just as the human decided there might be internal damage, the Ssana coughed up a gout of blood.

"It's all right," McCoy found himself saying. Running his tricorder over the boy as quickly as he could, he pinpointed the trouble: a lung had been punctured by a fragment of a broken rib.

Grabbing his communicator, he flipped it open and

barked, "McCoy to Fed Med One. Beam this kid up, damn it."

There was no reply from their facility upstairs. A moment later, however, the child was embraced by the transporter effect, and a moment after that he was gone.

Standing, McCoy forged ahead again, part of a line of doctors and trainees poring through the rubble for survivors, trying to follow the cries of pain to their sources with smoke-stung eyes. But for every living Ssana they found, there were half a dozen others who had perished in the explosion.

There were no words, no curses, no dirges that could adequately lament the blood that had been spilled in this place, the lives that had been cut short. There was only the impossible burden of outrage and despair and disbelief, and the mounting need to strike out at those who were responsible.

Abruptly, they were given that chance. As they swept across the vast ward, McCoy thought he could see white-robed forms moving through pockets of fire and ruin. With grim certainty, he knew that some of the assassins who had visited this plague of plagues were still here.

But why? Why wouldn't they have fled before the bomb went off? Unless . . .

The human swallowed. Unless they had left and come back—to finish what they'd started.

"Watch out!" he cried. The words had barely escaped his throat before something sizzled by the side of his head, close enough for him to feel the accompanying rush of air. "It's the assassins!" he snarled.

As if they'd rehearsed it, the line of doctors dropped to their knees. All except one, who stood his ground as if daring the assassins to skewer him on one of their blades. And that one, McCoy saw, was Vinnie Bando.

He held a child in his arms, an adolescent by the look of her. Unfortunately, she would never have the chance to grow into an adult. Her throat had been laid open in the explosion and gaped now like a bloody second mouth.

"Get down!" someone hissed. Through the smoke, McCoy recognized Bud Glavin by his shock of red hair. "Get down, damn it!"

But Bando wasn't listening. He was just standing there, his broad shoulders heaving, tears running down his face as he peered into the face of the murdered child.

"Come on," he bawled at the vague forms of the assassins. "You want to kill someone? Kill me, for god's sake! Kill me!" It was the cry of someone not altogether sane.

But strangely enough, the assassins didn't take him up on his invitation. They didn't even make an attempt. Their only response came in the form of a single figure who stepped out from behind a barrier of smoking rubble—a tall, blunt-featured Ssana with a red cross in a red circle stitched onto a spot over his left chest.

Someone muttered a single word: "Moboron." And McCoy felt a surge of awe mixed with hatred. The rebel leader, the author of all the destruction he had seen since his arrival on Ssan . . .

Moboron.

"We do not kill offworlders," snapped the High Assassin. "Go back to your Federation, intruder. Leave Ssan to us."

Something seemed to snap in Bando then. With a strangled snarl that was more feral than human, he dropped his burden of dead flesh and charged the assassin like a maddened bull. At first Moboron didn't move. Then, as the CMO came within a meter of him, he spun like a dervish and lashed out with his foot. There was a dull thud, and Bando stopped dead in his tracks.

For a full second he wavered there, head lolling, a thin rivulet of blood emerging from the corner of his mouth. Then he sank in a heap at the High Assassin's feet.

"Vinnie!" bellowed Glavin. "No!"

Without thinking, he raced out to the CMO's side. Moboron just watched. He obviously knew the red-haired man wasn't a threat.

"Thank God," Glavin whispered. "He's alive."

"I say it again," rasped the assassin. "We do not kill offworlders."

Then he retreated to where his comrades were waiting for him. And a second or two later, they had all vanished, as if absorbed by the spreading smoke.

Creeping forward, leery of the assassins' return, McCoy joined Glavin at Bando's side. But by then, the CMO was already shoving away anyone who wanted to help him.

"I'm all right," he muttered. "I'm all right."

McCoy watched as Carver and the other trainees moved forward into the smoke, answering a renewed chorus of childish cries for help. He grunted and surveyed Bando's tortured features, wondering at the man's courage.

With his foolhardiness, he had stopped Moboron from killing the rest of the young survivors. By putting his own life on the line, the CMO had achieved some semblance of the victory he'd been looking for.

But it was evident Bando didn't look at it that way. Wiping the blood from his mouth with the back of his hand, the man dropped his head into his hands and cursed himself in a bizarre, singsong rhythm.

He was still cursing when the government-aligned assassins arrived, and when the last living child was removed from the ward. Only after the doctors had done all they could there did the CMO allow himself to be beamed back up to his office.

The couple of days that followed were remarkably orderly, remarkably calm. Li Moboron launched no new attacks, so there were no new casualties. The government's assassins were quiet as well, so there was no prospect of a bloody counterstrike. It was as if both sides had pulled back to lick their wounds for a while.

McCoy didn't see much of Vinnie Bando in the corridors. The CMO spent a lot of time in his office, apparently in an attempt to come to grips with what he'd seen and experienced in the children's ward.

Back in Georgia, McCoy's father had told him that the toughest person for a doctor to heal is himself. The trainee saw the wisdom of that statement now.

Truth to tell, he had some healing of his own to do. They all did, veterans and newcomers alike. Anyone who had beamed down into that vision of mind-numbing horror would be a long time forgetting it. A very long time.

Many of the Ssana in the convalescent ward were transferred elsewhere in the building or to one of Pitur's other standard-care facilities. The only ones still ensconced in their metallic blankets on Federation biobeds were those whose injuries had been the most severe to begin with and, of course, the children rescued so recently from the High Assassin's wrath.

Unexpectedly, despite everything he had endured, McCoy slept well the first two nights after the attack. But the third night, he woke again in a cold sweat, his heart thumping so hard he thought his ribs would break.

He had dreamed that his daughter, Joanna, was lying in

the rubble of the children's ward. Her hair was dark with gore and matted across her face, her soft, little girl's cheeks drained of color until they looked like candle wax.

Thinking she might still have been alive, he ran his tricorder over her. But there was no sign of life in her frail, battered form. There wasn't a thing he could do for her. Helpless, enraged, he bent his head over her and cried hot tears.

Suddenly her eyes opened. But like the rest of her, they were dead. Staring at him accusingly, Joanna said in a dry, wavering voice: "You killed me, Daddy. You killed me."

Following her gaze, he looked at his hands and saw how bloody they were, how tattered the skin of his knuckles had become. Had he beaten her to death? Was that what she was talking about?

And then he knew, with a certainty found only in dreams, that he *had* killed her. Not the assassins, but he. And that's when he awoke.

McCoy had taken psychology courses in med school. He had learned a bit about interpreting dreams. So what did this one mean?

That he had killed whatever love his daughter had held for him when he left Earth? That he had betrayed her by running off into space?

Or was it himself he had betrayed, by valuing the end over the means in his dealings with the assassin whose care he'd been charged with? Was the shattered innocence he held in his arms his own?

It was as good an answer as any. Cold, still shuddering from the shock of seeing Joanna's corpse, McCoy pulled out his uniform and his boots as he had the other night and made his way down the darkened corridor toward the ward.

200

Why? Because that was where he felt most at home these days. With no fellow trainees and no commanding officer to talk to, he could at least commune with the biomonitors. It wasn't much, but it was something.

Strangely, there was no guard at the entrance to the ward. Had the Ssana been forced to answer nature's call? Or had the CMO's distractions afforded the authorities an excuse to deploy the guard elsewhere—perhaps in the children's ward?

It was of no real consequence to the trainee. He had never quite approved of having an armed Ssana there in the first place. There was something about lethal weapons and convalescing patients that, in his mind at least, didn't mix.

Walking out onto the ward, McCoy instinctively looked for the doctor on duty. He didn't know who it would be, but the man or woman would be easy to spot in a medical blue tunic.

After a moment, he found the shadowy figure he was looking for—in his own area of responsibility, as luck would have it. Heading that way, the trainee noticed that the doctor, whoever it might be, was scrutinizing the biosigns of the assassin.

As McCoy came closer, he was surprised to observe that the physician was Vinnie Bando. The man was standing by the Ssana's bed, looking down at his sleeping face as if it held some mystery he just couldn't fathom.

Odd, thought the trainee. He had never seen the CMO come out into the ward before. But then, the assassin was a rather special case, wasn't he? And one that Bando wasn't likely to see again for a long time.

Reluctant to intrude on Bando's reverie, McCoy cleared his throat. It was enough to alert the CMO that he had company. A moment later their eyes met across the darkened floor, and the trainee nodded.

Bando smiled—a little sadly, McCoy thought. In any case, the older man didn't seem to be holding a grudge about the words they'd exchanged earlier.

"What brings you out at this hour?" asked the CMO.

McCoy shrugged. "It's getting to be a habit," he replied. "And you?"

Bando grunted. "I wasn't always the chief medical officer, you know. Once I was a trainee, just like you. In a ward just like this one, except the patients had black skin and silver eyes and necks as long as your forearm."

"Kasserites?" the younger man guessed.

"Kasserites," his companion confirmed.

McCoy swallowed. "I . . . er, hope you're not too angry about those things I said. Before the attack, I mean."

"Not *too* angry," the CMO confirmed.

The trainee grinned. "Good. I have a lot of respect for you, sir. It's just that I couldn't go on with what I was doing and still be faithful to what I believed in. I was trained to be a doctor and from now on, that's all I want to be. A simple country doctor."

Bando gazed at him appraisingly. "Then be a good one," he told McCoy. "Tell you what. Let's continue this conversation in my office. I've got a bottle of Romulan ale that'll knock the back of your skull off. You're not likely to find a better cure for insomnia than that."

The trainee found himself frowning. "What if we've got to get up early?" he asked.

The CMO put an arm around his shoulder. "Listen, even a doctor has to unwind a little now and then. It's part of the Hippocratic Oath. In the fine print, at the bottom."

McCoy chuckled. "All right, you're on. Just let me check up on my patient here for a moment."

Bando pulled him away. "Come on, I just checked him. He's never been better."

The younger man almost allowed himself to be herded toward the door. Hell, a drink sounded pretty good right now, and he wasn't going to find anything the CMO wouldn't have found already.

But something in Bando's voice gave him pause. That and a sense that things weren't quite right when a CMO invited a trainee to share a bottle of Romulan ale with him.

"Maybe I'd better go over his biosigns myself," McCoy insisted. Tearing himself away, he glanced at the display above the assassin's bed.

That glance was all it took. The Ssana's signs were off—*all* of them. Not so far as to constitute a reason for panic. But no doctor worth his salt could have mistaken them for normal levels, which meant . . .

"What did you do to him?" McCoy demanded.

Bando's features suddenly turned to stone. "You weren't supposed to come by at this time of night," he said. "You weren't supposed to see this until it was too late."

"Blast it, what did you do?" the younger man asked again. He turned to the display and scanned the assassin's signs a second time. But they gave him no clue as to what the CMO might have injected him with—

Injected. Bando would still have the hypospray on him. And it would still be set to whatever compound he'd used to poison McCoy's patient.

"Don't you see?" the CMO argued. "I had to do it. He's an assassin. He's just like the murdering bastards that killed those children."

"He's also my patient," the trainee insisted. "And I need to know what you shot him up with."

Bando shook his head, his eyes wild with determination. "Over my dead body," he snarled. "He deserves to die. They all do."

"What he deserves," McCoy shouted back, "is justice, Ssani justice, not the kind you or I dispense. Now I'm not going to ask again. I want to know—"

"What's going on here?" thundered a voice from the other side of the ward.

Turning, the trainee squinted through the darkness. It was a moment or two before he recognized the square, shadowy form as that of Burly Curley.

"I asked what's going on here," the nurse repeated, this time a little more loudly.

"It's Bando!" cried McCoy. "He's poisoned one of my patients!"

Curley didn't need to hear any more. With surprising speed he negotiated a path between the biobeds, his ultimate goal to confront the CMO before he could get away.

Unfortunately, Bando had a trump card up his sleeve—or to be more precise, a phaser pistol concealed beneath his medical tunic, something he might have taken off a corpse at one of the disaster sites. Pulling it out, he pointed it at the onrushing nurse.

"Watch out!" McCoy bellowed, grabbing for the weapon. "He's got a phaser!"

But before the trainee could seize the pistol or even deflect the CMO's aim, Bando fired off a seething red stream of phased energy. It hit the nurse square in the sternum and drove him back a good thirty feet. He came up hard against the base of a biobed, his chest a bloody smoking ruin.

Horrified, McCoy turned to the CMO at the same time the CMO turned to him. There was a hot, murderous madness in Bando's eyes the likes of which the younger man had never seen before.

Suddenly Bando hauled off and backhanded the trainee across the face. McCoy's head snapped back with the impact. Sprawling over his patient, he fell onto the hard floor beyond.

As he gathered himself up, his mouth filled with the warm, faintly metallic taste of blood, he saw the CMO train his weapon on a second target: the unconscious assassin. Without thinking, McCoy grabbed the phaser and twisted with all his strength.

The beam of ruby red light that emerged from it missed his fingers by a fraction of an inch and kept on going until it burned a hole in the ceiling. Bando pulled at the weapon to regain control of it, but the younger man wasn't letting go, not even when the CMO dragged him back over his patient's inert form and wrestled him to the ground.

McCoy struggled to get his arms and legs between him and his adversary, but it wasn't easy. The CMO might have been older, but he was also a lot more powerful. For a moment McCoy saw the muzzle of the phaser fill his field of vision. Then, uncoiling his legs with one mighty thrust, he sent Bando flying backward into a space between two of the biobeds.

He scrambled forward onto his feet again, his mind racing. What had happened to the guard? The doctor on duty? The CMO must have dismissed them for this shift so he could go about his crazed revenge scheme unhindered.

Soon some of the other patients would wake up, if they hadn't already. But the only ones left were hurt too badly to help.

So there was no one to aid him in his fight against Bando's bull-like strength. McCoy was all that stood between his drugged patient and a lunatic who wanted him to pay for his people's crimes.

Before the older man could get up or aim his weapon again, the trainee launched himself through the air and was on top of him. They rolled one way, then the other, but McCoy hung on. That is, until Bando jarred him with a blow to his chin that made him see stars.

Damn it, thought the trainee, I'm not going to give in. I'm not going to let him kill that Ssana.

Abruptly, a sizzling phaser beam lanced up alongside McCoy's head, near enough to cut the very edge of his earlobe. Ignoring the pain, he battled to turn the damned thing away from him. The beam moved only incrementally, slicing into the biosigns display on the nearest bed.

The display erupted in a shower of sparks. The trainee could feel them on the back of his neck and on his hands, searing him. His adversary must have felt them too, because he uttered a strangled cry and swept at his face with his free hand.

Seeing his chance, McCoy took advantage of it. Drawing his fist back, he drove it into Bando's jaw as hard as he could. Again. And again.

However, it only seemed to make the other man madder. With a roar of rage, he grabbed McCoy around his windpipe and squeezed. Gasping for air, the trainee tried desperately to break Bando's grip, but it was like trying to bend duranium.

With a quick, savage motion, the CMO flopped McCoy over onto his back and planted a knee in his chest. Lips drawn back over clenched teeth, veins standing out in his neck like cords, Bando increased the pressure.

The younger man tried to kick himself free, to pummel away at his antagonist's arms and shoulders, but it was no use. His face was swelling with blood like some kind of exotic fruit, his strength ebbing with each flailing effort.

As the vice around his throat got tighter and tighter, McCoy thought his head was going to burst. He croaked, grunted, did everything he could to cry out, but Bando wasn't going to let him call for help a second time.

The world, which included little more than his adversary's face and a phaser barrel, started going black around the edges. Then the edges began working their way inward. The trainee struggled for all he was worth, but it wasn't enough, not nearly. Little by little, he felt his life slipping away.

He'd known that there were dangers in space. He'd even been prepared to die in the service of Starfleet. But this was one scenario he hadn't quite envisioned: to be choked to death by an insane chief medical officer . . .

EIGHT

Out of nowhere, McCoy felt a jolt, and suddenly the pressure on his windpipe was gone. With an urgency that sent shoots of agony through his chest, he drew in one greedy gulp of air after another, unable to fill his lungs fast enough to suit his weak and shuddering body.

But he had the presence of mind to look up and see what had happened to give him a respite from death. To his surprise, he spotted a familiar face. No, not one but three.

Carver and Jiminez and Huang. And they were all struggling with Bando, Paco wrestling him for the phaser while the other two tried to pin him against an empty biobed.

As McCoy sucked in huge, life-giving draughts, he tried to join the fray. But he couldn't. All he could do was watch as his fellow trainees strove with the CMO for possession of the phaser.

Come on, he cheered silently. Don't let him work his bloody revenge. Don't let the bastard kill my patient.

Abruptly, Jiminez tore the weapon free. And as Bando turned toward him to try to get it back, Carver slugged the unsuspecting madman, putting all his weight behind the blow. The crack of fist against bone reverberated throughout the ward.

For a second or two the CMO blinked as if he wasn't seeing quite right. Then he dropped to his knees, taking Huang with him, and finally sank to the floor, unconscious.

With almost comical haste, Warren scurried out from underneath Bando's bulk, no doubt uncertain as to how long the man was going to stay knocked out. But it didn't matter anymore, because Jiminez was holding the phaser now.

That's when McCoy remembered what this battle had been about in the first place. Crawling toward the CMO on wobbly limbs, he croaked: "The hypo."

Carver came over and knelt beside his fellow trainee. He was massaging his bleeding knuckles. "Leonard, are you all right?" he asked.

McCoy shook his head. They could talk about him later. Right now, with no way of knowing how long ago Bando had injected the assassin, there were more urgent matters to take care of.

"The hypo," he rasped again, this time a little louder. "In his pockets. The blasted hypo."

Merlin obviously had no idea what he was talking about, but he followed McCoy's instructions anyway. A moment later, he drew a hypospray out of one of Bando's tunic pockets.

"Is that what you were looking for?" he inquired.

Snatching the device out of his friend's hands, McCoy

checked its setting, noting the components of the compound the CMO had used on his victim. A moment later, he saw the full scope of Bando's plan.

He had injected the assassin with the bloodfire virus—the same stuff that made the Ssana a superman in times of need. But this wasn't the strain that existed in the Ssana already. This was a variant, which, not content to coexist with its host, would procreate at a vastly increased rate, gradually building a biological time bomb.

Over the short term, the variant's presence would only work to raise such indicators as pulse and respiration incrementally. But in a matter of hours, there would be so much of it that the slightest stress would flood the assassin with the Ssani equivalent of adrenaline. The result? Instantaneous and irreversible cardiac arrest.

And the beauty of it was that no one would ever be blamed for the Ssana's death. Unless one took pains to look closely, the variant strain would appear identical to the existing virus, and the incident would have been attributed to "natural causes."

Fortunately, the variant strain could be eliminated—killed—provided it hadn't been in the assassin's system for more than a few minutes. McCoy hoped to heaven they'd caught it in time.

"What is it?" asked Merlin. "What's wrong?"

There was no time to explain. Taking hold of his friend's shoulder, he hauled himself to his feet. "Get me to the assassin's bed," he said. "Now."

Carver, who'd been watching him with narrowed eyes, seemed to put two and two together. Wrapping an arm around McCoy's middle, he half-carried him over to where the assassin lay dead to the world.

The first thing the trainee did was check the biosigns display. Sure enough, the Ssana's heartbeat and respiration were up even higher than when he'd seen them a few moments ago. The variant strain was making its presence felt.

Frowning, focusing on the hypo, McCoy forgot about the damage Bando had inflicted on him, which he was only now starting to feel. What was the antidote to the virus again? He had read about it only a couple of days earlier.

Damn it, he told himself. Think. You've got a brain, haven't you? Show that it's good for something besides getting you into trouble.

And then he remembered. Making the necessary adjustments in the selector mechanism, he said a silent prayer to Hippocrates and pressed the hypo against the assassin's arm. Instantly, the antiviral medication was injected into the man's bloodstream.

Again, McCoy looked up at the display. If he'd come up with the antidote in time, the biolevels would start to descend in a minute or less. If he'd taken too long, or selected the wrong antidote . . .

"What's going on?" asked Jiminez, who had come up behind them.

"Quiet," urged Merlin.

"What are we looking at?" inquired Huang, who had joined them as well. And then: "Wait a minute. Those levels are too high, aren't they?"

"They *are* too high," agreed Jiminez. "Even for a Ssana."

But they were beginning to drop, McCoy observed with a great deal of relief. Not a lot, not fast, but they were beginning to come down.

He'd caught the thing in time. He'd saved his patient's life. But then again, wasn't that what doctors were supposed to do?

"Whatever you did," remarked Merlin, "it worked."

"Yeah. It worked," McCoy added hoarsely. He glanced at Merlin and found himself wondering about something. "What in blazes were you all doing out here anyway?"

Carver turned to him. Slowly, a rueful smile spread across his face. "I saw you get up in the middle of the night—again. You looked like you could use a friend."

McCoy scrutinized him. "But all three of you?"

"You looked like you could use three friends," responded Huang.

"Hell," said Jiminez. "You know we're all joined at the hip. One trainee gets up, we all get up."

Merlin nodded. "Especially when one of us has been in exile long enough. If it's all right with you, Leonard, I'd like to bury the hatchet."

McCoy found he suddenly had the urge to smile—an urge he couldn't resist altogether. "Oh yeah?" he retorted. "And just where would you like to bury it?"

Without breaking stride, Carver replied, "Down the middle of your head might be nice." He glanced at Huang. "Or better yet, down the middle of Warren's head. Let's do his hundreds of prospective patients a favor."

By way of a response, Huang jerked a thumb over his shoulder. "Speaking of burying the hatchet, we'd better tend to our leader there. He looks like he's starting to come around."

Fortunately, they had company by then—lots of it, in the form of all the doctors who had been woken up by the commotion. It took awhile to explain what had happened, and even longer to make them believe it, but in the end a couple of Ssani guards showed up and took a seething, swearing Vinnie Bando away.

* * *

212

A month later, Captain Hillios and the *Republic* arrived with a fresh load of trainees. Hillios's orders were to collect the five neophytes she had dropped off on Ssan and bring them to their next assignment, on Beta Aurelon Three, where a mysterious plague was decimating the population.

By then, of course, things at the medical facility had changed considerably. Chief Medical Officer Vincent Bando was long gone. He had been picked up by the *Enterprise,* commanded by a captain named Pike, to stand trial for murder.

Bud Glavin was serving as chief medical officer in Bando's stead and doing a damned fine job of it. And McCoy's assassin-patient had recovered well enough to be sent to the medical arm of a Ssani penal facility, never knowing that his doctor had saved his life a second time.

Also, they had beamed into three more disaster sites. But none of them was as bad as the scene they had encountered in the children's ward. It almost seemed that Li Moboron's people were losing their enthusiasm.

Another thing had changed as well. McCoy and Carver were somehow managing to see eye-to-eye a lot more, much to the amazement and consternation of their fellow trainees.

McCoy looked around the breakfast table at his fellow trainees. "I know we've been pretending otherwise, but this Ssani food is for the birds," he announced.

Merlin nodded. "It's bad. Really bad."

"It's terrible," said McCoy, pushing his plate away.

"The worst," noted his friend, emulating the gesture.

McCoy grunted. "I'm not going to miss it," he remarked, "I can tell you that. Though with our luck, the food on Beta Aurelon Three won't be any better."

That evoked a wavelet of laughter from the others. Underneath it was the easy camaraderie of people who had been to hell and back together, and lived to tell of it.

Jiminez sighed. "So. Beta Aurelon Three," he mused out loud. "From the frying pan into the fire, eh?"

Huang rolled his eyes morosely. "No rest for the weary. It's a good thing I'm so dedicated, or I might go back to Earth and open a private practice."

"Could be worse," McCoy told him. "My father's got one back home and he wouldn't trade it for the world. *Any* world."

"What would you say," asked Taylor, "if I told you I wasn't going with you to Beta Aurelon?"

McCoy looked at her, scarcely able to believe his ears. "What are you talking about?"

She shrugged. "I'm talking about staying. You know, seeing this through to the end."

"But we've been assigned somewhere else," said Jiminez. "You can't just decide not to go."

"I can if I get the commanding officer's permission," Taylor insisted. "I've already spoken to Glavin and he's given me his blessing."

McCoy shook his head. "You'd break up the team?" he asked, only half-seriously.

His fellow trainee smiled sadly. "I'm afraid so," she confessed. "It's important to me. You all understand that, don't you? Well, don't you?"

Huang spoke for all of them. "Of course we understand. We don't like it, mind you, but we understand."

"I'll catch up with you," she assured them. "If not at Beta Aurelon, then somewhere else. It's a long haul. We're bound to bump into each other, right?"

"Right," said McCoy, not believing it for a second.

"Right," confirmed Jiminez. He grinned. "Definitely."

She took them all in with a glance. "Make no mistake about it, I'll miss you guys."

Carver shook his head. "Not me, you won't."

Taylor looked sympathetic. "Don't say that, Merlin. Of course I'll miss you."

"No, you won't," he maintained stubbornly. He cleared his throat. "Because I'm not leaving either."

McCoy shot him an accusing look. "What is this, an epidemic? You never mentioned anything about wanting to stay here."

"You're just jealous that Janice is getting all the attention," decided Huang. "That's it, isn't it?"

Merlin shook his head again. "I'm afraid not, Warren." He turned to McCoy. "And the reason I didn't mention it is because I wasn't sure until just this moment."

"So you haven't gotten permission yet?" asked Jiminez hopefully.

"No," Carver admitted. "But if Janice got it, I think I can get it too. In fact, I'm sure I can."

"But this is ridiculous," McCoy argued. "You're needed on Beta Aurelon as much as you're needed here."

"You're probably right," Merlin agreed. "But Ssan's in my blood now. I think I have an understanding of this place, its people, its philosophies. I want to be around long enough to see them to the end of their troubles, to see them prosper."

McCoy scowled. "You can see the Beta Aurelonites prosper. Won't that do?"

Merlin grinned. *"You* can see the Beta Aurelonites prosper. And then you can tell me all about it."

McCoy sat back in his chair and forced himself to accept the situation. "That's a promise," he said.

"Like I'd give you any choice in the matter." Merlin smiled. "Remember to be one hell of a good doctor, Leonard. The kind you were meant to be."

"I will," returned McCoy. "You can bet on it."

By harvest season on Beta Aurelon Three, the plague was finally under control, thanks to a vaccine developed by the Federation's medical team. McCoy had just beamed back from a remote island, the last pocket of Aurelonese culture to be vaccinated, when the long-faced doctor in charge of the transport area handed him a subspace message disk.

"For me?" asked the trainee.

"Says so," the man pointed out. He was perusing a portable computer padd in anticipation of some supply transport. "That's probably a clue."

Ignoring the sarcasm, McCoy glanced at the handwritten notations on the outside of the cassette. "It's from Ssan," he said out loud.

The doctor glanced at him. "That's where you were stationed last, isn't it?"

As deadpan as the other man, McCoy shrugged. "Says so. I guess that's a clue."

Frowning, the doctor harrumphed. "Smart aleck," he muttered and went back to his supply list.

With a skip in his step, the trainee made his way out of the transport area and down the hall that led to his dormitory room. But even though the layout of this place was a great deal like the one on Ssan, the atmosphere was much different.

They'd caught the plague in time to prevent all but a very few casualties. There was a sense of accomplishment about the medical facility, a feeling of having worked hard and won. He had no regrets about leaving Ssan, no regrets at all.

Swinging into the dorm, McCoy headed straight for the disk reader and popped it in. Immediately the particulars came up on the dark green screen in gold letters.

Subspace communiqué
Standard Earth Date 8.3.2254
To: Doctor Leonard McCoy
Monfarra City, Monfarran Union, Beta Aurelon Three
From: Dr. Janice Taylor
Pitur, Southern Continent, Alpha Gederix Four

The trainee smiled. It would be good to hear from his friends after all this time. He would have liked to share the message with Huang and Jiminez, his fellow expatriates from the Ssanitation Detail, but they were still collecting data on one of the other islands and weren't expected back for another couple of days.

That's all right, he told himself. Whatever's on the cassette, it'll still be news when they return—not that I have any intention of waiting that long.

Tapping the button that would bring up the message itself, he sat back in his chair and read.

Dear Leonard,

I have some bad news. Unfortunately, I'm still too upset by what happened to think clearly, so if this message is jumbled, please forgive me.

As you may have heard, the Assassin Wars are all but over here. Several days ago, Li Moboron was killed in a raid on a rebel facility, and the government has been on the verge of claiming victory ever since.

Merlin and I and a couple of the newer trainees went out to one of the local watering holes to celebrate. While you and Paco and Warren were here, they never let us out for fear we'd be attacked by the assassins. But after Moboron was found dead, they loosened those restrictions quite a bit.

Anyway, we were sitting around and talking over a bottle of brandy. One of the new people asked how it felt to see the end of the conflict after we'd been here for six long months.

Merlin said it felt fine and raised his glass to toast all the Federation doctors who had served on Ssan—even Vinnie Bando. Then his eyes went all round and white, as if he saw something reflected in his glass.

The next thing I knew, he was flying toward me and we were crashing to the ground in a jumble of arms and legs. A second later—at least I *think* it was later—there was a terrible, loud sound.

By the time I got my wits about me, I saw a half-dozen assassins standing at the other end of the square. Five were running away. But one was just standing there, glaring at me. And this is the horrible thing, Leonard: I recognized him.

It was the Ssana you treated, the assassin Bando tried to kill that night in the ward. I've asked myself if I could have imagined his face in all the confusion, but I didn't. It was him.

The bastard did what he promised, though I don't know how. He escaped from the authorities and went back to doing Moboron's dirty work.

Merlin died in the explosion. We tried to help him, but it was too late. Too much trauma, too much loss of blood. If he hadn't flung himself in my direction when he did, I probably would've been dead too.

I know how much it's going to hurt you to read this. You were his best friend. You were the only one he would always forgive, no matter what was said or done between you.

I can tell you he was proud of what we accomplished in our stay on Ssan. Damned proud. But especially of you—of what you did and what you learned. He said that you'd look back someday and know that rescuing that assassin from Bando was the most important thing you'd ever done in your life. And he'd still say that, that you were right to save the assassin's life, regardless of what came of it, because that's what a doctor does. He saves lives no matter *whose* they are.

See you around.

Janice

For a long time McCoy just sat there, staring at the screen. He could hear the sound that Taylor had described. He could see Merlin flying across the table to shield her.

And he could see the face of the Ssana, the one whose life he'd saved, standing on the other side of the plaza, indigo eyes narrowed, inspecting his handiwork with grim satisfaction. And why not? He'd murdered another innocent, hadn't he?

McCoy knew he'd never forget that face as long as he lived.

Book Three

——————— ☆ ———————

JOCELYN

ONE

☆

McCoy had long ago run out of activities to occupy his time in sickbay. There wasn't a single device that hadn't been checked and rechecked, a single supply item that hadn't been accounted for two or three times.

So he paced. And paced some more. Up and down the length of the facility, until Choi and Frederickson, the two nurses on duty, couldn't ignore it anymore and started casting doubtful looks at each other.

The doctor didn't care. His nurses hadn't been offered a chance—albeit a slim one—to renew their claim to life, to happiness. They hadn't just rediscovered the person they loved and had always loved, only to have that someone snatched away again and dropped into the jaws of the local Hell.

He was so wrapped up in his thoughts, so racked with concern for Jocelyn—not to mention Kirk and Spock—that he almost didn't notice when the double doors began to slide away, opening the way to the corridor outside. Then he heard the sound of voices, so rife with anxiety that they made his head snap around and drained all the blood from his face.

"My God," he rasped, seeing the two bloody figures laid out on antigrav stretchers. Spock and Clay were helping a couple of security officers guide the things into the operating room.

The doctor converged with them at the entrance to the facility and helped haul the stretchers inside to a space between two operating tables. Without asking, his nurses directed Spock and the other nonmedical personnel to set the patients down on the tables and then ushered them outside.

As the Vulcan left, however, McCoy called out, "Where are the others?"

Spock didn't have time to answer before he was shoved out the door, but the look on his face told the doctor everything he needed to know. For some reason the captain and Jocelyn had been left behind.

It was just as McCoy had feared. The assassins had slaughtered them.

Putting his feelings about Kirk and his ex-wife aside, the doctor forced himself to concentrate his attention on his patients. He recognized them: Peterson and Diaz. Security officers. Good men.

One was now a good *dead* man. Frowning at the biosigns display above Diaz's operating table, he swore beneath his breath and exchanged glances with Nurse Frederickson, as if to say: He's past our help. Then he scanned Peterson's readout and cursed again.

The gray metal bolt protruding from his back had done a lot of damage. The security officer was bleeding inside like nobody's business, and with every passing second he was slipping deeper into shock. Of course, on the positive side of the ledger, the bolt hadn't hit the spine or any important organs.

"Ten cee-cees of penthorbaline," he told Nurse Choi. The woman had placed the hypospray in his hand almost before the words were out of his mouth. With a hiss, he emptied its contents into Peterson's arm.

It would be a moment before the drug could take effect. Come on, come on, McCoy exhorted it. I can't *do* anything until the boy's stable, damn it.

Though it made him wait for what seemed like an eternity, the penthorbaline finally did its job. Despite the terribly invasive object in Peterson's body, his vital signs had come down within normal parameters, and the nerve ends in the vicinity had been thoroughly deadened. Now McCoy could see to getting that invasive object the hell out of there.

Punching the appropriate buttons in the base of the table, he called up overhead and cross-section views of the bolt. It didn't look like there was any head on it, just a shaft with a sharpened point. In fact, it probably would have gone right through its victim if one of Peterson's ribs hadn't gotten in the way.

That fit with what the doctor knew about the assassins. They were purveyors of a quick, clean death, not torturers who wanted their weapons to inflict as much damage as possible if and when they were removed.

The next step, however, was to get rid of the security man's padded scarlet jacket. "Scalpel," he ordered, extending his hand again palm up.

This time it was Frederickson who was one step ahead of him. Setting the scalpel for a shallow cut, McCoy trained it on the fabric to one side of the bolt and activated the tiny beam.

225

In moments he'd sliced away a circle about a hand's breadth in diameter, exposing the torn, blood-soaked shirt beneath. The doctor frowned at the sight of the dark, tormented flesh around the wound.

He glanced at Choi. "We're taking it out," he warned her. "You hold him, I'll pull."

The nurse nodded. Coming around to the other side of the table, she took hold of the patient, using the space between the thumb and forefinger of each hand to form a hole around the bolt.

"Ready," she announced.

"All right," said McCoy. "Here goes."

The bolt slipped out more easily than he'd hoped. Frederickson was waiting with a plastic bag; slipping it inside, he turned to the wound again.

Choi had placed a temporary patch over it to keep the bleeding to a minimum. The doctor looked up at the displays of the wound. According to the device's built-in sensor array, the bolt had come out in one piece. There were no metal splinters to worry about.

It always made McCoy a little nervous to rely on a machine this way. But at least this machine was one he'd overhauled only the day before, when he was still trying to keep his mind off . . .

He stopped himself in midthought. No, he insisted. No time for that. I'm not done yet, I've still got to close up.

And close up he did, with some help from Choi and Frederickson. It was just a matter of inserting a tiny shunt to drain away the blood that had collected inside Peterson's chest cavity, trimming the wound's raw edges and pulpy tatters, and applying the dermaplast patch that would serve as a skin wall until new flesh could be coerced into growing underneath.

At last, his surgery complete, the doctor glanced again

at his patient's biosigns. Still stable, he observed with some satisfaction, and a little stronger than when he'd started. All the man really needed now was rest.

Leaning close to Peterson's waxy-skinned face, McCoy promised: "You're going to be fine now, son." He knew the security officer probably couldn't hear him, but he said it anyway. Then, leaving Peterson in the capable hands of Choi and Frederickson, the doctor made for the exit.

Spock and Clay, along with their helpers from security, were still waiting outside, just as McCoy had hoped. As he emerged from the operating room, they all turned to him.

"Are they . . . ?" began one of the security people. He seemed to have an inkling that he might be asking for bad news.

"Diaz is dead," the doctor reported flatly. "Peterson will live." But he was no longer looking at the officer who had posed the question. He was homing in on the diplomat, who stood with his back resting against the bulkhead and his face cupped in his large, well-manicured hands.

"Treadway!" snarled McCoy.

Clay looked up. His eyes widened as he saw the fury reflected in the doctor's, and he very nearly raised his arm in time to ward off McCoy's blow. But he wasn't quite quick enough. As Bones followed through, putting all his weight into it, the diplomat's head snapped back and he went sprawling over a hard, plastic counter. He landed on the other side of it with a loud thunk.

The doctor rushed around the counter to get at Clay again. Grabbing the stunned diplomat by the front of his tunic, McCoy raised his raw-knuckled fist a second time, but someone grabbed him by the wrist and wouldn't let go no matter how hard he struggled.

It was Spock; it had to be. No one else present had that kind of strength.

"Let me go," he growled, tightening his grip on Clay's tunic. "Let me give this weasel what he deserves, damn it!"

"I cannot," the Vulcan informed him. "Please, Doctor. Release Mr. Treadway."

McCoy had no intention of complying with that request. It took the combined efforts of Spock, the two security officers, and Clay himself to work his fingers finally free of the tunic's fabric.

"You're insane," the diplomat hissed as he got to his feet, touching his fingers to the mottled swelling on his jaw where the doctor had connected.

"*I'm* insane?" raged the doctor. "I'm not the one who insisted on beaming down into the assassins' den. *You're* the one responsible for *that* little demonstration of genius!"

Clay's face grew dark with anger. "I did what I had to do," he argued. "What the mission demanded!"

"You got Jim and Jocelyn *killed* is what you did," McCoy spat. He tried to get at the diplomat again, but Spock held him back. "You wouldn't listen to anyone but yourself and now you've murdered the two people I love most in the world!"

"I loved her too," countered Clay, his handsome features contorting into something primal and ugly. "I'm her husband, for God's sake!"

The doctor shook his head. "Not anymore you aren't. You've lost her—or didn't you know that?"

Apparently that was about all Clay could take. With a guttural cry from deep down in his throat, he launched himself at McCoy. The doctor didn't see the fist that smashed into the side of his brow until it was too late.

"Mr. Treadway!" bellowed one of the security men.

As Bones recovered, he saw that both of the officers had wrapped themselves around the sputtering, cursing diplomat. "I loved her too," Clay grunted through clenched teeth. "I would never have hurt her, not for anything."

McCoy wiped at the blood he could feel meandering down the side of his face. "Really?" he remarked. "You had a damned funny way of showing it."

Suddenly, he realized that they were talking in the past tense. Talking about *Jocelyn* that way. Swallowing hard, he turned to Spock.

"She's dead," he stated. "Isn't she?"

Seeing that the doctor had expended all the violence he had inside him, the first officer released him and shook his head. "I do not know," he confessed. "The last I saw of her, she was alive. Both she and the captain."

McCoy was confused. He said so. "If they were alive, why weren't they beamed up? Why in blazes are they still down there?"

Spock sighed. "I cannot say for certain, but I would guess it was the maldinium in the area. It may have prevented Mr. Scott from getting a lock on them."

"Maldinium," the doctor muttered. He eyed the Vulcan. "In other words, you and our diplomat friend had the good fortune to be clear for transport but Jim and Jocelyn didn't."

"I am only speculating," Spock reminded him. "But I cannot think of a more likely explanation."

"I want to know for sure," barked Treadway, slithering out of the security officers' grasp. "I want to know what happened and what we can do to get her back. And I want to know *now.*"

The Vulcan frowned ever so subtly. "I will do my best to determine what happened to both the captain and your wife," he assured the diplomat. "And then we will formulate a plan of action."

"You're damned right we'll formulate a plan of action," Treadway promised. And with a final, withering glance at McCoy, he stormed out of sickbay.

Bones turned to the first officer. "When you find out, Spock . . ."

The Vulcan nodded. "I will notify you as well, Doctor. I had no intention of doing otherwise."

With a look of sympathy, insofar as he was able of such a thing, the Vulcan led the security officers out of the medical facility. In their wake, there was silence, a grim, torturous silence which proved more difficult for the doctor to endure than even the most hideous certainty.

Spock reminded himself that he was a Vulcan and that, as such, he did not engage in shouting matches. Otherwise he would have been sorely tempted to return Clay Treadway's remarks decibel for decibel.

"What do you *mean* I'm no longer in charge?" the human demanded. He'd been on his feet ever since the meeting convened a little more than a minute ago, at which time he'd been apprised of his unexpected fall from power.

No doubt Treadway had expected that since he had initiated the proceedings, he would also be the one to preside over them. But that was not the Vulcan's intention at all.

"I meant precisely what I said," Spock replied. "This is no longer a straightforward diplomatic mission. Therefore, I am reassuming control of it on behalf of the ship's command structure under Starfleet Order Nine-five-eight, article three, paragraphs seven and eight."

Out of the corner of his eye, the Vulcan saw that his

move was meeting with approval from Mr. Scott, Lieutenant Uhura, and Mr. Chekov, the other officers Treadway had seen fit to include in these proceedings. The chief engineer even went so far as to wink at him in a conspiratorial way.

"That's absurd," Treadway snapped. "It's ridiculous. Order Nine-five-eight pertains only to situations in which the diplomatic envoy has been killed or incapacitated."

"Which may be the case," Spock rejoined grimly, "at least insofar as your wife is concerned."

The human's eyes narrowed dangerously. "My wife? What about me? I'm not dead *or* incapacitated."

The Vulcan shrugged—an economical gesture which barely required any movement at all. "Perhaps not, Mr. Treadway. However, as far as I can tell, you are only half of the diplomatic team assigned to this endeavor. And the absence of the other half suggests—at least to me—an impaired ability to carry out your diplomatic duties."

The human shook his head. "You're flirting with a court-martial here, Spock. And you know it."

"I know no such thing," Spock countered. "However, if you insist on pressing your point, that is certainly your privilege. You may voice your objection with Starfleet Command any time after I have given the order to lift subspace radio silence."

Treadway's face darkened. "Radio silence?" he echoed, his voice thick with irony.

"That is correct," the Vulcan confirmed. "It is possible that the assassins are monitoring our communications. I would not want to encourage them by letting on that there is even a hint of dissent in our ranks."

Treadway's nostrils flared above his dashing, neatly trimmed mustache. He seemed to be mulling his options and rejecting them one by one. When he finally spoke again, it was with the voice of a man who had resigned himself to defeat.

"I'm being railroaded here, Mr. Spock."

The first officer arched an eyebrow. "I do not see how," he commented. "I am merely abiding by the same set of regulations to which you yourself referred in taking command. I regret," he added, not regretting it at all, "that you do not agree with my interpretation of them."

Treadway didn't answer. It was clear to him, as the Vulcan had intended, that he wasn't going to make any headway with his protest. With calculated dignity, the diplomat lowered himself into his seat.

"All right then, it's your game, Spock," he declared pointedly. "How are you going to play it?"

Before the first officer could answer, the doors slid aside and Dr. McCoy walked in. With an angry glance at the diplomat, he said: "Were you going to leave me out of your little get-together, Clay?"

The other man responded without emotion. "Was there a reason to invite you?" he asked.

"You're damned right there was a reason," snarled McCoy. "I still know more about Ssan than you'll ever learn in the ship's library. With Jocelyn's life at stake here, I'd have expected you'd put what's between *us* aside and let me lend whatever help I can." He shook his head. "I didn't think even you would stoop this low."

Unmoved, Treadway smiled coldly. "No lower than you," he replied.

Spock had no idea what the diplomat was talking about. However, he thought it best to haul their discussion out of the muck before it degenerated any further.

"Gentlemen," he interjected, "we have a very serious

matter before us. I suggest we put our differences aside and address it. Dr. McCoy? Mr. Treadway?"

"Fine with me," remarked the doctor, pulling up a chair at the end of the table opposite his adversary.

The diplomat nodded. "I have no problem with that," he alleged, though his frozen smile stated otherwise.

"Very well then," said the Vulcan. He turned to the engineer. "Mr. Scott, what were your findings regarding your inability to recover the captain and Jocelyn Treadway?"

Scotty scowled. *Inability* was not one of his favorite words.

"It was as ye suspected, sir. We were confounded by the maldinium in the area. In retrospect, it's a wonder we got the rest of ye out."

Spock nodded. "And were you able to pick up Captain Kirk's coordinates at any time after you beamed us aboard?"

"We were nae," he confessed. "The maldinium's playing havoc with our sensors as well. Of course—"

"So we don't even know if they're dead or alive?" asked Treadway, his voice taut with barely contained dread.

"We dinnae," the engineer told him. "But as I was startin' to say, we can recalibrate our instruments, and in time, that'll enable us to discern the captain and Ms. Treadway from their captors."

"If they're still alive," McCoy amended. "If the assassins haven't killed them by now for their trouble."

"How long will it take?" asked Spock, maintaining eye contact with Scott and ignoring the doctor's pessimism.

The engineer shrugged. "Two, maybe three hours."

The doctor leaned forward like a snake uncoiling for battle. "By then," he observed harshly, "they may be past any help we could give them."

"Ve could send down a rescue party," noted Chekov. "Perheps a helf-dozen security officers trained to vork in mountainous terrain."

"You'll need a communications specialist," Uhura pointed out. "Someone who can find a way to maintain contact with the ship, maldinium or no maldinium."

The Vulcan shook his head. "We will need neither security officers nor communications specialists at this juncture. We will not be beaming down until we know for certain whether Captain Kirk and Miss Treadway are still alive."

"What?" sputtered McCoy. "I don't believe what I'm hearing, Spock! Jim is your friend, for god's sake!"

The first officer met the criticism head-on. "That is certainly true, Doctor. However, the captain would be the first to caution us against risking the lives of our comrades for what is at best an uncertain gain."

But McCoy was only warming up. Glaring at Spock, he said, "He went after *you*, damn it. Against regulations, against the odds, against reason itself, he went after you on that blasted Genesis planet. And he brought you back."

The Vulcan felt the sting he was intended to feel. After all these years, the chief medical officer knew how to get to him as few others could.

Thrusting his chin out, he replied: "I do not need to be reminded of what Jim Kirk has done for me, Dr. McCoy. It is forever etched into my soul, as you well know. However, that does not change anything. I must still pursue logic in making my decision. And logic dictates that I refrain from spilling more blood than is . . . than is absolutely necessary."

"Than is absolutely *necessary?*" Uhura echoed.

It was not for nothing that she had been the ship's preeminent authority on communications for most of the last twenty-five years. She had detected the change in the Vulcan's position even before he could recognize it himself.

For Spock *had* changed his position, hadn't he? Somewhere between McCoy's swipe at him and his reflexive response, he had weighed the evidence anew and realized it could be seen in another light—and all without its invading his conscious mind until Uhura had brought it into the open.

To be sure, Spock was still a Vulcan through and through. He had dedicated his entire life to that ideal. He had worked hard to embrace it.

But he had also learned a great deal since the crash of the ill-fated *Galileo* shuttlecraft more than a quarter-century earlier. He had learned that he could be wrong. And he had learned that humans, for all their illogic, could sometimes embrace a wisdom he could not.

Life-and-death decisions were not always reducible to mathematical equations. The welfare of the *one* was sometimes all that mattered.

"Yes," the Vulcan confirmed, remembering to answer Uhura's question. He took a breath, let it out. "Perhaps I was . . . somewhat hasty in rejecting the notion of a rescue party."

"Somebody pinch me," muttered McCoy, in what seemed like genuine awe. "You actually changed that steel-trap mind of yours. It's a miracle."

"However," Spock went on, undaunted, "I maintain

that security and communications personnel are inappropriate. In fact, no amount of security will protect anyone who beams down into the assassins' territory. Nor will we be able to communicate, I believe, unless they wish us to." He turned again to McCoy, making a promise to him that far transcended the spoken language he was about to employ. "I will beam down alone," he said. "And if it is possible, I will bring them back—both the captain and Jocelyn Treadway."

"No."

The word had come from Clay Treadway. His eyes as hard as duranium, he shook his head.

"I will not sit here," he announced, "while Jocelyn's in danger of losing her life to those assassins." He looked around the table, at each face in turn—McCoy's included, the Vulcan's last of all. "I'm her husband. One way or the other, I will be part of the rescue attempt."

"That's crazy," the doctor told him. "You don't know the first thing about clandestine operations. You'll just get yourself killed and screw up the mission to boot."

"I'm in shape," Treadway argued, matching McCoy's intensity. "I can rock climb with the best of them. It's in my file, if you care to look. And I'm a fair shot with a phaser. That's in my file as well."

The doctor dismissed his adversary's contentions with a wave of his hand and turned to the first officer. "You don't need a rock climber, Spock. You need someone who can tell you what those damned assassins are thinking. Someone like me."

"You?" The diplomat made a face. "You're a doctor. What do you know about alien agendas? Alien points of view?"

McCoy got to his feet. "I knew enough to tell you not to

beam into the assassins' front yard, didn't I? I knew enough to predict that your little foray would turn into a bloody disaster!"

Treadway leaned forward to address the Vulcan again. "You need me, Spock. What if there's an opportunity to pursue our original purpose and bring these assassins to the mediation table? If there's a chance for peace, even a slim one, you'll want me there to identify it and take advantage of it."

"That's a pipe dream," the doctor jibed. "I said it before and I'll say it again; in the real world, those assassins are never going to negotiate. *Never.* And if you believe otherwise, that's just your ego getting in the—"

"Gentlemen," interrupted the Vulcan. Both the diplomat and McCoy turned to him as one, their eyes still full of the rancor they harbored for one another. "There is no need to debate this any further. If you believe your presence will be an asset, you may both come along."

McCoy's eyes screwed up. "Both?" he repeated.

Spock nodded in response. "You, Doctor, are correct in pointing out that no one else on this ship has any experience with the Ssana. Also, the captain and Miss Treadway may turn out to be in need of medical assistance. However," he continued, addressing the diplomat now, "Mr. Treadway has a point as well. There may yet be an opportunity to achieve peace, and he is better trained in such matters than any of us. What is more, I may need someone besides myself to carry a phaser and, as he indicates, his file does describe him as a good shot."

Treadway glanced at McCoy with undisguised contempt. But he didn't complain about Spock's decision. He'd gotten what he wanted, after all, and, being a member of the diplomatic corps, he knew enough to quit while he was ahead.

"Of course," the Vulcan went on, "this presupposes that you both understand from the beginning who is in charge of this effort and agree to follow my orders, regardless of your feelings about one another. Otherwise, I assure you, I am still quite willing to go by myself."

The doctor scowled. "I think I can put my personal judgments aside long enough to drag Jim and Jocelyn out of there. Count me in."

"I accept your kind invitation," said Treadway, suddenly the picture of southern gentility once again. "You may rely on me as well."

"I should also tell you," Spock added, "that if we are lost, there will be no further rescue attempts. I will leave orders to that effect."

"Understood," the diplomat responded.

McCoy harrumphed. "I never expected anything else."

Spock eyed them appraisingly. "Good," he concluded. "We will beam down in twenty minutes, after I have consulted with Commander Scott and Lieutenant Uhura. Mr. Chekov, you may return to the conn."

The Russian nodded. "Aye-aye, sir." He rose and turned smartly toward the exit.

Treadway followed a moment later and McCoy a moment after that. As the doors slid closed behind them, the Vulcan looked to the chief engineer and the communications officer. They were alert, ready for his instructions.

"I will need a data map of the assassins' lair," he told Scotty, "with references to those spots where the maldinium deposits are the most troublesome."

"Ye've got it, sir," Scott promised.

"You'll also need communicators set to a frequency the Ssana aren't likely to monitor," Uhura noted. "And amplification inserts, just in case you need to contact us while you're still inside the caverns."

Spock grunted softly. "You anticipate me, Lieutenant. But at least you anticipate me accurately. I will indeed require the devices to which you refer."

"I'll get right on it," the lieutenant told him.

But as she and Scotty got up, she seemed less than eager to leave. Noticing her hesitation, the engineer hesitated too.

"Is there something else?" the Vulcan inquired of them.

Uhura frowned. "Mr. Spock . . . I don't think you were entirely honest with us. About your reasons for allowing Dr. McCoy and Mr. Treadway to accompany you."

The first officer cocked an eyebrow. "Really," he observed. "And what were my true reasons?"

"I believe," Uhura contended, "that you saw two men willing to sacrifice their lives for someone they loved. And out of respect for that, you let them."

Spock pretended to consider the possibility. "Fascinating," he commented at last. "I wish we had more time to discuss this theory, Lieutenant. However, as Dr. McCoy said, it is urgent that we get this mission under way as soon as possible."

Uhura gazed at him a moment longer. A smile came over her face. "Of course, sir," she responded. "I'll bring the communicators to the transporter room."

"That will be satisfactory," he informed her and watched as Uhura and Scott took their leave of him.

Alone in the conference room, the Vulcan leaned back in his chair. Uhura had been right, he mused, though he would never admit it.

He had given in not only on the question of whether to stage a rescue at all but also on the point of whether or not to bring the doctor and the diplomat for company. His father would not have approved of his less-than-logical approach to the situation.

But then, Sarek had not been wrested from the Genesis planet by a group of humans who had had no chance to retrieve him—and retrieved him anyway. Had brought him back from death, in fact.

For all his wisdom, Sarek had no grasp of the power of love.

TWO

☆

As they made their way along the corridor to the transporter room, Scotty did his best to keep up with the Vulcan's long strides. When Spock had his eyes fixed on a goal, the engineer mused, it was difficult to slow him down.

"So ye see," Scott went on, "there's really no place on that bloody shelf where ye can beam down and keep from being spotted."

"That is unfortunate," the first officer commented. "Is there an alternative?"

"Aye," said the human, "but nae an easy one." Punching the buttons on the tricorder he'd brought along, he held it up so Spock could see its tiny screen. "If ye look closely, sir, ye can make out a slope just above the place we've designated as their main entrance. It's a pretty steep incline and it does nae appear to offer a great many hand- or footholds. What's more, it's a rather long slope, one that'll take several hours to descend. But by the same token, I dinnae think it'll be watched very closely."

The Vulcan peered at the tricorder screen and nodded. "We will be of little help to the captain and Jocelyn Treadway if we are discovered by the assassins. I agree with your assessment, Mr. Scott. We will make our approach via the slope."

"Very good, sir," the engineer acknowledged. "The slope it is. In that case, ye'll need this tricorder. It's got all the maldinium data ye requested and a profile of the best descent route as well."

Spock looked at him. "Thank you," he said to Scotty. "That is most thorough—though, to be honest, I expected no less." Accepting the tricorder, the Vulcan tucked it away into one of the pockets of his cold-weather jacket.

Abruptly, the entrance to the transporter room loomed ahead. And a good thing, too. Scott didn't know how much longer he could keep up this pace.

As the doors slid aside, they could see that Uhura was already inside, waiting for them. She had the communicators that Spock had requested cradled in one arm. Apparently she'd been able to make the necessary adjustments in the devices on time and without any trouble.

Fariss, Scott's most experienced transporter operator, was also present. Her sleek, black hair drawn back into a tight ponytail, she looked to be all business, ready for anything.

Not that the chief engineer would let anyone but himself beam down the rescue party. But he couldn't create a maldinium map, profile the descent route, and prepare the transporter unit all at the same time—albeit in a younger day, he would certainly have tried.

As the doors started to close, Scotty heard the sound of

footfalls in the corridor he and Spock had just vacated. Glancing over his shoulder, he saw Dr. McCoy and Clay Treadway marching toward them, their jaws set in grim determination not only to recover Captain Kirk and the diplomat's wife but apparently to do it without talking to one another.

With the approach of the two men, the doors reversed their course and slid fully open again. Treadway made a beeline for the transporter platform, where he came to a halt beside a stack of climbing ropes and duranium wedges and appeared to gather himself for the effort ahead. The doctor, on the other hand, joined his fellow officers in the center of the room.

Uhura smiled. "Your communicators," she said, offering them to Spock and McCoy.

Bones took one. The Vulcan took two—one for the diplomat and one for himself. Then they joined Treadway and the pile of climbing gear on the platform.

That was Scotty's cue to assume command of the transporter console. Fariss moved to one side, not the least bit miffed. She knew how important this was to her superior; if there were any mistakes made, he didn't want to have anyone to blame but himself.

The chief engineer glanced at the controls, just to be certain Fariss had done her job. With some satisfaction, he saw that she had. Now it was all up to him. He looked up at Spock, awaiting the word.

The first officer gazed across the room with hooded eyes. His intellect was focused to a fine point, as only a Vulcan could focus. Scott had seen that look before and was heartened by it. No matter how good the assassins were down there, they had never dealt with the relentless resourcefulness of the being named Spock.

Without actually meeting the engineer's gaze, the Vulcan said, "Energize."

Scotty did as he was told. The tightly controlled energies inherent in the transporter process took hold of and enveloped the three figures on the platform. And then, in the time it took to blink, they were gone.

Good luck, the engineer wished them. Back safe.

He noticed that Uhura was looking at him. She smiled, knowing exactly what he'd been thinking. He smiled back, knowing she'd been thinking it too.

"Well," Scott exhaled, "I guess that's that." Turning to Fariss, he said, "It's all yours, Lieutenant." And with Uhura alongside him, he departed the transporter room, anticipating the long minutes and perhaps hours ahead.

After all, the worst part of serving as an officer on a starship was waiting helplessly for a landing party to come home. And Scotty had seldom felt so helpless as he did now.

"Captain?"

He was lying in a field, peering up at a dark blue sky framed by the corn stalks that rose about him on every side. Flies buzzed lazily near his feet; his sunburned face stung where perspiration touched it in its slow, meandering travels. From a distance the breeze carried the pungent smell of fertilizer.

And he wasn't a captain, no matter who had decided it might be fun to call him that, though, if dreams could come true, he might get to be a captain some day.

"Captain Kirk?"

The sky and the cornstalks gave way to the arched, copper-colored ceiling of one of the gyms at Starfleet Academy. His back hurt and his cheeks were suffused with a terrible heat. As he lay there, a face loomed above him and a hand reached down for him, and they belonged to an upperclassman named Finnegan who was offering him two falls out of three.

He still wasn't a captain—not by a long shot. And if Finnegan threw him a couple more times as hard as that first time, he wouldn't live long enough to become one.

"Captain Kirk? For god's sake . . ."

The gym melted around him and he was in the open again. It was night and the sky was full of stars. There was someone standing nearby, a man with a thick yellow mane and what looked like a tiny jewel set into his forehead, just above the bridge of his nose. The man's name was Tyree. They were friends, and Tyree had taken the first lookout this night, while Jim and the rest of his Federation survey team slept.

And he wasn't a captain yet, though he was well on his way. If all his assignments went as well as this one, he'd have his own ship before—

"Captain Kirk, wake up!"

Spurred by the tone of urgency, Kirk bolted upright and felt his head bob in a sea of sickening pain. Bringing a hand up to his temple, he touched the source of that pain—a hot, throbbing knot at the corner of his brow.

"Are you all right?" asked the voice.

Opening his eyes, the captain saw who had posed the question. It was Jocelyn Treadway, her face half in shadow and half awash with the light of a candle that she held in her hand.

"I've felt worse," he told her truthfully.

He looked around and saw that they were in a low-ceilinged cave. The candlelight didn't reach far enough to tell him how big the floor was, only that there was a supply of fresh air, because the tiny flame guttered in a faint breeze.

"Where are we?" he asked.

Jocelyn sighed. "In the assassins' lair. The very place we were hoping to get into." She glanced at something off in the darkness beyond their circle of illumination. "They brought us here after the others beamed up."

After they . . . beamed up? Kirk's head hurt too much for him to think clearly, but it came to him that he'd seen Spock and Clay Treadway vanish in the transporter effect. And that he'd expected to pull the same kind of disappearing act a moment later. Except he hadn't. And neither had Jocelyn.

"What went wrong?" asked the captain. "Why didn't we get beamed up along with them?" But even before he finished his question, he had the answer. "The maldinium."

Jocelyn nodded. "Of course. We must have been too near a deposit for Mr. Scott to get a lock on us." She bit her lip. "Some luck."

Kirk saw her eyes move as she pondered the injustice of it. But he didn't see a whole lot of resentment there. Or for that matter, a whole lot of fear, considering the fact that they were at the mercy of a violent cult.

"Well," she said, focusing on him again, "at least the others got away. I suppose that's something to be grateful for."

"I suppose it is," the captain agreed. And then it occurred to him that his companion might have injuries as well—injuries that were just less obvious than his. "They haven't hurt you?" he asked hopefully.

Jocelyn smiled a little and shook her head. "No. They said as long as I didn't offer them any resistance, I wouldn't be harmed. At least," she added ominously, "for the time being."

Kirk frowned. Just a threat, to keep them in line? Or

genuine notice of the assassins' intentions? He had no way of knowing.

"Of course," he said out loud, "the fact that they bothered to bring us in here at all is a good sign. If they didn't kill us right off the bat, it probably means they want something from us. Information, hostage value, something."

Or maybe they're just not sure yet, he mused. Maybe they're still mulling it over. But he didn't tell Jocelyn that.

The woman's eyes shone in the meager yellow light. "Will Mr. Spock try to get us out of here?" she wondered.

The captain shook his head—and winced at the pain it cost him. Reaching out blindly, he found an outcropping he could hang onto until the wave of nausea and vertigo passed.

"I don't know," he told her. "It depends on a lot of things; first of all, whether they think we're dead or alive. If the maldinium configurations in these caves prevent them from obtaining a reliable sensor scan, Spock might not want to put anyone else's life on the line."

Jocelyn didn't look happy about that, but she didn't break down in tears either. She was one tough cookie, Kirk noted.

"And if they can find us?" she asked. "If they can determine beyond a shadow of a doubt that we're still alive?"

"Still no guarantees," the captain warned her. "Those same maldinium configurations might prevent them from beaming down with any certainty of survival. And Spock's too good a commanding officer to take that kind of risk."

His companion nodded. "I had a feeling you'd say something like that." She glanced into the darkness again.

"So very possibly, we're on our own. And if we get out of here, it'll be either by the grace of God or through our own devices."

Kirk couldn't have put it better himself. He said so.

Absorbing the information, Jocelyn regarded him appraisingly. Then she turned away and chuckled softly to herself.

"What?" the captain prompted.

Looking up again, the diplomat suppressed a smile. "I was just weighing what I knew about the assassins—their physiology, their training, their psychological makeup—against the physical skills of two over-the-hill specimens like you and me."

"And?" he asked.

Jocelyn's expression turned apologetic. "I wouldn't bet the family farm on our side, if you know what I mean."

Kirk grunted. "You wound me, madam."

"Too late for that," she quipped dryly. "Someone beat me to it."

Before the captain could return the volley, he heard something move beyond their circle of light. Putting his index finger to his lips in a request for silence, he heard the distinct scrape of boots against a hard, coarse surface.

One set, he remarked to himself. They slowed down at what must have been the entrance to their cave. There were voices—two at least—engaged in a conversation too quiet to overhear. Then the footfalls sped up again and faded into the distance.

Jocelyn inquired with her eyes whether it was all right to speak again. Kirk nodded to show her that it was.

"I hear that every so often," she told him. "The changing of the guard."

"Any idea how often?" the captain asked.

The woman thought for a moment. "Not really," she decided. "Maybe every hour, maybe every two hours. I've heard them do it five or six times since they put us in here." She paused. "It's amazing how quickly you can lose track of time in this place."

"And the number of guards?" he pressed. "Just one or more than one?" Though he'd heard one set of footfalls approach and one set leave, there could have been several of them out there on a staggered schedule.

Jocelyn shrugged. "There were quite a few of the assassins with us when they brought us in—ten or twelve, I'd say. But as to how many are still out there . . ." She shrugged a second time. "Sorry. I just don't know."

"That's all right," he told her. "We'll figure it out."

But despite his encouraging words, he had a bad feeling about this. A very bad feeling. Even if Spock knew they were alive, even if he could get in here to rescue them, their captors were trained killers who knew these caverns a lot better than any *Enterprise* security officer.

Kirk had been in more than his share of tight spots, the most recent of them no less hopeless a place than the Klingon work camp on Rura Penthe. But even in that frozen purgatory, he'd never quite let his doubts get the best of him. He'd always known, deep down inside, that someday he and McCoy would again warm their hands by a friendly fire.

And despite everything, he had turned out to be right. They eventually escaped Rura Penthe, as they had escaped so many other places in the past. They beat the odds, came out on the winning end of the equation, triumphed over every difficulty their enemies could throw at them.

Given his track record, his penchant for bluffing and improvising and clawing his way around every obstacle, the captain should have harbored a certain amount of confidence that he could cheat death yet again.

Instead, there was a nagging fear that this small, dark cavern in the northern mountains of Ssan was where his luck would finally run out.

"The offworlders must die," said Cor Lakandir, his eyes glittering in the light of the fire. "What other option is there?"

There were murmurs of assent from the other young assassins. Andrachis noted this. The prevailing sentiment was not at all to his liking, and sentiments had a way of lurching out of control unless someone put a stop to them early on. He would have to be that someone.

"There *is* another option," he countered. "There is always another option. Particularly when tradition frowns on the taking of such lives."

"In what way does it frown?" asked Lakandir.

Andrachis met his challenge squarely. "It is dishonorable," he explained, "to shed blood that has never flowed through Ssani veins. I learned that before I made my first kill. Assassination is a right, a privilege—not to be bestowed on offworlders."

There was a time, he recalled, when he diverged from that principle. However, that was a long time ago, when he was very young, and he regretted it now as he regretted little else.

"We have already killed," one of the other young ones reminded them. "At least one of the Federation people is dead, and perhaps a second."

To the Ssana who offered the information, it was an argument for going ahead with Lakandir's proposal. To Andrachis it was quite the contrary.

"This is true," he conceded. "We have already carved

offworlder flesh. But is that a reason to do so again? Does an assassin build shame upon shame? Or does he learn from his mistakes and seek to rectify them?"

Lakandir grunted softly. "You call it shame to defend ourselves, Master?"

"I call it shame to break with tradition," Andrachis told him, "no matter the provocation. I assure you, Li Moboron would have slit his own throat and those of all his comrades before staining his blade with an offworlder's blood." He paused for effect, taking the opportunity to eye half a dozen of Lakandir's contemporaries. "It was not necessary to kill out there on the shelf. Had I been there, I would have found a way to prevent it."

"But you promised we would *break* the offworlders," said Lakandir.

The master assassin shook his head. "Break them, but not kill them. Send them away, but not to join the souls of their ancestors."

"What's done is done," commented another Ssana, neither youth nor grizzled veteran. "The question before us is what to do with our captives."

"We cannot let them go," counseled Lakandir. "They have seen our lair. They will return to their ship and use their knowledge to purge us from this place."

An older assassin nodded. "They have the power to do that. To do it easily, in fact, as someone recently pointed out."

It was Lakandir, of course, who had made mention of the offworlders' weapons. If the older Ssana didn't remember that, the master did. He remembered everything.

Andrachis shook his head derisively, but not too derisively. After all, he did not wish to alienate his followers, only instruct them.

"Has it not occurred to you," he asked, "that the

251

offworlders know the location of our lair already thanks to their advanced-technology detection devices, which someone mentioned recently as well? Or does one of us here think it is a coincidence that the Federation people happened to be walking around in these mountains?"

Silence, except for the spitting of the fire.

Good, he thought. His remark had found its target. He was not as skilled an orator as Li Moboron, but it seemed he was skilled enough.

"Then why were they walking around?" wondered Lakandir, breaking the spell. "Perhaps their instruments could not tell them everything. Perhaps there was something else they needed to know before they could attack us."

"Yes," said another youth. "And our assault kept them from gaining that knowledge. But if we were to send the captives back to them . . ."

Another challenge that had to be suppressed before it got out of hand. Andrachis threw himself at it the way he had thrown himself at countless adversaries during the Assassin Wars.

"Think," he exclaimed, his voice cracking like a whip in the still air of the cavern. "Have the Federation people ever attacked us? Have they displayed a desire to attack us?" He spat into the flames to demonstrate his disdain for the whole idea. "That is not their way," he pressed, "just as I told you earlier. They talk. They cajole. But they do not use force except when all else fails."

"How can you be so sure of this?" asked Marn Silariot, one of Lakandir's allies.

"As I told you," he related, "I had firsthand experience with them. It was during the wars. I came to know them better than some of them know themselves. And I tell you that this expedition did not approach us with violence in mind. They came to speak to us on behalf of the city-states, to counsel peace."

"It is true," noted one of the young ones, "that they did not kill any of us with their weapons. We were knocked backward, stunned, but no assassin lost his life out there."

"But if they are so naive, so harmless, why not just turn them loose?" Ars Rondorrin posed the question not so much because he wanted to know the answer but to give Andrachis a chance to expand on the ground he had gained.

"Because," the master answered dutifully, "they may prove valuable to us. Even if the Federation people do not attack us in our lair, the master governors will not be so reluctant. Eventually they will attempt to organize a strike. But if we have a couple of their human allies in our midst, they will be limited as to the types of weapons they may use. In the end, they may not storm us at all, for fear of losing the friendship of the offworlders."

Lakandir eyed him across the cooking fire. "You speak of our traditions, Master. But holding prisoners is hardly the function of an assassin."

Andrachis nodded. "You are correct. But neither is there any lore to relegate against it. Do not mistake me, Cor. I too see the need for us to adapt to our situation, to respond to a set of exigencies that Li Moboron and his predecessors never envisioned. I only ask that we remain true to the *spirit* of our laws, that we show respect for those Ssana who walked the assassin's path before us."

It would be difficult to argue with his stance after he had clothed it in such a way. Andrachis knew that. And apparently Lakandir knew it too, because he refrained from posing yet another challenge.

"The captives will remain alive," said the High Assassin, so there would be no confusion in the matter. "For now, that is all we need decide about them."

This time Andrachis had faced the challenge and surmounted it. But he knew it was not the last challenge he would face from Cor Lakandir.

His breath freezing on the thin air, McCoy looked around. He and his companions had materialized on a large, snowy plateau. On two sides, the mountain offered easy, gradual descents, distinguished by other, smaller plateaus at intervals. On a third side it displayed a rocky, gray flank, which climbed to even greater heights.

But it was the fourth side with which they would concern themselves, for that way lay the slope of which Scotty had spoken—the steep, almost vertical slope that would eventually deposit them at a point over the entrance to the assassins' lair.

"This way?" asked the doctor.

Spock nodded. "Yes."

McCoy scowled. He couldn't help it.

Clay said nothing, obviously preferring to guard his emotions. But that was fine with Bones. Better for them both to be silent than to be at each other's throats.

Approaching the collection of ropes and wedges that Scotty had beamed down alongside them, the Vulcan hoisted some gear onto his shoulder. Following his example, McCoy and the diplomat did the same.

As the doctor watched, Spock walked to the edge of the plateau, knelt on the cold stone surface, and, using one wedge as a hammer, drove another one into a small fissure in the cliff. The impact made the air sing, but not so loudly that it could be heard below.

It would no doubt be the first of many wedges that the Vulcan would drive that day. McCoy recognized that fact as Spock hit it a second time, and a third. Then he attached his rope to it and let it slink down the almost featureless slope, a first step toward their ultimate destination.

Finally, he looked up at the doctor. With a raised brow, he made a wordless inquiry. After all, Spock was well aware of McCoy's fear of heights. The doctor had mentioned it some years ago, when he had seen Jim Kirk climb El Capitan. And even if the Vulcan hadn't heard it from McCoy's own lips, he would certainly have known it from the look in his eyes.

But Bones wasn't shrinking from this descent—not when it might make the difference between Jocelyn living and dying. As wordlessly as Spock had framed his question, he communicated his answer: You're blasted right I'm still with you.

Satisfied, Spock took hold of the rope and lowered himself down over the brink of the plateau. McCoy swallowed. He only hoped these damn-fool heroics would eventually be rewarded.

Kirk knew there was no point in trying to be discreet as he headed for the way out of their cavern. As he had told Jocelyn before taking possession of their single candle, a Ssani assassin would hear him no matter how quiet he was. And if the Ssana thought one of the humans was trying to sneak up on him, he might decide to strike first and ask questions later.

Of course, this was all assuming there was one guard and one only. It was entirely possible there was more than one, in which case it would have been twice as foolhardy to go skulking around the cave opening.

So he did just the opposite. He came toward the opening candle in hand, whistling softly to himself, alerting whoever was out there that there was a captive approaching.

As the exit began to define itself in the meager yellow light, Kirk heard the shuffle of feet out in the stone passageway beyond. Even then, however, he couldn't tell if it was one assassin out there or more than one.

So, clenching his teeth, he put one foot in front of the other and kept on whistling. And he wouldn't stop, he vowed, until he had found out what he needed to know.

Abruptly, a white-robed figure stood in his path, filling most of the opening with his bulk. Kirk hadn't seen the Ssana move into place. It was as if he had just appeared out of the thin, cold air.

"Where are you going?" the assassin asked.

The captain frowned. "Even animals don't mess their dens," he pointed out.

"No," the Ssana agreed. "But you will. That is, if you know what is good for you."

As he spoke, two other assassins moved into position behind him. They probably didn't expect an unarmed human to be any real threat, but they weren't taking any chances.

More importantly, it told Kirk that there were at least three guards out there. Three armed guards, he noted, his eyes drawn to the knifelike weapons inserted into their belts.

Given the frequency with which they were replaced by fresh personnel, they weren't likely to doze off. And if they weren't providing their captives with simple amenities, it wasn't likely they would respond to the old sudden-sickness ploy either.

Not good news, the captain mused. Not good news at all.

"Thanks for the hospitality," he said, smiling thinly at the Ssana who had confronted him. "I guess I'll be going now."

The assassin didn't reply. He just stood there and watched as Kirk made his way back into the recesses of the cave. It wasn't until the captain had retraced about half his steps that he heard the Ssana move away from the opening.

A moment later Jocelyn's image swam back into the range of the candle's illumination. "Any luck?" she asked.

Kirk grunted. "I got what I set out for," he told her.

"And?"

He shook his head. "You don't want to know."

"More than one?" she pressed.

"More than two," he reported.

Jocelyn's spirits seemed to flag. "Oh," she commented.

Joining her, the captain sat down with his back against a more or less vertical plane of rock. "Sorry I couldn't have been the bearer of better news," he added.

She looked at him. "That's all right," she said. "It's not your fault we're in this position." A pause. "It's mine. Mine and my husband's."

"Spilt milk," he remarked. "And you know what they say about that."

Jocelyn smiled a little. "Yes, I do. So now what? We just wait for something to happen?"

Kirk thought about it. What indeed? There was still a chance that they could get out of here, of course. There was always a chance.

But he didn't believe they could do it on their own. Some sort of opportunity would have to present itself, and when it did, they had better be ready for it.

"I don't see that we've got any choice," he responded at last. "At least for the time being."

His companion accepted that conclusion in silence. It wasn't an easy thing to accept, this helplessness. But she was giving it her best shot.

Abruptly, she said, "You've known Leonard for . . . what? Almost thirty years?"

"Twenty-seven," he told her. "Ever since he signed on with the *Enterprise.*"

"Almost half his adult life," Jocelyn mused.

"I guess that's right," the captain confirmed. Where was she going with this? He tried to divine the answer in the set of her eyes.

"What is he like?" she asked suddenly.

Kirk looked at her. "What do you mean?"

Jocelyn frowned a little. "I mean, what kind of person is he? What kinds of food does he like? Has he got any hobbies?"

The captain had to smile. "Hobbies?" he echoed. "Bones?" It was difficult to picture his friend building a Rigellian terrarium or playing one of those zero-grav games that enjoyed a comeback a few years earlier.

"No," he told her. "No hobbies. But as for the rest of it . . ." He pondered the question for a moment. "Well, come to think of it," Kirk said at last, "he's not exactly a gourmet either. We've had the chance to sample some pretty interesting meals in the course of our travels together, but I can't remember him really liking any of them. Bones has always been more partial to home cooking. In fact, unless I miss my guess, his favorite dish is chicken-fried steak."

"You're joking," she replied, her eyes widening.

The captain shook his head. "No. Why?"

"I used to make chicken-fried steak when we were married," Jocelyn explained. "And he hated it. Absolutely wouldn't touch the stuff."

Kirk grunted, appreciating the irony. "Maybe you made it too well," he suggested. "Not greasy enough."

She looked grateful. "Maybe. What else can you tell me about him?"

The captain leaned back against the cavern wall. "Let's see. He's one hell of a good doctor. Really cares about his patients."

"That doesn't surprise me," Jocelyn commented. Was there just a hint of pique in her voice? A subtle note of resentment?

"He loves his family." Kirk could feel himself blushing as he realized the implications of that statement. "I mean—"

"You mean Joanna's family," she amended, saving him the trouble of trying to get his foot out of his mouth. "Don't be concerned. I didn't expect to be included in that description. Not in the last several decades, anyway."

Clearing his throat, he went on. "Bones hates machines. All kinds, I suppose, but transporters in particular. He's told me over and over how he can't stand getting his atoms scrambled and shot through space."

His companion seemed intrigued by the information. "How about that?" she declared. "I don't like getting transported much myself." A beat. "You mean we actually turn out to have something in common?"

The captain didn't know what to say to that. Fortunately, Jocelyn got him off the hook a moment later.

"Sorry," she told him with obvious sincerity. "I didn't mean to get all sarcastic. It just comes naturally, I'm afraid. Please, continue."

Kirk scratched at his jaw. "Well, he keeps a pretty well-stocked bar. Always has, as long as I've known him. He's got a taste for brandy, Saurian in particular. And he doesn't like to drink alone."

Jocelyn nodded. Her gaze had lost focus. "I do believe," she said after a while, "that I knew that."

The captain ignored the comment. He had a feeling it was none of his business. "And beyond that," he stated, "I'm not sure there's a whole lot to tell."

His companion seemed disappointed. "But you've been his friend for so long," she insisted. "Surely there must be something else."

"He's a man of simple tastes," Kirk pointed out. "Outside of his family, his friends, and his profession, there isn't much in life that really grabs him."

Jocelyn pondered his observation. "Well, then, who are his friends? Aside from you, of course. Mr. Spock?"

The captain couldn't help but smile. "In a way," he replied. "Mind you, they don't exactly go around slapping each other on the back. To listen to them, you'd probably think they were bitter enemies. But when push comes to shove—and believe me, it has—there's a bond of affection between Spock and McCoy that even I can't quite fathom. Nor do I try."

He could have said more, about how the doctor carried the Vulcan's katra in him for a time, or how Spock had given up a life of bliss with Zarabeth to return Bones to his rightful time and place. But that was between the two of them and no one else.

"I see," noted Jocelyn, perhaps sensing that Kirk was leaving something out but declining to press her luck. "How about Mr. Scott? Chekov? Uhura?"

"Old comrades," the captain answered. "They'd give their lives for him. And vice versa. I'd include Captain Sulu in that group as well. And Christine Chapel, who served as his nurse."

McCoy's ex-wife took it all in. "And . . . lady friends?" she asked. "There must have been some of those, right?"

Kirk smiled. He should have seen this coming. "I don't feel right," he said, "talking about a friend's romantic liaisons. Almost anything else, but not that."

Jocelyn harrumphed. "Listen," she countered, "I know about Leonard's relationship with Nancy Crater, or whatever her name was when she was single. It was all in your ship's logs."

Nancy Crater was a woman the captain and Bones had encountered on one of their first missions together. Sometime after she and her husband established an archaeological site on planet M-113, Nancy was killed and replaced by a shape-changing, salt-sucking creature indigenous to that world, though Kirk didn't find that out until after several of his crewmen were killed by the thing.

"I know about Natira as well," Jocelyn continued. "About how Leonard was dying of xenopolycythemia and decided to stay with her on her doomed asteroid. What was it called? Yonada? And how he changed his mind once he discovered both a cure for his medical problem and a way to save Natira's world." A pause. "I'm just asking if there was anyone else—anyone not mentioned in your logs."

"There were a few," the captain told her, careful not to tread on any confidences. "But no one he loved the way he loved Natira." Or the way he loved you, he added silently.

"Was she beautiful?" Jocelyn asked.

Kirk nodded. "Yes. She was."

His companion shook her head. "Leonard should have stayed on Yonada. He probably would have been happy there with his high priestess."

The captain shrugged. "At the time, he said his life on the *Enterprise* was more important to him. And I don't think he's ever regretted the decision."

261

She regarded him frankly. "I very nearly made him regret it."

Kirk wasn't sure what she was talking about. "Jocelyn," he said, "if this is something that should remain private—"

"Nonsense," she said. "You're Leonard's best friend. If he didn't tell you, it's only because he didn't get a chance." She looked wistful in the flickering candlelight. "You see, we almost had a little tryst last night, he and I. Almost, but not quite."

Suddenly all the pieces fell into place. The air of tension between the Treadways that he'd noticed back in the transporter room. His observation that something had happened the night before. Now he knew what that something was. And he knew also why it had driven a wedge between them.

"Captain?"

"Mm?"

"You're gaping," Jocelyn told him.

Self-consciously, the captain closed his mouth. "Sorry," he muttered.

"It's all right," she replied. "It's my fault. I just didn't think you'd be all that surprised."

Kirk swallowed. This wasn't right. He shouldn't be hearing this, not from her. Not from anyone. There were some things that weren't meant for public consumption.

"Look," he said, "whatever happened last night was between you and Bones. If I'm ever going to face him again, I don't want to—"

"You're not," Jocelyn interrupted. "Going to face him again," she expanded. She spoke unflinchingly, her voice steady, her eyes unblinking.

The captain frowned. "Don't sound so certain of it."

"You haven't given me any reason to sound otherwise," she reminded him.

"We're going to get out of here," he said more assertively. "We're going to make it. How do I sound now?"

"Like a much better liar," his companion answered. "But a liar nonetheless. And if you're not going to see him again . . . if neither of us is . . . there are some things I want to say. No—*have* to say."

Kirk understood. "Confessions, you mean."

"They say it's good for the soul," she returned.

He grunted. "I'm probably not the person you should be confessing to."

Jocelyn's eyes suddenly grew shiny in the soft light. "Captain," she told him, her voice a bit huskier than usual, "you're the only one here."

That much was certainly true. He took a breath, let it out. "All right," he said. "I'll listen."

THREE

"Have you ever been to a high school social?" asked Jocelyn.

Kirk thought for a moment. "Yes, I guess I have," he recalled. "Though to be honest, I don't remember it very well. Just that there was a girl named Cindy Mellon and that she was a much better dancer than I was."

His companion nodded. "That's usually all you do remember, I think. Whom you danced with. And whom you didn't dance with." She paused. "At this one particular social—I'd just turned seventeen, if I recall correctly—I was dancing with the most popular boy in town. The best athlete, the best-looking, the best everything. That was Clay Treadway, of course."

The captain looked at her askance. "You knew him all the way back then?"

Jocelyn sighed. "Guilty as charged. Come to think of it, he wasn't very different from the way he is now. Handsome. Polite. And jealous as hell. But in those days, I really didn't mind the jealous part. After all, it meant that he cared for me."

"This was before Bones?" Kirk ventured.

"Yes," she confirmed. "But only just before. Clay and I had been an item for at least a year, I suppose, by this time. In a way, though, we'd been matched up much longer than that. Our families, the Darnells and the Treadways, were kind of the town aristocracy, you see, and our parents had practically had us betrothed since we were infants. It was like some kind of ancient society, where people arranged marriages and the parties involved didn't have the least bit of say in it."

"Sounds delightful," the captain noted.

"Funny thing was, I kind of liked it. I liked it a lot, in fact. Of course, if I'd been paired with someone other than Clay, I might not have. But I was." Jocelyn smiled. "So there I was, tripping the light fantastic with old Clay, and this other girl comes along. I forget her name now, but she was prettier than I was. And taller. And when she smiled at a boy, it was a sure bet he'd smile back."

"She smiled at Clay?" Kirk guessed.

"Sure as blazes," she said. "And not thinking I was looking, he grinned like a raccoon with his nose in a picnic basket. But I *was* looking. And let me tell you, I didn't appreciate it very much."

"You stormed off?" the captain suggested.

"In the proverbial huff," she expanded. "Naturally, Clay came after me, protesting that I hadn't seen what I thought I'd seen, and even if I had it was probably just a tic. But I wasn't buying it. I was mad. And when a Darnell got mad in those days, people knew to watch out."

"What did you do?" asked Kirk, genuinely curious by now.

"What I did," Jocelyn told him, "is head for where the wallflowers always congregated, under the chronometer. I take it you had wallflowers where you came from?"

"A few," the captain reported. Hell, he'd even been one, once upon a time. But this wasn't his story, so he let it go at that.

"Well," said Jocelyn, "we had more than our share. Nice boys too, just a little shy is all. Anyway, I marched right over to the lot of them and grabbed the nearest one."

"Could that have been Bones?" Kirk inquired.

"It could have been," she agreed. "But the fact is, it wasn't. He was the second boy I grabbed, after the first one fainted dead away. And judging by the way your friend was looking at me, all wide-eyed and waxy-pale and all, I had a feeling he was going to swoon too."

"But he didn't?"

"No," Jocelyn reported. "Thankfully, he stayed on his feet and let me lead him onto the dance floor. And in front of Clay and everyone else, I danced with him. It was a slow song too, but I didn't care. I was making a statement, for god's sake. I was asserting my independence—and boy, did it feel good."

"What about Bones?" the captain wondered.

She thought about it for a moment. "I think it felt pretty good to him too." Reflecting for a moment more, she said, "No, I'm sure of it. He wasn't smiling or anything, probably because he was so intent on avoiding my feet. But I knew he liked it all right, because when the song was over, he asked me to stay on the dance floor with him."

Kirk smiled, caught up in the innocent, awkward emotions that were woven through the story. "Don't tell me you said no," he entreated.

Jocelyn shook her head. "I said yes. And not because I

266

wanted to make Clay jealous, though that had certainly been foremost on my mind in the beginning. It was because of the expression on Leonard's face, sort of sweet and trusting and hopeful all at once. And, of course, the color of his eyes. Even today, I don't believe I've ever seen a more beautiful shade of blue."

"And Clay," the captain noted, "was no doubt getting angrier by the minute."

"By the second," she corrected. "He was trying to keep it from showing, trying to make it seem like he didn't care that I was dancing with someone else, particularly one of the wallflowers. But if I didn't know better, I would've sworn there was steam coming out of his ears.

"Anyway, I asked my dance partner what his name was, and he told me it was Leonard McCoy. He said he and his family were new in town, so I probably hadn't heard of him. He was right; I hadn't. On the other hand, he knew my name. In fact, he confessed, he'd seen me around school. But he never expected he'd get the chance to dance with me, much less be *asked* to do so."

Kirk thought he knew what came next. A long walk in the shadow of some peach trees, an exchange of heartfelt secrets, a moonlit idyll. He was dead wrong.

"That's when Clay spun him around, hauled off, and punched him right in the nose," said Jocelyn. Her forehead creased with the memory. "I don't know who was more shocked, Leonard or myself. All I remember is Clay grabbing my hand and pulling me away, muttering something about me coming to my senses. I tried to get free, but Clay was strong, and he had had just about enough of my antics. Oh, I suppose he would have let go if I'd screamed or something, but I wasn't about to make a scene that my parents would hear about."

The captain shook his head. "But then, you and Bones . . . ?"

"I'll get to that in a second," his companion promised. "So there I was, being dragged away like some cavewoman. And there was Clay, fit to be tied over what he perceived as a punishment he didn't deserve. In our anger with each other, we'd both pretty much forgotten about the boy I was dancing with. But Leonard hadn't forgotten about *us*.

"There was a sound like a branch cracking in a windstorm and suddenly Clay was sitting on his rump, holding his hand to his mouth. And my dance partner was standing over him, eyes blazing, nose and knuckles bleeding, ready to go at my antagonist again if need be. *My* antagonist, not his. Leonard didn't even seem to notice that his nose was swelling up like a great big old cherry blossom. All he cared about was that someone had offended his lady fair. He was like some noble knight, come to defend my honor."

Kirk couldn't help but be reminded of the amusement-park planet in the Omicron Delta region and the Black Knight McCoy had encountered there. He cringed at the thought of the doctor lying on the greensward, dealt an apparently lethal blow by the Black Knight's lance.

"I know," said Jocelyn, mistaking his expression for a reaction to her story. "I know. It still makes me shudder a little to think about it." She took a breath, let it out. "Perhaps needless to say, I was enchanted by the whole scene. When you're a young woman, having two men fighting over you the way Leonard and Clay were fighting was the height of ego gratification. And besides, Clay was in need of a comeuppance after the way he'd behaved."

The captain looked at her. "You mean you let them continue to go at it?"

Her eyes widened. "Are you crazy? Of course not. Clay would have killed him. So I very quickly stepped between them and made it clear I wasn't moving until they withdrew to opposite ends of the room."

"A wise course," Kirk observed.

"I thought so, too. And by then we were the focus of attention, so I had some help from the other kids in separating the combatants. Clay and Leonard went off to lick their respective wounds, though they didn't stop glaring at one another. Or glancing at me, to see what I would do next.

"It was only then that I realized I had a choice to make, and a big one. Should I go home with Clay as expected, considering he was the one who brought me to the dance in the first place? Or should I throw the town gossipmongers for a loop and take the arm of the awkward-looking boy who'd defended my honor at the risk of a serious pummeling?"

"I'm betting you chose the latter," said the captain.

"You're betting right," Jocelyn confirmed. "I went home with Leonard, much to poor Clay's dismay and chagrin and the consternation of not only the Treadways but the Darnells."

"Your family didn't like McCoy?" asked the captain.

Jocelyn shook her head. "Not in the least. You have to understand the way it was when I was a girl. In many ways, the South hadn't changed since before the Civil War. There was still an aristocracy in towns like ours, a caste of kinship groups who had been living there for what seemed like forever and liked it that way. And those people preferred that their children marry their friends' children, the way they always had and—unless the Earth fell to some kind of alien invasion—always would."

"A closed society," Kirk observed. "I've seen plenty of

them on other worlds. I just didn't know they still existed on Earth."

His companion grunted. "Not so much anymore," she said. "But they exist, all right. A family like the McCoys, nice as they were and as well-to-do, weren't good enough for the Darnells or the Treadways or any of the others who traveled in their social circles. They were outsiders, inferior somehow. And here I was, going out with one of them. It didn't sit well with my parents or a lot of other people.

"But that didn't stop me. In some ways, I guess, it spurred me on. I kept on seeing Leonard. Mind you, Clay tried to change my mind, tried constantly. It seemed like he'd never give up, and I guess some part of me was flattered by that. But I never led him on. As far as I was concerned, I was Leonard McCoy's girl and that was that.

"It went on that way all through high school. Then came college. By that time Leonard had decided he wanted to be a doctor like his father, and Lord knew he had the grades for it. He was the brightest young man I knew. The only question was whether he'd go away to school or stay close to home.

"Dr. McCoy—his father, I mean—told him to go away. He said that with the affinity he'd demonstrated for medicine, Leonard could have his pick of any school on Earth. I wasn't telling him anything. In my head, I knew that his father was probably right. But in my heart, I was afraid that if he went away, he would find someone else and never come back."

"But he didn't go away," the captain noted. "He stuck around."

"He stuck around, all right. For *me*. Because he was just as afraid as I was—but not that he'd be the one to lose interest, of course. He was afraid that if he left me alone with Clay, I'd eventually give in to his charms and go back to him."

Jocelyn paused for a moment, lost in some private thought, too private even for a confession, perhaps. Then, with a deep breath, she plunged on.

"Funny," she said. "The way it worked out, he might as well have been away. With all the studying he did, I hardly saw him anyway. There were nights when I had to go to the library and physically drag him out just to shove a little food down his throat." A pause. "I was going to college too, but I didn't take it as seriously as he did. I can't even remember anymore what it was I was studying, except it was easy to get a degree in it. In those days I didn't want to be anything more than some wonderful man's wife, and that wasn't something you could learn about in school.

"Anyway, one night when I went to haul him out of the library, he wasn't at his usual table. I looked for him everywhere, asked people who knew him, even called his parents' house. But no Leonard. Confused and more than a little worried, I finally went home. And as I went up the steps in front of the house, I almost tripped over him in the dark." Her eyes shone with sudden sentiment. "The goon had gone out and gotten me an engagement ring," she explained. "When my parents told him I wasn't around, he'd decided to wait for me, and he'd been waiting for the last couple of hours."

For a little while, Jocelyn was silent. Kirk respected that and did nothing to mar the stillness.

"I accepted," she added at last. "As you may have guessed. A couple of months later, we were married."

Cor Lakandir had grown up on a crowded sea coast where the sun was always hot and a boy's biggest concern was finding some shade. He wasn't used to places like this, cold places where the wind rasped at one's face with frigid fury.

Of course, the northern mountains had their good points, too. They offered the kind of sprawling, blue-white vistas that Cor could only have imagined a couple of years earlier. And they scoured the mind along with the skin, creating a clarity that suited his assassin's temperament.

"Andrachis is wrong," said Cor's friend and fellow sentry, a youth named Marn Silariot. "The captives should be killed like our other enemies."

Cor shrugged. "The High Assassin represents tradition. And tradition dictates that we allow the offworlders to remain alive."

Marn made a sound of disgust. "Andrachis and his friends are still living in the time of the wars. They think they know the Federation, but what they know is forty years old. Who knows how the offworlders may have changed in that span?"

"I have asked that question myself," Cor admitted. "Not in public, of course. And I have not come up with a satisfactory answer." He scanned the shelf that stretched for kilometers from the entrance to their lair. "On the other hand, their behavior during the encounter supports the master's assessment of them. Even when one of them fell dead, they did not retaliate with killing force. Their weapons only dazed us."

"It could be that their weapons were not capable of doing more," Marn suggested. "Or perhaps they had no time to change the setting to something lethal."

Cor grunted. "Then that says something about them too, does it not? That they would bring weapons capable only of stunning their enemies? Or if their weapons could kill, that they would not employ a killing setting to begin with?" He shook his head. "In this respect, I believe Andrachis was correct."

The other Ssana smiled. "In *this* respect?" he echoed.

Cor nodded. "Perhaps in this respect only." He turned to his companion. "Since when do assassins kill only the strong? Or those bent on lethal violence? We kill because that is our nature, because it is our place in life to do so."

"Then you agree that the captives should die?" asked Marn. "Despite the High Assassin's arguments to the contrary?"

The wind blew down the mountainside, bringing with it granular snow that shone in the sunshine like tiny jewels. Cor could feel the snow prick his face like a thousand tiny knives.

Off in the distance, a couple of dark V-shapes appeared against the sky. Uterra, he mused, seeking their daily prey.

Cor frowned. "Yes," he said at last. "I agree that they should die."

Marn clapped him on the shoulder. "I thought so. So, what will we do about it? Sit around the fire and talk ourselves breathless or act on our convictions?"

Indeed, what would they do? Cor knew where this conversation was headed. But was he ready to take that step? To oppose Andrachis in such a manner that their ranks would be split by it? And to risk substantial bloodshed by doing so?

On the other hand, could he stand by and watch while the High Assassin led them in the direction of weakness? Was it not their duty to wrest the reins of leadership from Andrachis, to guide the movement in the direction of strength and courage?

When Cor first came to these mountains, one of the

earliest to do so, his allegiance to the master had been unshakable. But times had changed. He had grown up—as an assassin and as a Ssana.

"Well?" Marn searched his eyes for an answer.

Cor gave him one. "We act," he said.

As if in response, the wind whistled ominously down the mountainside. But whether it approved or disapproved of his decision Cor could not tell.

"I liked being married to Leonard McCoy," said Jocelyn. "And I liked it even better when Joanna arrived. Of course, we were only twenty-one at the time. We hadn't planned on her and we didn't know the first thing about being parents. But somehow or other we learned."

For a moment, Kirk thought about his own son, lost at the hands of the Klingons back on the Genesis planet. He wished he had been there to raise David, to watch him grow. But that chance was long past, and no amount of regret would ever restore it to him.

Unaware of the captain's ruminations, his companion went on. "That was the happiest time of my life," she confessed. "The three of us had our own little world, insulated from everyday realities. Who cared about a major swing in our world's politics when Joanna was starting to turn over on her belly? Who gave a damn about a first encounter with some alien race when our daughter was about to cut her first tooth?"

Jocelyn leaned back against the cavern wall and smiled wistfully. "The happiest time," she echoed. "Too bad it didn't last all that long. Two years, maybe three. Then Leonard started immersing himself in his studies again. He said that it was getting harder and harder to keep up. They were getting into exophysiology, exoimmunology, exothis and exothat. It all sounded very exotic, very difficult. I had no trouble believing it was hard work to comprehend it all.

"But that wasn't much consolation when Joanna and I would look at one another across the dinner table and wonder when Leonard was going to come home that night. Actually, she handled it better than I did. When her father finally did stagger in the door, she was gladder to see him than if he'd been around all day. Absence makes the heart grow fonder, they say. In my case, however, it as often as not made the heart grow cold."

"It couldn't have been easy," observed Kirk. "I've seen plenty of relationships fall by the wayside because one or both parties involved couldn't tear themselves away from their work." He paused. "In fact, I was in such a relationship."

Except that he and Carol had at long last put aside their careers and turned their attentions to one another. Had fate allowed them to do that, only to pluck the captain away at the last minute? Could even *fate* be that cruel?

"Then perhaps you have some idea of what it was like," Jocelyn went on. "The loneliness. The feeling that you have to raise a child all by yourself. The resentment when you finally do get hold of some time together, and all he wants to talk about is his work and all the good he'll do when med school is over. Not about the vacations he's going to take with his family or the evenings he's going to spend with his wife but the career he's got planned." She sighed. "Fortunately, I had little Joanna around to keep me company. It kept me from finding out how miserable I truly was."

Jocelyn frowned, as if grappling with something. "That's when Clay came back into the picture," she said. "He'd moved out of town for a while, to go to some fancy northern college—not that he'd ever had much interest in learning, but the Treadways had gone to that school for several generations, and he wasn't going to be the first to break with tradition.

"Anyway, I hadn't seen him since my wedding day. But one afternoon, I was taking Joanna for a walk in the park. We were going to feed the ducks and she was carrying a little bag full of old, crusty bread she'd saved up. But as we passed the tennis courts, she dropped the bag and the bread fell out on the grass.

"Before we knew it, a flock of pigeons had descended and were pecking away at the grass, eating all of Joanna's bread. She started to cry as loud and hard as can be, and I didn't know whether to try to shoo the pigeons or comfort her or pull my hair out of my head in clumps. Suddenly the birds took off as quickly as they'd arrived, frightened by something that had come up behind us. As I turned around, I saw this tanned, handsome man in tennis whites standing over us with his racket in his hand."

It wasn't hard to guess the identity of Jocelyn's savior. "Clay," said Kirk.

"Clay," his companion confirmed. "Bigger than life and twice as unexpected. He smiled at me, then at Joanna, then at me again. And he knelt down there on the grass while his tennis partner waited less than patiently, and he helped us collect all the bread the pigeons hadn't gotten to."

"Nice of him," remarked the captain.

"Very nice," Jocelyn agreed. "He asked me how Leonard and I were doing, and I told him we were doing fine. But Clay knew me well enough to hear the discontent in my voice. He was too much like me to believe I could be happy sitting home all the time while my husband pored over medical texts in some library.

"On the surface, though, he didn't take issue with anything I said. He just patted Joanna on the shoulder, told me it was pleasant to see me again, and returned to his tennis game. He couldn't have been any more of a gentleman if his life had depended on it."

Kirk felt a queasiness in his gut. But he let his companion go on without interruption.

"It was fine to see Clay again after all that time. Like a breath of fresh air to someone who had had the windows closed too long. I almost felt guilty for thinking about him that way. So guilty, in fact, that meeting Clay was the first thing I told Leonard about when he walked in the door that evening. But he barely seemed to hear me. In his mind, I think, he was off on another planet, performing an emergency appendectomy on some strange but sentient life form. One thing was for sure, he wasn't in that kitchen with me.

"A few days later, I got a call from Clay in the middle of the day. He wanted to know if I could get away to play some tennis with him. I told him I couldn't, of course. My parents were out of town and there was no one to watch Joanna. Seeing the reason in that, he said he'd try again some other time.

"Weeks went by, however, and he didn't call. I was beginning to wish I'd found a way to take him up on that first invitation. After all, it would have been a lot more fun than playing jacks with a five-year-old. Or listening to your husband mutter medical inanities into your ear instead of sweet nothings.

"Finally, when summer was all but over, Clay tried again. And this time I was ready. I grabbed my racket, packed Joanna off to my parents' house, and made a beeline for the park. When I got to the tennis courts, Clay was there waiting for me, tall and dark, and grinning with those perfect teeth of his. He made me feel so young, as if we were kids playing hooky from school."

The feeling in the captain's gut was getting more and more unpleasant. But he managed to keep his mouth shut, to let Jocelyn go on.

"I've got no proof that he let me beat him that day, but I'm pretty sure of it nonetheless. After all, I hadn't played the game in a couple of years, and that had been with Leonard, who wasn't much for games of physical prowess. In any case, I took two out of three sets, and it felt great. Not just to win, but to sweat, to feel the sunshine on my skin, to have somebody pay attention to me for once.

"Clay wanted to take me out for a late lunch to show he wasn't a sore loser, but I didn't think that would be such a good idea. People might see us and start to talk, and that wouldn't do at all. So I asked him to just take me home, if he didn't mind. He didn't, of course.

"It felt funny to have Clay dropping me off at the door. Just like back in high school. But we weren't kids anymore. It didn't seem right for me to just send him off without so much as a glass of iced tea. And besides, I was hungry for adult company. I didn't want the afternoon to end quite yet. So I invited him in."

Kirk squirmed. He could see where this was leading, and he desperately didn't want it to go there. But he had no choice. He was just along for the ride.

"For the last forty years," Jocelyn told him, "I've tried to remember who made the first move, who initiated what came afterward. And I can't. Maybe it doesn't matter. But Clay's visit didn't end with a glass of iced tea. It became much more than that. I didn't plan it, at least I think I didn't. But it happened anyway, Lord help me. It happened anyway."

The muscles in the captain's stomach knotted painfully. It was almost as if it wasn't Bones she had cheated on, but him. And there was more. He could see it in her eyes as the candlelight searched out the truth in them.

"Unfortunately," she went on, "it was that afternoon that Leonard decided to come home early and surprise me with a bouquet of flowers. I was surprised all right." Her hand came up to her mouth as she relived the memory. "We both were. No—make that all three of us."

McCoy looked up at Clay and Spock, who were working their way along the ropes above him, their breath coming in frozen puffs. The descent was going more slowly than they had hoped. The three of them were still quite a distance from their destination and the day was beginning to wear thin.

No matter what, they didn't dare remain out here after nightfall. It would be too difficult to find hand- and footholds in the rock and too cold to take advantage of the ones they could find. Nor could they use any kind of artificial light source, as it would be too easily spotted by the inevitable sentries at the base of the slope.

The doctor's reverie was shattered by a dark blur in the corner of his eye and the sound of something big and leathery flapping in the wind. He turned just in time to catch a glimpse of a long, open beak and several sharp rows of carnivorous teeth before the thing was on top of him.

Uterra, he thought. The pterodactyl-headed, winged predator of the northern mountains. Until now he'd only seen the things at a distance; he wished that were still the case.

Lashing out as hard as he could, he backhanded the flyer across the side of its head. It screamed so loud McCoy thought his ears would burst, but it didn't give up.

Before he could gain his balance for a second blow, it had sunk its claws into the thick fabric of his jacket.

The thing tugged at him, trying to drag him away from the slope. It was big, as big as he was, with a wingspan twice his height. The uterra was strong, too, stronger than anything the doctor had ever wished to encounter at this height with only a single wedge separating him from a crushing death on the rocks below.

Just above, he could hear the shrill cry of its mate, plucking at one of his companions. Unfortunately, McCoy had his hands too full to offer them any help. He found himself gagging on the creature's fetid breath, rank with the smell of raw meat as it opened its jaws wide.

FOUR

☆

McCoy kicked out at the uterra's ravening beak and clung desperately to the rope in his thermo-gauntleted grip. The thing squawked and tried another angle. The doctor kicked again, buying himself another second or two.

He used that time to see how the others were doing. A little farther up the slope, Clay was hanging by one hand, groping for the phaser inside his Starfleet jacket with the other. He didn't seem half as agitated as McCoy, though.

Of course not, thought the doctor. The man didn't have any good reason to hurry. What did it matter to Clay Treadway if McCoy became some leathery predator's dinner? It would only make his life that much simpler.

"Get away from me, blast you!" he snarled at the winged carnivore. "Go find something else to peck at!"

But the thing wouldn't listen. With frantic intensity, it clawed at him, ripping the outside layer of his cold-weather garb to shreds. And for all his efforts to deal it a stunning blow, the creature seemed not even to notice.

Finally, it accomplished what it had been trying to do all along: it got a firm grip on his jacket. Flapping fiercely with its huge, batlike wings, it did its best to tug him away from the smooth rock surface.

McCoy didn't want to let go. He didn't want to be dropped from a dizzying height, the way a seagull might drop a big old clam, so some Ssani bird could pick his bones clean at its leisure. But he could only hold on for so long using his hands alone. They were already starting to cramp, to lose their grip. . . .

Abruptly, there was a flash of something narrow and bright red, something that hit the uterra with sledgehammer force. The flyer writhed under the impact and made the air shiver with the violence of its scream. More important, the doctor was free again.

Looking up as he gratefully entangled his leg in his rope, McCoy saw that Clay had found his phaser pistol and was trying to keep it trained on the darting predator. But the uterra was too fast, too unpredictable in its flight, and the diplomat couldn't seem to adjust quickly enough.

Without warning the thing took a right turn and slammed directly into Clay, flattening him against the slope and sending his phaser flying out of his grasp. He clutched at it, but it was too late. And while he was stunned, off-balance, the creature came at him a second time.

With a cry of pain, the diplomat hit the rocky surface and seemed to bounce off, his grip on the rope negated by the savagery of the uterra's attack. And before McCoy knew it, Clay was plummeting past him to his death.

The doctor didn't think. He just reached out and

grabbed. As luck would have it, his gloved fingers closed on the other man's wrist.

Unfortunately, Clay was a big man, heavier than most, and McCoy had never had the impulse to build up his muscles. As it was, the shock of bearing the diplomat's weight nearly ripped the doctor's arm off at the shoulder.

"My God!" groaned McCoy, enduring agony worse than anything he'd encountered on Rura Penthe. His bicep screamed with pain, as if it had been torn to shreds and was tearing still. He gritted his teeth, shut his eyes tight, and saw streaks of red lightning carve a path across the inside of his eyelids.

For a moment he thought he would pass out. He could hear his blood banging like a hammer in his ears, feel a wave of ice water trying to separate him from consciousness. But somehow, despite it all, he held on.

"Don't let go!" bellowed Clay. "Dammit, McCoy, don't you dare let go!"

He sounded far away, well beyond the tightly focused universe in which the doctor strove against unbelievable torment. McCoy was sorely tempted to release his burden and end the punishment, but he couldn't do that. He couldn't let a man die—any man—if it was within his power to prevent it. "Much as I want to," McCoy gritted his teeth and rasped, "I'm not going to drop you, Clay. Don't worry."

But the panic in Treadway's eyes didn't subside one iota.

And then his fingers began to slip. Not the ones that held Clay, but the ones wrapped around the rope that supported them both. Cursing, the doctor tried to tighten his grip, but it was no use. Slowly, inexorably, they slid down the slope, the diplomat's weight doing its best to be the death of them.

"Hang on," McCoy grunted. "Hang on, damn it."

But no matter how much he chastised himself, the rope continued to snake through his fingers. Another couple of feet and they'd be at the end of it. And after that . . . a cruel and grisly doom.

Unless the doctor lightened his load. Wasn't that the only sane thing to do? To let go of Clay and save himself? Why should they both die when one of them could live?

Yet there were times when two minus one didn't leave one. It left something less—some fraction that couldn't live with itself, not after the oath McCoy had taken all those years ago. He would rather die, he thought, than give in to that kind of arithmetic. No matter what, he wasn't letting go.

Not even when the rope continued to slide through his fingers. Not even when he felt something pop in the shoulder that was supporting Clay, firing up spasms of red-hot anguish. Not even when he started to see death as something welcome, a relief from his insupportable suffering.

Down below, the diplomat's face was caught in a rictus of fear. He must have known what his rival was going through to keep him from falling, but he obviously thought it was preferable to the alternative.

Through eyes that could barely see for the tears in them, the doctor watched the rope continue to run through his trembling fingers until there was barely anything left of it. Another hand's breadth and it would slither out of his grasp altogether.

And then he noticed something else, something big and dark and leathery looking. The uterra, he thought. It's coming back for another shot at us.

Thing is, it could save itself the effort. In a second or

two we'll be easy pickings at the bottom of the slope anyway.

But just as he told himself that, a thin, red phaser beam slammed the creature full in the chest. With a strangled cry, it half-swooped and half-plummeted away from the slope.

McCoy looked up and saw the source of the intervention. It was Spock. Of course. Who else but the Vulcan had that kind of timing?

Too bad, the doctor mused. Spock could have saved himself the effort as well. He heard a scraping above him, a twanging of the rope against the rocky surface. And then, despite his best efforts, the last of his lifeline wriggled out of his cramped and clawlike hand.

For a split second, he and Clay seemed to hug the slope, to be suspended in a limbo of neither here nor there. Then gravity seemed to remember they existed and exerted its pull on them, dragging them down to their ultimate destruction.

But before they could go very far, McCoy felt something grab him by the wrist of his still outstretched hand. It was a very strong something, and in some ways a very familiar something.

There was a jolt in both the doctor's shoulders as Clay's weight pulled his arms taut. Gritting his teeth against the pain, McCoy looked up to see if his suspicions were correct.

They were.

"Spock," he gasped.

"Do not speak," the Vulcan advised him. "Save your strength."

He was hanging on to the rope with his left hand and the doctor's wrist with his right, his arms outstretched as McCoy's had been. But instead of supporting one person, he was supporting two. How long even Spock could keep that up, the human had no idea.

Before he could wonder for very long, the Vulcan began to shift his position. Wrapping his leg around the rope, he let go with his left hand and used his right hand to pluck a wedge from one of his jacket pockets.

Finding a tiny fissure in the slope, Spock drove the wedge in as hard as he could. Not nearly hard enough to make it dependable, of course, but it was a start. Rummaging in his jacket again, the Vulcan removed a second wedge and hammered at the first one, forcing it deeper into the fissure. Again. And again.

Then, his facial muscles showing the toll all this was taking on him, Spock reached into a third pocket and produced a coil of rope. Tying it around the wedge with one hand, he tugged on it as a test. It held.

Only then did the Vulcan let the line trail down the face of the slope, where not only McCoy could grab hold of it but Clay as well. Seconds later the doctor felt the diplomat's weight taken off his tormented arm. His shoulder still hurt, but at least it wasn't threatening to tear loose of its moorings any longer.

Swinging his arm around as best he could, McCoy wrapped his numbed and bloodless fingers around the rope. Then, without even waiting for Spock to let go of his wrist, he latched on with his other hand as well.

Pressing his face against the slope, the doctor took a deep, tremulous breath. "You're a damn miracle worker, ya know that, Spock?" McCoy was halfway between laughter and tears.

"Please, Doctor," the Vulcan said, clearly embarrassed by McCoy's show of emotion.

The doctor didn't care, really. Even the cliff's rocky surface felt good against his hot, sweaty cheek.

He was safe. *Safe.* He wasn't going to die—at least not yet. And, thanks to his unrelenting will, he thought as he glanced downslope, neither was Clay Treadwell.

There were three candles burning in the long, narrow alcove Andrachis had claimed for himself as a sleeping place. Set into niches in the rock, the candles had been placed at the disparate heights required by tradition: the lowest to signify the death that preceded life, the middle to signify life itself, and the highest to signify the death that came after life.

As Ars Rondorrin entered the alcove, Andrachis noted with satisfaction how the older man inclined his head toward the highest candle. After all, the death that came after life was the birthright of every Ssana. It was from this vine that all assassin ideology hung, like a cluster of sweet, deadly fruit.

"Well met, old dagger," said the master.

Rondorrin smiled grimly. "Well met, tir-Andrachis." He used the title of respect, though he alone, of all the assassins gathered in the caverns, could have avoided it if he had wished. It was an indication that he had come on serious business.

"What is on your mind?" asked Andrachis.

The other Ssana glanced over his shoulder, to make sure no one was within earshot. Then he turned again to the master.

"I have heard a great many stories in my life," he replied. "Some have been to my liking. Others have not." His indigo eyes narrowed meaningfully. "The ones I hear now I like perhaps least of all."

Andrachis sighed. *Stories* could only mean rumors, the kind that would not be repeated in the presence of the assassins' leader, though someone like Rondorrin might have access to them. And if Rondorrin had not liked them, the master had a feeling he would not like them either.

"What sort of stories?" he inquired pointedly.

His visitor grunted. "Tales of death," he answered. "The demise of a great leader, before his time."

The master assassin frowned. He knew what Rondorrin was talking about, and he was not altogether surprised. He had not expected their patched-together movement to hold forever; nonetheless, it was infuriating. More than that, it was ridiculous. For all his hard work, Andrachis was to be cast aside like a worn-out sheath.

No, he told himself. Not if I can help it.

"Who desires this?" he demanded.

Rondorrin chewed the name for a moment, as if it were the marrow of a uterra bone. Then he spat it out: "Lakandir. The firebrand."

Lakandir, thought Andrachis. Of course. Who else would have had the courage, the ability to gather others around him? Who but Lakandir would have dared?

It was a pity such fine traits were matched with such an unwise purpose. A great pity, the master mused. For now he would have to seek another to train as his successor.

"I regret having to bring you this news," Rondorrin said. "I know in what esteem you held him."

Andrachis shrugged. "Assassins come, assassins go, eh, old blade? As good as Lakandir was, there will be one better. All I need do is wait."

But he did not sound confident, even to himself. For all he knew, all those who would ever flock to him had already done so. And even if their ranks swelled tenfold, he might never find a protégé with the potential of a Cor Lakandir.

Unfortunately, he did not have the option of sparing

the youth. Rebellion was dealt with swiftly and surely. That was another of the assassins' unwritten laws—a tradition, like all the others, that only the most foolish Ssana would fail to follow.

"They have a plan," Rondorrin informed him. "One that is to be carried out in the morning, just before your accustomed time of waking. There will be eight of them, as far as I can tell. And when it is over, Lakandir will be the new master."

"Unless," Andrachis amended, "I am ready for them with some allies of my own." He thought about it, then nodded. "Gather ten Ssana you can trust. And when my young friend comes calling tomorrow, I will do him the honor of killing him before any of his accomplices."

Rondorrin inclined his head. "As you wish, Master." And with a gesture of respect to the highest candle, he disappeared into the darkness.

"Don't judge me too harshly," said Jocelyn.

Kirk grunted. "To be honest, that's a little difficult, considering I know the people you're talking about. And Bones in particular."

She frowned. "I'm not trying to deflect any responsibility for what I did. Lord knows, I was wrong. Horribly wrong. But I won't take all the blame for the circumstances that led up to it. Leonard has to accept his role in them as well."

The captain nodded. His companion was right about that. Infidelity usually didn't just happen. It was the culmination of a lot of things. A lot of imposed loneliness, a lot of miscommunication, a lot of forgetting the reasons two people came together in the first place. And it sounded like Bones was guilty of at least some of that.

"In any case," she continued, "the rest is sort of a blur.

I remember Leonard turning white as a cotton ball, his mouth making words without sounds. I remember him dropping the flowers he'd brought me and staggering out of the room. And I remember feeling as if someone had taken hold of my heart and was squeezing as hard as he could.

"I threw something on and ran after him. I didn't know what I was going to say, what I could say, but I ran. Of course, I wasn't fast enough. By the time I got to the front door, he was pulling away, leaving a cloud of dust in the driveway. Somehow I knew he wouldn't be coming back. Not ever."

Kirk watched as tears stood out in Jocelyn's eyes and began to run down her face. He must have moved to take her hand, to comfort her, because she held up a hand to stop him.

"It's all right," she told him. "I just need a moment to collect myself."

A moment later, she shuddered and was herself again. Wiping away some of the tears, she took a deep breath.

"Lord," said Jocelyn. "I've had that on my conscience for forty years. It sure felt good to tell someone about it."

The captain winced. To carry something like that around for so long . . . he didn't envy the woman. But for that matter, he didn't envy Bones either. He'd been carrying something around just as long, hadn't he? And he was carrying it still.

"That was when he joined Starfleet," his companion explained. "Blinded by the pain I'd inflicted on him, crushed beneath its terrible weight, he wanted to get as far away as he could. At least, I guess he did. I never actually knew the details."

Kirk did. But this was her confession, not his. Even now he was reluctant to betray any confidences.

Maybe Jocelyn perceived this, because she didn't press him for any information. She just went on with her story.

"The hardest part for him must have been leaving Joanna. He loved that little girl like the Georgia sun loves its red-clay soil. But he knew that he and I weren't going to be together anymore, and it wouldn't have been good for her to see us struggle for control of her. So he just let me have her, no questions asked."

She muttered a curse beneath her breath, swearing not at McCoy but at herself. "And I had to explain to her why her daddy was gone. Not just for the day or the evening, but maybe for a very long time, and how it wasn't his fault he hadn't said good-bye. I did my best to make it seem like a brave and noble thing he had done, a thing Joanna could only be proud of. And if she suspected that it was something else that had sent him out to the stars, she put on a pretty good act.

"From that point on, my life turned upside-down. My husband was out in deep space somewhere. I was a single parent now in fact as well as in theory. We were all right financially, because Leonard had Starfleet send us most of his salary. But Joanna and I were easy prey for the wolves."

The captain shook his head. "The wolves?"

Jocelyn nodded. "My family. The Darnells. They'd always thought Leonard was no good, and now they had proof of it. He'd run away to chase his selfish dreams and left his family to fend for itself. Or at least, that's what they gathered, and I didn't have the nerve to tell them the truth. My parents insisted that Joanna and I move in with them, and after a while, no longer being the iron-willed specimen I was in my youth, I agreed.

"It was a while before Clay dared show his face again. What had happened between us would have been the

291

biggest scandal our town had seen in years, and he was too much of a gentleman to drag my name through the mud if he could at all help it. So he'd laid low for a while, waiting for things to settle down. Then, one day, he came knocking at my parents' door.

"It was almost as if we were back in high school and he was taking me to some silly dance. Except we were both older and wiser, and I had Joanna to think about now. Clay and I went on walks together, met for lunch, took in a play every now and then. It was all very genteel, very restrained. And then, one afternoon at the zoo, he told me he wanted more."

Jocelyn's features seemed to soften with the memory. "By then," she said, "so did I. And it didn't seem right to continue masquerading as Leonard McCoy's wife when nothing could be farther from the truth. So I sent a message to my husband that I wanted a divorce. His consent came a week later, by subspace packet. And the next day, it was official. Our marriage had been stricken from the record, as if it had never existed in the first place."

She scowled. "It must have hurt Leonard a great deal to give his consent to that. Hell, I had to have known it would hurt him when I asked. But it didn't matter to me when I compared it to my own loneliness, my own sense of incompleteness. I was the only one that really mattered, wasn't I? It had always been that way, ever since I was a child." She chuckled bitterly. "That was the trouble with our southern brand of chivalry. It turned women into useless objects of desire, and I was the prime example.

"But when I received notice that our divorce had come through, something about it stopped me in my tracks. Maybe it was the finality of it, I don't know. But it made me very, very sad. And I vowed then and there that I wouldn't become involved with anyone—Clay included —until I had come to grips with the flaws in my character that had led me to destroy my marriage."

"A wise move," Kirk remarked.

"A wise move indeed," agreed Jocelyn. "Naturally, Clay wasn't too happy about it. He told me I was making a mistake, that I was throwing out a second chance for happiness. But I stuck to my guns, and it was the best decision I ever made. The first thing I did to celebrate was move out of my parents' house. Then I went back to school and enrolled in courses. And this time, I really studied, mostly at night so I could spend time with Joanna. And I made something of myself."

She had, too. The captain recalled it vividly.

"You know the rest," she told him. "How, after Joanna grew up a little, Leonard came back to remind her she had a father. How he and I almost had a rapprochement shortly after that but couldn't make it work. And how another thirty years or so went by without our saying so much as a word to each other." Jocelyn shook her head. "All that time, Clay kept courting me. He wouldn't take no for an answer, no matter how many times I turned him down. But I couldn't marry him. He was vain, shallow, selfish—all the things I had been before I decided to change. Then, about twelve years ago, he decided to go into the diplomatic corps."

"Just like that?" Kirk asked. "Seems like a strange choice for a man who hadn't been out in space before."

"I'd agree with you," she told him, "except Clay had diplomacy in his blood. His grandfather, his father, and two of his aunts had been in the corps. All they had to do was pull a few strings to get Clay a shot at it too."

"So he was a natural?" the captain surmised.

"Not exactly," Jocelyn replied. "In the beginning, he was just all right. He didn't make any mistakes, but he didn't notch any big successes either. Then Clay asked me to accompany him on a mission to Yarnos Seven, where he was mediating a civilized but rather intricate dispute among three separate factions. I only came along because I thought it sounded interesting, but before I knew it I was sitting next to him at the bargaining table. And much to my amazement, it was one of my suggestions that broke the impasse."

"So you got the bug," Kirk said.

"I did at that. With Clay's help, I joined the corps. And once we were working together, and doing such a damned fine job of it, it only seemed to make sense that we should be partners in other respects as well. So we went back to Georgia and got married, just as our families always thought we should. I had finally pleased both the Treadways and the Darnells."

The comment was dripping with sarcasm. "Hadn't you pleased yourself as well?" the captain asked.

Jocelyn met his gaze. "I've come to the conclusion," she informed him, "that I'm not the marrying kind. For a number of years, we were reasonably happy. Then I started getting antsy, just as I had with Leonard forty years earlier. Except this time, I didn't have an inattentive husband to blame for my restlessness, or a less than stimulating intellectual life. I was doing interesting work, I was loved, I had everything anyone could ask for. And yet I still wasn't content. There was something missing."

"And that was?"

She shrugged. "I still don't know to this day. But after what happened up on the ship, I can guess." She licked her lips. "I think I never stopped loving Leonard or feeling guilty about what I had done to him. And until I had resolved those feelings, I just wasn't going to let myself be happy."

Kirk thought about it. "An interesting theory," he concluded.

Jocelyn nodded. "Clay tried to convince me that it was just a phase I was going through, and that I'd come to my senses before long. But the feeling of restlessness didn't go away. It lasted for a year, two years, three. Finally, just a few months ago, I couldn't deny it any longer. I asked Clay for a separation. He said it was out of the question. We were a team. How could he go on with his work without me at his side?

"The work we were doing was important. I knew that. So we compromised. I agreed not to break up the diplomatic team. And he agreed that we would sleep in separate quarters. And until we got to the *Enterprise,* that arrangement seemed to work. Then . . ." His companion shrugged. "Then it *stopped* working."

She peered at the captain across the candlelit space. "Now you know everything," she told him.

It was a great deal more than he had ever wanted to know. More than he had a right to know, he mused. But like it or not, he had heard Jocelyn's confession from beginning to end.

And now, he knew, she wanted him to give her some kind of absolution for what she had done. For the crime of inflicting pain on those she was supposed to have loved— not only McCoy but Clay Treadway as well.

It wasn't an easy thing to do. Bones was his friend, one of the two men he trusted most in all the galaxy. To tell Jocelyn that what she'd done was understandable, was only human, would be to condone the agony and humiliation Leonard McCoy had carried with him for nearly all his adult life.

And yet his friend had considered loving this woman all over again. Despite the horror she'd put him through, despite the long, lonely years spent contemplating his disappointment and his failure. Somehow he had found it in his heart to forgive her.

If Bones were here, he would relieve Jocelyn of her burden of guilt. Could Kirk could do any less in the doctor's place?

He picked his words carefully. "I'm no judge," the captain told her. "No jury. I don't take any satisfaction in assigning blame." He licked his lips. "Things happen sometimes, things that drive people apart. But it's our nature as human beings to remove those things if we can. I think, given time and the right circumstances, that's what my friend would have done—he would have put the past behind him. Because the bigger tragedy would have been to go on hurting and feeling guilty, never knowing that you could still love another."

Jocelyn looked at him. On one hand, he sensed, she knew he was trying to find a way to be kind to her. But on the other hand, she seemed to want to believe every word he said. Which part of her would ultimately win? He couldn't say.

"Thank you," Jocelyn said, in a controlled voice. "That means a lot to me."

FIVE

☆ —————

As it turned out, it was dark already by the time McCoy and his companions reached the icy ledge that hung just over the entrance to the assassins' lair. They couldn't see the inevitable sentries standing guard over the place, but that was good, because the sentries couldn't see them either.

Of course, thought McCoy, as he nursed his painful and pretty much useless arm, it was possible that they *had* been seen, or maybe even heard, despite their efforts to make their descent as quiet as possible. Also, there was the matter of Clay's phaser, which he'd dropped when the uterra dropped *him*.

But they couldn't worry about any of that now. They could only proceed on the assumption that their appearance would come as a surprise to the Ssana.

The Vulcan had been the last one down. As he divested himself of a coil of rope and the wedges they no longer had need of, something in the snow seemed to catch his attention. Leave it to Spock, the doctor mused, to find something "fascinating" even in a place like this.

But a moment later, he understood the first officer's interest. What Spock had discovered was Clay's phaser—a little ice-encrusted but none the worse for wear. Apparently the snow had cushioned the sound of its fall.

His arm hot and throbbing, McCoy hadn't expected to get involved in the assault on the assassins' guards. He wasn't the least bit disappointed in that expectation. Without a second thought, the Vulcan returned Clay's weapon to him and jerked his head to indicate the ledge's forward limits. Hefting the phaser, the diplomat nodded to show he understood.

As Spock approached the brink, he lowered himself to all fours. Clay did the same. At a signal from the Vulcan, both of them took a peek at what was down below. Then they pulled their heads up again.

Spock looked back at the doctor, probably more as a courtesy than anything else. After all, he was still part of the team, even if he wasn't carrying a weapon. The first officer held up two gloved fingers.

Two sentinels blocking their way. Apparently they were unaware of the trio's proximity. It was probably the best situation they could have hoped for.

Turning again to Clay, Spock held up all five fingers now. One by one, he folded them over—a trick only a Vulcan could easily perform. When he'd folded over the last digit, both men peeked past the end of the ledge again and fired their bright red beams.

McCoy heard a moan, then two soft thuds. Judging by the satisfied expression on the diplomat's face, he and Spock had taken the Ssana out with their first shots.

Beckoning for the doctor to follow, the first officer slipped over the snowy brink and temporarily out of sight.

Clay waited, however, to see if McCoy and his damaged arm needed help getting down. Frowning at the thought of needing the other man's help, the doctor advanced to the edge and jumped.

Unfortunately, it was a lot more slippery down below than he'd expected. If Spock hadn't reached out and steadied him, he would have fallen flat on his face. As Clay descended behind them, McCoy turned his attention to the fallen assassins.

They were stretched out before a small, triangular-shaped opening in the rock, their white robes blending in with the white snow. The doctor knelt between them to get a better look, then grunted his approval. No bruises in evidence, but then, there seldom were when you set your phaser on stun. More important, the Ssana would be out for a while.

Without waiting for further comment, the Vulcan led the way into the cave. Clay was right behind him. McCoy brought up the rear.

It was dark inside but not much darker than the moonless night through which they'd descended the last part of the slope. Around a bend was a soft, yellow glow. Moving forward, the trio discovered it to be the light of a single candle, resting in a concavity that seemed almost to have been designed for the purpose.

Clinging to the opposite wall lest they cast discernible shadows, Spock led them into the bowels of the mountain. As it happened, they had no choices to make, since there was only one tunnel that led inward from the cavern mouth. But that also made it more likely that they'd run into someone else coming from the other direction.

Following the passage, concentrating on listening for

the sound of assassin footfalls, the doctor weighed their chances of accomplishing this mission. With the maldinium data Scotty had encoded into Spock's tricorder and their communicators, it might not be all that hard to execute the second part of the plan—the return to the ship. But the first part—determining where in these caverns the assassins were likely to have hidden their captives—was going to be plenty difficult.

Of course, there was always the possibility that they'd arrived too late, that Jim and Jocelyn had already been killed by the Ssana and the best McCoy and his comrades could hope for would be to recover their bodies.

He recalled Li Moboron's words, spoken so long ago in that nightmare of a children's ward, about how assassins didn't kill offworlders. But Li Moboron's philosophy had apparently died when he did or the doctor's friend Merlin Carver might have been alive even today.

Up ahead was another glow. Another candle. Just beyond it, the tunnel widened considerably but remained unbranched. Still, for consistency's sake, the first officer continued to lead them along the same wall.

It almost proved their undoing. One moment Spock was making steady progress, the next he seemed to be losing his balance, grabbing at the almost featureless rock. When Clay reached out and pulled him back a step, the Vulcan seemed to recover.

McCoy didn't dare inquire about the incident out loud. But as he peered around the diplomat, he saw the answer with his own eyes.

There was a hole in front of them, a crevasse that began here at the cavern wall, widened until it consumed nearly the entire width of the passage, and then tapered again at the far end. It had no visible bottom, either, which meant it could have been seven feet deep or seventy. In either case, not the kind of opening Spock would have been eager to stumble into.

Frowning slightly at his close call, the first officer scrutinized the outline of the crevasse as carefully as he could. Then he set out again, skirting it by half a meter or so, and the humans fell in behind him.

Shortly after they passed the hole, the passage narrowed again into something even smaller than before. And just a couple of meters after that, it split into two entirely different corridors, each illuminated by a distant candle.

Which way? Their choice might make the difference between success and failure. Nor was there any real information to help them decide.

In the dim light, the doctor saw Spock cock an eyebrow. This was going to take a gut reaction, McCoy thought, and that was one activity Vulcans normally didn't excel at.

A moment later, the choice was taken out of Spock's hands. The sound of voices came to them from the passageway on the right, voices that seemed to be getting closer with each passing fraction of a second.

Turning to his companions, the Vulcan motioned for them to proceed into the tunnel on the left. Neither the doctor nor Clay wasted any time in complying. Then they waited, holding their respective breaths, phasers at the ready.

The voices grew louder. There was barking laughter. In the corridor the Federation team had just left, shadows appeared and lengthened as the Ssana passed one of the candles McCoy had glimpsed a moment earlier.

More than likely, these were replacements for the pair they'd left stunned at the entranceway. That was good news and bad, all in one package. Good, because they would pass the branching corridor by and keep on going.

And bad, because they would eventually find the unconscious sentries and sound the alarm.

Needless to say, the doctor mused, Spock wouldn't allow that. A moment later, two assassins went by in their white robes, unaware of the intruders' presence in the adjoining passageway, and McCoy's thoughts proved prophetic.

Without warning, the Vulcan fired his phaser. Its ruby red beam slammed one of the assassins against the far wall with stupefying force. As he sank to his knees, the other Ssana whirled, reaching into his robes for whatever weapon he'd concealed there.

But as he drew it out, Clay discharged his own weapon. The spear of phaser energy caught the assassin in the shoulder and spun him around, sending something decidedly sharp and dangerous-looking flying out of his hand.

Still, it didn't have quite the desired effect, because a split second later the Ssana was hurdling his comrade's stunned body and heading back down the passage the way he'd come. If he got away, McCoy knew, their chances of recovering Jim and Jocelyn would be nil.

Fortunately, Spock was nearly as fast as the assassin. Springing after the Ssana, he took aim and fired. As the doctor followed in his wake, he saw that his companion's shot had had the desired effect. The white-robed figure was sprawled face first in the middle of the corridor.

McCoy darted a glance down each of the passageways that radiated from this juncture. There were no signs of any other assassins. He listened. No telltale sound of approaching footsteps.

With luck, the incident would go unnoticed—for a while, anyway. And by then, the doctor hoped, he and his fellow rescuers would have come and gone.

But first things first. Without waiting for the Vulcan to ask, McCoy bent and took hold of the ankle of the nearer Ssana and dragged him toward the lefthand corridor.

Having served with him all these years, the doctor had a pretty good idea of the way Spock's mind worked, Lord help him. He was sure the first officer would take them down the corridor from which the assassins had emerged now that it had been proven there were signs of life at the other end of it.

Signs of life probably meant captives as well. People like these assassins were likely to have kept Jim and Jocelyn in their midst, where they could keep a close eye on them.

And if those signs also held deadly danger for them . . . so what? They knew the job was dangerous when they took it.

In the large cavern that served as sleeping quarters for many of the young assassins, Cor Lakandir sat with his knees clasped to his chest. Soon it would be time.

His blade, close at hand, reflected just the slightest glimmer of distant candlelight. It was the same blade that Andrachis had said was not for cutting meat but only for separating Ssana from their souls. When he used it to separate the High Assassin from *his,* there would be no one to tell him he could not use his weapon as he liked.

In a way, that was a pity. It was good to have someone to tell them of the laws, the traditions, even if they did not necessarily wish to embrace them. Surely Cor himself could not do that. He would have to defer to Ars Rondorrin or one of the other old-timers in such matters.

That is, if they would follow him. More than likely, they would not. They would leave, perhaps form their own cult, possibly even oppose Cor's position as High Assassin by naming one of their own.

There could be a war like the one that took down Li Moboron forty years earlier. Except this time, there were fewer assassins to begin with; their movement could be destroyed utterly.

But that was only a possibility, a chance they would have to take. There was just as good a possibility that, under his young and vigorous leadership, their brotherhood would become stronger than ever.

Besides, what choice did he have? They could not go on following a master whose philosophy had withered and become weak with the passage of time. They needed a leader who would show no pity, give no quarter, whether their enemy was Ssana or not.

At any rate, thought Cor, he had already made his decision. He had given Marn his word. In a little while he would honor Andrachis with a quick and well-deserved death.

Thud.

Kirk turned at the sound, which seemed to have come from the passageway outside their prison cavern. Until now, the only sounds he'd heard were the murmured conversations of their guards and the scrape of footfalls when one of them was relieved by a newcomer.

Thud. Thud.

There it was again. The captain took a couple of steps toward the entrance to listen more closely.

Jocelyn, who'd been staring into the dwindling candle flame, turned to him. "Did you hear something?" she asked.

He nodded. "Two somethings, a second or two apart."

His companion suddenly looked worried, maybe because Kirk looked worried himself. "What do you suppose it could be?"

He shrugged. "I don't know. But I'm going to do my best to find out."

Jocelyn got to her feet and caught up with him. He sighed.

"What do you think you're doing?" the captain inquired.

"I'm coming with you," she told him.

"I'm not so sure that's a good idea," he replied.

"Why?" she asked. "Because if the guards decide to get rough, you're more durable than I am?"

Actually, that was his rationale exactly. But if Jocelyn wanted to put her life on the line, who was he to stop her?

Hell, what was he saying? Her life was on the line already and had been for some time now.

"Come on," he conceded. "Just follow my lead, all right?"

She smiled ironically. "Naturally."

Ignoring the sarcasm, Kirk approached the entrance cautiously. Something was definitely going on out there. There were urgent whispers, the sound of rapid footsteps.

He wasn't sure what it all meant, but if it was a distraction, they might be able to take advantage of it and escape. They'd better, he mused. The longer they remained in this cave, the more time their captors would have to realize how useless they were and destroy them.

Abruptly, the whispers and the footfalls died. There was silence in the corridor outside. The captain bit his lip. It was now or never.

Taking his fellow captive's hand, he took a step out of their prison cell, only to be blinded by something bright and red and close. A reflex told him what it was long before his brain figured it out.

Releasing Jocelyn's hand, he flung himself sideways before the phaser blast could catch him full in the chest. As it was, it smashed into his hip, flipping him around and sending him skidding along the rocky floor of the passage until he came up against a barrier.

As Kirk struggled to recover, to get to his feet despite the numbness in his hip, he saw three forms backlit by the light of a distant candle. They weren't wearing white robes, oddly enough. And they had a phaser—certainly not the assassins' weapon of choice.

All of that added up to a situation the captain hadn't even dared hope for. Squinting in the gloom, he tried to make out any details that would confirm his suspicions.

"Damn," said one of the silhouettes. "It's Jim!"

Kirk would have known that voice anywhere. "Bones?"

"My God," said one of the figures, separating himself from the others. "We finally find them and what do we do? We try to take their heads off with a phaser beam."

Suddenly the figure stopped, in mid-stride, as if something had caught his eye. Or some*one*, the captain remarked inwardly.

"Leonard?" ventured Jocelyn. "Leonard, is that you?"

She emerged from the cavern as if drawn to McCoy by some inexorable force, the way an iron filing is drawn to a magnet. Kirk could see her fling her arms about him as she melted into his silhouette, becoming one with it.

"Ouch!" he rasped.

Jocelyn withdrew a bit, looked up at him. "What's the matter?"

"My shoulder," he explained. "I tore it up a bit getting

here." He drew her to him again. "But it was worth it. It was *all* worth it."

Brushing past McCoy and his ex-wife, another of the figures approached the captain. Even before he grasped his commanding officer by the shoulder, Kirk knew it had to be Spock. No one else could have led a team this far into the assassins' lair.

"Jim, are you all right?" the Vulcan asked, his voice uncommonly laden with concern.

"I'm fine," the captain breathed. "Or at least I was, before you hit me with that phaser blast. How did you find us?"

"We found your guards first," explained Spock. "Since we could think of no other reason for a trio of assassins to be standing out here in the passageway, we surmised that they were here to prevent your escape."

For the first time since he'd emerged from the cave, Kirk looked around for their jailers, and noticed the three white-robed forms lying on the cold stone a little way down the corridor behind him.

They were very definitely unconscious, no doubt as the result of the kind of phaser blast the captain himself had just avoided. Hence, the thuds he'd heard a few moments earlier.

The first officer reached into his pocket, took out a phaser, and handed it to Kirk. Hefting it, the captain nodded to signify his gratitude.

"We've got to get out of here," said their third rescuer. "Before they find some of the bodies we've been leaving around."

The voice wasn't as familiar to Kirk as the first two. It took him a moment to realize that it belonged to Clay Treadway.

The captain's heart sank in sympathy. The diplomat

had risked his life to save his wife's, only to find out her heart belonged to someone else now. He could only imagine how the man felt.

Jocelyn turned to Clay in the near-darkness and murmured, "I'm sorry."

Her husband didn't seem to have a ready response. He just averted his eyes. For a moment, there was complete and utter silence. Then Kirk shattered it, because someone had to.

"Treadway's right," said the captain. "If you've been leaving a trail of bodies, they're going to trace them to us sooner or later."

The Vulcan tilted his head to indicate the direction from which he and his companions had come. "This way," he urged. "The nearest maldinium-free area is back along our original route."

As he started down the passage, the others fell into line behind him. Kirk took one last look at the fallen assassins before he hastened to join them.

The candles in Andrachis's sleeping alcove had burned so low that they hardly gave off any light at all. In the normal course of events, he would not have noticed this. He would simply have woken up in the morning, seen that the candles had expired, and replaced them with new ones.

However, this was not the normal course of events. This was the night the master assassin was scheduled to die, at least as far as Cor Lakandir and his comrades were concerned. That was why Andrachis was neither asleep nor alone.

He searched the recesses of the alcove and saw a host of tiny lights glittering back at him, the dark eyes of Ars Rondorrin and the ten assassins he had trusted enough to recruit for this ambush. Their blades, however, did not glitter in the least; they were careful to keep them out of sight until the time came to use them.

Andrachis himself had hidden his knife under his blanket. He pretended to sleep, knowing the conspirators would never try to kill him if he was awake and could yell for help. But the pretense was a difficult one to effect, considering the bloodfire that raged in his veins like an enraged beast.

It had been some time since the master had felt that particular madness. After all, the assassinations of the master governors had been carried out by his followers. He himself had been too busy planning to actually take part in them.

Andrachis missed the chase, the confrontation, the kill. He yearned for the look on his victim's face, the sound of death in his throat.

But his anticipation was dulled by the knowledge that it was an assassin he'd be slaying. And not just any assassin but the movement's best hope for the future.

Where were they already? What were they waiting for? His fingers caressed the handle of his knife, the only outward sign of his impatience. Had Lakandir and his friends lost their courage? Had they changed their minds?

Suddenly he heard the scrape of footfalls on the stone outside his sleeping space. Not loud enough to wake him if he'd really been asleep, but more than loud enough to be heard by someone listening as intently as he was. Tightening his grasp on his weapon, he tensed for action.

The next sound he expected to hear was that of his antagonists' shallow breathing as they entered the alcove. He wasn't disappointed, either. Except the group was smaller than the eight he had expected. *Much* smaller.

In fact, it sounded almost as if it were a conspiracy of

one. But how could that be? Why would the young ones send a lone assassin when so many desired the master's death?

"Tir-Andrachis?" said a voice. Lakandir's voice.

It was all the master could do to keep his brow from wrinkling and giving him away. Since when did assassins, even young ones, announce themselves on arrival? Unprepared for such insanity, his mind raced, seeking understanding. What in blazes was going on?

"Tir-Andrachis?" the voice repeated. "Are you awake yet, Master?"

Still puzzled, still off-balance, Andrachis opened his eyes and saw Lakandir standing at the entrance to the alcove. The young one was alone. And as far as the master could tell, he was also unarmed.

"Cor?" he muttered, still clinging to the pretense that he had been asleep. "Is that you?" he asked.

Lakandir nodded. "Yes, Master. It is I. I apologize for the hour, but I needed to speak with you as soon as possible."

Slowly, without revealing the knife in his hand, Andrachis sat up on his sleeping mat and squinted at his visitor. "What would you speak about?" he inquired.

Even in the meager light, he could see the muscles working in the younger assassin's jaw. "About your death," he replied calmly.

"My death?" the master repeated, as if he was still fuzzy in the head. "What in Moboron's name are you talking about?"

"The death you were to have met this morning," Lakandir explained. "The death I and others had planned for you."

"You had planned?" Andrachis echoed.

He wasn't convinced that the scheme was no longer in effect. He looked past the young one and listened, but he couldn't detect the presence of any others.

"What happened to this plan of yours?"

"We gave it up," Lakandir told him. "At my urging."

The master grunted. "And what is it you would have killed me over?"

"Your adherence to tradition," said the young one. "That is what we would have killed you over." Lakandir paused, searching for words. "You see, tir-Andrachis, there are those of us who do not see wisdom in the old ways as you do. There are those of us who feel the bloodfire burning us up from within, urging us to kill the offworlder captives and every other adversary who crosses our path."

The master eyed him. "Then why did you not back up your arguments with the edges of your blades?"

Lakandir licked his lips. "Because as I lay awake pondering your death, it came to me that the perpetuation of our movement is more important than any individual opinion, no matter how valid that opinion may be. I realized that, in the end, it does not matter whether we follow tradition or some new slate of ideas, as long as we follow it together. As assassins. As brothers."

Andrachis loosened his hold on his knife. "I trusted you, Cor. And you would have betrayed me with rebellion."

"I would have," Lakandir admitted. "But I did not. I *could* not. Nor could I let this morning pass without confessing my intention to you."

The master weighed the young one's words. They had the ring of sincerity to them and, no less important, the weight of courage. Lakandir could have quelled the rebellion and let it go at that. But, at considerable risk to his own life, he had informed Andrachis of his intended treachery.

Even Li Moboron would have been impressed with such a gesture. How could his disciple fail to be impressed as well?

"I forgive you," he told the younger man.

Lakandir's eyes narrowed. "Forgive me?" he repeated numbly.

Andrachis nodded. "Yes. For your honesty. For your unremarkable valor. But most of all, for having the good sense to keep your disaffection from turning into treason."

For the first time since he had entered Andrachis's alcove, Lakandir seemed to relax. "I . . . I do not know what to say," he muttered.

The High Assassin smiled. "Say nothing. Simply remember what transpired this night and how close you came to a mistake that might have torn this movement asunder. That will be all the response I—"

Suddenly a couple of younger assassins burst into Andrachis's alcove behind Lakandir. At the same time, Rondorrin and the master's other self-appointed bodyguards sprang out of concealment, knives at the ready, uncertain whether the newcomers intended violence against the High Assassin or not.

The master was on his feet as well, knife in hand. He hadn't thought about it; his body had simply reacted that way. Lakandir had reached for his weapon as well but, being unarmed, he had come up empty.

There was a moment of high tension, when anything seemed possible. And in the middle of it all stood Andrachis and Lakandir, who firmly established with an exchange of glances that they were both surprised by the young ones' entrance. There was no treachery here, only coincidence.

Turning to his unexpected guests, the master said, "Speak."

Obviously taken aback by the presence of Rondorrin and his comrades, the newcomers nevertheless did as they were told. Or rather, one of them spoke for both.

"An enemy has penetrated this place," he barked. "Several of our brother assassins, including those who watched the entranceway, have been found unconscious. And the prisoners have escaped."

Andrachis could barely control his fury—but control it he did. After all, a High Assassin could not give in to the passions that others could.

"Cut them off," he ordered. He took in Lakandir, Rondorrin, and most everyone else with a seething glance. "They will *not* elude us."

And shoving his knife into his belt, Andrachis himself led the rush to carry out his command.

McCoy knew they were still a long way from finishing what they'd started. If they failed to reach the beam-up site Spock had in mind, they didn't have much of a hope of getting out of here alive, an outcome that didn't appeal to the doctor in the least.

At first they met with no opposition. In fact, they saw no assassins at all except the ones they'd already knocked out in their search for the captives.

In the meantime, it felt good to hold Jocelyn's hand in his, to know that she was beside him again once and for all. This was the way it was meant to be, he told himself, the way it would have been if he hadn't been so damned blind when he was young.

And if they did escape this infernal rabbit warren full of

indigo-eyed killers, he would make sure he never made the same mistake again. He'd shower her with so much attention she'd have to pry him loose with a crowbar.

All of a sudden, as if by magic, the tunnel just ahead was full of ghostly forms. With a start, McCoy recognized them as the fluttering robes of the white-garbed assassins, pouring out from around the next bend.

But why would they come hurtling at them this way, knives dancing in their hands, bellows of rage tearing from their lips, unless they knew in advance that there were intruders about? And perhaps that their captives had been set free by them as well?

As all this flashed through his mind, the doctor drove Jocelyn sideways against the lefthand wall of the passage and covered her with his body as thoroughly as possible. At the same time, he saw the assassins' white garments illuminated by the crimson gleam of a couple of phaser beams.

The foremost pair of Ssana went flying backward into the others, stunned by the force of the phased energy blasts. A moment later, a third beam laced into the mass of assassins as the captain fired past McCoy and his ex-wife.

Something whizzed by within an inch of the doctor's ear. He turned instinctively to see if it might have hit Kirk. However, the captain had protected himself by flattening against the wall opposite McCoy's.

The doctor thought he heard another knife go by as several more phaser beams lanced through the damp, cold air of the tunnel. Then, as quickly as they had appeared, the assassins seemed to have disappeared.

But as McCoy stood to get a better view, he realized that they hadn't disappeared at all. They'd only fallen to the ground, the victims of his companions' phasers.

"Damn," breathed Kirk, stepping forward to survey the carnage. "Looks like they're onto us, Spock." A beat. "How much longer until we reach the beam-up site?"

The Vulcan thought for a moment. "Not more than a couple of minutes."

The captain sighed. "Let's go," he commanded.

McCoy looked down at Jocelyn, saw the lack of fear in her eyes, and drew strength from it. Helping her up, he took her by the hand again and followed Spock down the corridor.

There must have been ten or twelve of the assassins cluttering the floor of the narrow space, but they managed to pick their way past them. Then it was clear sailing for a while. The doctor began to wonder if they'd gotten past the worst of the opposition when the passageway began to widen.

He knew where they were now. They were approaching the cavern that contained the crevasse the Vulcan had almost fallen into. Apparently Spock and Clay realized that as well, because they slowed down to signal everyone over to the righthand side of the tunnel.

"Bones, what is it?" hissed Kirk.

"There's a drop up ahead," McCoy tossed back. "Just follow me and you'll steer clear of it."

Then he heard something else—not from the captain but from far behind him. A cacophony of voices from deep within the caverns. Nor was there any mistaking their murderous intent.

All the more reason to reach the beam-up site as quickly as possible, the doctor thought. All the more reason to get the hell out of here.

The two figures ahead of him stopped abruptly. The doctor bit his lip. Had they reached their destination already? Was it just a question now of opening their communicators, giving Scotty the word, and closing their eyes while the transporter did the rest?

He would have loved to believe that. But something was wrong. He could tell by Spock's posture, by the way he held his phaser in front of him, by the way his head moved from side to side.

It was as if he sensed the presence of something dangerous up ahead—something he couldn't see but nevertheless knew was there. As McCoy peered into the same darkness, it seemed to him there *was* something there, and it was breathing softly like a huge, subterranean beast.

"Drop your weapons," snarled a distinctively Ssani voice. "Do it now, or you will become sheaths for a thousand knives."

The voice had barely finished speaking before the cavern suddenly erupted with a half-dozen flares of light. And as the flares stabilized into candle flames, McCoy and his companions finally saw what they were up against.

"My God," whispered Jocelyn, as awed by the sight as the doctor was.

On the other side of the crevasse were at least a hundred Ssana blocking their way, all dressed in their white robes, all armed with something sharp and deadly looking. Their indigo eyes smoldered beneath thick, overhanging brows, expressing their hatred for the offworlders who had polluted Ssan with their ideas. And their shadows, looming large on the cavern wall behind them, were like the souls of all the assassins who had gone before them, hungry for blood even in death.

SIX

"Drop your weapons," one of the assassins repeated, in the voice that had spoken to them from the darkness. "I will not say it again."

He stood in front of all the others, an older Ssana whose face spoke of dignity and purpose—whose robe bore an emblem of a red cross inside a red circle just below his left collarbone. Instantly McCoy recognized the symbol.

This was the High Assassin, he realized. This was Shil Andrachis.

But that wasn't all the doctor recognized. As he stared at the dignified visage of the High Assassin, he realized that he had seen it before.

Amid the ruins of a government tower in Pitur. And later, in a Federation biobed. And still later, in nightmares where Merlin Carver lost his life over and over again to the blast from a killer's bomb.

It was the young Ssana whose life McCoy had saved

all those years ago. *He* was the High Assassin. *He* was Shil Andrachis, the one behind the latest wave of killing and death.

Suddenly, McCoy's fear was gone, replaced by a boiling, blistering malice. Without thinking about it, he stepped forward, ignoring Jocelyn's attempt to hold him back, ignoring the prospect of death at the hands of the assembled assassins.

"You bastard!" he bellowed. "You coldhearted, murdering bastard!"

The High Assassin leveled a molten look at the human. But recognition must have dawned in him too, because his eyes narrowed and his mouth shaped the doctor's name.

"McCoy?" he muttered. The word carried in the vastness of the cavern.

Behind him, the white-robed assassins looked at one another. Obviously they didn't know what to make of this.

"You're still kicking," the doctor spat, eyeing his adversary. "Why shouldn't I be kicking too?"

At some point the captain had come up beside him. "Bones . . . you *know* this man?"

McCoy nodded. "Remember that friend I started to tell you about? *He* killed him in cold blood, when the wars were almost over."

Overhearing them, the Ssana shook his head. "I killed no offworlders. There is no honor in such a deed."

"I couldn't agree more," the doctor growled. Raising his voice accusingly, he said, "But another of my comrades saw you. It was at a public house. You were with four others. One of you threw a bomb . . . and my friend died in the explosion."

Andrachis's brow creased as if he were trying to remember. "I was young then," he replied at last. "And angry. It is difficult to remember some of the things that happened in those days." He dismissed the subject with a quick sweep of his hand. "But we are no longer living in the days of Li Moboron's wars."

Suddenly McCoy saw an opportunity and, stifling his anger, grasped at it.

"Part of me," argued McCoy, "will always live in those days. I can't forget all that took place back then, High Assassin. Can *you?*"

Of everyone assembled there, only Andrachis would understand what he meant by that. Only Andrachis would recall the way the human had saved his life, bringing him the sort of dishonor that time and accomplishment couldn't erase.

That gave McCoy a certain amount of power over him. Because if he told the other assassins that tale, the master would be disgraced, and they would have to seek another leader.

On the other hand, a well-thrown knife would eliminate that threat. After all, the Ssana had helped to kill Merlin Carver forty years ago; why not kill McCoy now?

If it were only Shil Andrachis he was dealing with, he could predict the ultimate outcome—and it wouldn't be a good one. But the man was no longer merely Shil Andrachis. He was the High Assassin, sworn to uphold his predecessor's principles. And Li Moboron had stated plainly that his kind did not kill offworlders.

That was why they hadn't simply been cut down in the darkness, wasn't it? Because Andrachis couldn't kill a bunch of offworlders and still call himself a master in the mold of Li Moboron.

"In the spirit of those days," McCoy said, loudly and clearly, "I ask you to let us go. We have no quarrel with

319

you. We came only to see if we could resolve your conflict with the city-states."

"Silence," hissed another of the Ssana, a younger man. "We do not care why you came. Your methods and objectives are of no interest to us."

"You hurt us simply by being here," bellowed another. "By exposing Ssan to your alien notions of life and death."

The doctor ignored them. After all, Andrachis was the one who wielded the power. His word was the only one that really mattered.

"But surely," McCoy went on, "among civilized people —and I *know* you are civilized people—there's no just cause for imprisonment. No reason to keep people in cages as if they were animals. That brings no more honor to the jailer than the jailed."

The other assassins turned to Andrachis to see what he would say. For a time he mulled the human's words. Then he opened his mouth to answer them.

But before he could get a word out, one of his followers provided another kind of answer. There was a whisper of metal on the air and a glimmer of reflected candlelight and a single, angry cry:

"Marn, no!"

Fortunately the knife missed them, clattering against the lip of the crevasse at McCoy's feet. With such a clear shot, a veteran assassin wouldn't have missed—so it had to have been a youngster who'd thrown the thing.

Which meant there was still a chance to contain the potential for violence. As long as they stayed in control and no one fired back . . .

But someone did. Clay's phaser erupted with blood-red fury before anyone could move to stop him. As the doctor watched, horrified, the beam crossed the crevasse and struck Andrachis himself, sending him spinning out of control at the very brink of the pit.

One of the assassins at his side reached for the master, but it was too late. With a roar of pain and anger, Andrachis plunged into the yawning fissure.

But not before he gained a measure of retribution. For even as he fell, the High Assassin produced a knife from his robes and pitched it in his assailant's direction.

Unfortunately the Ssana's aim was spoiled by his fall. Missing Clay, the blade came whirling at McCoy instead. The doctor had no time to avoid it, only to brace himself for its lethal impact.

But somehow it found another target en route— another body with the speed and agility to slip in front of Bones and absorb the knife's breastbone-shattering force. It was a moment before McCoy realized which of his companions had saved his life.

And by then, Jocelyn was already teetering over the edge, clutching at the blade that protruded from the base of her throat. Eyes wide, knuckles white with her effort to pull out the weapon, she plummeted into the crevasse just as the High Assassin had a moment before.

"Jocelyn!" he cried, as the realization of what had happened sank in. Like a madman, he tried to leap in after her.

"Bones, no!" bellowed the captain. He took hold of the doctor's right arm even as Spock grabbed the sleeve of his left. "You don't know what's down there!"

It was true, he didn't. But he didn't care. Tearing free of both Kirk and the Vulcan, he jumped away from the edge of the fissure and felt a cold breath of air engulf him as he dropped into nothingness.

Abruptly, much sooner than he had expected, something hard and unyielding rushed up to meet him. It jarred him, awoke spasms of agony in the arm he'd injured earlier.

As he recovered, he could hear a moaning in the darkness. Assassins didn't moan, even in mortal pain. It had to be Jocelyn.

As Kirk watched McCoy vanish into the sea of darkness that stretched between himself and the assassins, his first impulse was to jump in after him. But he resisted, reminding himself that he had more immediate concerns.

Paramount among them was to make sure there was no more violence—no more phasers, no more knives. To that end, but with a certain amount of satisfaction as well, he belted Clay Treadway square in the jaw.

The diplomat staggered backward with the force of the blow, right into Spock's waiting arms. The Vulcan caught Treadway with one hand and grabbed his weapon with the other. Then, before the human could even think about getting it back, Spock placed him at arm's length.

Instantly the diplomat rounded on the captain, hands balled into fists, eyes burning with the desire to pound Kirk into the ground. But to his credit, he held himself back.

"That's right," said the captain. "You don't want to hit me. You don't want to do anything that will tempt our friends to send a shower of knives our way."

Treadway glowered at him, but that was the extent of it. Little by little, he unclenched his fists and came out of his hostile crouch. Finally he tore his gaze away from Kirk and peered into the blackness at their feet.

"My god," he whispered hoarsely. "Jocelyn . . ."

The captain turned to the assassins gathered on the

other side of the fissure. They were watching the intruders, poised for any eventuality. But they weren't flinging any of their weapons this way. Not yet, anyway.

That in itself was something to be grateful for. Obviously there were some cooler heads among the white-robed killers, despite their reputation to the contrary. Or was it just that they were confused without Andrachis to guide them?

After all, the High Assassin might still be alive. And if he was, it was still his right to determine the offworlders' lot.

Either way, Kirk couldn't trust fate alone, he had to establish a dialogue. And he had to do it before one of the assassins decided to change his mind.

"My comrade made a mistake in firing at your master," he called across the crevasse. "He will *not* fire at you again. None of us will."

The Ssana eyed him warily. Finally one of them came forward to answer him. He was young, but his voice had a ring of authority to it.

"I hope you are right," he said. "For your sake. We have practiced forbearance because that is the High Assassin's way. But if we find out you are trying to deceive us—"

"We're not," the captain assured him. "All we want now is to find out what happened to our people—and your master. If you could shed some of your candlelight into the depths of this crack . . ."

The Ssana regarded him for a moment or two. Then he turned to the nearest candle-holding assassin and nodded.

Following the sound of her moaning, McCoy felt along the floor of the crevasse for Jocelyn. Before long, he came up against something soft, something that trembled with fear and sadness. It was her hand, turned palm up as if in supplication.

Immediately her fingers closed around his, albeit weakly. With his free hand he groped for the knife that had lodged so hideously at the top of her sternum. It was still there, still hard and unspeakably ugly to his touch.

His first inclination was to pull it out, to rid her of the evil that had invaded her. But he didn't, because the resulting torrent of blood would only hasten her death.

Swallowing against the ache in his throat, he could hear the sound of urgent voices above, the hiss of protests and the crack of commands. But that was none of his concern. All he cared about was the woman who lay dying on the cold rock floor, the woman who had borne his child and broken his heart and, at long last, restored it to him.

"Leonard?" Her voice was little more than a burbling whisper.

"Hush," he told her, gritting his teeth lest he break down and become useless to her.

Slipping his tricorder out of his jacket, he worked the controls by rote. As the tiny monitor lit up, automatically compensating for the darkness, he played the device along Jocelyn's body. Numbers flashed on the screen, which to a layman would have meant nothing. But to him they meant a great deal.

It confirmed his initial fears. Jocelyn was dying, quickly and painfully, and it was beyond his power to save her. All he could do was ease her suffering.

McCoy set his tricorder down on the ground. By the light of its monitor, and little light it was, he removed a hypospray from another pocket. Working quickly, for he didn't know how many more breaths she had in her, he punched in the formula for a painkiller that would mitigate the torment but still leave Jocelyn lucid. Then he injected her with it.

It took effect immediately. In the blue light from the tricorder screen, his ex-wife's eyes met his. They looked as clear and beautiful as the evening he'd met her, when he was too young to guess what life might have in store for them. Now, as then, he would have done anything for her—but unfortunately, he'd already done all it was possible for him to do.

"Leonard," she said, even more softly than before. She seemed to take pleasure in saying it, as if it were an incantation against the darkness.

"I'm here," he told her, grasping her hand more tightly. He didn't know what else to say.

She took in a ragged breath. "I'm sorry," she said. "For everything."

McCoy shook his head. "There's nothing to be sorry about. Not anymore."

Jocelyn smiled at that, or at least tried to. "I don't want to leave you," she sobbed. "Not now. Not after we—"

Suddenly her eyes opened wide, as if she were seeing some truth she had never seen before. And they simply didn't close again.

"Jocelyn?" he ventured. And then again: "Jocelyn?"

But there was no answer. No answer at all.

Heaving with emotion, McCoy buried his face in her still-fragrant cheek and, shamelessly, he bawled like a newborn baby.

Sometime later he remembered they weren't alone at the bottom of the crevasse. There was another presence there, another living being, who hadn't uttered a word.

Andrachis.

The man who had killed not only Merlin Carver but

now Jocelyn as well. The single individual who had caused McCoy more grief than any other.

Through his pain, McCoy listened, and he heard a shallow wheezing in the otherwise perfect silence. He crept toward it and the sound grew louder. Finally, his eyes better adjusted to the lightlessness, he made out a vague outline that could only be Andrachis.

"Come no closer!" the Ssana snapped. But his voice didn't have the strength it should have. There was something wrong with him.

Knowing better than to ignore the High Assassin's warning, the doctor stopped just shy of Andrachis's reach. Then, ignoring the ache in his throat, he ran his tricorder the length of the Ssana's body and read the results.

It was as he had suspected. Andrachis had broken several ribs. One of them had punctured a lung. The assassin's pain must be incredible.

"You're bleeding to death," McCoy said aloud, eyeing Andrachis's silhouette where he figured the Ssana's face was.

"I know that," Andrachis rasped. "It is my time, Doctor. Let me die."

"Your *time?*" Suddenly McCoy was furious. "Like it was *hers?*" he demanded. "Like it was Merlin's?"

Andrachis gasped in pain, and rolled away from the doctor. On his tricorder, McCoy saw the assassin's vital signs dip even lower.

"Leave me now," the High Assassin said. "As you should have left me then."

The words struck McCoy like a physical blow. He *should* have left Andrachis to die in the wreckage of the Pitur council chamber long ago, or let Bando kill the Ssana that night in the infirmary. He should have. If he had, Merlin would still be alive.

And so would Jocelyn.

And now, he could make up for that. He could even the scales. All he had to do was let the Ssana perish. It was so simple. How many Ssani lives would he save that way? A hundred? A thousand? Without its leader, the assassins' movement might even die out completely. At the very least, it would be severely weakened.

All he had to do was let Andrachis die.

Next to him, the assassin cried out involuntarily.

And McCoy felt tears well up in his eyes.

"Damn it," he said hoarsely. He looked over at Jocelyn. "Damn it, I'm a doctor, not a blasted politician."

If Andrachis wanted, he could take his own life later on. Right now, right here, McCoy wasn't going to let him perish.

Punching new instructions into his hypospray, he drew closer to the assassin. Despite his infirmity, Andrachis lashed out at him, catching his wrist in a steely grip.

"Let me die!" the assassin repeated.

"You can go to hell," McCoy told him, "on your own time." With his free hand, he injected a stabilizing agent into Andrachis's arm.

It was significantly more effective than the drugs he'd used on the Ssana the last time; Federation medicine had come a long way in forty years. Andrachis's hold on his other hand grew stronger as the medication took effect.

"No!" the Ssana gasped. "You must let me—"

"Shut up!" snarled McCoy, sounding more like an animal than a man. "Break my wrist if you want, but you're not going to keep me from doing my work."

Abruptly, the darkness lurched and parted, as he and Andrachis were caught in a wave of flickering candlelight from above. Looking up for a moment, he saw faces peering down at him from either side of the abyss.

Jim Kirk, Spock, and Clay Treadway were arrayed along one edge, the assembled assassins along the other. Their expressions contained varying proportions of surprise, horror, relief, and repugnance.

"Jocelyn!" cried the diplomat. "Jocelyn, answer me!"

"Bones, are you all right?" called the captain.

"I'm fine," the doctor snapped, forcing himself to concentrate on the task at hand. Resetting his hypo, he injected the Ssana with an antibacterial compound.

"What are you doing?" bellowed one of the assassins.

"I'm *trying* to keep him alive!" McCoy barked.

"Jocelyn!" Clay called again, refusing to believe the evidence of his own eyes. "She's not dead, she *can't* be dead!"

"Stop," insisted Andrachis, too weak to enforce the directive. "It is wrong for you to save my life. You know that."

"I know no such thing," countered the doctor. He saw the Ssana's cursed visage through the prism of his own tears. "Life is precious. I won't be a party to your wasting it."

The assassin grimaced at the indignity being heaped on him. "I will cut your heart out," he threatened, "and feed it to you on a stick. I will shred your flesh and grind your bones to dust."

"No," said McCoy just as venomously. "You won't. Because that would bring you dishonor too, wouldn't it? I'm an offworlder, remember?"

"The human is attempting to heal Andrachis!"

"He cannot! It is sacrilege for such as he to preserve the master's life!"

The hell with them, McCoy thought, setting the hypo-spray a third time. What's the worst they can do? Kill me?

I feel dead already, he told himself. When he'd obtained the medication he was looking for, he injected the Ssana yet again.

"Damn it, what is he doing down there?"

Clay again, noted the doctor, through a haze of misery.

"That's the one who killed my wife. Doesn't he know that? Why is he helping the bastard when he murdered Jocelyn?"

Because I'm a doctor, McCoy thought, swallowing back his sorrow. Because that's what a doctor's supposed to do.

"Stop it!" blared the diplomat. "Let him die for what he did, you fool!"

But McCoy didn't. Not for Clay, not for the assassins. Not even for Jocelyn. Instead, he reached for his communicator to arrange an emergency transport.

Cor Lakandir's heart was racing so fast he could barely make sense of his own thoughts. He couldn't allow the human to save the master's life. It would dishonor not only Andrachis himself but all those present who allowed it to happen.

And yet, if the High Assassin did not survive, the movement would be without a seasoned leader, without someone to guide it through this time of adversity. Marn Silariot had thought Cor himself could be their leader, but he knew now how absurd that was. He was no master; he was barely an assassin at all.

For a long moment he stood there, not knowing what to do, aware that all the younger assassins were looking to him for a decision. But his dilemma was like a puzzle with no solution. Try as he might, he couldn't see a way out.

Perhaps, he thought, there *is* no way out. Perhaps the choice is only between one form of disaster and another.

Until now the High Assassin had been glaring at the offworlder. Now he looked up, fixing his eyes on Lakandir. He said something, but it was too low for the young one to hear, what with the whispering of his brethren and all the commotion the intruders were making on the other side of the pit.

Still, Lakandir didn't have to hear the master's words to understand his plea. He could see it in his expression.

Frowning, bloodfire scalding his veins like acid, he raised his knife to the level of his ear. And with a quick, deadly motion, he flung it end over end toward the flesh that awaited it below.

McCoy looked up too late to avoid the blade that came whizzing toward him. But as it turned out, it wasn't meant for him at all. Missing his head by the width of a finger, it plunged point first into Andrachis's chest.

The assassin grimaced with the impact, but only for a fraction of a second. Then he was past expression, past feeling, past everything.

Looking up, the doctor found the Ssana who had hurled the knife. He wasn't difficult to spot. His hands were empty, his eyes were narrowed with sadness, and he was the object of every other assassin's scrutiny.

Taking a deep, desolate breath, McCoy let it out and looked down at Andrachis again. The Ssana would be happy, he mused. There was one less shadow on the sun. But the human who had tried to save his hateful life would never be happy again.

Slowly, methodically, McCoy put his tools away. What now? he wondered, feeling scoured out inside. With

Andrachis dead, would someone else take his place? Someone who would want the offworlders killed for what they'd done?

Not that he gave a damn. There was nothing left for him to give a damn about. With his jacket pockets full again, he got up, walked over to Jocelyn, and knelt down beside her.

Her skin was heartbreakingly pale in the dance of candlelight, her lips heartrendingly still. Brushing her cheek with the backs of his fingers, McCoy found she was cold to the touch.

Why was that so hard to acknowledge, so difficult to accept? He'd seen corpses before. Every doctor had. In the larger scheme of things, how could one more make any difference?

But it did, didn't it? It made all the difference in the universe.

"Go," he heard someone call out, in a voice tinged with bitterness. "If it were up to me alone, I would take your lives in exchange for his. But the master would not have had it that way. He would have let you live, out of deference to tradition. So be gone from this place, and quickly."

By way of a reply, someone flipped open his communicator. "Kirk to *Enterprise*," said the captain.

There was an answer, surprisingly clear and intelligible, and obviously eager to receive word. *"Enterprise* here. What are your orders, sir?"

A pause. "Five to beam up, Lieutenant, including one fatality. You'll find her beside Dr. McCoy."

A corresponding pause, as the implications of Kirk's command sank in. "Aye-aye, sir," came Uhura's emotion-tinged response.

The doctor shook his head. He'd beamed down here to get Jocelyn out of this place. And he was doing that, wasn't he? Only not the way he would have liked.

Just as he thought that, he saw the figures of the captain, Spock, and Clay Treadway begin to shimmer with the first telltale signs of the transporter effect. A moment later the crevasse was gone, replaced by more familiar surroundings.

EPILOGUE

☆

Captain's Log, Stardate 9582.1:

The assassination cult on Ssan is crumbling. Without Andrachis's experience and charisma to keep it unified, the organization appears to be splitting up into individual factions, each with a different interpretation of assassin traditions and objectives.

The Ssani city-states believe they can deal with these factions much more easily than they could with the High Assassin's acknowledged genius. In fact, they have already had some notable successes in finding and incarcerating Andrachis's followers.

Sometimes the death of a leader can galvanize a movement — even more than the leader's presence ever did while he was alive. Fortunately, that is not the case in the present instance. To a people who believe death is something to be desired, there is no such thing as martyrdom.

333

In short, the crisis has been averted, though certainly not the way we originally intended. For the foreseeable future, there is no reason for additional Federation involvement on Ssan.

On a more personal note, I would like to commend the courage and the spirit of Jocelyn Treadway, diplomatic liaison. It is an indication of her devotion to the principles of peace and justice that she gave her life to see our effort on Ssan succeed. We are saddened but also proud to convey her body back to Earth for burial.

Kirk had barely completed his log entry when his quarters echoed with the sound of chimes, signifying the presence of someone outside his door. Disconnecting his link to the ship's computer with the flick of a toggle switch, he stood and turned to confront whoever was out there.

"Come in," he said.

The doors slid open to reveal Mr. Spock. With the slightest nod, he walked into the anteroom and let the doors shut again behind him.

There was no need for amenities between them; they knew each other too well for all that. The captain gestured to a chair, but he had a feeling his friend would decline it. As it turned out, he was right.

"I will not stay long," Spock explained. "I only came to tell you that Dr. McCoy's behavior has not changed. He continues to view his ex-wife's body in its stasis receptacle." He paused. "I have attempted to speak with him, to help him accept his loss . . . but to no avail. He is inconsolable."

Kirk sighed. "It's frustrating, I know. I've tried to help him get over this as well, with no more luck than you had." He shook his head. "On occasions like these, words are often inadequate. I think . . . I think he just needs time. When he's ready to be part of us again, he'll let us know."

The Vulcan raised an eyebrow. "I will defer to your assessment of the situation," he remarked. "As you know, I have always had difficulty understanding human emotions."

The captain didn't miss the irony in Spock's voice. "Of course you have," he told his first officer, playing the game out of habit. "I wouldn't expect anything else from such an impeccable Vulcan."

Spock's brow climbed just a tad higher in response.

McCoy stood in one of the ship's lounges and looked around him. The place was empty, as he'd expected. He wouldn't have come if he'd thought otherwise.

Instinctively, he knew that he had to be among people again eventually. He knew that he had to put Jocelyn's death behind him and rejoin the human race or wither away like a tree denied its ration of sunlight. And Jocelyn wouldn't have wanted that to happen to him.

Hell, even when they were kids, she'd managed to get him to embrace life the way she did. It would be a brilliant Saturday afternoon and he'd locked himself away to study for some test or something, but Jocelyn would show up at his window and drag him out to feel the sunshine on his face. And inevitably, he'd join her in her almost holy fervor.

So he couldn't become a hermit now. That wasn't the way to honor the memory of someone who would climb a hill just to smell a particular flower.

Except . . . he wasn't ready to emerge from his shell. Not even for Jim and Spock, who had tried time and again to get a word out of him over the last several days. Not for Scotty or Uhura or any of the other friends he'd made over the years.

He just wasn't ready.

The doctor was about to leave the lounge, to return to Jocelyn's side, when out of the corner of his eye he saw someone standing in the open doorway.

McCoy turned and saw that it was Clay.

"What the hell are you doing here?" he asked. He hadn't meant the question to reek of bitterness, but it did. Across the room, the other man flinched.

Go ahead, the doctor told himself. Lash out. Never mind that he hurts as much as you do. Never mind that his loss was every bit as great as yours, and maybe even greater.

"I thought you might like some company," replied Clay, his voice empty of rancor. "I know I would."

McCoy frowned. "Sure," he said. "Come on in."

The other man took a seat near the doctor's and fixed his gaze on the brilliant rush of stars. "I never thanked you," he remarked. "For saving my life, I mean. That wasn't very polite of me."

McCoy shrugged. "We had other things on our minds."

Clay turned to him and smiled crookedly. "We still do, don't we?" He swallowed. "We still have *her* on our minds, for god's sake."

The doctor took a breath, let it out. "I suppose we do. And we no doubt will for the rest of our lives."

"You know," Clay confessed, "I hated you when we were young. For knocking me down at the social. For being smarter than I was. And, of course, for taking Jocelyn away from me."

McCoy grunted. "I hated you too. For being tall and good-looking and having a way with women. And for what happened . . . that day I came home early from school."

The diplomat nodded. "I guess we both know how that feels now. One might say we were even on that count. That is, if one were tempted to keep score."

The doctor eyed his longtime rival. To his surprise, he felt nothing but sympathy for him.

"There's no score anymore," he said softly. "The game's over—and we're both losers. We lost the person we held dearest in all the universe."

Clay's forehead creased with the weight of that realization. He turned away to look at the stars again, finding some solace there.

For a long while, they sat in companionable silence, more like old friends than old enemies. Then Clay sighed and got up to leave.

"What now?" asked McCoy. "Back to Earth?"

The other man shook his head. "No. I'm staying in the diplomatic corps. It'll keep me distracted. And you?"

The doctor smiled wistfully. "Retirement. They're putting this ship in mothballs, you know. And I really don't feel like putting out on another one."

"Well, then," said Clay. He held out his hand. "See you around."

McCoy took the other man's hand and squeezed. "I guess so," he replied.

Lips stretched taut against a flood of emotion, the diplomat started across the lounge. Then, as if he'd forgotten something, he stopped and turned around.

The doctor looked at him, wondering what else there was to say. Clay wasn't long in telling him.

"Score or no score, Leonard, there's something that has to be resolved." Clay's eyes grew hard with determination. "Jocelyn only really ever loved one of us. Sure, she went back and forth, confused about what she really wanted out of life. But when you dug deep, there was only one *true* love in her life." He lifted his chin slightly. "And that love, I'm very sorry to say, was yours."

Without waiting for a response, the diplomat turned again and made his exit, leaving McCoy to ponder his words in private.

Kirk sat in his command chair and watched a familiar sight loom before him on the forward viewscreen.

"Entering Sol system," announced Chekov.

The captain nodded. "Slow to impulse," he said.

"Slowing to impulse," Christiano confirmed.

Leaning back, Kirk frowned and tapped his fingers on his armrest. It wasn't right, he thought. It just wasn't right.

This was the last leg of their last voyage. They should all have been on the bridge together, all the fine, self-sacrificing officers who had served him so long and so well over his many years in space.

Of course, most of them were. Spock was at the science station, intent on some esoteric bit of Ssani physiology, the glow of his monitors turning his face as green as his blood. Uhura was at her communications board, monitoring subspace traffic for anything pertinent to their situation, her brow creased ever so slightly in concentration.

Scotty was at the engineering console, looking for all the world like a big kid as he admired the workings of his precious warp engines from afar, trying not to think about the moment he'd have to say good-bye to them. And Chekov, still as full of wonder as when he'd first stepped aboard the old *Enterprise,* was keeping an eye on navigation with characteristic vigilance.

Only one was missing: McCoy. But he could hardly be blamed for his absence.

The doctor had lost someone he dearly loved, someone who had only recently been restored to him. He needed to come to grips with that fact. He needed to absorb the injustice of it, cry his bitter tears and find some meaning in what he had left.

Of all of them, the captain knew how long and difficult a road that could be. Like McCoy, he had cheated death more than he had a right to. But death, in its inimitable style, always seemed to have a way of evening the score.

Fortunately for the doctor, he still had a lot to be grateful for. Joanna and her children were waiting for him back on Earth, and while they would have their own load of grief to deal with, at least they could deal with it together. That was what families were all about.

Still and all, Kirk mused, it would have been nice to have McCoy standing at one shoulder and Spock at the other as they pulled into Earth orbit for the last time. It just didn't look as if it was going to turn out that way.

The thought had barely crossed his mind when he heard the turbolift open and the sound of footsteps on the deck.

Of course, it could have been anyone coming up to the bridge. A half-dozen officers and functionaries had arrived already in the course of the captain's hour-old shift, seeking to fulfill one duty or another. Odds were it was more of the same.

But some sixth sense told Kirk otherwise. Turning in his chair, the captain saw his friend Bones standing in front of the lift, its doors sliding closed in his wake. He looked a little disoriented, as if he was seeing the bridge and all its personnel for the very first time.

Slowly, perhaps even hesitantly, the doctor negotiated a path to the command chair. No one said anything. They just watched, Kirk among them. When McCoy finally reached his destination, he gazed at the forward viewscreen, where the stars swept by in pristine splendor.

"Are you all right?" the captain asked him, in a voice so low only the two of them were likely to hear it.

His friend didn't take his eyes off the screen. "I'm fine," he said. His forehead wrinkled momentarily. "Or anyway, I will be."

That would have to do. Kirk started to swivel around to face forward again when he saw his first officer move away from his post at the science station. Deadpan as ever, Spock crossed to the captain's chair as well and took up a position at Kirk's other shoulder.

For the briefest moment, the Vulcan and Bones looked at one another. There were no words, no overt gestures, just an exchange of glances.

The captain had heard these two engage in bitter conflicts, playful dialogues, and deep, philosophical debates. What passed between them now was none of these things. It was something at once more basic and more profound.

Something akin to: *I share your pain.*

McCoy's mouth twisted into something of a smile. Then he turned again to the viewscreen, his soul just a shade less burdened than before.

Kirk smiled too. Their careers might be over, but it was just possible that life's adventure was only beginning—for all of them.